Windrush

Windrush

Jack Windrush Series – Book I

Malcolm Archibald

Published 2016 by Creativia
Paperback design by Creativia (www.creativia.org)
ISBN: 978-1530641215
Cover art by http://www.thecovercollection.com/

Contents

Prelude

Chillianwalla, River Jhelum, India, 14 January 1849

'Are your men ready, Sir John?'

'All ready, Sir Hugh.' Colonel Murphy scanned the ranks of the 113th. They stood at attention along the fringes of the scrubby jungle, listened to the batter and howl of the artillery and tried not to flinch as the occasional Sikh round-shot landed in front of their position.

'It's their first action isn't it?' General Sir Hugh Gough glanced to his right and left, where his army was preparing for the battle ahead. He had 12,000 men, tired after a three day march through the Punjab heat, while Shere Singh commanded at least 32,000 Sikhs, well dug in and supported by sixty-two pieces of artillery.

'Yes, sir; we are a new regiment, and this is our first time outside England.' Murphy felt that familiar flutter of excitement as a bugle called far to his right. He hid his smile.

'Not your first though, eh?' Gough controlled his skittish horse as the Sikh artillery probed for the range. 'You knew the Peninsula I believe.'

'Yes, Sir Hugh; Talavera and Salamanca, and Kabul in Afghanistan more recently.'

Gough nodded, 'well good luck Sir John; blood the men well and bring honour to the flag.' With his white fighting coat distinctive in that array of scarlet British and Indian soldiers set against the dark green and dun of India, Gough kicked in his heels and moved to speak to the colonel of the 24th Foot. A score of vultures circled above them, waiting to feast on the carnage to come.

'Blasted birds always know when there is to be a battle,' Major Snodgrass grumbled. 'They are a harbinger of death.' He withdrew a silver flask from inside his jacket and sipped at the contents. 'I hate them.'

'Put the spirits away, Snodgrass,' Murphy ordered. 'The men will be nervous enough without seeing their officers tippling.'

'The brandy helps,' Snodgrass took another pull before he obeyed. 'Here we go then.'

The 113th was in three lines, eight hundred fighting men in formation with their sergeants placed with each section and the officers leading from the front. In the centre, hanging limply in the appalling heat, the Queen's Colours and the Regimental Colours acted as a talisman and rallying point, as British colours had done in a hundred battles in India in the past and would in a hundred battles in the future. A puff of air as hot as any blast furnace ruffled the regimental colour, so the number '113' was partially displayed against a virgin yellow-buff field.

'Time to put a battle honour on our colours,' Murphy roared out to his regiment. 'Heads up lads: the Sikh *Khalsa* has a reputation for being brave and resourceful warriors, but he has never met us before! Keep together, keep in step, never mind the noise and win glory for yourselves, the regiment and the queen. Come on the 113th!'

Most of the men looked to their front, as required by discipline and tradition. Others slid their eyes sideways to their colonel; some swallowed hard, a few chewed tobacco or sucked on a stone to combat the ever-present thirst of India. One man was praying, the words a low mutter underneath the grumble and roar of the guns.

In front, the 24th marched bravely forward, flanked on one side by the sepoys of the 25th Native Infantry and on the other by their colleagues of the 45th. The mid afternoon sun was like brass above, bringing thick beads of sweat to faces not yet accustomed to the Indian heat. The red coats vanished into the scrubby jungle.

'Keep the distance!' Murphy roared; he looked along the ranks of his regiment, 'show them your Colours, 113th!'

'Only the bayonet!' the words were passed from senior officer to junior officer and along the ranks of the private soldiers, 'General Gough's orders are no firing; only use the bayonet.'

Murphy looked at Major Snodgrass and raised bushy eyebrows. He made no adverse comment about his senior officer, but he looked at his inexperienced infantry and wondered how they would cope. The Sikhs had proved to be the toughest enemy the British had ever faced in India, and General Gough had now further handicapped the already outnumbered and tired British soldiers.

The nearest men to Murphy were marching steadily with their muskets at the correct angle and boots thumping on the brick hard ground. Sweat glistened on red faces that peeled with sunburn, while their uniforms constricted their bodies in tight swathes of red serge. They looked uncomfortable, hot and nervous as they marched forward to face the enemies of the Honourable East India Company and, by association, enemies of the Queen.

'Will the Sikhs fight?' Snodgrass asked. He reached for his flask again but withdrew his hand as Murphy frowned. 'We've fought and beat them so often that surely they must know they haven't a chance.'

'They are the *Khalsa*,' Murphy paused, nodded approval as a sergeant roared to get his section to straighten the line. 'The Sikh Army is the finest native fighting force in India, tough professionals with European training, artillery as good as ours and a history of victory. They also outnumber us and are in a strong defensive position. Yes, they will fight.'

As they entered the jungle, the British had to break their formation to negotiate tangled bush and dense thickets of trees and undergrowth. From ahead there was a sharp outburst of musketry and again the deeper, savage boom of artillery.

'It's begun,' Murphy said. 'Steady the 113th! Onward to victory!'

There was a surge of cheering as the British made contact with the enemy, and the cannonade increased. The acrid smell of powder smoke drifted through the scrub, faint but stronger with each step they took.

'That's the Sikh infantry firing on the 24th,' Snodgrass said. 'The 24th might need our support soon.'

'Quicken the pace, boys!' Murphy ordered. 'We don't want to meet the *Khalsa* in penny packets.' He looked right and left. In the confines of the scrub, he could only see a fraction of his regiment at any one time, but it appeared to be steady enough, although some sections were dropping back as they became entangled in the undergrowth.

The cheering from the right and ahead mingled with screaming, and still, the Sikh artillery roared. There was regular volley fire from the Sikh muskets, a sure sign of well-disciplined infantry.

'The 24th is getting a pounding, 'Murphy said and nodded as a glistening-faced messenger approached.

'General Gough's compliment's sir, and could you move the 113th to support the 24th as quickly as the occasion permits.'

Murphy nodded. 'Thank you, my boy, and please tell the general that the 113th will be in support directly. He has my word on it.' He watched as the ensign turned about and vanished into the bush. The boy could not be more than seventeen, the same age as Murphy had been when he first went to war forty years ago.

'Come on men! The 24th need us!' Dismounting, Murphy ran forward to lead his regiment. He drew his sword and lifted it high in the air, then swung it in the direction of the enemy. 'Quick march the 113th!'

He heard movement behind him as he strode toward the Sikh lines. His men were following; one of the only two regiments in the British Army that had no battle honours on its colours, the hundred and thirteen virgins, the Baby Butchers, his men, the 113th Foot was advancing into battle.

Murphy hacked at an overhanging creeper and emerged in a large sun dappled clearing. He saw uniformed men ahead, drawn up in a tight formation. They wore the yellow turbans of Sikh gunners, and they stood behind a row of cannon. As the 113th emerged from the jungle in dribs and drabs, a section here and a company there, the Sikh officers barked orders, and the gunners crouched to their cannon.

A shiver ran through the scattered 113th; men stared at the wicked mouths of the waiting artillery in alarm or glanced over turned shoulders at the concealment of the jungle.

'Forward lads!' Murphy encouraged. 'There's no going back now; take the bayonets to them, capture these guns!' He led the charge, knowing his regiment supported him, knowing that British infantry always reacted best when the danger was at its height.

The clearing, the *maidan*, stretched before him, with the Sikhs waiting in disciplined lines, matches smoking at the locks of their cannon, bearded faces smudged in the late afternoon sun. Murphy brandished his sword and ran into the heat. He no longer shouted; he had not the energy or the breath.

The Sikh officers waited until they had a sufficiently large target before they gave the order to fire. Their line exploded in a succession of orange muzzle flares, and gushing white smoke followed instantaneously by a volley of twelve and eighteen- pound cannon balls that raced toward the disorganised 113th. Men fell in ones and twos and entire sections, but Murphy was untouched.

He took a deep breath of smoke tainted air. 'Take the bayonet to them, men!'

The Sikhs fired again, grapeshot and canister this time; lead balls that spread and butchered men by the dozen. Murphy felt a feather tickle his left arm. He shouted again: 'charge!' and stepped forward, but his legs would not answer.

He looked down; the ground was rising to meet him as he fell. It was soft beneath his face. He turned to watch his men win their glory. 'Come on the 113th' he tried to shout, but the words emerged as a meaningless ramble. 'Where are my men? Where is my regiment? Where are my darling boys?'

He saw only bodies on the ground and the screaming, writhing wounded; that and the backs of the 113th as they turned and ran back into the jungle. He saw Snodgrass standing with tears pouring down his crumpled face and the brandy flask held in a trembling hand.

'My regiment,' Murphy said. 'My brave boys, my 113th,' and then there was only blackness.

Chapter One

Smeared across the sky, grey clouds bellied downward, depressing the already sombre mood of the funeral procession that wound in the shadow of the hills. Black horses walked slowly, heads bowed and plumes nodding as they dragged the hearse along the bumpy, rutted road. A procession of mourners followed; some in black draped carriages, most on foot and only the occasional scarlet uniform added a splash of colour. In front, walking with head bared and shoulders hunched, a drummer tapped a beat slow to accompany the steady tramp of two hundred feet.

Nobody spoke. Nobody heeded the thin rain that descended, damp and insidiously miserable, to seep through woollen cloaks and turn the road into a ribbon of sticky mud under the surrounding wooded slopes. Nobody sobbed or wept as the long column eased between leaning lichen-stained gate posts and entered a graveyard where grey tombstones sheltered beneath weeping trees. Bare branches thrust to the sky as if clutching forgiveness from an uncompromising God.

With a creak that sounded like a cry of despair, the hearse stopped. The horses stood silently in their traces, and the mourners shuffled to a halt, standing unmoving under the steadily increasing rain. Only the drummer continued with his repetitive, unending tap.

A man emerged from the hearse, his face set into professional solemnity as rain dripped from his tall black hat. Stepping slowly to the rear of the carriage, he called for the pall bearers to step forward.

'That's us,' Jack whispered to his brothers, aware that every eye was on him. Taking his place, he slipped his shoulder under the coffin and took the strain. His brothers filed into place behind him, silent save for the slush of boots through muddy grass. There were six pall bearers; the three sons of General William Windrush and three officers of his regiment. They moved forward in unison as the drummer continued his slow, rhythmic tapping and the priest, erect and slim with his black cloak sweeping the ground, held his Bible as if his soul depended on it.

As they manoeuvred around a dismal yew tree, Jack looked at his surroundings, from the mist that dragged across the long ridge of the Malvern Hills to the ancient graveyard centred on a church whose walls were slowly crumbling back into the soil. Gravestones protruded from the ground like despairing hands, some decorated with skulls and bones, others surmounted by weeping angels, but most indecipherable as years and weather removed all traces of the names and pious statements that long-dead hands had carved there. In such an intense parish as this, there were only a handful of names, but none of the stones bore the name Windrush. The masters of the land had their own crypt, and it was to this that the mourners made their slow way.

Windrush: the name erupted from the marble slab that surmounted the pillars at the entrance. The letters were bold, uncompromising and when the iron gates between the pillars opened, lamplight highlighted seven steps leading downward into chilling darkness. Unhesitating, Jack moved on, unheeding of the weight of the coffin that dug into his right shoulder.

Beyond the steps, the ground was stone flagged, the air chill and damp. The light cast weird shadows, highlighting a host of names. Unconsciously he repeated them to himself:

Colonel William Windrush killed at Malplaquet. Major Adam Windrush died of wounds in Germany. General Adam Windrush died of fever in India. Colonel William Windrush lost at sea.

Nearly every Christian name was William or Adam. Jack wondered as he had often before, why he had been named differently, breaking centuries of tradition. Ever since the Glorious Revolution, the oldest son had always been William, with any succeeding male being Adam, and then George. His name was an anomaly, but his mother had ignored any questions he had asked.

The stone lid was open, the tomb waiting to enclose the latest Windrush to die for the Regiment and in the service of the country. The dark space was friendly somehow, welcoming a Windrush home rather than confining him to eternity. This crypt was where every male Windrush hoped to repose; this was where Jack would end in ten, twenty if he were lucky maybe thirty years' time. With hardly a pause, he helped ease the coffin down as the mourners filed inside, their numbers crowding the crypt, their breathing echoing from the stones, their feet shuffling in soft harmony.

At a signal from the priest, the drummer lifted his drumsticks and stood at attention. Silence crushed them like a thick blanket. Jack fidgeted, looking to his brothers; William ignored him as usual, but Adam gave a nervous half grin and mouthed something until the priest began the service. The sonorous words growled around the crypt, penetrating into each corner, rebounding from the hard stone, reaching every silent mourner with their reminder of inevitable mortality. Jack listened unmoved. He knew his destiny; he would follow his father into the Regiment and die in the service of his country. Every first born Windrush male joined the Regiment and very few retired back home; he would be no different. That was what Windrushes did; it was as fixed as the stars in the filament, as unchanging as the tides; it was the destiny for which he had prepared since he was old enough to walk.

At last, the priest stopped speaking, and one by one the Windrush males moved forward to give their final farewell.

'Well, father,' Jack looked down at the lid of the coffin, already closed and screwed down. 'I hardly met you, but now I must take your place. I would have liked to have served under you, but that was not to be. I'll carry the family name and honour forward as you would have wished.'

There was no more to say. Jack's father had done his duty, and he would do his.

His brothers came next, murmuring their good byes to a man they had never known, and then the officers of the Regiment filtered forward. The brave scarlet uniforms contrasted with the grey stone and the black of mourning, as the officers spoke crisply, following their duty to a man of their regiment, their caste and their breed. There was no emotion.

'Well young Windrush,' Major Welland stood erect, balancing his sword against his hip as he held Jack' eye. 'Are you ready to join the regiment?'

'I am, sir.' Only the solemnity of the occasion prevented Jack from smiling. 'I've waited all my life to be a Royal.'

'Good; it's a fine career and the best regiment in the British Army.' Welland nodded. 'We'll speak again later, once you have attended to the formalities.' He paused and added as an afterthought: 'Oh, I'm sorry about your father. He was a fine man.'

'So I've been told, sir.' Jack agreed. 'He insisted I complete my education before I joined.' He hesitated for a second, 'there was mention of Sandhurst, sir.'

'No need for that, young Windrush. The Regiment will teach you all you need to know.' Welland nodded. 'Well, we'll be seeing you in the Mess shortly, and you'd better not be long. The Royals are not the same without a Windrush.' Tall and dark haired, Welland's face was weathered, with only the tracing of a white scar spoiling his regular features.

Jack gave a small bow. 'I'll try not to be, sir.'

Welland lowered his voice slightly. 'Is there a young lady in your life, Windrush?'

'Not yet, sir,' Jack wondered what was coming next.

'Good,' Welland seemed satisfied with the reply. 'Keep it that way if you are serious about your profession. Don't even think about marriage, youngster, not until you are a major at least and you have to keep the family line alive. Women are for procreation, not recreation; they will only distract you.'

Jack nodded. 'Yes, sir.'

There is little possibility of any woman distracting me, Major Welland.

With the General safe in his crypt, the mourners made their separate ways home, with only the Windrushes' private carriage rolling to Wychwood Manor, the ancestral home of the family since time immemorial. Snug beneath the Malvern peaks, it was a sprawling place, centred on a fourteenth- century manor house but with additions from half a score of builders and owners, marking the passage of architectural time. Lawns rolled green and smooth on either side of the entrance door, while centuries of English weather had all but obliterated the Windrush arms carved in the limestone arch above the main door.

As grooms ran to attend to the horses, Jack stood in the outer hall with its soaring Corinthian columns and oak panelling. He glanced at the array of portraits and pictures that virtually related the story of his family over the past hundred and fifty years. Grim faced or solemn; his ancestors stared at him from above the scarlet uniform of the Royals. Some were alone, others painted against a backdrop of battle, but all had added to the lustre of the Windrush family.

'Uncle George's still hidden,' Adam pointed to the black curtain that concealed one of the portraits. 'I'd have thought Mother would have released him by this time.'

Despite the gravity of the day, Jack grinned. 'Poor old Uncle George; always condemned to be the black sheep of the family.' He glanced behind him to ensure his mother was not present, and carefully eased back a corner of the curtain. George Windrush stared out, resplendent in his regimentals and with a devil-damn-your-hide glint in his eyes that Jack had rather admired as a youth.

'Best not let Mother catch you,' Adam advised. He tried to force the curtain shut again, but Jack pushed his hand away for a longer look.

'Imagine joining John Company and marrying a native woman,' William pushed in. He sounded aghast at the audacity of his uncle.

'Terrible,' Jack shook his head in mock horror. 'It's just as well that he was lost at sea.'

'He was a blight on the family,' William snatched shut the curtain. 'Better his portrait is burned rather than just covered up.'

'Oh indeed,' Jack fought to keep the mockery from his voice.

'Here's mother now.' William stepped back from the portrait in case its very proximity should contaminate him.

'Well, thank God that ordeal is over,' Mrs Windrush rolled off her black gloves and dropped them on the hallstand for a servant to put away. 'Funerals are such tiresome affairs.' Tall, slim and handsome despite her years, she stood erect and calm as she surveyed her sons. 'All right boys,' she said quietly. 'We have family business to execute. Meet me in the library in five minutes, if you please.'

The library was the holy of holies, a room in which only the most important decisions were made and one which Jack had visited only a score of times in his life. He felt his heart begin to pound as he mounted the stairs with the nearly invisible servants shrinking from him as he passed. The forthcoming business must be vital, and he guessed what it was. His mother was calling them into the library to hand him his commission papers; there could be no other reason. By this time tomorrow he would be an ensign in the Royal Malverns; by this time tomorrow, he would be a man following his destiny.

The room was broad and chill, with two tall windows overlooking the Herefordshire Beacon that thrust its terraced slopes through the low lying mist. Glass fronted bookcases lined two walls and crept into part of the third, while a large writing desk sat square in the centre of the room. Mrs Windrush lit the three candles that stood to attention in their brass candlesticks and waited until the light pooled increased. She did not say anything as she pulled back the leather chair and sat solidly behind the desk while her children stood in a row in front of her. Jack noted the determined thrust of her chin and the strange, nearly triumphant light in her eyes and knew she was about to announce something portentous. Save for the ticking of a long case clock in the landing below, and the occasional distant bleat of a sheep that sounded through the cracked-open window, there was silence as Mrs Windrush opened the top drawer of the desk and pulled out a small pile of papers.

Jack felt his heart beating like the thunder of martial drums. He could see what looked like an official seal on the top document and guessed that it came from the Royals. That would be his ensign's commission which opened up his real life. Tomorrow he would catch the mail coach to London to purchase his uniform, and within a couple of weeks he would take ship for his new home; the only real home he would ever know: the Royals.

'Stand still boys,' Mrs Windrush commanded and waited for only a second until they obeyed. 'With the death of your father, some things need to be said, and some matters must be addressed.' She allowed the last word to hang in the air for a few moments, sitting upright in the chair as she slowly pushed the top document to one side and opened the others, one by one. She placed them in a neat row in front of her.

'Now boys; your father has left me instructions for each of you, but I fear that certain circumstances force me to modify them a little.' When she looked directly at him, Jack felt his heart beat increase further, the drums rattling the charge rather than a quick march. Modify them? What the deuce does that mean? He thought there was something nearly malicious in the glitter of her eyes, a hint of satisfaction that he had witnessed and dreaded on each occasion she had announced he was due for punishment. He jerked his attention back to his mother's face. She was watching him, and he knew she understood every thought that crossed his mind.

'I will begin with your father's intentions,' Mrs Windrush said and lifted the sheet of paper closest to her. 'You, Jack, were due for a commission in the army; in your father's regiment. William: your father intended that you care for the family estate. You, Adam, were either to enter the army or to pursue a career in law. Neither your father nor I intended that any of you become a gentleman of leisure.'

Jack permitted himself a small smile. He could not imagine his mother ever allowing one of her sons, or anybody else in her power, the luxury of leisure.

'However,' Mrs Windrush continued, 'I have had to make some alterations.' Her voice hardened as she lifted the next sheet, looking directly at each of her sons in turn as she proclaimed their fate.

'Jack: you will still enter the army, but not in your famous Royals.' She spoke the last word as if it was a curse. 'Instead, you will be commissioned into a different regiment.' There was triumph in her eyes.

'What? Why is that, Mother, pray?' Jack felt the shock strike like a hammer to his heart. There was only the one family regiment. No other held any appeal for a Windrush.

'Kindly permit me to finish.' Mrs Windrush chilled him to silence with a single look. He felt all his childhood fears return although the threat of physical correction was long past. 'Now, William, you are now destined for the army. I have ordered the family lawyer to purchase a commission for you in the Royals.'

William bowed slightly from the waist, while his eyes flicked sideways to meet Jack's, before slowly sliding away. 'Yes, mother.' He accepted the alteration in his fortune so quickly that Jack guessed he had known about the decision in advance.

'Mother!' Jack stepped forward, so he was touching the desk. 'How can this be?'

'Silence!' That single word cracked like a huntsman's whip. 'Adam; you will now take over William's duties in the estate.'

With a glance of mixed apology and sympathy to Jack, Adam bowed his acceptance. 'Yes, mother.'

'Now you may speak, Jack,' Mrs Windrush allowed. She leaned back slightly in her chair, placed her elbows on the desk and pressed the fingers of both hands together. Her eyes were unyielding as ice-covered granite.

'Mother; I have to join the Royals. The eldest son has been commissioned into the Royals for two centuries; why should I be in a different regiment while the second son is in the Royals?' He glanced toward

William, who stood with an expression of smug foreknowledge that Jack found extremely disturbing.

'You made one valid point there, Jack, and asked one question, but both are intimately connected.' Save for the deep grooves around her eyes, Mrs Windrush appeared quite relaxed 'Your point was nearly correct when you said that the eldest son in this family had been commissioned into the Royals for two hundred years. You would have been more accurate to say that the eldest *legitimate* son has always been commissioned into the Royals.'

For a moment Jack could only stare at his mother. 'Legitimate?'

Mrs Windrush's smile contained only malice. 'And in this family, the eldest, or more correctly, elder, legitimate son is William, who we have indeed commissioned into the Royals.'

'But, mother...' Jack was unsure what to say as his world collapsed around him.

'I am not your mother.' The smile was tighter now, the gleam of triumph shattering the ice around the granite eyes. 'And you are not my son. Your mother was a kitchen maid or some such you are merely the by-blow of your father's youthful indiscretion.' The smile broadened as if this woman was, at last, revealing something that circumstances had forced her to conceal for many years. 'You are an accidental child, Jack, born on the wrong side of the blanket. In short, you are an unwanted little bastard.'

A bastard?

Jack gasped at the disgrace. Five minutes previously he had been destined for an honourable career with the finest line regiment in the British Army. He had thought of himself as the eldest son and the heir of one of England's most ancient and honourable families, but now he was merely the bastard son of a kitchen maid, and his future lay in utter tatters.

'As a *bastard*, of course,' his step mother was talking again, relishing the roll of her voice around the dishonourable name, her words controlled but her tone full of justified satisfaction, 'as a *bastard*, you cannot be commissioned into the Royals, or indeed into any decent regiment.' She permitted herself a short snort of derision. 'No gentleman would agree to serve with you.' She paused for a meaningful glance at her elder son. 'However I did promise your father that I would see you commissioned, so I have purchased you a commission as an ensign into one of the few, one of the very few, regiments that would accept you.'

Shocked at this downturn in his fortunes, Jack waited, saying nothing. Already he felt something alter within him and he wanted to give no more satisfaction to this woman who no longer acted as his mother. He felt sick; his legs were shaking so much he grabbed hold of the desk to steady himself.

'Don't you want to know which distinguished regiment agreed to have you?' That was deliberate cruelty as Mrs Windrush watched him suffer.

'Yes, mother; if you please.'

'Don't call me mother, Jack. With the death of my husband, your father, we have no remaining relationship. Madam would be better, but Mrs Windrush might be acceptable.'

'But mother...' Jack saw the slight, sneering smile slide onto his step mother's mouth and forced himself to stand upright, 'my apologies, Madam.' Determined to give this suddenly cold stranger as little satisfaction as possible, he gave a formal bow. 'I would be obliged if you could inform me into which regiment my father's money has purchased me a commission.'

The smile vanished. Lifting the still sealed document from the desk in front of her, Mrs Windrush threw it contemptuously across to him. 'There is your commission, sir. My husband's money has bought you the necessary uniforms and my generosity had added a one-off sum of two hundred guineas. That is all. This family has cared for you for the past eighteen years but this is the last, and very generous, act of kindness we will do for you. From this minute you are on your own.'

Lifting the commission, Jack deliberately did not open it. He had to strike back, for if he left like this, with his tail between his legs, he could no longer look in the mirror. 'This will be a terrible scandal of course, once it is known.' He allowed the words to hang in the air. He knew there was nothing his step mother dreaded more than a slur on her family name. 'People will talk, and your friends will close their doors once they learn how your husband cuckolded you.'

He felt his step mother's anger as she half rose from her seat. 'The scandal will rebound on you,' she said softly.

'I have less to lose.' Jack reminded. 'I am only a dishonourable bastard. But if I had, say, a thousand guineas a year in perpetuity, I would certainly have no reason to speak.'

'That's blackmail.' Mrs Windrush sat down again.

Jack lifted the commission; 'you have deliberately twisted the promise of my deceased father, which is as dishonourable an act as I can conceive.'

'Two hundred guineas a year and you promise never to return.'

'Seven hundred and fifty guineas deposited on the first day of February every year and I will never return to Wychwood Manor in your lifetime.' Jack faced her across the width of the desk, forcing himself to act with a strength he did not feel. 'Do we have a contract?'

'The second you resign your commission or set foot on Windrush land again, your money stops.'

'And the first time you fail to pay my money, I will be back.'

Rising from her seat, Mrs Windrush pointed to him, her finger trembling in anger. 'Show this bastard out of our house, William, if you please. We will not see him again.'

'I'll pack my things first,' Jack kept his voice cool-as-you-please. 'And take my money. When I have an address, you can send the rest of my belongings along.' He gave a slight, mocking bow. 'Good day to you, madam and I hope you can try and keep your next husband more faithful than your last.'

It was a telling parting shot that did nothing to assuage the sick despair that engulfed him.

Chapter Two

Herefordshire, England, February 1851

Gripping the commission in hands that seemed to have turned to claws, Jack squared his shoulders and stalked from the room. He ignored the stares of the servants and the scornful face of his step brother as he gathered such of his possessions as were readily accessible, swept a handful of gold and silver coins into his pocket book and swept through the entrance hall with its portraits and pillars, its memories and solid grandeur.

Wychwood Manor had been the home of his ancestors for centuries, but now it was lost to him. He was as much a stranger here as any inhabitant of China or Hindustan or the South Sea Islands. The tears began to prickle at the back of his eyes, but he forced them away, for he had no desire to allow his mother or William the satisfaction of knowing how deeply he was hurt.

It was hard to step through the front door beneath the worn Windrush coat of arms, hard to walk down the sweeping entrance stairway for the last time, hard to put on a swagger when all he wanted to do was huddle into his despair. At the end of the driveway he turned for a last long look at the scythe-shorn lawns, the turrets and towers that told of his history, but William stood in the doorway, master of Wychwood Manor, sneering at him over an uncrossable bridge of birth and blood. The sun had eased through the clouds, reflecting on two score windows and highlighting the ancient stonework of his one-time home.

His father's amorous adventures had closed that door, and he was no longer welcome. It would be no good to run screaming back, to beg forgiveness for a sin he had never committed, to plead and cry and grovel, for his mother was as bound by convention as she was by law. As a bastard, he was not the legitimate heir, and that was unalterable.

And then it was the sad walk out of the estate and on to the high road that led toward Hereford, with the Malvern Hills greenly familiar behind him and the countryside unfolding for mile after fertile mile. His countryside no longer: he had no place with the one-time tenants of his father's estate, he would no longer fish the Cradley Brook, no longer sit on the green heights and dream of glory, no longer gallop his horse across the hills or shoot pheasant or wild fowl in the pleasant woods. His past was gone, and his future written in the piece of simply-sealed paper he gripped far too tightly.

After half an hour the commission was burning a hole in his hand: he had to discover which regiment he was destined to join; he had to know where his future lay. If the famous Royals did not want him, perhaps he was destined for the Buffs or the Rifles; maybe the 24th Foot, a regiment known for hard fighting. They would suit. He must find out, but not here. If he stopped near the Malverns then sure as death somebody would recognise him and ask what he was about; he could not face the shame. He would wait until he reached Hereford, many miles away.

The Inn was on Church Street, a few scores yards from Hereford Cathedral. Its creaking signboard proclaimed it to be The Gwynne Arms and the black and white exterior was as inviting as the convivial sounds of men and women talking together. Jack hesitated for only a second; his mother would not approve of him entering such a place. *By God, that is as good a reason as any to go in.* He pushed open the door. The noise enveloped him like a friendly arm, and he eased to a seat in a dusty corner and examined the seal of his commission. It was a simple red blob of wax without even an official crest when he had expected something much grander. Apparently, an ensign counted for less than he had thought, or perhaps some petty clerk could not be concerned to finish his work properly. Breaking the seal, he unfolded the parchment.

At sixteen inches by ten, it was also much smaller than he had expected, and when he read the contents, he felt once more the sick slide of despair. Skipping over the heading that stated that 'the Commander in Chief of the Army reposed special trust and confidence in his loyalty,' he came to the 'do by these presents constitute and appoint you Jack Baird Windrush to take rank and post as Ensign in the 113th Regiment of Foot.'

The 113th Foot.

Jack stared at the fateful number and swore quietly to himself. 'I'm going into the 113th Foot; oh good God in heaven; the Baby Butchers, the lowest of the low.'

The 113th Foot was the regiment that nobody wanted to join. There had been other regiments that bore the same number; the 113th Highlanders who had lasted for two years before being disbanded in 1764, and a later infantry regiment that had been raised and disbanded in 1794. Both these regiments had been fine, honourable units with no stigma attached; this latest incarnation was not. If his step mother had wanted to make her revenge on his illegitimacy as hurtful and shameful as she could, she had succeeded. Jack knew little about the 113th except for their nickname of the Baby Butchers, but that was enough to make his heart sink. Leaning back against the plaster wall of the inn he once again fought the tears that threatened to unman him.

Gaining the seven hundred and fifty guineas a year had been a tiny victory in a day of catastrophic defeat. From being a landowner and officer in one of the finest regiments in the British Army and an income of ten thousand a year, he had descended to an unwanted bastard with a commission in the most inferior of all formations and barely enough money to scrape along as a junior officer, yet alone a gentleman. His mother had barred him from his home and the only way of life he knew, and with such a meagre allowance he would never be able to purchase his way into a decent regiment.

113th Foot!

He heard the song even through his gloom, the words familiar from his youth.

> *'Squire Percy well mounted, away he did ride*
> *James careless with hounds coupled close by his side*
> *Then off to St Margaret's park did repair*
> *For Reynard long time had been harbouring there.'*

'And what's the matter with you?'

'I beg your pardon?' Jack looked up. The voice had been female, but rough; it had been the voice of a countrywoman. The Herefordshire accent was pronounced. He shifted uncomfortably in his seat.

'I asked what the matter was.' She was dark headed and perhaps seventeen, with an attractive plumpness that would probably turn to fat within a few years but which suited her very well at present.

Jack first inclination was to ignore such a personal question from a girl so obviously below him socially, but her smile was friendly, and he needed to talk to somebody. 'I have just lost my family, my status and my life,' he told her. He edged further away when she perched herself on the wooden bench at his side. Her scent of grease and soap and cooking was not unpleasant.

Her sympathy was obvious. 'Was it the fever that killed them?' He flinched as she placed a warm hand on his arm. Her blue eyes prepared to fill with tears on his behalf.

About to explain what had happened, Jack shook his head. He was duty bound not to speak of his misadventures. 'I'd prefer not to talk about it.'

She patted his arm and snuggled even closer. 'I understand; losing your family is too painful.' Her eyes were soft with sympathy. 'And you sound like a gentleman, too.'

Jack said nothing to that; at that moment he was unsure exactly what he was. The edge of the bench foiled his attempts to pull away.

'Not talking? Poor little man.' She was smiling again, rubbing her hand up his arm in a very familiar manner. 'They call me Ruth.' Her smile was broader than ever.

'And I am Jack.'

Her kiss took him by surprise; he recoiled and put a hand to his cheek.

'What was that for?'

'Because you needed it,' Ruth told him seriously. 'If somebody needs something, and it's in our power to give it, we should do so. That's in the Bible.' She tried to kiss him again, but he moved aside.

Used to the reserved girls of his own class, or shrinking and respectful servants, Jack was unsure how to react. He recoiled slightly until the innkeeper asked if he wanted anything.

'Two tankards of ale, please,' he said, paid with the loose change in his waistcoat pocket and watched Ruth hold the tankard with all the aplomb of a man.

'So you have no family left,' Ruth smiled over the rim of the pot.

'None left now,' Jack agreed. He held up the commission, 'and I'm in the 113th, not the Royals.'

Ruth frowned. 'You're going to be a soldier?'

'An ensign in the 113th,' Jack looked for sympathy but found none.

'You're going to be an officer?' Ruth recoiled slightly as her eyes widened. 'So you've no responsibilities for anybody, and you're going to be an officer? What are you complaining about?' She pulled further away, with her smile fading. 'All you have to do is get promoted to a general, and you'll have all the money in the world.'

'It's not as easy as that…'

'Life is never easy,' Ruth told him. Her frown made her look older than her years. 'How is it not easy?'

'You have to buy your way up,' Jack began to explain the system.

In common with every officer and potential officer, Jack knew exactly how the system worked. A British Army officer would purchase his commission as an ensign in the infantry or cornet in the cavalry, and then systematically buy his way rank by rank until he was in command of a regiment. It was a system that produced men such as Wellington, but one which favoured the wealthy, whether inefficient or not, while even the best of the poor were condemned to fill the most junior ranks unless by some freak of foolhardy bravery they caught the eye of an influential superior.

Jack realised that Ruth was listening intently to him.

'I have not got enough money. I might manage to purchase one step, from ensign to lieutenant in a fourth-rate regiment, but no more. I have to be known.'

'So the toffs have it all their own way then,' Ruth's tone betrayed her opinion of the upper classes. 'Ordinary officers can't get on at all then.'

'Only if they are extremely lucky and are seen being stupidly brave.'

Those words led Jack to his next logical step. As well as money, and every bit as important to an officer was courage, but here again the wealthy, the aristocracy, held all the advantages. They were brought up to danger in the hunt and hardship at public school; it was part of life. While a private soldier, a sergeant or an unknown officer may spend a lifetime of hardship and courageous acts, he was doomed to be unreported and unknown while every action of an aristocratic officer was gloried over and exalted. The son of General Windrush would be known; the illegitimate son of a kitchen maid was doomed to anonymity.

Jack heard his words trail away. He was saying far too much to this unknown girl.

It's all the fault of my blasted mother!

In some ways, Jack could not blame his step mother for her attitude. She had, after all, kept her dislike of him nearly hidden for eighteen years when every time she saw him must have been a reminder of her husband's infidelity, but still, he felt sick, discarded and bewildered. He closed his eyes against the shameful tears.

Ruth's voice had a hard edge. 'Look around you, Jack, and tell me what you see.'

He did so; weavers and small farmers, a shepherd or two, a group of hirsute Welsh drovers with silver belt buckles; their associated women and children. All the people in the inn huddled together in small groups, some eating, some drinking, but all wearing work-worn clothing and with faces bearing traces of hardship and hunger.

'And how many have a chance, even the smallest of chances, of doing what you do? None,' she answered her own question. 'They are born into poverty, live a few reckless years of youth and then grow old toward pauperism.'

Jack nodded, unsure what point she was trying to make; these people were different from him; they were from the labouring classes while he was a gentleman; he could not compare his life to theirs. But Ruth obviously could and suddenly, frighteningly, so could he. The realisation was appalling in its simplicity. As a bastard, he was no longer a gentleman. As a maid servant's son, only a combination of fortunate circumstances had allowed him a decent education and granted him a commission. These people, these dirty, uncouth, loud, poverty ridden people, were closer to him in blood than his step mother.

'Dear God.' He leaned back in his seat, staring at her.

'Dear God? I don't know about that, Jack, but I do know you've been given a better chance than any of these people will ever have.'

'Dear God,' Jack repeated. He took a deep breath and looked around the inn. The hurt and shock were raw, tearing away everything he had so recently taken for granted. Maybe this was where he belonged, living with these basic, unlettered people, a man with no future and no prospect of anything save infirmity, poverty and death. Maybe he was more like his mother, the unknown, unnamed and unconsidered maid servant, used only for sensual pleasure, than his father, the honoured, feted and distinguished general.

Ruth was still watching him, her eyes curious in her broad, friendly face. 'I think that commission thing gives you a chance of escape,' she told him.

'By God you're right.' The commission into the lowly 113th, which had seemed an insult only a few moments before, was now a golden key to a future far brighter than anything the denizens of this inn could ever know. He held it again, seeing not a descent into the abyss of a poor quality regiment, but the first small step back to respectability, honour and a position to which he had always felt entitled. The thick paper seemed suddenly fragile as if it might crumble or blow away, taking his newly precious future with it.

He had to move. He had to find his new regiment and start his career; he had to clamber onto the slippery ladder of success and reach for the heights. With no money, he could not purchase promotion, but he could earn it and step into the shoes of officers killed in action. 'Here's to a bloody war,' he drained his tankard and rose, contemplated touching Ruth's arm but pulled away. 'I must return to my lodgings. Tomorrow I catch my coach to London.'

Ruth lifted her ale. 'God speed, Jack.' She winked at him over the rim of the glass.

It was only when he tried to pay for his ale that he realised Ruth had picked his waistcoat pocket. He shook his head; she had taken her opportunity when she could and had taught him a lesson far more valuable than the few coins she had removed. Luckily he had the sense not to keep all his money in one place when entering a public inn; he was young but not that green, and besides, her advice had proven more valuable than a pocketful of coins.

Jack had been aware of the noise outside for some minutes, but now he looked up as it escalated. 'What the devil is happening out there?'

Ruth had disappeared, but the other denizens of the pub looked equally interested as the racket increased. One woman hurried to the door and peered into the street outside. She withdrew her head hurriedly. 'It's a riot! The redcoats are attacking the blues!'

As the woman spoke, something heavy crashed against the window, cracking one of the small panes of glass. The woman at the door screamed; men rose from their seats to stare outside.

'What the devil?' Jack said again. He stalked forward, joined the woman at the door and ducked when a bottle smashed against the wall a yard away from his face. A sliver of glass nicked his forehead. He blinked away the thin trickle of blood and looked around. There was enough light left to see the group of men who clustered outside a row of half-timbered houses across the road. The men were gesticulating at three uniformed police who stood side by side, gripping long staffs.

'Get moving you blue-bottle bastards,' one shouted, 'we don't need your kind here.'

As Jack watched, the police began a slow walk across the road, each tapping his staff in the palm of his left hand.

'Get back to where you belong,' one of the police advised. 'Or you'll spend the night in the lock-up.'

The words acted as a catalyst. The men unfastened their belts and began to chant 'down with the blues!' One wrapped the belt around his fist, so the brass buckle acted as a vicious weapon, the others swung the belts around their heads, with the buckle blurring and lethal. As they came into the wavering light of the street lamp, Jack realised that they were all wearing military scarlet. He fingered his commission and wondered if he should try to use his new rank to pacify the situation.

Would they listen to me?

Would they listen to a Johnny-raw ensign? My presence would likely make things worse.

There were a few seconds of frantic activity as the police defended themselves. Jack saw the staffs rise and fall, heard the ugly crack of wood on heads and the whirr and snap of the belts, and then the soldiers surged around the thin blue line, boots thumping into police ribs, faces and legs.

'Down with the blues!' A soldier with a pock-marked face continued to chant.

'Stop that!' the voice was of a young woman. She hurried over from the other side of the street, 'you brutes! Stop that at once, I say!'

Jack shifted uneasily from foot to foot. It was one thing to stand aside from a straightforward contest between police and the army and another to allow a woman to take charge.

The women stepped fearlessly toward the grunting mass of redcoats. 'You have done enough to these poor fellows,' she poked at the nearest soldier, a man of about thirty with a cropped head and a face seamed with scars. 'Leave them alone.'

When the crop-headed soldier looked up his eyes were wild. He swore and pushed the woman away.

A gaunt faced private grabbed her. 'You're a saucy little whore aren't you?' He put a hand over her mouth, swore and pulled clear. 'The bitch bit me!'

'She's got a dash of temper then,' crop-head gave a high-pitched laugh. 'Give her this way, and I'll cure the poxy little flirt!'

The other soldiers stopped their relentless kicking of the prone policemen and looked up. 'She's a looker,' a sandy haired soldier said in a hard London voice. 'What are you doing here, Mary-Jane?' He stepped on a prone policeman as he approached the woman. 'Want a real man do you?'

The woman did not back away. 'There are ten of you attacking three policemen,' she said, 'that is an ill game.' She looked from one soldier to the other, perhaps hoping for support or sympathy, but finding neither. Her voice rose, 'I think you should all return to your barracks.'

'Oh, that's what you think is it?' The gaunt soldier pressed his face against hers as his companions gathered around, encouraging him with animal sounds and gestures.

'Go on, Pete, you show her.'

Pete put a hand on the woman's shoulder and pushed her back; she staggered, and her bonnet fell off. Large boots trampled it underfoot.

'Take your hands off me,' her voice was high now as her confidence drained away.

'I'll put my hands wherever I bloody well choose,' Pete grabbed her shoulder and pulled her close. 'Come on boys; let's have a little fun here.'

Jack had been watching, hoping that the situation would resolve itself without the need for him to become involved, but now he left the shelter of the pub doorway and strode across the street. As he got closer to her, he realised that the woman was younger than he had first supposed. She was perhaps twenty, while her accent and bearing suggested she came from a refined background.

'Enough of that!' He tried to inject authority into his voice. 'Leave that woman be.'

Pete put one arm around the woman's throat and the other round her waist. 'What has it to do with you?' His eyes were flat, poisonous, 'who the hell are you?'

Jack tried to stare the man down. 'I am Ensign Jack Windrush,' he said grandly, 'and I order you to leave that woman alone and return to barracks.'

'A bloody boy soldier,' the crop-headed redcoat said, 'a babe fresh from the cradle. Piddle off home to your mama, Ensign Jack Windrush, and don't interfere with men's work.'

'It's no work for a man to bully a defenceless woman.' As soon as Jack said the words he knew he sounded like a school prefect rather than an officer who held the Queen's Commission.

Pete laughed and planted a rough kiss on the woman's lips, which brought a cheer from his companions. The woman tried to push him away, her eyes now desperate as she looked at Jack.

One of the police groaned and tried to sit up, 'leave that woman' he called.

'You shut your mouth, bluebottle bastard!' As the sandy haired soldier began to kick the policeman into insensibility, Jack ran forward. He knew he would not have any chance against ten hard bitten redcoats, but he might manage to unsettle one.

'Quick!' he barged straight into Pete, unbalancing him by surprise more than force, and pulled the woman clear. 'Run!'

'I will not!' The woman said. 'Who are you to give me orders, sir? I am...'

Jack stepped between her and the crop-headed man. 'This is no time to argue!'

The woman hesitated and gestured to the policemen on the ground. 'We can't leave them...'

Jack pushed her in front of him. 'We have to,' he said. He looked down the street; there was nowhere to hide except the pub, and the soldiers would follow in there. Already Pete was beginning to recover, swearing foul vengeance as his companions urged him on.

'Get the bastard, Pete, rip his innards out!'

'Knock his head off, Pete and take the bloody woman!'

As they spread out and sidled toward them, Jack shouted: 'Run!' and pushed the woman in front of him. Unsure which direction was safest he headed for what he hoped was the centre of town. There might be more people there, and numbers could mean help and safety. The woman hesitated. 'Run, damn it!' Jack repeated. He dodged a drunken punch and struck back, feeling the satisfaction of his knuckles crunching on bone. The sandy haired soldier reeled backwards, cursing, and the woman moved at last. Hitching her long skirts above her ankles, she scuttled up the road.

'After her!' Pete roared, pushed Jack aside and followed, with his companions in his wake.

Hampered by her long skirt and with only a few yards of a start, the woman hardly crossed the street before George caught her. He grabbed at her sleeve and yanked her backwards. 'Come here my pretty.'

Rather than scream, the woman whirled around within Pete's grasp and kicked him solidly on the shins. A few steps behind, Jack barged the soldier to the ground and pushed the woman in front of him. 'Keep running!' he ordered, but he knew they could not get far. There were too many soldiers, and now their blood was up they sounded like a pack of hunting dogs, baying for the kill.

A bottle whistled past them, turning end over end until it smashed against a wall and sprayed vicious shards of glass onto the paved street. Another followed, to bounce from a doorway and land on the ground, where it rolled harmlessly and erratically toward the road.

'Head them off!' That was Pete's voice. 'Don't let them get out of the street.'

The gaunt faced man giggled hysterically, 'look, reinforcements!'

Jack swore as another body of soldiers appeared at the end of the road.

'What's to do, boys?' One of the newcomers yelled.

'Get these bastards,' Pete replied, and the newcomers spread out across the street, grinning.

'We're trapped!' the woman shrieked.

Jack hustled her into the recessed door of one of the black-and-white timber-framed houses. 'Get in there,' he ordered and turned to face the soldiers. There were eighteen now, either drunk or nearly so and they formed a semi-circle around the doorway, blocking any hope of escape.

'Now we've got you, you bastard,' three missing teeth defaced Pete's grin.

'You monsters!' the woman shouted, 'fight fair!'

Jack took a single step forward, so he was clear of the woman and adopted the classical prize-fighting stance his school had taught him. 'I'll fight any or all of you,' he said, 'but leave the woman alone.'

The soldiers jeered, with Pete making obscene gestures that left no doubt as to his intentions toward the woman.

'Oh, you cowards!' the woman said. She pushed level with Jack and tossed her head back; blonde curls bounced around her face. Twenty of you against one man and a woman! No¡ she said as Jack tried to hold her back, 'I will not keep out of the way. 'We will fight them together!'

'You're a spunky little piece, I grant you,' Jack told her, 'but it would have been better if you had held your tongue!'

Her smile took him by surprise. He could feel her trembling, but whether out of fear or anger, he did not know. 'Some things just have to be said.'

'What a bold ensign,' sandy hair said, his east-end London accent slurred with alcohol.

'He's game right enough,' crop-head added, 'a right little fighting cock we have here.'

They remained where they were, encouraging each other with loud boasts and high pitched laughter at their crude jokes.

'Come on then, if you dare!' Jack challenged. He could feel the woman close beside him and lowered his voice. 'Could you back off, please? I'll need space here.'

'You can't fight them all!' she replied.

Pete led the rush with an unsophisticated head-down rush that Jack parried easily. He landed a single punch that missed Pete's jaw but landed squarely on his cheekbone. As Pete staggered, Jack swung at crop-head; his target dodged and the blow bounced from the forehead of a squat, evil eyed man of about thirty and then the soldiers were on him. Jack grunted as a kick landed high on his thigh, and then staggered as a punch landed on his shoulder. He heard the woman's defiant shout alter to a scream.

'Leave the woman alone!' he yelled.

Jack kicked at one soldier who lunged for his groin, elbowed another that grabbed his arm and swore as something hard crashed into his leg. He did not see the arm that wrapped around his throat and pulled him backwards.

'Get in here Jack for God's sake.'

Jack could not resist as somebody dragged him inside the building and banged shut the door behind him. He looked around; the woman was already inside, and Ruth was shaking her head at him.

'You do need looking after, don't you?' she said. 'Somebody has to take you in hand.'

'Thank you,' Jack panted. Only then did he become aware of the various aches and pains in his body. He struggled to control his ragged breathing. 'You came at the right time.'

They were in a stone flagged corridor, illuminated by the flickering light of a single candle that did not penetrate far into the gloom. There were darker shadows behind the low beams.

Ruth nodded and jerked her thumb at the woman. 'Who is your trouble-making friend?' She shook her head and addressed the woman directly. 'That was a foolish thing to do, interfering in a fight between the peelers and the redcoats.'

'I am Lucinda Harcourt,' the woman sounded very calm, 'daughter of…'

'You can be the daughter of the Devil for all I care,' Ruth said as she drew a massive bolt across the door. 'But we'd better get you somewhere safe. The sojer-boys have you in their mind now, and they won't rest until they get you or until they are locked up and sober.'

'We're safe now,' Lucinda said.

Again Ruth jerked a thumb in the direction of the soldiers in the street outside. 'Not with that lot.' She stepped back as something heavy hammered on the outside of the door. 'See what I mean? They'll kick the door right in to get you. If they had half the sense of a dog they'd use the window, but…' She shrugged, 'who ever said that sojers had sense. If they had, they wouldn't join the army.'

'And just who are you?' Lucinda straightened her skirt and bounced her curls back. 'I've lost my hat! Oh,' she looked at Jack as if expecting him to run out and fetch it for her. 'Did you hear me? I've lost my hat!'

'I'm the woman who saved you from getting raped,' Ruth was very blunt. 'Now follow me and don't do anything foolish, if that is possible.' She flinched as there was another massive crash against the door. 'We'd better hurry; that door won't last for ever.'

Lifting the candle, she headed along the corridor with her skirt swishing around her bare feet. 'Come on Jack; you, Lucinda, you can come or go as you choose. I don't care which but if you stay the sojer boys will have their sport with you.'

Hitching her skirt, Lucinda followed as Ruth led them through a succession of dark rooms and to another door. 'This will take you to a lane that leads to Broad Street,' she said. 'Now you're on your own.'

'How can I thank you?' Jack asked, but Ruth shook her head.

'Just get out,' she opened the door wide and pushed him between the shoulder blades. 'Go now.'

Broad Street was nearly empty, with only a handful of people walking and a stance for hackney-cabs on the opposite side of the road.

'I think I'd best take you home,' Jack said.

'I think I will decide where I go,' Lucinda told him.

'Come on,' Jack ignored her protests, took hold of her arm and led her to the cab stance. 'Where do you live?'

'That is hardly your concern,' Lucinda shook herself free.

'Miss Harcourt isn't it?' The middle-aged cab driver leaned across. 'If you care to step inside sir, I will take you both to the young lady's house.'

'You know her?' Jack asked.

'Everybody in Hereford knows Miss Harcourt,' the driver said. 'In you come, Miss Harcourt and I'll see you safely home. You too sir, if you care to.'

No! Women will blight my career; I should walk wide of this one.

But Jack knew he could not do that. He was a gentleman by instinct and training. As such it was his duty to protect women; even women such as this vocal hedgehog who everybody except he knew. 'In you go, Miss Harcourt,' he gave her an ungentle push inside the cab and followed her in. He raised his voice. 'Take us to Miss Harcourt's house please driver.'

'You've no right to do this,' Lucinda protested, 'I will tell my father.'

'You can tell the Queen and the Archbishop of Canterbury if you wish,' Jack was tired of the company of Lucinda Harcourt. 'It matters not a dot to me.'

That was true, he told himself. In a few days or perhaps even a few hours he would be with his regiment and out of range of the spleen of any civilian from Hereford or anywhere else. He leaned back against the leather cushion; he would soon be an ensign of British infantry, and then he would climb the ranks and regain his former prestige and position, somehow. All he needed was a few bloody wars and the chance to prove himself against a foreign foe. He stared out of the window as they growled through the dark streets of Hereford.

There always seemed to be some enemy on the fringes of the British Empire. He wished he had grown up a decade before when he could have tested his mettle against the Afghans, the Kaffirs or the Sikhs. Now the Sikhs were vanquished, and the Afghans were licking their wounds behind the Khyber Pass. There was still the Kaffirs to fight, but there was little glory in chasing naked savages across Africa. Jack grunted involuntarily; he needed a more worthy foe than that to earn his spurs and start the climb back to respectability. He closed his eyes, wondering if he would ever lead his men to face the French; another Peninsula campaign would be bloody and glorious, with General Jack Windrush...

'Here we are sir, Miss Harcourt,' the driver's voice interrupted his imaginings. 'The Harcourt residence.'

'I'll take you to the front door,' Jack said.

I may as well do the thing properly.

'I am sure I know the way,' Lucinda's glare could have curdled milk.

'All the same,' he said cheerfully, 'a job half done is not done at all.' He slid out of the cab, asked the driver to wait for him and walked at Lucinda's side.

The Harcourt's house was neo-classical, with Doric columns displaying the master's wealth and power. Jack waited while Lucinda skipped up the flight of stairs that led to the front door. Before she was half way the door opened and a large man with an impressive set of white whiskers appeared.

'Who the devil are you, sir,' he said to Jack, 'and what do you mean by bringing my daughter home at this time of night?'

'I am Jack Windrush, sir,' Jack said, 'and I am endeavouring to bring your daughter home in safety.'

'I'll be damned if you are,' Harcourt said. 'Jack Windrush eh? I'll remember that name, mark my words. Now be off, or I'll set the dogs on you!' He grabbed Lucinda by the shoulder and hustled her inside the house. The door slammed shut.

For a moment Jack stood still. Major Welland had warned him to keep clear of women, and by God he was right. He had met two today: one had picked his pocket, and the other was a flighty, prickly piece of pure trouble. Both were reminders that his career lay in a world of military glory and not in domestic disharmony.

'Where to, sir?' The cab driver asked.

'City Arms Hotel,' Jack said. 'I have a coach to catch at five tomorrow morning.'

Chapter Three

At Sea, Winter 1852

Ten years. Jack leaned on the rail of the Peninsula and Oriental liner *Ripon* and watched the harbour lights of Southampton fade into the bleak distance. The homesickness increased as nausea rose in his throat. The authorities had told him the 113th would be in India for at least ten years. He would not see England again until he was thirty years old; if he survived. The steady chunk of *Ripon*'s paddles only increased his depression.

'Cholera, fever, loneliness, a hundred different types of diseases they have not even identified yet.' The educated tones drawled out the words in between long pulls at his cheroot. 'You are going all the way out East are you not?' His eyes were fringed with lashes as long as any girls.

'I am,' Jack agreed. He did not feel like talking.

His companion did. 'I thought so; you have the look of a man who is saying goodbye to England for a long time.' He took another pull at his cheroot. 'It can't be long enough in my case.' He tossed the cheroot over the rail and watched it spiral down until the dark water extinguished it.

He wants me to ask why.

Jack said nothing. The lights of Southampton were a dim glimmer through the haze.

'Do you know India?' The man lit a second cheroot.

'I was born there,' Jack said unguardedly.

The man raised a languid eyebrow. 'Oh: an Anglo-Indian are you?'

'No; military.' Jack resented the implication that he was from one of the civilian families who made their careers in India.

'Military background? I did not see you at Addiscombe.' The dark brown eyes were as innocent as Eve's serpent.

Addiscombe: that is the training school for the army of the Honourable East India Company; he is a John Company officer.

'I was not there,' Jack said.

'You're in a Queen's regiment then; which one?' The questions were relentless as the officer probed deeper into Jack's situation.

Jack nearly gagged as he spoke the name. '113th Foot;' he could not hide the bitterness as he added: 'the Baby Butchers.'

The officer gave a little smile. 'I am George Lindsay, soon to be of the Madras Fusiliers.' He held out his hand, 'what name did fate bless you with?'

Jack took the hand. 'I am Jack Windrush.'

Lindsay leaned slightly closer. 'Windrush; now there's a famous name. You're not related to the Windrushes are you? The famous Fighting Will of the Royal Malverns?'

Jack instantly denied any family connection. 'Only by name.'

'I thought not. If you were you'd be going into the Royals and not the 113th.'

'Exactly so,' Jack nodded. 'But I am only going into the 113th.' He thought he saw smug contempt flick across Lindsay's face. 'You'll be spending your entire John Company career in India then?' Jack shook his head slowly, 'I have heard there is plenty of money to be made if you survive.' He stepped back from the rail; the lights of England had disappeared behind a wall of mist: his past must vanish as completely. 'Now, I must get ready for my career serving the Queen. You fight for the profits of fat merchants; I fight for my country.'

And to get my name and honour back, but that is none of your damned business.

'In the 113th, old man, you only fight children and civilians,' Lindsay appeared unruffled. 'Your regiment has an unfortunate tendency to run away from real soldiers; especially Indian ones.' He waved his cigar in the air, winked and sauntered away.

He's right, damn him!

Jack opened his mouth to argue, decided he could not and stomped to the deck below. He shared his cabin with two other young India-bound officers, both of whom talked of nothing but glory and women.

'I have fixed my eye on that brunette looker,' Ensign Rands decided, 'she's the gal for me.'

'Oh my word,' Cornet Simpson's affected drawl did nothing to hide the acne that disfigured his face, 'she's a delicate piece and makes the most of it, don't you know?' He yawned openly. 'My preference is for that lively blonde. She'll be a Cheapside bargain.' He looked at Jack, 'how about you Windrush old man?'

'Women are a distraction,' Jack said and sought solitude on a ship where that was a scarce commodity. When promenading passengers crowded the upper deck, Jack found a small space in the darkness of the cable store, lit the stub of a candle and studied his profession.

When the weather turned wild in the Bay of Biscay, the upper deck was remarkably clear, so Jack positioned himself beside the upside down launch and began to study military manuals. 'Courage, above all things, is the first quality of a warrior,' he read as the spray spattered around him. He lowered Clausewitz's *On War* when he heard a familiar laugh.

Ensign Lindsay and Cornet Simpson faced toward him as they spoke animatedly to a tall woman in a blue boat-cloak. As Jack watched, the women laughed again and turned her head, allowing him to see her face.

Good God, what are you doing here?

Lucida Harcourt looked directly at him. 'Is that Ensign Windrush?' She raised a white gloved hand in salutation. 'Won't you join us?'

'Do you know that bookish fellow?' Lindsay asked. 'I'm afraid he much prefers his own company to that of ours.' He slipped a hand through the crook of Lucinda's arm. 'I do believe he does not care for ladies either.'

Jack opened his mouth to retaliate but closed it again. *Clausewitz says: 'If the leader is filled with high ambition and if he pursues his aims with audacity and strength of will, he will reach them in spite of all obstacles.' Lucinda is merely another obstacle to my aim. I will not weaken at the first hurdle.*

'Oh,' Lucinda gave him a look of astonishment. 'I see. Well, Ensign Windrush, we will leave you to your own devices on this occasion, but your future company would please me very much.'

'Oh leave him, Lucinda, he's a queer fish,' Simpson dismissed Jack with a sneer. Lucinda awarded Jack with a small smile and waved her hand at him behind her back as she promenaded along the canting deck with her companions.

Clausewitz welcomed Jack back.

'Are you joining us for a hand of whist, Windrush? Lucinda and Harriet will be there.' That was a daily invitation in spells of clear weather, and Jack gave a reply that gave rise to much amusement and not a little contempt.

'I have too much to do; you carry on.'

'Oh he certainly does not like the company of ladies,' Lindsay said.

When they called at Gibraltar to re-coal, Jack accompanied Lindsay and the others for a tour of the fortifications, asked many questions and took notes of the answers. He nearly missed the ship as the Grand Harbour fortifications in Malta engrossed him, ignored a squall as they neared Egypt and stood aside while his peers rushed ashore in Alexandria to test out their theories about the delights and souks of Egypt.

'Oh do come along Ensign Lindsay. I have heard so much about these romantic Oriental bazaars, and I need a chaperone, father says.'

As Lindsay tipped his straw hat and rushed to obey Lucinda, Jack hefted his single trunk over his shoulder and negotiated the gang plank.

'Is he a pederast I wonder?' Simpson asked in a shocked whisper.

'I imagine that might be the case,' Lindsay replied.

A pederast! Jack shuddered. One hint of homosexuality will blight my career and ruin my reputation for all time. Whatever acts of courage I perform, however good a soldier I am, will not matter if they think I am guilty of that most unspeakable of all sins. I must try to talk to Lucinda at least. There will be an opportunity when we travel along the canal.

Jack followed the others into an open boat that someone may have cleaned in the previous year. He watched clamorous boatmen attaching the tow, wiped sweat from his forehead and mustered a smile for Lucinda and dragged his brain for something to say. 'Did you have success at the bazaar, Miss Harcourt?'

'Oh we bought the most wonderful things,' Lucinda sat close. Jack flinched at the touch of her hand on his arm. 'A carving of a sphinx that is three thousand years old,' she displayed her treasure for Jack's education.

It was rough sandstone, crudely carved. 'Are you sure this is genuine?' Jack held it up.

'Of course, I'm sure!' Lucinda snatched it back at once.' Hot eyes replaced her incipient smile.

'Of course, Lucinda is sure,' Lindsay echoed. 'You ignore him Lucy; he's not worth your time.' He put an arm around her as the tow began with a jerk.

'I meant no offence, Lucy.' Jack said.

'My name is Lucinda,' she silenced him with a look that would have caused the Biblical plagues to flee from Egypt.

The ten- hour journey up the Mahmoudieh Canal to Aftieh would have been uncomfortable enough with just the hot sun and rough benches to contend with, but Lucinda's turned shoulder and Lindsay's barbed comments made things infinitely worse. Jack barely noted the fellaheen working on the canal bank or the long strings of camels that patiently plodded past.

When they reached Aftieh, Lindsay helped Lucinda up to the quay and guided her on to the slightly scruffy steamer that took them to

Cairo. Jack huddled in the lee of the paddle-box and looked miserably at the beautiful feluccas that sailed the Nile waters as they had for centuries.

'I'll be grilled long before we even get to India,' Rands complained as he looked at the carriage that was to draw them across the desert from Cairo to Suez. Six mules stood patiently waiting for the eighteen- hour drag. Behind the rickety wagon, a score of Egyptian workers piled British baggage onto a string of lean camels.

'You'll get used to the heat,' Jack found himself enjoying the high temperatures. 'I was born out East.'

'That might explain rather a lot,' Lindsay said as he fanned Lucinda.

'The English never get used to the heat,' Lucinda raised her face to the draught of hot air. 'Father told me that.'

'Perhaps Windrush is only part-English,' Simpson said. 'He certainly has dark enough hair to pass for a native, and I have noticed he does not suffer in the heat as we do?'

'Withdraw that!' Jack knew he could not let such an insult pass.

'It was said in haste,' Lucinda shook her head, 'really, Jack, you must put a curb on that hot temper of yours!'

'His hot temper must come from a hot climate, eh Windrush?' Lindsay turned away, leaving Jack with nobody on whom to vent his frustration.

From Suez, it was another voyage on Oriental across the painted Indian Ocean to Madras. They disembarked at the dock, with the ensigns and cadets split up with handshaking and promises of eternal friendship. Jack watched Lindsay accept a folded note from Lucinda, took a deep breath and lifted his single trunk. He had neither need nor money for a porter.

'Our life begins here,' Rands looked around at the confusion of noise and colours, the press of people, the beggars that held out hopeful hands and the thin thread of British officers who pushed through, each man an island amidst a breaking ocean of Indian humanity. 'I wonder if we'll ever get used to this place.'

'You hate India for a month and then love it for ever,' Jack quoted a family saying. He had vague childhood memories of all the noise and bustle and colour of this country and here he was experiencing it again as if the intervening fifteen years had never been.

'Where are you off to?' Rands asked.

'Calcutta,' Jack said, 'and wait for marching orders.'

'I'm off to the Frontier,' Rands said, 'Peshawar and all points north.' His grin was triumphant, 'where is the august 113th based?'

'All over the shop,' Jack tried to keep the despondency out of his voice, 'but nowhere near the Frontier. Assam, Arracan, Bengal ... Everywhere they are not needed.'

Rands sucked in his breath. 'All on the East side of India? Hard luck old man.' He lifted a hand in farewell, turned his head to the north and stalked away, with his head and shoulders rising above the mass of the crowd.

Lucky beggar.

Jack watched him go, balanced the trunk on his shoulder and then searched for transport.

Fort William was the principal military base for Calcutta, but Jack felt nothing but gloom as he mingled with hordes of soldiers sick with identified or unidentified fevers all clutching medical certificates to take them back home. The streets were dim and the humidity oppressive; during the day the population was ill tempered, and at night the streets were dark, with the few oil lamps emitting as much smoke as light.

He stood outside his quarters, a tiny dark building where the air that penetrated only added malodour from the street outside to the stinks from the lack of sanitation within.

Well, this is India, my home now. I hope I don't have to wait long for my marching orders.

He looked up as a massive bird hovered above, so close that it blocked the only shaft of sunlight to brighten the street. Jack looked up and waved his hand in a vain attempt to scare it away.

'I wouldn't do that, ensign,' a malarial-faced major with hollow eyes scolded him. That's an adjutant bird. There are standing orders that to kill or even injure one is gross misconduct and you don't want that as the start of your career.'He peered at Jack's uniform and demanded: 'how long have you been out East?'

'I just arrived, sir.'

The major grunted. 'Oh, you are a complete Griffin. Of course, that sort of thing is expected from Griffs.'

Don't argue with a superior officer. 'I won't shoot any adjutant birds, sir, despite my inexperience.'

The major frowned, 'watch your words, Ensign; they'll get you into trouble if you're not careful.' He looked upward. 'There's a storm coming in. You'd best get shelter for the night.'

'Yes, sir,' Jack watched as the major marched away. He could not have been more than forty but looked like an old man. But he was still a British soldier, straight backed and proud.

'Ensign Windrush?' The corporal was gaunt and worn, with a face bronzed by a decade out East.

'That's me, Corporal.'

'General Beaumont sends his compliments, sir, and could you report to him at once.'

'Thank you, Corporal,' Jack returned the salute as formally as he could.

Beaumont is somewhere on the other side of Calcutta. How the devil am I to find my way there? There's never a gharry-wallah when you want one, and anyway, they might not be working with the weather deteriorating as it is. I have to walk.

Jack signalled to one of the many natives who crowded near the British quarters hoping for employment. 'You, fellow, do you know where General Beaumont might be?'

The man nodded and bowed, holding his hands before him and his palms pressed together.

'Take me there will you?'

Jack did not see from where the man obtained a lantern. 'This way sahib,' he set off at a smart walk, turning every few seconds to ensure that Jack had not fallen behind. Jack watched the lamplight flicker on the wiry, near -naked brown body and found he was smiling with half-forgotten memories from his childhood.

I remember you, or men very like you. You're as tough as teak and you never give up.

The wind increased minute by minute until pieces of rubbish skipped through the streets and people looked for shelter within the dingy houses. Within fifteen minutes tree branches flew free and white European faces peered anxiously from windows as brown faced servants struggled to close clattering shutters. Darkness fell as swiftly as it always did in the tropics, so only the dim light from the lantern was left, flicking back and forth as the wind caught it.

The street ahead was narrow, empty of people except those who had nowhere else to go: a Company cornet fighting to hold his hat on his head, a pair of pencil-thin sweepers searching for shelter, a beggar hiding his battered bowl within the scanty folds of a filthy loincloth. Jack saw their faces as a series of vignettes, big eyes and open mouths set against faces scared or resigned and then vanishing again as the wind flicked the lantern light away.

Then the light was blown out. The dark was sudden, frightening with the violent gusts of wind as the unseasonal cyclone battered Calcutta.

'Halloa! The light's gone out!' Jack yelled. 'Come back, fellow! Lantern wallah!'

There was no response except the rising howl of the wind, the batter of flapping shutters and the clatter as gusts blew objects around the narrow street. A large section of wood crashed against the ground a few feet from Jack, then something that shattered into a thousand shards on his other side. Palm fronds flapped in a crazed frenzy somewhere close by, heard but unseen in the dark.

There was a terrible crack of thunder followed immediately by a flash of lightning that temporarily illuminated the street ahead, showing whirling rubbish, crashing shutters and torn branches of trees. The returning darkness seemed all the more intense after the brilliant light. Jack took a deep breath and moved on, hoping to dodge the worst of nature's missiles and find General Beaumont's quarters.

He walked straight ahead, trusting in luck not to fall over anything and cursing when something caught him a glancing blow on the leg. Only when the lightning flickered again did Jack realise he had taken the wrong route. Rather than walking along a relatively broad street, he was in a morass of tiny flat roomed houses separated by alleys so narrow he wondered how any human could negotiate them. He sensed that a score of predatory faces had turned to watch him intrude into their private world.

'You don't belong here.' The voice came from the deep dark.

'I am a British officer,' Jack felt for the pepperpot revolver at his belt.

'I know sahib, and this is no place for a British officer.'

Jack peered into the night. 'A British officer can go anywhere in India.'

The resulting laugh was more amused than insulting.

'Show yourself, damn you! Stop hiding in the shadows and face me like a man!' Jack pulled out the revolver.

'Is this British officer so scared of a voice in the dark that he has to use a pistol?' The tone was gently mocking.

'Who are you, damn you?' Jack stood still, aware he was being ridiculed but not sure what to do. Mercifully another flash of lightning showed a broad shouldered man in a blue turban a few feet from him.

'Ranveer Singh,' the man said, and added as instant darkness returned, 'I was once a soldier of the Khalsa.'

'You are a Sikh,' Jack aimed his revolver.

'I am a Sikh,' Ranveer agreed, 'and I fought against the British in two wars, but we are no longer enemies, so you do not need the pistol.'

'What do you want with me?' Jack asked.

'I want to stop you from getting killed,' Ranveer had to stand sideways to squeeze through the narrow alley. 'A pack of these dogs might murder a lone British officer on a dark night. Where are you going?'

'I am heading for General Beaumont's headquarters.' Despite Ranveer's words, Jack did not holster his pistol.

'I will take you,' Ranveer said, 'follow me, sahib.' When he left the alley, Jack saw that the *tulwar* in his belt had a silver handle.

This man was no ordinary soldier of the Khalsa. He is an officer and a gentleman.

'My name is Windrush,' Jack tucked his revolver away, 'Ensign Jack Windrush of the 113th foot.'

General Beaumont hardly glanced up as Jack stepped into his office. 'Your servant can wait outside,' Beaumont said. His own Indian servants stood in a silent row of uniformed men behind his desk. In the darkest corner of the room, the *punkah-wallah* wore only a loin cloth as he worked at the unending task of keeping the great fan in the ceiling moving by the string attached to his big toe. Jack thought it best not to mention the typhoon that battered at the corners of the building.

Beaumont looked at Jack over a tall pile of documents, all tied with ribbon and fastened with a seal. 'Which one are you?' As Jack looked bemused, Beaumont snapped, 'what's your name, Ensign? Who the devil are you?'

'Windrush, sir, 113th Foot; I was ordered to report here...'

'Piece of nonsense, Windrush; your orders are being sent out together with all the other officers.' Beaumont sifted through the documents in front of him. 'With all this uncertainty in Ava, half the officers in India are being sent east, even griffins that are no good to man nor beast.' He hauled out a document, glanced briefly at the front and tossed it casually across to Jack, 'there you go, Windrush; there are your marching orders, now get out. You're dismissed.'

That was very casual and where in creation is Ava?

Jack stood outside the office with the document in his hand, aware that Ranveer watching without any expression on his face. He broke the seal and unfolded the paper.

Moulmein: I have to report to Moulmein, wherever that may be.

'I'm off to Moulmein,' he spoke without thinking.

'You will need me,' Ranveer stated.

'Why will I need you?' Jack stared at him.

Ranveer's grin was white through his neat beard. 'You got lost walking across Calcutta, Sahib. What hope is there for you in Burma?'

Burma? Is that where I'm going? The disappointment was like a kick in Jack's stomach. *That's the opposite side of India from the Frontier.*

'I will get us prepared,' Ranveer said solemnly.

Jack felt too sick to argue.

Chapter Four

Moulmein 1852

'Welcome to the 113th Foot.' Colonel Murphy stared at Jack across the width of the desk while a *punkah-wallah* slowly pulled the cord that rotated the fan that stood above his head. He dropped his eyes; 'home to all the sweepings that the gutter rejects.' He poured gin into a heavy glass and tossed it back in a single swallow, refilled the glass and repeated the procedure. Jack noticed that he only used his right hand; the left sleeve of his tunic was empty.

Sweat eased from Jack's scalp under the regulation forage hat and trickled down the length of his spine. 'Thank you, sir.'

'Thank me?' Murphy paused with the next glass half way to his mouth. 'You've little to thank me for, Windrush. You know what Wellington called the British Army? He called them the scum of the earth. Well, the 113th gets the refuse of that scum, rapists, thieves, blackguards of all descriptions.' He drank the gin and poured himself another. 'I would not be surprised if we had a murderer or two, or a blasted Whig like as not.'

'Yes, sir.' Jack had never taken any interest in politics, but he knew his father had been a Tory and the Whigs were the opposition, so he supposed that Colonel Murphy shared his father's opinions on matters political.

'And cowards,' Murphy's eyes were red-rimmed as again raised them to hold Jack's gaze. 'You'll have heard the stories, no doubt.'

'There have been rumours,' Jack said cautiously.

Colonel Murphy banged his glass down on the desk. 'So don't expect any glory here, boy.' He shook his head. 'Not for us the celebrated battles and newspaper headlines. Oh no, we had one battle, and we ran away. Now we get garrison duty at the arse end of empire, so we die of fever and ague. If there is a hell hole or disease ridden swamp anywhere, that's where they will send the 113th.'

'Yes, sir.' Jack could not think what else to say. Certainly, this port of Moulmein did not appear to be the healthiest place in the world.

Colonel Murphy wheezed in a breath of humid air. 'As you are no doubt aware, Windrush, every regiment of the British Army carries their reputation and history on their colours.' He did not wait for Jack to agree or disagree but continued. 'Do you know how many battle honours the glorious 113th displays?'

'Yes, sir.' Jack had scoured London's bookshops for every book on the regiment and had read them on the interminably long voyage from England. There had not been many; the 113th was not the sort of regiment about which people wrote books or published memoirs.

'Well?' Murphy's hand hesitated on the neck of the gin bottle. His eyes were like shining sable at the foot of blood red pits. 'How many?'

'None, sir,' Jack said quietly.

'Exactly; none, sir,' Murphy tore his hand away from the bottle. 'So what heinous crime did you commit to join this illustrious regiment? Did you bed the wrong woman? Steal the family silver? Cheat at cards?'

'None of these, sir.' Jack had expected a vastly different interview when he first met his commanding officer.

'None of these, sir,' Murphy repeated. 'Of course not. Well, Windrush, you are with us now, God help you, and I have work for you. I expect you have heard that we are at loggerheads with the Court of Ava?'

'I have heard we have a dispute with the King of Burma,' Jack agreed cautiously. Every British officer he had met since his interview with General Beaumont had spoken hopefully of a possible war with Burma. He watched as a great-winged moth fluttered around the lamp.

'Yes, well, I will explain the situation for you.' For a moment Murphy looked like a colonel of the British Army and not a hopeless lush as he concentrated on the matter at hand. 'We fought the Burmese back in '25 when they invaded our territories, and the war ended with the Treaty of Yandaboo which guaranteed our trade and the security of our merchants.'

Jack nodded. 'I have heard of it, sir.' He had frantically read about the Burmese War on his journey to Moulmein.

'Aye, well, the Burmese have broken the treaty,' Murphy said. 'They insulted our merchants and stuck one poor beggar on a pestiferous island in the Irrawaddy River. It was the rainy season, so the river naturally rose, and only blind luck saved him from drowning. Then the governor of Rangoon did worse than attempted murder.' Murphy pushed the gin bottle away as he warmed to his subject. Lantern light gleamed from pink scalp between his thinning red hair. 'He put a ship's master in the stocks – a British captain, mark you – so we have demanded compensation from the Emperor of Ava or the King of the Golden Foot or whatever fancy name he chooses to call himself.'

'Yes, sir,' Jack flinched from a flying beetle.

'You may know that the King, Emperor or what-not of Ava tried to intimidate us before, back in '39 when we were embroiled in that Afghan nonsense.' Murphy's voice was growing in clarity. 'Mister Gold Foot promised to drive us from the lands of Tenasserim that we conquered in the war of '25. He led a large army, or the rag-tag that the Burmese call an army, to Rangoon but when we send over a brigade and a couple of steamers the Lord of the White Elephant and Brother of the Sun and Moon – as he also calls himself - decided that peace was better than war. Perhaps our victories in China helped convince him that fighting us put him on a hiding to nothing.'

'Yes, sir,' Jack nodded again. He waited to hear why the Colonel was telling him all this. He watched as the beetle balanced precariously on the edge of the gin tumbler.

'And you are wondering what all this has to do with you,' Murphy echoed Jack's thoughts. His eyes, hazed with drink only a few moments previously, were now sharp. 'Well, Mr Windrush, His Excellency Lord Dalhousie in his wisdom sent HMS *Hermes*, Captain Fishbourne, an interpreter called Captain Latter and Uncle Tom Cobley and all to sort the matter out.' He shook his head, 'all that for a king who calls himself the Brother of the Sun and the Moon.'

'Yes, sir.' Jack wondered anew where this conversation was leading.

'Dalhousie may have thought the Burmese would bow before the presence of the Royal Navy, but Captain Fishbourne found otherwise. There was more trouble and more insults, as one would expect of a savage race that believes it is superior.' Murphy put the gin bottle away in the desk drawer. 'Don't look so wearied, Windrush, there is a point to all this. I have not called you here purely to give you a lesson in politics.'

Jack hoped that his boredom had not been too evident.

'To cut a long story short,' Murphy said, 'Fishbourne acted with a high hand, as one would expect from the Royal Navy. He used his bluejackets to board and seize one of the Burmese king's ships.' Murphy's smile was unexpected, 'so that set the ball rolling. Fishbourne emptied Rangoon of everybody who was in danger from the Lord of the Golden Foot and his minions and brought them to Moulmein. And there we have it. We are now at war with the Empire of Burma; the navy, the army, the Honourable East India Company, you, me and the 113th Foot.' Murphy's smile faded as he leaned closer to Jack.

'That is not official yet of course, but it is a fact. I think Fishbourne wanted to burn Rangoon down there and then but his men were sailors on land, ducks out of water. We are soldiers and,' the smile dropped completely, 'we are the 113th, Windrush, the Baby Butchers, the pariahs of the British Army and we have to prove ourselves.'

For the first time, Jack felt the injured pride beneath Murphy's exterior. 'Yes, sir. I wish our regiment to be regarded as the equal to any in the army.'

Murphy's eyes were level. 'That will be a hard task, Windrush, a hard task to win back lost honour.' He stared at Jack as if working something out. 'I know your father. He is a good man, but a Royal Malvern through and through.'

The change of tack took Jack by surprise. 'I did not know you knew him, sir.'

'What did you do to anger him?' The question was brief and straight to the point.

'He's dead,' Jack was equally blunt.

Murphy re-filled his glass. 'All soldiers die.' Jack was pleased that he did not pursue the question. 'Very well, Windrush; you will want to redeem yourself from whatever misdemeanour you naturally do not wish to discuss, and I wish to raise the reputation of my regiment.' He scowled, 'Baby Butchers by God; I'll show them Baby Butchers!' The colonel looked directly into Jack's eyes. 'You see me as a drunken old wretch, Windrush, but I see you as hope for the 113th.'

Jack raised his eyebrows. He was not sure what to say. Murphy continued.

'Tell me, Windrush, who do we remember when we think of the Buffs at Albuera? Is it the Colonel of the regiment? No, it is young Ensign Thomas, who wrapped the Colours around his breast to save them from the French.'

Jack nodded. 'Yes, sir.'

'And take Chillianwalla when our regiment ran like stricken rabbits, there was one ensign of the 24th, a boy no older than you, Windrush, who took the Colours from the staff and wrapped them around his body so the Sikhs could not capture them.'

'Yes, sir,' Jack said again.

'There are others,' Murphy half stood at his desk, possibly in honour of the youths of which he spoke. 'You will have heard of Lieutenant

Dick, the Engineer who was first on the wall at Jhansi and of Ensign Havelock who stormed the abattis at Vera?'

'Yes, sir.' Jack had heard of some of these heroes.

'That is what I want from you, Windrush. I want you to win glory and renown so when men talk of the 113th they think of your exploits and not the infamy of Chillianwalla.'

'Yes, sir.' *Most of these men died winning glory: does the colonel want a martyr?*

When Murphy sat down again, his eyes were clear. 'A man with your name does not belong in this place of regimental disgrace. You belong in a more distinguished regiment, Windrush, but for whatever reason, you are with us.' He scuffed the beetle from its perch on the rim of his glass. 'If you had the funds you would be elsewhere so you must achieve glory to have your name spoken of in the same manner as these other heroes, and in so doing you will raise the reputation of the 113th.'

Jack nodded and repeated 'yes, sir,' once again.

'Now: to business,' Murphy pulled a small sheaf of documents to the centre of his desk. 'There will be an expedition to fight the Burmese, but the Powers-that-be will not send the 113th. We are being split into penny packets and used to garrison the eastern frontier of India from Assam to Arracan in case the Burmese launch an attack.'

'Will they attack, sir?' Jack asked.

Murphy ignored the question. 'However, I know the Colonel of the 18th Foot, the Royal Irish. He and I served together when we were about your age, and I have persuaded him to accept some of our men as replacements.' Murphy paused for a moment. 'I am sending you into Rangoon with a dozen men. God help us but finding a dozen good soldiers from the 113th is not easy, but we'll do our best. I want you to push yourself forward at every opportunity, Windrush. Show the world what the 113th is capable of.' Murphy leaned back in his chair and tapped long fingers on the desk. 'The Burmese are a proud and warlike race. They will not like us being in what they think is their territory and I anticipate strong resistance.' His grin was fierce. 'Your job is to face the enemy, Windrush, treat them with courtesy and respect, and then destroy them.'

'Yes, sir.' Jack nodded. He did not hide his smile. When he first entered this room, he had thought Colonel Murphy a broken old drunk, but now realised he was only a disillusioned veteran soldier who wanted the best for his regiment. 'When do I leave, sir?'

'You will join the expedition as soon as it's created. Until then get used to the climate and the people and get to know the regiment.' Murphy shuffled his papers before looking up again. 'Try and find a decent sergeant to take with you. Perhaps you could locate a fellow called Wells; he appears a cut above the usual standard.'

'Yes, sir,' Jack hesitated, 'thank you, sir.'

Murphy did not answer; his hand strayed to the gin bottle.

'Right you misbegotten bastards!' Sergeant Wells glared over the line of men that stood at what they fondly imagined was attention in front of him. 'You were sent to this regiment because your own did not want you.' A head taller than most of the men, he marched along the line, counting slowly. 'One, two, three, four and five: five rejected blackguards.' He lowered his voice to a roar; 'and you are all mine now!' He stepped closer to them. 'I don't know why you were unwanted, and I don't care what crimes your dirty little paws have committed. I only know that you think you have had a shabby hand in life.'

Jack watched the performance from the shade of a grove of peepul trees. He knew Ranveer was behind him but did not notice the tall officer who strutted to join him.

'You got here then, Windrush.' The voice was familiar but not welcome.

'Good morning Lindsay,' Jack did not attempt to sound friendly.

'He's a strange man Sergeant Wells,' Lindsay ignored the snub. 'He's an old India hands; when his regiment sailed for home, he transferred to your lot. God knows why. I would not trust a man like that.' He snapped his fingers and shouted, 'cigar' to a Burmese servant who stood a few feet away.

Jack wiped the sweat from his face. 'Maybe he likes the climate.'

'Oh no,' Lindsay casually slapped the servant on the head and dragged smoke into his lungs. 'These niggers are lazy scoundrels.'

Jack vaguely remembered the attentive servants who had looked after him when he was a young boy in India and said nothing.

'Now you idle, useless bastards,' Wells was shouting again, 'I will teach you how to shoot, although God alone knows why anybody would ever trust things like you with a broken stick, yet alone a bundook.'

Wells lifted the musket he carried. 'This is your friend; you do not treat her like your wife. I know how blaggards like you treat women; you are rapists and rogues and not fit to be near a woman. No; you treat Bess as if she was your immortal soul if you still have one, which I doubt.'

Insults with dark humour: does it work? Jack remembered the ugly group of soldiers in Hereford and wondered how accurate the sergeant's words were.

'Let's begin with the basics,' Wells said. 'This is a Brown Bess musket. It is what you will use to kill the queen's enemies. Bess weighs ten and a half pounds, and a good marksman can hit his target at eighty yards. However, Bess is a difficult lover; she has a stiff trigger, and you are weak and stupid. That means that when you pull the trigger, you will open your hand like so,' Wells extended the fingers of his right hand. 'Because you believe that gives more power to your hand. In doing so of course, you lose control of Bess, and she recoils. The first time she does so, you are taken by surprise, and she cracks you one.' Wells stepped suddenly forward and smacked the butt of his musket against the jaw of the tallest recruit. The man stepped back. 'I did not say you could hold your face! Stand at attention!'

Lindsay gave a little snort of amusement. 'Take note, Windrush; that is how you treat rankers and women. I know you avoid women.'

Jack said nothing as Ranveer withdrew. Wells continued.

'The second time you try, you will expect the recoil and hold back your head. By doing so, you cannot aim, so your enemy, be he Pathan,

Sikh or Frenchie, will charge up, slaughter you and piss on your disembowelled body. Now, that is a bad thing and disappoints the Queen whose shilling you took and who keeps you in smart uniforms and good rations. Now you don't want to disappoint Her Majesty, do you?'

The recruits shook their collective heads. The tallest man had the beginnings of a bruise on his chin.

'No: good. So we will do something to ensure that Her Majesty is pleased, won't we?'

The men nodded without enthusiasm.

'Lift Bess!' Wells ordered. 'And follow my lead. First, we take a cartridge, like so,' he held up the short stubby cartridge so that even the densest of the private soldiers could recognise it, 'and we tear it open, like this...' he tore the top with his teeth. 'Of course, you could use your fingers, if you have a third hand, but the good Lord, in his wisdom, granted us only two, unless you are some many-armed Hindu goddess.'

Jack smiled at the expected subdued laugh. *Wells is playing them like a violin.*

'This Sergeant Wells is good,' he said to the silent Lindsay.

Lindsay grunted. 'He knows how to keep discipline. That seems to be hard for your lot. My sepoys do what they're told if they know what's good for them.'

'The 113th will do better next time,' Jack said.

Lindsay snorted. 'I doubt it. Not with Colonel Lushy in command, and officers who are scared of women.' He snapped his fingers for another cheroot.

Jack felt the words rise to his mouth. A lush was a drunkard: he had seen Murphy with the gin bottle. 'Are you implying cowardice, Lindsay?' He knew that he had to respond to such an accusation. Cowardice was the worst possible insult for a British officer.

Lindsay held the cheroot for the servant to light. 'What makes you think I was referring to you at all, Windrush: unless the boot fits of course.' He puffed smoke and pushed the servant away before lazily addressing Jack. 'Are you scared of women? You had no interest in the delightful Lucinda.' His smile had all the sincerity of a cat enticing a mouse into its paws. 'Or in any other woman, I believe.'

Jack felt the colour rise to his cheeks as Lindsay's smile broadened.

'Sahib...' Jack had not heard Ranveer come up. The Sikh gave a brief bow.

'Not now, Ranveer,' Jack heard the tension in his voice. 'Ensign Lindsay and I are having a discussion.'

Should I call him out? Is duelling legal in India? Is it worse to break the law or have one's honour insulted and abused?

'Yes, Sahib, but you did ask me to come to you immediately I find the women.'

'What? What nonsense are you talking Ranveer?' Jack looked around, irritated at this new distraction.

Ranveer was not alone. He had three women with him. Two were obviously local girls with cheap *longyis* wound around their slender bodies and sandaled feet nervous in the dust. Both wore orchids in their black, coiled hair. The third was from further west, a Dravidian from southern India, Jack guessed, with caste marks on her forehead and a large brass ring in one ear. He tried to hide his sudden unease.

'You asked me to find a girl for you, sahib,' Ranveer bowed again. 'I could not find the particular girl you requested. Perhaps these three will make up for that?'

He's trying to help. How the devil did he know?

Jack saw the sudden interest in Lindsay's face. He took a deep breath. 'No, take them away, Ranveer. I only want that one woman: no other will do.'

'Yes, Sahib,' Ranveer said. He ushered the women away less gently than Jack would have wished.

'You are only interested in one particular woman then?' Lindsay's eyes watched the departing women, never straying from the slide of longyi around their backsides.

That's disgusting. 'So it would appear,' Jack tried to sound mysterious.

'I see,' Lindsay flicked ash toward Sergeant Wells, who continued to harass his squad with well-worn invective. 'Well, better to play the field old man, remember that marriage ruins the prospects of young officers,' he shook his head slowly, 'not that there are many prospects in your unhappy regiment if that lot is an example of their prowess. My sepoys would tear holes in them.'

Jack controlled the anger that Lindsay roused in him and continued to listen to Sergeant Wells.

'I already told you to ignore the taste of the powder,' Wells shouted. 'Ram the cartridge well home, then the bullet, and put the cap on – easy.' He swung the musket to his shoulder and aimed directly at the face of one of the men. 'Now repeat what I said, Coleman or I'll blow your bloody head off.'

Coleman visibly paled. 'Jesus Sergeant! Careful! That thing's loaded!'

'Then you had better be correct, Coleman: repeat what I said.'

Coleman took a step back as he gabbled the sergeant's instructions.

'Not quick enough, Coleman; now prepare Bess.' Wells kept the musket pointed at Coleman's face as the man fumbled to tear the cartridge, remembered to bite it but trembled so much that a third of the coarse black powder spilt down his chin.

'That's you dead, Coleman,' Wells took one step closer, so the muzzle of his musket was only eight feet from Coleman's face. 'You dropped half your powder, so your ball will not fly true, and the Sikhs are now running at you and hacking at your guts with a great big *tulwar*. Duck!' He screamed the last word even as he pulled the trigger. There was a click as the hammer of his musket cracked down but no report and no puff of powder smoke.

Wells grinned as Coleman threw himself backwards. 'That was a misfire, Coleman; you are still alive, God knows why. You have to watch for misfires and depend on your left or right- hand man or your rear marker to watch out for you, and you for him.'

Wells pulled his musket back to the on-guard position. 'You are a soldier and part of a section in a company, in a regiment, in the British

Army, but when the *Ghazis* come screaming *Allah Akbar* from the high hills, then you will feel all alone in the big wide world.' He unsheathed his bayonet and clicked it home. 'But you are not alone, Coleman. Even you have this little lady; you and she are lovers; the only lover an ugly useless bastard like you will ever know. Together you can destroy anybody that gets close enough.' His smile encompassed all the men there. 'Now I will teach you how to kill.'

'Time we were gone Windrush,' Lindsay continued to stare at the retreating women. 'The hand to hand stuff is all very well for the men, but hardly for gentlemen, I think.'

'I don't agree,' Jack did not move. 'The more we learn about our profession, the better, surely.'

'Oh God you griffs are such bores,' Lindsay tossed his cheroot aside. 'I have better things to do than spend my day chatting to the Queen's Griffins. Good day to you,' tipping forward his forage cap, Lindsay sauntered in the wake of Ranveer and his trio of women.

I hope you catch the pox

'Blood!' Wells screamed the word. 'Blood, blood, blood; come on lads, shout out!'

Jack had started at the sheer volume of sound that came from Wells' lungs. Now he watched as the sergeant trained his men in the gentle art of slaughter by bayonet. He showed them lunges and parries, how to use the point and the edge, and had them yell 'Blood' and 'death' and 'kill' as they rammed the bayonets into the boles of the nearest tree.

'Next time,' Wells promised, 'I will find you a live pig to practice on.' His men watched through eyes that were dull with fatigue.

I want him, whatever his history, I want that man with me.

'I'm not sure which is worse,' Major Snodgrass sipped at his gin and growled at the *punkah-wallah* to work harder at the fan, 'the heat, the humidity, the insects or the blasted natives.'

Jack looked around. The officers' mess of the 113th consisted of a thatched Burmese hut with a fan in the ceiling, a table, a dozen wickerwork chairs and a cabinet of drinks. Ranveer stood, smart in the livery of the 113th but was only one of the dozen or so Indian servants who outnumbered the officers three to one, while the Regimental and Queen's colours were encased in half-cleaned glass as if ashamed to admit they did not bear a single battle honour. Jack remembered peering into the officer's mess of the Royals when he was a child, staring in awe at the glittering silver and the trophies from scores of campaigns, the cased colours held in pride and the aura of assured victory.

'I hear you are going up-country?' Snodgrass raised a lazy eyebrow.

Jack nodded. 'Colonel Murphy wants the regiment represented in the war.'

Snodgrass shrugged, rolled the gin around the glass and swallowed it. He leaned across the table toward Jack. 'Here's some free advice, Windrush; keep your head down, never volunteer and let the sergeants deal with the men. Maybe flog a few now and then so they respect you but aside from that, avoid them.'

'They can't be that bad,' Jack said hopefully.

'They're gutter bred scoundrels to a man. You've heard the stories no doubt?' Snodgrass asked. He snapped his fingers and pointed to the drinks cabinet. A soft-footed servant brought him another bottle of gin, opened it and poured a generous glass. 'You will have heard how the regiment was raised to put down the Radicals in England and how they charged a meeting in Liverpool, bayoneting and clubbing the civilians?' He tasted the gin and screwed up his face in disgust. 'This is watered down pony-piss.'

'Yes, sir,' Jack said. 'The regiment is known as the...'

'Baby Butchers,' Snodgrass finished the sentence for him. 'And don't call me 'sir' in here. They killed a dozen civilians and wounded over a hundred at that Radical meeting. Among the dead were two babies under a year old.'

'That was a long time ago,' Jack said.

'It was in 1819,' Snodgrass finished the gin in the glass and signalled for a servant to pour him another. 'The regiment was never abroad until the 1840s; our first action was in the Sikh Wars.' He sipped the gin. 'This is not so bad once it numbs your palate.'

'I heard we were in the Sikh Wars.' Jack looked away. 'That was another less than glorious occasion I believe.'

'Chillianwalla,' Snodgrass said only the one word and then glanced at the servant to ensure he was not listening. 'One of the hardest fought battles in India; the regiment's introduction to glory and what did they do?' He shook his head and dropped his voice to a whisper. 'They ran away. As soon as the Sikh artillery got our range, we threw away our muskets and ran as fast as God would let us.'

Jack drew a deep breath. The thought of a regiment of British infantry running before any foe was disturbing; the idea of British soldiers fleeing from an Indian army was frightening. The British could only control the huge population of India because of their reputation for moral and military superiority; once that was damaged who knew what the outcome might be. He glanced at Ranveer; what must that inscrutable, shrewd man think of this defeated and disgraced regiment.

'Colonel Murphy wants the 113th to redeem its reputation,' Jack said.

Snodgrass snapped his fingers for more gin. 'Not quite Windrush old fellow. Colonel Murphy does not want the 113th to redeem its reputation; Colonel Murphy wants *you* to redeem the reputation of the 113th.' He pushed the servant aside and grabbed the gin bottle for himself. 'He knows that none of us will be willing to risk life and limb for a lost cause, but you are young and idealistic. You did not see the men's faces as they broke and ran: we did.'

'Did you try and stop them?' Jack asked.

'I fired shots in the air and walloped them with the flat of my sword,' Snodgrass said, 'but they were too far gone. I've never seen such a disgusting display. British soldiers!' he shook his head. 'These are not soldiers, and I doubt that they are even men!' He surveyed Jack over the rim of his glass. 'Murphy is an old woman, Windrush; the affair at Chillianwalla broke him. You are a fool if you think you can restore any pride or courage to this regiment and a bigger fool if you think any other regiment would accept you now. The curse of the 113th has already tainted you. God help you.'

I have no interest in women, the stigma of an illegitimate birth and now the curse of the 113th: what do I have except some mad act of bravery. God, I hope that the Burmese fight.

Chapter Five

Rangoon River, Burma: April 1852

The mosquitoes were waiting as soon as they reached the deck. Not in ones and twos, or in companies, but in entire regiments and brigades. They swarmed everywhere, like a biting black swarm that attached proboscis to every square inch of exposed flesh in their search for blood. Jack swore and scraped a hand across his face. With the insects came perspiration that broke out immediately and soaked through the thick serge of his uniform within minutes.

'If this is the Kingdom of Ava they can keep it,' an anonymous Hereford voice murmured, and somebody else barked a short laugh.

'They can keep the whole bloody East,' Coleman grumbled until Sergeant Wells roared them all to silence.

'Just get on deck,' Jack ordered, 'and prepare to support the Navy.' He said no more, for Sergeant Wells would take care of the details.

They clambered up, one by one, with their once scarlet tunics faded to a dozen shades of red from ochre to ominous blood, and lined up against the rail of *Rattler*. The wash of the corvette broke on the banks on either side of the river and set small fishing boats rocking in the current.

'Bloody mud, bloody forest and bloody mosquitoes,' Coleman hawked and spat over the side into the Rangoon River.

'Keep your mouth shut Coleman and watch for the Burmese.' Wells' ordered.

Rattler chugged on with her screw churning the brown river to a creamy froth and unseen birds calling in the background. Jack looked over his dozen private soldiers; there was no need to inspect Wells. There were other infantrymen on board, but only these twelve were his. They lined the rail, held their muskets and stared at the slowly unfolding landscape.

Burma stretched on either side of the river, an unknown, alien land of jungles and rice fields, mud flats and mosquitoes, small villages of thatched huts and the strange calls of unseen animals. A flock of parrots exploded from the branch of an overhanging tree, their plumage bright against dark leaves.

'Do you think they'll attack us, sir?' Wells asked.

Jack shook his head. 'I don't know sergeant,' he remembered what he had read about this land. 'They are an aggressive people, well used to warfare. They won't like us invading their territory like this.' He glanced along the spar deck, where the thin line of British soldiers faced outward. 'The King of Ava has mustered twenty thousand men I heard, so he must be confident of facing us.'

Wells glanced around. Representatives of different regiments lined the rail, all sweating under the punishing sun and waiting for something to happen. 'We're a long way from England, sir.'

Well, that was stating the obvious. Jack nodded. 'Indeed we are,' he nodded to the guns of the corvette and the other ships of the flotilla, both steam and sail powered, that accompanied them on this expedition. 'But we have firepower, backed with infantry.' Every turn of the corvette's screw carried them further up the river and further away from Moulmein and the main British base. He watched their wash set small ripples easing across the boggy rice-fields that lined either bank. Men and women stopped working in the fields to see them pass; a child gave a hesitant wave until his mother hurried him away from these strange intruders in their land. A family clustered around a huge water-buffalo, the man in a broad hat, the woman in a brilliant blue *longyi* with a baby at her breast. High above, vultures circled in an azure sky.

Jack watched as a single ship chugged from upstream and passed with a flurry of signals. Two officers stood on the raised poop-deck behind a tall funnel, while an ominous row of bodies lay wrapped in sail cloth on her spar-deck.

'That's *Serangipatam*' one of the ship's officers said quietly, 'John Company's black ship.'

Jack watched her pass. 'Where has she been?' He could smell the jungle from her.

'Only God and the commander know,' the officer nodded to a tall man in an immaculate uniform who stood on the poop. 'And you've got more chance of hearing from God than getting information from the commander. Best tend to your own business, Ensign.'

'We're slowing down,' Private Easterhouse said softly, and Jack realised that the beat of the engine had altered, the creamy lines of their wake lessened, so they vanished into almost nothingness before reaching the rice-fields.

'What's that?' Coleman pointed ahead. Even through the slight mist that had risen to obscure one bank of the river, Jack could see the glinting light.

'What the devil is that?' Smith repeated the words as every eye on that side of the corvette peered into the mist.

'It's the Golden Pagoda of Rangoon,' Jack guessed quietly. 'That is Burma's chief religious site and one which they will fight to defend.'

'We're in the province of Pegu; the locals don't consider themselves as Burmese,' Wells spoke so quietly that only Jack heard him. *How the devil does a ranker know that?*

Mention of the word gold had an instant effect. Heads turned, and fingers pointed over the side of the boat. The pagoda's tall cone thrust upward from misted trees to soar toward the clouds. Set a good mile back from the bank of the river it still dominated the area.

'Get back to attention!' Wells roared.

'Don't concentrate on the pagoda,' Jack said quietly, 'but be prepared for hard fighting. The Burmese have built stockades and are
masters of defending them.'

*I am approaching my first action; I should be scared and excited, but
this does not feel real. I am somebody else looking down on me.*

'We are anchoring,' Wells said as *Rattler* eased to a halt on the
pagoda side of the river. The other ships of the flotilla followed suit
until there was a long line of British vessels anchored bow to stern,
sails furled, smoke oozing from tall funnels and the multi-crossed flag
of the Union hanging limply in the sulky heat. It was an array of British
military power blatantly displayed far up a river in this south eastern
corner of Asia. Shafts of sunlight escaped from the fraying fingers of
mist to seep between the banyan trees and create sparkling ribbons
on the brown water.

'Impressive, isn't it, Wells?' Jack nodded to the ships.

Wells glanced and shrugged. 'Yes, sir.' He did not look impressed.
'The mist is clearing, sir.'

As a boy, Jack had often stood on the ridge of the Malvern Hills and
watched the ground mist smeared across the Worcestershire plains.
He had seen the spires of the churches protruding from the silver grey
blanket, and the tops of the tallest trees, and then the mist had gradually cleared to reveal the countryside. This Oriental mist was different,
denser, sinister even, lacking the cosy friendliness of his native land.
It seemed to cling to the tall pagoda that swept upward from the huddled buildings of Rangoon as if reluctant to reveal the intricate details
to the British invader.

'That's impressive, sir,' Wells indicated the pagoda. It was easily the
largest building in Rangoon with the apex of its cone glinting gold
under the kiss of the sun and the sliding mist below. It soared above
the squat domestic buildings and lesser pagodas that huddled together
to make up the new town of Rangoon. Wells nodded toward the guns
of *Rattler* and the other British ships that were forming into a long
line in the muddy water of this tributary of the Irrawaddy. 'It's a sin
that we have to blow it to bits.'

Now that's another unusual sentiment for a ranker.

Jack nodded to the ground between the banks of the river and the temple where the old town of Rangoon had so recently stood. Now that settlement was gone, destroyed by word of the King of the Golden Foot and the materials had been used to build a series of stout stockades.

'The Burmese agree with you,' he said quietly. 'We have to get past that lot first.'

From their position in the centre of the river, Jack could see the ugly snouts of cannon protruding above the log ramparts and the heads of inquisitive defenders bobbing around as they watched the creeping British advance.

The enemy is there; even now some Burmese soldier might be pointing me out and planning to shoot me.

Jack watched as the British ships lifted anchor again and manoeuvred for the best position for the attack. The officers on *Rattler* shouted orders that saw the corvette throw great hawsers astern to the forty-four gun frigate *Fox*. The pennant of Commodore Lambert hung in the humid air. Somewhere an animal screamed high pitched; a monkey perhaps.

'That's the man in charge then,' Wells indicated Lambert's flag.

Jack said nothing. It was not an officer's place to reply to a sergeant. He watched the scurry of activity on the frigate and wondered how these seamen, used to life on the broad reaches of the world's oceans, felt being confined in such a small space as the Rangoon River.

'Take the strain!' A lean lieutenant roared as *Rattler*'s engines increased their revolutions until the noise increased to a whine. The tow rope tautened and vibrated. The water under Rattler's counter churned to a creamy brown.

'Slow ahead!' the officer shouted, and the corvette inched forward with the sailing ship fifty feet behind and a handful of seamen watching over the towing cable. Over on the far bank, a man slowly guided a pair of water buffalo through a rice field, ignoring the spectacle that Britain had provided for his enlightenment.

Rattler moved on, slowly, towing the frigate astern as they eased closer to Rangoon with its impressive pointed pagoda and the outlying stockades that sat, squat and menacing, as guardians of the Burmese Empire. The atmosphere was heavy, humid; the air so dense it was hard to breathe while every movement brought the exasperating prickle of perspiration.

'Shoal water, sir!' a seaman in the bow shouted.

Jack had hardly seen the captain on their voyage from Rangoon, but now he took control.

'Cast off the tow,' the captain ordered. '*Fox* has deeper draught than us; she will run aground here. Slow ahead; stand by the guns!'

A seaman threw the tow rope into the muddy water and *Rattler* moved on alone. The seamen hurried to the guns as she eased yard by yard closer to the teak stockades that barred any landing. Jack could see the heads and shoulders of the captain and the first lieutenant on the bridge as they scanned Rangoon with their telescopes. Below them, the spar deck of *Rattler* was busy with white clothed, tight-trousered seamen readying the five huge 32- pounder broadside cannon or the even more massive pivot 68-pounder that occupied the bow. The officers gave sharp orders as the powder monkeys, the young boys who carried cartridges to the guns, scurried around, laughing and joking despite the stern words and occasional blows.

'So here we are,' Jack said to himself, 'thirty miles up a tributary of the Irrawaddy River in a flotilla of ships, facing an unknown and savage enemy.' For the first time, he felt a prickle of excitement. He was about to earn his pay. He had chosen this career; fighting was his only way back up to where he belonged.

'There's movement there,' Wells pointed to the nearest of the defending stockades. The defenders were clustering around cannon; the ugly black snouts protruded through embrasures on the parapet.

They're going to fire first. I am going to be under fire. Jack felt something cold run down his back and his buttocks involuntarily contracted. Why that particular part of me? He fought the desire to laugh.

Nerves! It's the same feeling as I had when summoned to the Rector's study.

The captain leaned over from the bridge to give explicit orders to his crew.

'Get ready men, but don't fire unless they do.' His voice carried across the corvette. 'Let them open the ball, but we'll close the final curtain. Do your duty, *Rattlers* and look out for one another.'

The sun had burned away the mist, so the Golden Pagoda was like a blinding blaze of splendour. A sough of furnace-hot wind stirred the palms and set a hundred bells ringing, with the faint tinkling a macabre musical backdrop to the impending scenes of slaughter. Without the mist, the defending stockades were clear, their tall teak walls formidable and the muzzles of cannons bared in dark defiance. Smoke rose from the interior.

Jack saw the heads of the Burmese scurrying behind the stockade walls. He saw the puff of white smoke a second before he heard the sound of the cannon, and for a fraction of a second, he saw the black streak of the shot coming toward him.

'Happy Easter,' Coleman muttered.

Jack nodded. He tried to ignore his suddenly dry throat. He was under fire; the war with the Burmese Empire had begun, and he was right in the front line. *Father would be proud of his illegitimate son.* He saw one of his men duck: that was Thorpe, a heavy set man with a pock-marked face.

'No bobbing!' Wells' voice was hard. 'You're British soldiers so bloody act like it.'

The Burmese gunners fired in a rolling barrage that concealed the delicate tinkle of the temple bells. He counted fifteen British steamers plus the frigate *Fox* and a sailing brig: have more come up when I was not looking? Or did I miscount? He saw the orange flares from the muzzles of the cannon, he saw the long jets of smoke, and he heard the sharp crack of Burmese artillery as they targeted the British vessels in the narrow river.

So this is war. Jack fought the impulse to duck.

'They're firing at us,' Coleman murmured.

'And we'll fire back,' Sergeant Wells replied. 'Now keep your tongue behind your teeth and act like a British soldier Coleman, you useless bastard.'

Jack saw a long column of water where a Burmese cannon ball landed only a hundred feet from the ship. Thorpe swore and began to tremble slightly. Wells stepped behind him.

'Easy lads,' Jack controlled his fear. He had not known what to expect when he was under fire, but it was the strangest feeling, a mixture of intense excitement, wonder and fear. 'Keep calm and face your front.' He glanced at the men of the other regiments; they would know the reputation of the 113th and would be waiting to jeer the first sign of wavering.

'Fire,' the captain ordered. He removed his cap and gestured toward the nearest stockade, 'rattle them, *Rattlers!*'

Rattler retaliated, with the five thirty- two pounders of her broadside firing simultaneously. The shock heeled the corvette to one side and unbalanced the unprepared infantry who lined her spar deck. Most staggered, and some fell.

'Get back to the rail!' Wells sounded almost apoplectic as his men clattered to the deck. He landed a full-blooded kick on Thorpe's backside. 'Stand up you idle blaggard! Get up there you black-hearted buggers!'

'Careful, redcoats!' A grinning seaman called. 'We're firing now.' He gestured to the cutlass he wore at his waist. 'Soon be time for hand to hand fighting, sojer-boys. You can watch that too and learn what to do.'

'Bloody tar-backs!' Coleman picked himself off the deck, grabbed his musket and glared at the sailor. 'Away and trim the webs from your toes you tarry-arsed bastard.'

Jack stepped forward before Coleman attacked the offending sailor. 'Get back to your station, Coleman! Show these sailors how the 113th behave.'

The Burmese were firing hard, with cannon balls howling overhead or raising tall fountains of water. White smoke hazed the stockade and smothered the surface of the river.

'They've got bottom,' Wells had to shout above the noise of battle. He blinked as *Rattler* fired another broadside. Soldiers and sailors alike coughed in the acrid smoke, wiped the sweat from foreheads and endured the rivulets that ran down their bodies. Jack watched with envy as the seamen stripped off their jumpers and worked bare chested.

'Permission to take off my tunic, sir,' a thin faced soldier named Leigh asked.

'Denied; look to your front,' Jack barked. Soldiers of the Queen did not act in such a casual manner as seamen; discipline must be maintained.

A Burmese round shot skipped off the surface of the river and bounced right across the deck without touching anybody or doing any damage. Jack gasped as the wind of its passage temporarily sucked the wind from his lungs.

'Are you all right, sir?' Wells looked concerned.

Jack nodded, unable to speak.

A few cables' lengths astern, *Fox* fired her complete broadside. The massive discharge filled the hot air with noise so loud that men clapped hands to their ears. *Nobody said that battle was this noisy!* Jack watched the closest of the Burmese stockades as the volley smashed home. The stout logs shuddered under the impact; one entire length of teak flew high in the air, spun and arrowed back down. *Rattler* fired again, and everybody in the ship flinched as there was a huge explosion within the stockade. An orange fireball ripped the logs apart, with yellow flames on the side, slowly subsiding as fragments of timber and people rose and fell, to patter onto the mud and splash on the river, burning dangerously close to the wooden British ships.

There was an instant's silence as men watched the terrible sight.

Wells was first to recover. He spoke to Jack and pointed toward the stockade.

Jack nodded; he could see Well's mouth move, but the tremendous noise had robbed him of his hearing. Splintered remnants of great logs were scattered over a wide area, some burning, others mere shreds of wood and all mingled with the remains of the Burmese defenders. Hearing returned slowly, gradually as partial sounds penetrated the enforced hush.

'Burn in hell, you bastards,' Leigh croaked until Wells jabbed a hard hand under his ribs.

'Keep your mouth shut you useless bugger!'

A lone cannon fired from a second stockade, with the shot falling short.

'They're game, these Burmese;' there was respect in Coleman's voice.

Half a dozen stockades defended Rangoon, each one with its quota of cannon and men. *Rattler*'s captain stood on the bridge, nodding as his ship fired broadside after broadside at the Burmese. Occasionally he gave a brisk command to the other officers on deck. In turn, they ran to the gun captains and pointed out the next target.

Leigh tugged at the leather stock at his neck. 'I feel a bit queer, Sergeant,' he stepped back from the rail. 'It's the heat.'

'Face your front!' Wells pushed him back to his position. 'You're a soldier; act like one.'

The Burmese shot was still coming and mostly still missing, falling short of the line of British ships. The occasional ball skipped over the water nearby as *Rattler* concentrated on the next stockade. The crewmen altered the angle of their guns, laughing, joking and sweating in the punishing heat of the mid-morning sun.

Greasy white smoke coiled around the cannon, swirled up the masts and lay waist deep along the spar deck as *Rattler* continued to fire. The sun hammered the deck, setting the tar bubbling between the planking and making every move a torment. Jack wiped perspiration from his forehead and glanced at a lieutenant of the Madras European Infantry, one of the Company regiments that had a contingent of men on board. Where the Queen's officers wore nearly the same uniform in the East as they did back in Britain, the Company officers wore a much looser helmet, adorned with yards of cloth to make a sensible turban and baggy jackets of cotton drill rather than tight shell jackets.

Jack was unsure whether to sneer at their lack of manliness or be jealous of their cooler appearance. He looked away, feeling the sweat prickle inside his white buckskin gloves and thought he was baking within the stifling confines of his uniform.

Leigh tugged once more at his stock, looked appealingly at Sergeant Wells and then slid to the deck. His musket clattered into the scuppers.

'Get up you idle bastard,' Wells stirred him with his boot. When Leigh did not respond, he kicked him sharply in the ribs. 'I said get up, damn you!' He knelt beside him, unscrewed the cap of his water bottle and poured some of the contents on the man's face and neck. 'Come on Leigh,' the tone of his voice had changed from a brusque bark to concern. 'Come on, son…' he forced open Leigh's mouth and upended the bottle. Water dribbled down the side of Leigh's face to form a small pool on the deck.

'Is he all right?' Jack knelt at Well's side.

'No, sir,' Wells looked up. 'I think he's dead.'

'It's the heat,' Knight pulled at his stock. 'He was always grousing about the heat.'

Jack shuddered. That's the first death under my command; the first of my men dead. He knew there would be more, but he would always remember Leigh. He fought his shock: he was a Queen's officer, he could not submit to emotion. 'Unfasten your stocks boys and undo the top buttons of your tunic.'

'That's against Queen's Regulations, sir,' Wells shook his head.

Jack pointed to Leigh. 'I want no more deaths from the heat.' He knew he was asking the impossible. Soldiers died of heat or disease; they always had and they always would. That was a soldier's lot.

'But it's against Queen's Regulations, sir.' Wells repeated. 'The stocks protect our necks from the sun.'

'Do as I order,' Jack injected authority into his voice, and Wells reluctantly removed the leather stock from his neck. The privates were gleeful as they followed his example, with Coleman rubbing two fingers around his sweating throat.

'It's worth losing Leigh to get that bloody thing off,' Graham said.

'Coleman, you and O'Neill take Leigh below decks,' Jack watched as the two men *dragged their comrade away. O'Neill was surprisingly gentle.*

I wonder how many more of my men will die before we win this war. How do I feel? Numb; the reality had not hit me yet. I have chosen this life, and the Burmese have to be defeated.

Rattler fired another broadside, with the vessel heeling over in the river and the roundshot howling toward the defences of Rangoon. Within minutes a second stockade was destroyed as its powder magazine exploded and tall flames leapt skyward. The second explosion did not have the same power to shock as the first had done.

'Burn you bastards,' Coleman jeered. He looked toward Wells and patted the lock of his musket. 'Can we fire at them as well, Sergeant?'

'Any more talking from you and you'll feel the cat,' Wells took out his resentment at breaking Queen's Regulations on his men. 'Now keep quiet until you are ordered to talk, damn you.'

The captain gave another order, and the gunners raised their sights. 'Go for the Golden Pagoda, boys!'

With two of the outlying stockades in flames, the Burmese fire had slackened, but most of their heavy artillery was based around the Golden Pagoda. *Rattler* fired broadside after broadside at this tall target, with her 68 pounder swivel gun adding its fire to those of the spar deck 32-pounders. The smoke became so dense that Jack could not see *Fox*, yet alone the full line of British ships, but the constant noise and glare of orange muzzle flashes assured him they were still there.

'We're giving them a hell of a licking,' a grinning powder monkey screeched, his voice high pitched with excitement. He immersed his head in a bucket of water on the deck and came up dripping wet and still smiling. 'There's no need for you redcoats to be here; the Navy will do all the work!'

Jack said nothing. *Rangoon is on fire, we've destroyed their outer defences, and only the Golden Pagoda is standing. This war may be over in one day.*

'Can we at least fire at them, Sergeant?' Coleman asked again. He tapped the butt of his musket. 'We are meant to be soldiers.'

'Stand firm,' Jack ordered. 'And do the 113th proud. We'll get our chance, never fear!'

We'll get our chance if the navy leaves us anything. How can I better the regiment's reputation by merely watching? More important, how can I distinguish myself and get into the Royals, where I belong?

Around two in the afternoon an order from the Commodore Lambert stopped the cannonade. A slight breeze shifted the smoke, pushing it away as if it was a sliding door. Visibility increased. Sunlight reflected from the pagoda and, faint on the wind, the musical tinkle of temple bells mocked the British fleet.

'They only have twelve pounders,' a naval lieutenant's voice sounded through a lull in the firing. 'They can see us, but they don't have the range.' He slapped a hand on the breech of his cannon, 'but neither have we. That temple will stand there until doomsday.'

'Over there, sir,' Wells nodded to the banks of the river. 'There's a group of men.'

Jack nodded. 'So I see.' At this point, the river was no wider than the Thames, muddy and green and turgid, with dismal rice fields or ugly green jungle on either side of Rangoon. There were a few dozen small Burmese boats along the bank, with a larger war-boat peeping out of a sheltered bend. Warriors in light clothes and carrying long muskets and the ubiquitous Burmese dha – the long, viciously sharp knife - clustered around the boats, gesticulating toward the British ships and firing the occasional shot.

'Load your muskets, men.' That was the first time Jack had ever given that order in the face of the enemy. He felt a thrill of mingled excitement and apprehension. *Are these Burmese going to try and board us? Will this end up hand to hand, bayonet against these terrible dhas?*

That is it. I am a real soldier now; we are under fire and preparing to fight back.

'Get ready to defend the ship if the Burmese attack.'

Somebody swore softly as the eleven remaining men loaded their long Brown Bess muskets much as their forefathers had done at Waterloo and Albuera, Long Island and Quebec. The weapon was the same and the uniforms very similar. Jack realised he was witnessing the same scene as his father and grandfather had seen.

He watched the Burmese moving around the boats, some waving their dhas in anger or defiance or both. The sound of gongs joined the sweet tinkle of the bells. There were drums as well, insistent, martial, strangely unsettling. 'If they board,' Jack said, 'fix bayonets.' He nearly felt the shiver that ran through them, but whether of fear or anticipation, he could not tell.

'Message from the commodore,' a lieutenant called. 'Recommence firing at the pagoda.'

The next broadside sent the Burmese scurrying back to find whatever cover they could find.

By late afternoon orange flames licked through the dense smoke that rolled across Rangoon. *Rattler* continued to fire until the liquid notes of a bugle sounded, and the guns fell silent. Men looked across at the wreckage that had been a bustling, vibrant town only that morning, grinned at the relief that they were unharmed and wondered what the future would bring. A seaman commented on their smoke-blackened appearance, and others laughed nervously.

'That was easy enough,' Wells said. 'The Burmese hardly put up any resistance.'

Jack glanced along the spar deck of the ship. He could see no casualties on *Rattler*; for all the fire and fury of the Burmese defence, not a single shot had hit the ship.

Leigh is dead. He is lying below.

'At least the bloody smoke keeps the mosquitoes away,' Coleman said.

'Mr Windrush!' A midshipman ran up. He was about sixteen and looked like a mischievous schoolboy with black powder smoke around his eyes and dirtying his white uniform. 'The Captain sends his compliments and would you care to support our boats with your men?"

It was not the Navy's way to stand idly by while there was work to be done. *Rattler*'s officers were already organising a landing party. A burly petty officer was handing out muskets to sailors who handled them with casual familiarity. Other seamen were sharpening their cutlasses on a circular whetstone while still more lowered three boats over the side into the river.

'Please inform the captain that I will be delighted,' Jack said. He raised his voice. 'Come on the 113th! Time to show these sailor men how to fight.'

A seaman stood in the bow of the small boat, holding a boathook to attach it to *Rattler*. 'Down you come lads,' he invited. 'Don't mind the rocking!' His grin was more amused than mocking as the soldiers dropped clumsily into the boat, tripping over the thwarts as they jostled for seats.

'Sit still,' Jack ordered. 'Keep your rifles upright between your knees and for God's sake keep your bayonets in the scabbard. I don't want anybody spitted.'

They look nervous. Thorpe is white faced, and Coleman looks sick. There is no bluster now.

He glanced at the river bank. The Burmese were waiting, waving their wicked looking dhas and loading their muskets in readiness for the landing. Despite the severe cannonade they had endured they did not appear cowed. With small turbans on their heads, dark quilted jackets and mostly bare legs they looked alien and somehow all the more dangerous for that.

Four more seamen boarded the boat, their nimbleness a contrast to the lumbering soldiers. They grabbed oars and even as the soldiers settled, began to pull toward the shore. The young midshipman sat in the stern giving crisp orders.

Windrush

'These Burmese lads look right handy,' Thorpe sounded nervous. 'I don't like the look of their swords.'

'They're called dhas,' Wells said, 'and they don't like the look of our muskets either. Now stop grousing and earn your pay.'

'We don't like the look of you, Thorpey,' Coleman added and looked over his shoulder at the rapidly approaching land. 'Oh, Thorpey there's thousands of them all waiting to cut your goolies off. Can you hear them? They're chanting: give us Thorpey, we want Thorpey.' Some of the other soldiers echoed his laugh, but most fidgeted uncomfortably on the wooden seats. Smoke drifted from the burning stockades, and the sounds of drums reached them, loud now, mingled with the wailing of women and the hoarse shouts of men. A gong clattered brassily from the wreckage of the nearest stockade.

'Jesus,' Thorpe said. 'They're going to massacre us.' He glanced back toward *Rattler*. 'Get back to the ship, boys, for God's sake.'

'Sit tight!' Jack yelled as Coleman began to rise. 'We have a job to do!'

Others of the 113th were looking nervous and following Thorpe's lead in staring at the Burmese soldiers that waited for them. The sound of drums increased, filling the air and making speech difficult.

It's going to be Chillianwalla all over again: another disgrace for the regiment.

'Sit back down!' Jack reached forward and pushed at the shoulders of Coleman, shoving him hard back onto his seat. 'You took the Queen's Shilling to be a soldier, and by God, you will act like one or I'll shoot you dead here and now!'

To their right, the second of *Rattler*'s boats surged past with the seamen on board cheering as they neared the shore. Men from the Madras Fusiliers looked curiously at the upheaval among the 113th.

'Right lads!' Jack shouted above the noise of drums. 'Now is our chance to show the bluejackets what the 113th can do! Let's make our children proud of us!'

There was a scattering of musketry, and a ball thumped into the boat, raising chips of timber and leaving a raw scar on the wood.

78

Thorpe screamed, and Coleman ducked, cowering beside the men around him for shelter.

'Sit to attention!' Jack ordered. 'Don't bob!' He looked astern. The young midshipman was standing by the tiller as he concentrated on steering the boat. Jack took a deep breath and stood up, balancing against the movement and hoping the Burmese did not use him as a target. They were within twenty yards of the river banks, and he could make out the facial features of the waiting enemy. He shivered; they were watching him out of expressionless eyes in flat faces, waiting.

'Ready lads!' Jack reached for the pistol at his belt. He had bought an Adams pepperpot revolver because of the firepower, and now he was glad of the six chambers. He touched his sword hilt; it was the 1845 pattern Wilkinson sword, designed by John Latham, with a thirty-two and a half inches long, slightly curved blade and with a sharkskin grip, yet it seemed inadequate and fragile compared to the lethal dhas of the Burmese. Suddenly Jack's force of twelve British soldiers seemed very inadequate compared to the number of Burmese that was waiting for them. He heard the harsh breathing of his men, and then the bow of the boat slithered onto soft mud, and the bluejackets were leaping over the side, drawing their cutlasses and yelling at the enemy.

There is no fear in these seamen.

'Fire a volley!' Jack ordered, 'then charge!'

His doubts had all vanished. Instead, he felt a wild elation as he gave the order, fired his revolver at the gesticulating Burmese, rode the kick that jolted his forearm, and ran forward hoping his men were at his back. He remembered one of the few occasions that his father had spent time with him.

'There are two types of officers,' his father had said. 'Those that say: go on and those that say: come- on. In the Royals, we only have room for the come-ons.'

Now Jack was a come- on officer, leading his men from the front. This was not how he imagined his first action, jumping into muddy water against a bunch of turbaned men in some obscure eastern town;

he had thought of leading the Royals against the French in some glorious European battle with a cast of tens of thousands.

Jack fired again, but the Burmese did not rush to meet him, as he thought all soldiers would do. Instead, they turned and fled before the two sides came within bayonet distance.

'They're running!' Wells did not sound surprised. 'We've sent them running!' He knelt and fired his musket at the retreating Burmese, 'come back and fight, you bastards!'

Belatedly, Jack checked his men. They were all with him, panting in the heat, white of face and more scared than war-like, but they had followed him. Twelve men of the 113th had proved they were not cowards. To that extent, the shadow of Chillianwalla was lightened. Even Coleman had kept up and now shouted abuse as the Burmese disappeared into the thick scrub that reached nearly to the walls of Rangoon.

Was that it? Was that my first battle? It was over in seconds.

'Follow them!' O'Neill lifted his voice in some Gaelic slogan that lifted the hairs on Jack's scalp. He grabbed hold of O'Neill's arm.

'No! They know the jungle. They will cut us to pieces in there.' He dragged O'Neill back. 'Stop here!'

'Cowards!' Coleman pushed to the front of the redcoats and waved a closed fist. 'Come back and fight!'

'You are very brave now they're running,' Wells was not smiling.

'More to the point, Sergeant Wells, is that none of our men ran.' He raised his voice. 'Well done men. We chased the enemy away.'

'Sir,' Wells nodded to the jungle. 'The Burmese have not run far.'

Jack was aware of the Burmese warriors gathering at the edge of the bush but more aware of the circle of bluejackets who listened to every word he said. *He had led his men to a minor victory. We have not spilt any enemy blood, but we faced them, and nobody ran away. That is a good way to end the day.*

Chapter Six

April 1852: Rangoon

'They won't stand a chance,' Coleman sat in the centre of the boat with a man on either side and his musket upright between his knees. He looked toward the still smoking remnants of the stockades that had barred the British landing on this bank of the Rangoon River. Now the route to the Golden Pagoda lay open. 'They ran away from us last time, and they'll run again.'

Jack let him talk. In the two days that had elapsed since the bombardment of the stockades, reinforcements had joined the British fleet. Vessels of the Honourable East India Company had brought up hundreds of soldiers, both Queen's and Company's, and now instead of three boats from *Rattler* and a handful of redcoats and bluejackets, dozens of boats were rowing across the river, each with its quota of soldiers. All peered eagerly into the pre-dawn dark and hoped for a brief victorious fight followed by plunder.

Jack surveyed the scene: he saw the proud Midshipmen or bearded petty officers in the stern of each boat directing the naval rowers while the redcoats sat in disciplined ranks waiting for their opportunity. There were the Royal Irish of the 18th Foot, the 51st Regiment and four hundred of the 80th Foot as well as immaculate sepoys of the Bengal and Madras Native Infantry from the Company's army plus some capable sappers and miners. Backing the infantry were pieces of artillery, precariously balanced in the boats. Together with the navy and company ships, it was the largest collection of British military might Jack had seen gathered in one place.

And my men of the 113th are part of it.

Jack grinned, unable to hide his sudden pleasure at living the life he had always wanted. Here I am fighting for the Queen in this strange humid land, facing the Queen's enemies and seeing exotic and captivating places.

'There's that Golden Pagoda,' O'Neill blinked away the sweat from his eyes. 'That's what we're taking today, boys.' He licked his lips. 'Gold and silver and jewels,' he said. 'I heard that that place is stuffed with rubies and emeralds for the taking.'

'How did you hear that?' Coleman jeered. 'Your thick Irish ears can't understand English yet alone Burmese.'

'One of the sweepers told me,' O'Neill ignored the insult. 'He said he had seen hundreds of rubies and piles of gold.'

'I heard there were dragons and monsters there,' Graham's Cumbrian accent was every bit as incomprehensible as O'Neill's Donegal.

'And guns,' Wells grunted as a single cannon shot sounded across the ruins of the stockades. 'This may not be as easy as the last time.' He nudged Thorpe with the side of his boot. 'None of your grousing, Thorpey-boy; I'm watching you, and I'm up to all your dodges.'

'They're firing at us,' O'Neill said as a spurt of smoke emitted from the Golden Pagoda followed a second later by a deep bang. 'They want you Thorpey!'

'Keep together boys,' Jack ordered. 'Remember that we're with the 51st Foot, and we're going after the White House Picket.' He indicated their target, a stockade that stood directly between the landing party and the Golden Pagoda. 'After that,' he pointed ahead, 'we are advancing on the Pagoda itself.'

'Will the Burmese fight?' Coleman sounded anxious.

'I bloody hope so,' O'Neill's words brought general laughter. 'The quicker they fight, the quicker we can kill them and get the loot!'

'113th!' The word cut crisp across the mud flats. 'Form up beside us.'

The 51st looked like veterans, sun bronzed and fit. They glowered at the newcomers and only reluctantly made room for them. 'Bloody Griffins and Johnny Raws,' a corporal complained. 'Well, I hope you know how to fight.'

'I'm Major Reid,' a stocky, tanned officer introduced himself, 'of the Bengal Artillery.' He jerked a thumb toward the stockade that blocked their path. 'We are the leading unit and your men have to escort us so we can blast the Burmese out of the way.'

'You can rely on us,' Jack hoped he sounded more confident than he felt. Not only Thorpe had started at the report of the gun from the pagoda: Coleman and a couple of others had looked decidedly nervous as well.

'You take the right flank,' Reid ordered and returned his attention to his artillery.

The right flank was that furthest from the landing place, and the least covered by the guns of the Navy. There was an area of open ground, a maidan between the advancing British and the dark scrub jungle that spread on either side of Rangoon.

'Open order, men, keep in front of the guns but not too far in case the Burmese get between us.' Jack tried to sound confident.

We are the foremost troops of the British Army: the 113th is in the van.

They moved forward slowly with the guns in the middle of the formation, and the sound of gunfire behind as the ships of the fleet exchanged shot and shell with the defenders of the pagoda. Thorpe ducked as a shell whizzed low overhead, then looked around with a guilty grin on his face.

'That was one of ours,' Wells' voice was flat. 'As soon as it sees your uniform the cannon ball will stop and go elsewhere.'

Thorpe's grin altered to a relieved smile. 'Is that right, sergeant?'

'Of course, it is,' Wells said, 'so keep your head up and don't bob.'

'Oh Jesus save us,' Coleman shook his head.

The cannon ball rammed into the ground a few paces in front of them, bounced and splashed into the mud.

'Jesus; they're firing at us!' Coleman's voice rose into a near screech.

'Stand!' Jack put a hand on Thorpe's shoulder to prevent him from running. 'We're British soldiers; they are only a raggy-arsed bunch of jungle-wallahs.'

'That was one of theirs,' Wells had not flinched.

There was further gunfire; more balls whizzing past or slogging into the mud. Coleman pointed a shaky finger. 'Look over there!'

At first, Jack could see nothing and then as his eyes accustomed themselves to the shape and shadow of the jungle; he saw human shapes flitting about between the trees. Drums sounded from somewhere, but whether from the jungle or the stockade he could not tell. A gong sounded brassily between the scream and crash of artillery.

'The Burmese lads are hard to see,' Wells said.

Jack nodded. 'Their clothes and colour blend with nature: unlike us.' He was suddenly aware that the scarlet of the British Army looked bold and martial on parade or when armies were manoeuvring in civilised warfare, but out East, in the jungle, the red-coated British soldiers made excellent targets.

'Open up,' Jack realised that his men had bunched together, 'and advance on these Burmese skirmishers.'

The gongs continued; he could not tell when they had started, he only knew that they were there, everywhere, in his head, surrounding him, penetrating his thoughts. They were the sound of Burma and a reminder that he an intruder in this beautiful, frighteningly alien land. Gongs and artillery, the muted swearing from his men, the sharp crack of musketry: this was his unique introduction to warfare.

Jack looked forward, where the Burmese gunners were firing from the White House Picket. It was a formidable stockade, larger and stronger than any they had destroyed so far in this war, and the Burmese defenders seemed determined and active. Their cannon fired again, and Jack saw some of the sepoys of the Madras Native Infantry fall; their line immediately closed up. A high pitched scream sounded across the battle field, just as the gongs raised their sonorous beat.

'Advance on the jungle skirmishers,' a red faced colonel ordered. 'You fellow' he pointed a plump finger at Jack, 'take your men and clear that blasted jungle. We're fighting on three fronts here, damn it.'

Jack saw the cannon on the White House Picket fire again, and the 51st Foot form up for the assault. There would be glory there, and honour for the regiment that overcame the Burmese in that stockade, but none for the 113th if they merely guarded the flank against jungle skirmishers.

We are no longer the front markers: now we are a sideshow.

'They're getting bolder, sir,' Wells said.

A score of Burmese emerged from the jungle, moving fast as they weaved from cover to cover. One dropped to his knees and fired his long musket.

'They're going to harass our flank as we attack the White House Picket,' Wells pointed out the obvious.

'Volley fire!' Jack ordered. 'One round: fire!' He stepped close to Thorpe. 'Take your time men and mark your target.'

Twelve muskets cracked in a ragged volley. None of the Burmese fell.

'Fix bayonets!' Jack said. More Burmese appeared from within the wall of the jungle, sturdy, active men with black padded jackets and long muskets or dhas. Some fired back with the white spurts of smoke swift to appear, slow to dissipate against dark foliage. Others slipped around the sides, intending to outflank the 113th. Muzzle flares momentarily gleamed on the naked blades of a dozen dhas.

'Spread out!' Jack ordered. He fired his revolver at the closest of the Burmese and saw the man stagger but recover. 'Hold the line! Don't let them entice you into the forest.'

'No bloody chance of that,' O'Neill said. 'Once we go in there they'll chop us to pieces.'

'Load!' Jack realised that his men were standing with empty muskets. *I have to tell them even the simplest thing.* He saw Thorpe glance behind him, searching for safety. 'Look to your front Thorpe! You took the Queen's shilling, now earn it!'

'But sir!' Thorpe's eyes were unfocused; his breath came in short bursts. 'Sir...'

'Come on Thorpey,' Wells encouraged, 'a shilling a day: good pay for the privilege of fighting the Queen's enemies!'

'Fight them, man!' Jack pointed to where the Burmese advanced from the jungle, crouched to fire and moved again. 'There is the enemy, Thorpe: kill them, and we'll be safe!'

The British artillery fired again as Reid slewed his four guns around to point at the White House Picket. Roundshot arced overhead and ripped down, too fast for the eye to see.

'That bloody fort is right in our path,' O'Neill glanced at the stockade. 'Until we destroy it we are stuck here for the Burmese to hit us on two fronts at once.'

'Ignore the stockade,' Jack loosed two shots at the flanking enemy and swore as the hammer clicked on an empty chamber. He fumbled for cartridges to reload. 'Our job is to contain the Burmese in the jungle.'

A panting corporal of the 51st ran up, musket at the trail. 'Are you in charge of the 113th, sir?'

'I am,' Jack admitted.

'Colonel St Maur sends his compliments, sir, and could you push the enemy back from the jungle edge sir? He's going to lead the 51st through the jungle to take that fort, and he wants his flank secure.'

Damn! We'll lose all our advantages in the jungle.

'Pray inform Colonel St Maur that the 113th will secure his flank,' Jack said. He raised his voice. 'Come on lads; we're needed! The whole advance depends on us!'

Jack estimated that there were between thirty and fifty Burmese on the fringe of the jungle, some firing, others merely making threatening gestures with their dhas. He paused for a moment to complete loading his revolver, dropped a cartridge in nervousness or excitement, he was not sure which and let it lie as a brassy memory on the grass. 'Right lads,' he tried not to duck as a Burmese bullet hissed past his head, 'fire a volley and this time hit some of the bastards, and then take them at the charge.'

Jack remembered an uncle who told him that very few soldiers ever stood against a British bayonet charge. The fear of facing men intent on spitting them like meat on the end of eighteen inches of sharpened steel was usually enough to break even the firmest confidence. Looking at the Burmese swordsmen, he hoped that his uncle's theory was proved correct. These dhas looked hideously dangerous.

'Present,' he gave the order. Twelve red jacketed men slammed their muskets against sweat-stained shoulders. Twelve Brown Bess muskets pointed toward the swarming Burmese.

'Fire!'

Twelve spurts of flame; twelve jets of white smoke; twelve lead balls hurtling toward the Burmese. Even as three of the enemy fell, two to kick and writhe on the ground, one to lie in a crumpled heap, Jack shouted:

'Drive them back boys! Bayonets and charge! Follow me, 113th!'

With his pistol in his left hand and sword in his right, Jack ran toward the Burmese, hoping that some at least of his men were behind him. He did not expect Thorpe to follow.

The Burmese stood longer than Jack had hoped. One brave man stepped toward him, wielding a dha with a long straight blade. Jack squeezed the trigger of his revolver, missed the first time but saw the second shot smack home and the man stagger. The Burmese looked at the bleeding hole in his chest, and Jack swiped wildly with his sword, caught him a glancing blow that opened a cut on his arm and rushed past, yelling.

'Kill them!' That was O'Neill, 'kill them all!'

'Blood, blood blood!' Knight had remembered the lessons from his bayonet drill.

'Jesus Christ; Jesus bloody Christ!' Coleman was alternatively cursing and praying, but he was there with the rest, slashing and thrusting at fresh air with his bayonet.

The Burmese did not stand long. Most fled into the jungle before the 113th arrived and only three put up any resistance. O'Neill finished the swordsman that Jack had wounded while Pryor bayoneted a stocky man who stood and swung his musket like a club. Coleman and Wells each thrust their bayonets into the body of the third Burmese, and Wells finished him with savage kicks from his iron studded boots.

'Well done lads,' Jack counted his men. All twelve were there, with Thorpe at the rear, panting, wild eyed and his cap askew, but still with them. 'Now keep within sight of each other. We're going into the jungle; dress the line, men.'

There was no gradual build up. The maidan ended at what seemed a solid green wall of scrub and bamboo, dark, seemingly impenetrable, familiar to the Burmese but utterly alien to soldiers brought up in the neat fields or urban slums of Britain.

Major Reid's four guns were firing hard with their shot crashing into the White House Picket, with the Burmese guns replying in an irregular ripple of orange flame along the parapet. Jack saw two of the Company sepoys bowled over by a Burmese shot, and another scythed by chain shot so he lay screaming with both legs shorn off just above the knees. Dark blood pumped onto the ground.

'Hot work,' Wells cleaned his bayonet with a piece of oily rag. 'Is this your first action, sir?'

'It is,' Jack admitted. 'I know it's not your first.'

When Wells shook his head, Jack saw a gleam of grey hair under his cap. 'No, sir.'

'You are a veteran then,' Jack decided that any question could wait until later. 'Good; I want you to lead the right wing, and I will take the left. Keep in touch, and we'll push these Burmese back as far as we can.'

'Yes, sir,' Wells looked relieved; fighting the Burmese was obviously easier on his nerves than answering what may have been awkward questions about his past.

'Thorpe, Coleman: you are with me.' Jack decided. 'Reload!' He waited until everybody was ready, glanced back at the main army and saw a general officer, presumably St Maur, marshalling a column of the 51st ready to assault the stockade.

'Follow me, lads,' Jack stepped over the threshold of the jungle and into another world. The heat on the maidan had been oppressive, but here it combined with intense humidity to bring out the sweat in great rivers that had his tunic soaked even before he had advanced ten paces. The mosquitoes that he had tried to ignore were joined by a dozen other types of insect, each of which seemed set to bite or sting as they buzzed around his head or fed on the sweat from his face and body. A female monkey crouched on a high bough cradling her young, and then turned and fled, shrieking.

'Keep in touch, 113th!' his words seemed hollow in the green dimness. 'Push on!'

He could hardly see the man on his left yet alone any Burmese. A bird called, the sound harsh and ugly compared to the blackbirds and song thrushes of the Malvern Hills. He stepped on, hoping there were no snakes or whatever other wild creatures were native to this hostile environment.

The noise must have scared them all away, like that monkey. Keep moving.

'All clear, sir!' Wells' shout echoed through the trees.

Jack shouted an acknowledgement and stepped forward. There was no sign of the Burmese; they had melted away as if they had never been. 'Push on,' he ordered, 'give the 51st as much space as they need.' When he looked behind him he saw only tangled undergrowth, creepers twisted around the boles of unknown trees and sunlight frond-filtered to a dull grey.

There was the distorted sound of marching feet as the 51st entered the jungle in a dense body, a succession of sharp orders and honest British swearing, echoing in the brush.

'Far enough, boys,' Jack shouted. 'Hold your positions and shoot any Burmese that comes close.'

Shoot any Burmese? I can't see anybody to shoot.

The 51st was marching now, crashing through the fringe of the jungle that Jack and the 113th had cleared of any opposition. A flanking file passed Jack, led by a lithe looking engineer officer with red hair and a peeling, sunburned face. He stumbled over a trailing creeper, looked down and shouted something to a squad of men who carried a storming ladder.

Go for glory 51st, while we rot in the jungle.

'Sir!' Wells shout brought Jack back to the alert. 'Burmese!'

There was a single musket shot, and then a small fusillade, a long drawn out scream that could have been part of that terrible dense forest and then thick silence. Powder smoke drifted acrid between the trees. Jack shuddered as a huge spider scuttled out of a hole in the trunk of the tree he sheltered behind. A bird called in the distance and the jungle noises started again.

'Wells!' Jack heard the tension in his voice. 'Wells; are you all right?'

'The bastards tried to sneak past, sir,' Wells shouted. 'O'Neill gutted one. He's still alive.'

There was a sharp squeal and then O'Neill's voice. 'He's not alive now, sir.'

'Keep alert,' Jack felt the hair on the back of his neck raise at the casual manner in which one of his men had disposed of an enemy, but this was war at the fringe of Empire. These men faced brutal reality, not the sanitised romanticism of the newspapers. He peered through the dim light, hoping to see a Burmese soldier before the Burmese saw him.

The 51st tramped through the fringe of the jungle with the artillery from the fort banging away and roundshot crashing and ripping through the trees.

'There go the 51st!' Knight shouted.

'Shabash the 51st!' O'Neill yelled, high pitched.

Staring into the green jungle, Jack could not see the actual assault on the stockade, but he heard the deep throated cheer of the 51st Foot and the sudden acceleration of musketry as the Burmese defenders fired at the advancing column.

Movement in the jungle in front attracted his attention. 'Here they come again!' he yelled and fired in the general direction of the noise. Jack saw leaves flicker and a flat, intent face and then the Burmese advanced with a rush, flitting from tree to tree, firing muskets and ducking away again.

Pryor stiffened and looked down at his arm, where a feathered stick seemed to have sprouted. 'That's an arrow,' he said in amazement and yelled as another whistled through the trees and thumped into his side. 'They're using bows and arrows!' Leaning his musket against the bole of a tree, he pulled at the arrow in his arm.

'Get down!' Wells yelled, 'get your bloody head down!'

'Look for cover,' Jack shouted. 'We're just targets standing. Get behind a tree and fire back.' He blinked as an arrow thumped into the trunk of a tree six inches from his head, and then there was a spatter of musketry from the Burmese. Jack suddenly realised that this was not a formal set piece battle such as characterised British military thinking since the peninsula and had come to its Indian apogee in the Sikh wars: this was warfare against a different type of enemy and needed different tactics. 'Fire at will boys! If you see the enemy, fire! Don't wait for orders!' That was not something he had ever expected to say in the British army, where volley fire had been the norm for centuries. *Wells will not agree.* He heard a spatter of musketry from his men. *Good lads! Fight them!*

'They're coming at us!' That was Thorpe. 'I can see them!'

'Get back Thorpe! Don't just look! Get behind a tree and shoot the buggers!' Wells' voice cracked through the forest. 'Fire lads! Send the bastards to hell.'

Now that the 113th were free of the restraint of waiting for orders, they loaded and fired faster than Jack had expected. The sound of their musketry was like rolling thunder until Jack realised there was no fire coming toward them. 'Stop firing boys! We're shooting at nothing.'

The firing died away leaving the acrid drift of burned gunpowder and the low gasps of the 113th. The silence was stifling. 'Anybody hurt? Call the roll!' Jack listened to the names as the men shouted out. Only Pryor was silent.

'Pryor? Where are you, Pryor?' Jack's voice echoed in the trees.

'Here he is, sir,' O'Neill sounded casual. 'He can't answer though; he's dead.'

Pryor stood erect beside his tree with five arrows in his body and one through his mouth.

That's two of my men dead.

'Hold still boys; check your ammunition and keep watching.' One by one the sounds returned to the jungle as birds and insects filled the void.

The cessation of violence was as unsettling as its sudden eruption had been. Jack controlled his ragged breathing and nudged Coleman, 'go and see what's happening at the White House Picket. Tell the colonel that the 113th has secured his flank and repelled a Burmese attack.'

The sound of firing from the stockade increased and then died away to a succession of single shots. Then there was cheering and then silence.

It was forty anxious minutes before Coleman returned, with his hat awry and his uniform ripped by trailing thorns. 'The stockade has fallen, sir.' He threw a belated salute.

'How?' Jack asked.

'The 51st did it, sir. They threw four ladders against the walls and some major, I heard he was a Sawney called Fraser, was first up.' Coleman blinked as a flying beetle investigated his face.

Jack brushed the beetle away. 'Carry on Coleman.'

'There were wounded, sir. The Burmese hit a lot of the 51st and some of the sappers. I think there was an officer killed as well but it was the heat that done for them more than the Burmese.'

Jack realised that his men had gathered to listen to the news. 'Get back to your positions, 113th! We have not won the day yet!'

Coleman continued: 'once the 51st mounted the walls, the Burmese fell. We have the stockade sir.' Close to Coleman was older than Jack had realised. He was about thirty, with the thin physique of a slum dweller or a man who was a habitual drinker, which description covered a large proportion of the British Army, Jack realised.

'Were there orders for us, Coleman?' Jack asked.

Coleman had the grace to look guilty for a second. 'Yes, sir. We have to move forward and allow the 51st to take over the flank guard.'

That was it; no thanks and no recognition for the 113th, but that was not unexpected in the army. We did our duty without glory or fuss. We stood our ground; we did not run.

Jack raised his voice. 'Well done men: you did yourselves and the regiment proud.' He gave orders for Pryor's body to be carried with them. Only eleven men left now.

Chapter Seven

Rangoon: April 1852

There was a scattering of bodies on the scrubby ground that led up to the still smouldering wooden stockade, victims of heat as well as Burmese resistance. Amidst the carnage, many men of the 51st lay in whatever shade they could find with their white caps and the sun flap over the neck their only protection against the relentless sun.

'It's hot,' Coleman said.

'It's bloody India,' O'Neill added.

'It's bloody Burma,' Wells corrected. 'Brave men to storm this place,' he nodded to the ladders that leaned against the logs.

That should have been us; we had as much danger but no glory.

Jack stepped through the wide open gate of the White House Picket. Ammunition for the Burmese cannon, iron balls and stone, was piled everywhere but it was the strength of the stockade that impressed him. He had expected a single palisade wall of undressed teak, but instead, there were three layers of defence, with a ditch that ran along the exterior, backed by an outer wall of timber about ten feet from an inner wall of brick. The Burmese had filled the space between the walls with earth cannon fire would be less effective. Jack inspected the reverse slope, up which the Burmese had dragged their cannon.

'These Burmese know how to fight,' he said.

'The 51st did well to take this place,' Wells gave his professional opinion. 'These Burmese lads know their stuff.'

The white house that gave the stockade its name was sheltered well within the walls. It was a wooden building of vague white appearance with a flight of steps leading to a large doorway. 'This way for the loot, lads,' Thorpe, last in battle, proved to be first in theft as he led his colleagues up the stairs, musket at the trail.

The interior was dim and busy with British and Indian soldiers all staring at a colossal statue of a sitting Buddha.

'Is that God?' Private Smith asked. He removed his hat as the vicar had probably taught him in his village church and stared, open mouthed, at the statue. 'Have we attacked a Holy place?' He sounded scared at the thought.

'It's like their god,' Wells told him. 'That's Buddha.' He looked around and lowered his voice. Jack moved closer to the colossal statue. 'Sometimes they have precious stones in these places, lads, rubies and diamonds and gold. That is loot for us, once the officers have gone.'

'This officer is going nowhere,' Jack told them. 'And being caught looting means the cat or even the noose.'

'Don't get caught then,' that was Lacey, a scar-faced man in his late twenties.

'Any more of that lip and you'll be first at the triangle, Lacey;' Wells' voice was sharp.

'You lot – what regiment?' The major was short, red faced and very erect.

'113th sir,' Jack reported.

The major's red face darkened to scarlet. 'Good God! The Chillian-walla wallahs! I see you've come after all the fighting is over. Well now you're here you can make yourselves useful and throw all these Burmese cannon balls and grapeshot down the well.'

'We were guarding the flank, sir,' Jack's attempt to defend his men failed as the major marched away without a further word.

'Come on lads,' Wells pointed to the nearest pile of ammunition. 'You heard the major.'

'If I wanted to be a bloody labourer I would have stayed in Donegal,' O'Neill said, but he was first to lift a cannon ball and drop it down the well.

'What a waste,' Coleman shook his head, 'we could sell this lot for a pretty penny in any metal dealer.'

'But think of the shipping costs,' Graham said, 'the carters always charge by the mile.' He looked upward at the azure sky. 'How far is it to Carlisle, boys? About three thousand miles at a penny a mile ... How much is that?'

'More than you can afford, anyway, Graham,' Wells growled.

'No sergeant. I was thinking I would do the carting; get hold of one of these Burmese bullock carts and charge you all to take your cannon balls...'

The firing interrupted them.

'Stand to!' an officer of the 51st shouted, 'man the walls!'

'Here we go again,' O'Neill dropped a cannon ball and lifted his musket. 'There's no bloody peace in Burma.'

Jack raced two ensigns up to the parapet and arranged his men alongside him. 'To me the 113th!'

'These Burmese lads know their business, sir,' once more Wells approved. 'They built the stockade well. We can see everything from up here.'

'It's their country: they should know it well.' Jack said.

Wells was quiet for a moment. 'It's not actually their country sir if you don't mind me saying. We're in Pegu province; the Burmese are invaders here.'

Jack frowned. *It's not a sergeant's place to lecture an officer.* 'I hardly think that matters just now, Wells.'

'Yes, sir.' Wells nodded toward the Golden Pagoda that dominated the whole area.

'That place will not be easy to capture either, sir.'

'Never mind that,' Jack heard the tension in his voice. 'Watch for these Burmese soldiers.'

Jack concentrated on the jungle where they had held back the Burmese, but from this height, he also saw that there were more patches of jungle, interspersed with scrubby plains.

'Watch the maidan, lads,' Wells shouted, 'that's the open bits, for the benefit of you ignorant Johnny Raw bastards.'

Moving between the forest land and crossing the maidan were bands of Burmese, some wearing black quilted tunics, others bare chested, some sporting spiked helmets, most bare legged and all carrying long muskets, or the ubiquitous if varied Burmese dha with its gently curving, vicious blade.

'They are not going to attack us are they?' Wells sounded more curious than apprehensive. 'They have no chance of taking the stockade back from British infantry.'

'They won't even get close,' O'Neill hefted his musket and sighted on one of the scurrying figures. 'They are far out of range, but the gunners will get them.'

'There's hundreds of them,' Thorpe said.

'And they're all after you, Thorpey,' Coleman nudged him. 'They told me that when we were in the jungle.'

'Just keep quiet and wait for orders,' Jack said.

O'Neill was correct. Every time the Burmese clustered into an appreciable group, the artillery opened up and either scattered them or sent them scurrying to the patches of jungle for shelter. The British soldiers cheered with each explosion. 'Shabash the gunners!'

When the bugles sounded stand down, most of the infantry returned to seek shade, except a few who remained to watch the fun.

'They've got one of our lads prisoner!' O'Neill shouted. 'Over there!' he pointed to a patch of barren maidan between two areas of jungle, 'there's a man in British uniform.'

Jack focussed on the group that O'Neill indicated, just as the British guns opened up. One shell landed close-by, throwing up a fountain of dirt and stones. When the dust drifted away the men were Burmese were gone and so was the man in the scarlet jacket. One body lay crumpled on the ground.

'They've taken him away with them,' O'Neill said flatly. 'God help the poor bugger. These savages will have him pulled to pieces by elephants.'

We should go and rescue him; that would bring the 113th to prominence.

'You,' a voice of authority intruded, and the stocky, erect major glared at them. 'What's your name, sir? Windrush? Why are your men not doing as I ordered? Get these cannon balls down that well sir!'

By mid- afternoon the interior of the stockade was insufferable, and the men were drooping with the heat. One by one they staggered to find whatever shade they could as all work within the stockade eased to a stop. Even the bustling major slid into the shelter of the White House.

'It's bloody hot,' Coleman said.

'You're always bloody hot,' Knight snarled at him.

The Engineers and Sappers had been busy destroying what they could not save. As the afternoon wore on, they set the White House Picket alight, so smoke and flames added to the torment of the sun. British soldiers drank copious amounts of water and waited for the relief of darkness. O'Neill stamped hard on a scuttling scorpion. Even the sepoys searched for shade.

'Get these cannon balls shifted,' Jack ordered. He swatted in vain at the insects that coiled around his face.

'Camp outside the walls!' the order came from officer to officer, so the soldiers withdrew from the stockade they had won and found rest for the night. Some slumped on the ground while others sought beds of straw beside the artillery or kept close to the ditch.

'O'Neill, you and Coleman take first watch. Smith and Armstrong relieve them at two in the morning.' Jack posted pickets, haggled for water and food, had the men check their ammunition and obtained more from a harassed supply officer before he could relax. All the time the ships fired over their heads in a pyrotechnic display that kept some men awake while others slept so deeply that it seemed nothing could have woken them. Ranveer's blue turban was unmistakeable as he ghosted around the camp, finding fresh water where there was none to be found, ensuring Jack was fed and keeping a low profile.

So this is campaigning on the outer fringe of Empire? I am not sure if I can live like this for the next forty years of my life. Or less if the fever gets me.

As the sun sunk, the walls of the White House collapsed in a welter of sparks, so only the huge figure of Buddha was left, sitting on his mound surrounded by flames and smoke. The statue looked disapproving of this army of northern barbarians that had broken his peace, his eyes inscrutable as he sat in silent splendour.

Simultaneous with the destruction of the White House, the woman appeared. One minute Jack was lying on the ground trying to rest before the troubles of the next day, and the next the woman was amongst them, watching the flames leaping around the statue.

'That will bring trouble,' she spoke English in a strange sing-song accent. 'It is not wise to interfere with Buddha.'

'There's always trouble in war time,' Wells lifted a hand to acknowledge her presence. His eyes smiled.

The woman stood in the middle of the bivouac. She was slim and quiet, with the ubiquitous light jacket of Burmese women and a blue satin longyi that wrapped itself around her hips and legs with such grace that Jack had to tear his gaze back to her face. She was unsmiling and unafraid, with her hair coiled in a tight cylinder on top of her head and long earrings dangling at the side of her neck.

He inhaled her perfume of sandalwood oil as he struggled to sit up.

'What are you doing here, miss?' He asked as the woman looked around her.

'What are you doing here, British soldier?' The woman's eyes were dark as they held his.

'Teaching a tyrant a lesson,' Jack knew he sounded pompous even as he spoke, 'and upholding the honour of the British flag.'

The woman looked pointedly to where the fire was dying down around the White House. A spiral of sparks rose above the head of the Buddha before it dissipated. 'Where is the honour in destruction?'

'There is honour in bravery and courage,' Jack said. *Who is this woman and what does she want?* Despite himself, he inhaled again. The sandalwood was intoxicating.

When she looked directly at him, Jack saw dark shadows in her eyes. *Who are you?*

'It is better to conquer yourself than to win a thousand battles,' she said.

'What the devil does that mean? Who are you, miss?' Jack looked around. There were no other women in this place of men. Soldiers of the Queen's army mingled with those of the Company's forces, infantry, engineers and artillerymen working, sleeping or trying to sleep as the guns of the Royal Navy and John Company kept up a desultory fire on the new town of Rangoon and the golden temple. Ranveer stood in the shadows, one of a handful of Indian servants.

The woman did not look afraid, although she was alone amidst hundreds of alien intruders. Nor did she smile as she folded herself onto the ground and sat, back straight and arms at her side, looking directly at Jack. 'You are an officer here,' she stated.

'I am,' Jack agreed.

'And tomorrow or the next day you will lead your men into the Shoe Dagoon, the Golden Pagoda.' She said the words as if they were facts.

'I cannot see the future,' Jack said. He felt vaguely uncomfortable.

'It will happen,' the woman said. The flames rising from the White House Picket sent shafts of orange light through the dark, throwing dancing shadows over the woman, so she appeared to be moving although she sat still and serene amongst the supine soldiers.

Jack waited for her to speak, surprised that his men did not make ribald comments and suggestions. Instead, they watched and listened as the guns fired and the orange flames reflected from the dark pressure of the Oriental sky. Only Wells seemed aware as he cleaned his musket and kept his gaze fixed on the elegant Burmese woman.

'Will my regiment win glory and honour?' Jack asked.

The woman seemed to consider for a long time before replying. 'It will be a victory soon forgotten,' she said.

'But still a victory,' Wells confirmed. He shrugged. 'Victory is better than defeat, and all victories in the East are distorted before they reach the ears of the West.'

God, that is deep from a sergeant! I will have to watch this man.

'Are there an East and a West, or is there just a world with false divisions created by tyrants and kings?' The woman's voice was musical, serene in that place of war and the drift of powder smoke.

'Without kings, there are no countries, and without countries, there is chaos and disorder,' Wells met her words. 'British victories will bring peace to more people.'

'There is always a reverse to any coin; a victory for one is a defeat for another, and always there is a loss for all.' The woman seemed to have a private conversation with Wells, with both speaking in riddles that Jack did not understand.

'That is true,' Wells agreed, 'but better peace under one flag than discord under many.' He relapsed into silence as the woman again focussed her attention on Jack.

'You have three battles, British officer,' she said. 'And you must be victorious in the one you do not acknowledge to have success in the others.' She stood up. 'Our paths will cross again.' When she laid a hand on his arm, Jack felt as if her light touch had thrilled right through him.

'At least tell me your name,' Jack asked, but the woman slid through the sleeping ranks without another word. Jack watched the shimmer and shift of the tight longyi around her hips until she merged with the dark.

'You've been in India a long time, Sergeant,' Jack said. 'Do many women appear in the middle of our camps?'

Wells shook his head. 'No, sir. That woman is different.' His grin was unexpected and took years from his age. 'I've never met a woman before who can quote Buddha in the middle of a British encampment. Burma is a most interesting place.'

'It could be,' Jack agreed, 'but how do you know she was quoting Buddha?'

Wells closed his mouth so firmly that Jack was sure he heard the click of his teeth. 'I read about it, sir,' he said. The tone of his voice told Jack that the sergeant would say no more.

Wells knows far more than he is saying. I thought that other ranks were only here to make up the numbers. This sergeant has his own personality.

Jack did not raise his voice; he knew his servant would not be far away. 'How about you, Ranveer? What did you make of her?'

Ranveer shook his head. 'I think she is trouble, sahib.' His smile was sudden and very white, 'but all women are trouble.'

Wells' laugh was loud enough to wake the Burmese. 'You got that right, Ranveer!'

Jack closed his eyes and tried to ignore the intermittent batter of the guns. The image of that Burmese woman filled his mind, and he was sure he could still smell sandalwood long after she was gone.

Smoke from the burning town of Rangoon rose thick enough to mask the sun as the 14th of April began.

'The Burmese will know we're coming,' Thorpe muttered as he checked the percussion lock of his musket and slid his bayonet in and out of its scabbard. 'They'll be waiting for us.'

'It's hardly a secret,' Coleman adjusted the length of *puggaree* that protected the nape of his neck from the sun. 'We spent all yesterday battering them with artillery, and we are forming up in the open to attack.'

O'Neill took a swig from his water bottle. 'Let them wait; let them do anything they bloody like,' he said. He tapped his musket. 'They can dance and sing and bang their bloody gongs from Monday until Christmas if they like, it won't make a bit of difference when we get in among them. There's not a Burmese alive will face British soldiers with musket and bayonet.'

The mocking laughter came from a passing group of the 80th Regiment. 'Not a Burmese alive by Christ! And that from one of the Baby Butchers; thank the Lord there are no Sikhs in Burma, lads or the 113th would turn tail and run!'

'They'll do that anyway, Sikhs or Burmese or Afghans,' another of the 80th said. 'Just pretend Rangoon is full of babies and women boys; then you'll be brave again!'

'You bragging blackguards!' O'Neill lunged for the men of the 80th but outnumbered twenty to one he was knocked to the ground, and the boots were going in before Jack arrived to calm the situation down.

'Can't you control your men?' He bellowed to the nearest officer, a thin faced youth with a sword that seemed intent on getting between his legs and tripping him. The lieutenant gave him a wave but said nothing.

O'Neill swore loudly as the 80th filed past, rank after rank of grim faced men. He sorted out his rumpled uniform, adjusted his cap and raised his voice. 'Shabash the 80th! Give them the bayonet, lads!'

'Poor buggers,' Wells said, 'they are the storming party.' He looked ahead where the walls and cannon of Rangoon waited, with the great golden cones of the pagoda thrusting skyward amidst the drifting smoke of the British bombardment.

The stocky, erect major pushed O'Neill aside and nudged Jack. 'Windrush: here's one of the engineers' plans of the Burmese stockade. Clear the way for the 80th. I want them to arrive at the walls in good order, so you and your blackguards ensure there are no Burmese skirmishers in their path.'

'Yes, sir!' Jack felt his heart lift.

In front of the main assault: we are leading the army; honour and glory for the 113th!

'Come on lads; you heard the major: at the double!' Jack led them forward. As before he knew he could not look backwards at his men. He had to trust them to keep pace with him and hope that Sergeant Wells kept them in line.

'Uriah the Hittite' Wells said quietly, 'sent to the forefront of battle.'

'Oh, sweet Jesus save me!' That was Thorpe's voice.

The 80th foot were veterans of the First Sikh War, hard bitten, hard eyed and hard of tongue. They gave a rueful cheer as Jack led his handful of 113th past them.

'Here come the Baby Butchers: we're safe now lads!'

O'Neill responded with obscene comments that Coleman and Armstrong copied, and then they were in the van of the army and moving quickly toward the walls of Rangoon.

'How far do we have to advance?' Coleman asked.

'About a mile,' Wells replied, 'and the Burmese will have men in every thicket and patch of jungle.'

Between the British and Rangoon was an area of mixed maidan and thick outcrops of jungle, with lesser areas of scrub and small trees.

'Do we have to take another stockade, sir?' Wells asked.

'More than that,' Jack unfolded the plan he had been given and tried to read it even as he trotted forward. 'There is a moat and then a bund even before we get to the wall.'

Wells glanced at the plan and then squinted toward Rangoon where only the great Golden Pagoda was visible above the patches of jungle. 'The map doesn't show a stockade,' he pressed his point.

'No,' Jack agreed. 'But according to this plan, there's a mud wall sixteen feet high right around the town.'

'The 80th will love that,' Wells said.

'There's more. The Burmese have cannon mounted on a rampart at the top and more artillery in pagodas through the town.' Jack checked his men. They were in an extended skirmishing line, moving quickly. 'And *jingals* as well, whatever they are.'

'They're like large calibre muskets,' Wells told him quietly. 'They are ugly things that outrange our muskets. If a ball from a *jingal* hits you, you'll know all about it.'

'Mary!' O'Neill was the nearest private soldier. 'The wall is sixteen feet high? How are we meant to get up that? Bloody jump?'

'We're not going up at all,' Jack told him. 'That's the 80th's job. We just clear the way for them.' He nodded toward the Golden Pagoda. 'That will be the hardest fight for the most magnificent prize. Our informants tell us that the Burmese have solidly fortified it with a double layer of cannon and...' he stopped as a cannon ball whizzed past him and thudded into the ground. A fountain of mud rose six foot in the air before subsiding with a brown spatter. Jack noticed that his men had instinctively bunched together. 'Spread out boys and watch your front!'

The 80th was immediately behind them, with the Madras Fusiliers and Madras Native Infantry slightly in the rear. The Bengal Native Infantry were to the left, advancing well.

'They're moving fast,' Wells said.

Of course: nobody wants to linger when the enemy is firing at them.

'Keep within sight of each other,' Jack ordered as they crossed the maidan, 'but spread out for God's sake.' He pointed to a patch of jungle that lay in their path. 'If I were the Burmese commander I would have men stationed in there.'

He glanced behind him: the 80th were in column, marching solidly behind their officers. There was the drift of regimental music: 'Come lasses and lads' as bow-shouldered men staggered under the weight of long storming ladders. They seemed distorted by the heat, as if they wavered, some looked elongated, others foreshortened, but they did not hesitate. Despite the Burmese artillery that blasted shot at them, they were as steady as if they were on parade.

A musket shot cracked from the patch of forest, followed by a dozen more that whizzed past without hitting a single man. 'Give them a volley and forward with the bayonet, lads!' Jack fired three shots from his pepperpot toward the drifting musket smoke and then broke into a run.

Should I be scared? Why am I not scared?

With his legs seeming too light for his body and his breath rasping in his chest, Jack covered the thirty yards to the forest in ten seconds that seemed like ten minutes.

'Don't stop,' he shouted as soon as his men were within the outer fringes, 'use the bayonet; kill anything in your path.'

He advanced slowly, one cautious step after another with the ground soft underfoot and the surroundings a hundred shades of green. There were no bird noises now, merely the pad of feet and the harsh gasp of nervous men, a single animal scream, the sudden crack of breaking twigs and the occasional loud report of a musket, whether British or Burmese he could not tell.

The green faded to grey then turned to brilliant light and Jack was out the other side of the jungle and on to a broad area of maidan. He saw a group of agile Burmese infantry in front, running to the next deeply forested patch, fired two shots without result and rammed cartridges into his revolver as he waited for his men to catch up.

'Roll call!' he announced and listened to the list of names. 'Where's Smith? Has anybody seen Smith?'

'No, sir.' There was a collective shaking of heads.

'He was my right- hand marker sir, and I thought I heard a noise,' Coleman said, 'I thought it was some bird or something.'

'Go back and look; O'Neill, you go with him.'

He watched his two men disappear back into the jungle. He saw the walls of Rangoon about half a mile ahead with spurts of smoke from the defending cannon and *jingals*. He heard the lively music from the advancing 80th and the fire of the British cannon and howitzers howling overhead.

'Forward lads: Coleman and O'Neill can catch up.' *I cannot spare the time to wait.*

Then it was onward again, pacing toward the walls of Rangoon with the tension building every second. *God, I wish I was leading an entire company and not a mere handful. I wish I had the colours on display. I hope the general is watching us.*

'Smithy's dead, sir,' O'Neill's voice broke his images of glory. 'We didn't find his body, but we got this.' He held up Smith's head with the mouth wide open in a silent scream and the eyes staring. Blood dripped onto the ground.

'Bloody barbarians,' Coleman sounded shocked, 'bloody evil barbarians!' He raised his voice 'they cut Smithy's bloody head off!'

'Keep moving forward,' Jack could not help staring at Smith's face. The eyes seemed to accuse him. 'Shoot anything that is not British.'

They walked on, holding their muskets ready, bayonets pointing forward and upward and each man waiting the chance to avenge

Smith. There was no talking now and no laughing, merely a deter-
mination to advance on Rangoon and slaughter the enemy. Jack saw
a roundshot hit a file of Bengal Native Infantry. The men closed up
at once. A *doolie* carrier jolted up with a *palankeen* for the screaming
wounded. A *jingal* ball passed in a black blur.

A group of black-jacketed Burmese appeared in front of them as
though they rose from the ground itself. Imbued with anger after the
death of Smith, the 113th fired without orders and roared forward.

'Blood, blood, blood!'

The Burmese fled, leaving one man still on the ground and two
writhing wounded. Armstrong and Graham plunged in their bayonets,
and the 113th moved on, still not sated, still vengeful after the death
of Smith. *They are more affected by his decapitation than if the Burmese
had shot him: why? He would be dead either way.*

A large calibre shot ploughed into the earth a yard from Jack's feet,
and a few minutes later another on the other side.

They are targeting me as an officer. Well, let them: murdering bastards.

'Come on the 113th! Remember Smithy!'

Standing erect to show he was not scared, Jack marched on. Twice
he saw movement among small patches of scrubby bush and each time
he halted his men, fired a volley and led a rapid advance. Both times
the Burmese fled before the 113th reached them.

'Kill the bastards,' Coleman knelt for better balance, aimed and fired.
'Missed again!'

'You're a cross eyed bugger Coleman,' Wells jeered.

'You try it!' Coleman looked up, eyes wide. 'You're always full of
words sergeant.'

'Keep moving!' Jack fired at the pagoda, knowing it was a waste of
bullets but he had to do something.

'Kill the bastards!' O'Neill loped forward, whooping high pitched.

The bulk of the Burmese fire came from a small pagoda directly in
front. It stood on a low wooded hill with open maidan on either side
that stretched as far as the outer defensive wall of Rangoon.

'That's a perfect killing ground,' Armstrong said.

To their right, the 40th Bengal Native Infantry seemed to agree. They took one look at the Burmese shot landing like metal hail on the open maidan and withdrew hastily behind the hillock. The Madras Fusiliers filed up in perfect order to join them.

The advance has stalled.

'Fix bayonets!' the order passed from officer to officer, and a sinister snicker ran through the ranks as each man clicked his bayonet in place. The sun glittered on hundreds of wickedly sharp blades; Queen Victoria's final argument. The army took a deep breath and waited for the next stage. High above, vultures circled in an azure sky.

'We'll be charging the ramparts soon,' Wells said.

'How soon?' Coleman looked up at the stout mud walls where the gilt hats of the defenders were clear, and *jingals* fired round after round at the attackers.

'As soon as the guns have blown a breach,' Jack told him. He ducked as a *jingal* bullet whistled above his head. The large calibre shot disappeared somewhere to the rear.

I recognise the different sounds already; the cannonball is like tearing cloth, the jingal whistles and the musket ball is silent unless it hits a rock, when it ricochets with a high pitched whine. I am becoming a soldier.

'Move on!' Jack did not see General Godwin give the order but he heard it pass from officer to officer.

'Right lads,' He stepped forward. 'The 113th is in the van.'

The entire attacking force rose behind him, Queen's and Company regiments creating columns of scarlet on the dun maidan. They continued their advance toward the walls of Rangoon. The world was concentrated into a series of disjointed images and thoughts, each one a picture of horror or bravery, each one vastly important to the man involved and each merging into a confused whole, a monstrosity of sound and agony of which Hieronymus Bosch would have been proud.

'Down!' the order was countermanded, and Jack motioned to his men to comply. They lay on the open maidan with the Burmese fire plunging above over the 113th as the gunners targeted the main attacking force. There were groans and cries as bullets and roundshot found their mark.

Jack watched a column of black ants march past his nose, relentless on their collective business.

'Are we to lie here all day?' Wells asked. 'We should either go forward or back. Sitting here being shot like targets is only encouraging the Burmese.'

'It's only been a few moments,' Jack bellowed back over the noise of the guns. He checked his watch. *Good God! It's nearly half past eleven! We set off before seven. What happened to the time?*

'Sir!' Wells nodded toward the Golden Pagoda. 'There's a storming party forming.'

Jack saw a mixed force gathering opposite the eastern side of the pagoda. There were around five hundred men, 80th foot, 18th Royal Irish and agile sepoys of the 40th Bengal Native Infantry.

'They have their work before them,' O'Neill said softly. 'Look at the ground they have to cross.'

Wells sucked in his breath, 'that's bad, bad ground,' he said.

Jack knew he lacked the experience these men had gathered in their campaigning in India, but even a Griffin like him could see that difficulties faced the storming party. The British rear positions, from where the artillery battered at the defences of Rangoon, were half a mile from the walls, with a shallow valley in between, scattered with patches of jungle and small clearings.

If the attackers managed to pass these obstacles, they faced a steep hill topped by the Golden Pagoda itself. That was the most heavily defended position in Rangoon, if not in all of Burma, with three terraces, each protected with a wall manned by Burmese infantry and artillery. The first wall held the lighter guns, then the medium and finally the heavy artillery on the tallest, broadest and strongest wall.

'How are they going to scale these walls?' Coleman asked. 'They don't have a single ladder.'

'See that gate?' Wells pointed to a large doorway in the centre of the main East wall. 'The artillery will weaken that, and the boys will storm their way through. After that…' he shrugged, 'after that its boot and butt and bullet and bayonet and bugger anybody who tries to stop them.'

'There they go!' Wells said.

The columns of British and Indian troops began to move across the broken ground.

The idea came to Jack fully formed. The 113th been ordered to lead the 80th to the walls of Rangoon. It had achieved that. Now, this advance had stalled. The attack was going in on the eastern wall.

'Thorpe! Run to General Godwin and advise him that the 113th is joining the storming party!' Jack spoke the instant he made his decision. *Colonel Murphy ordered me to raise the reputation of the 113th, and there will be no better opportunity than to take part in the storming of an important and heavily defended town.*

What did Clausewitz say? It is even better to act quickly and err than to hesitate until the time of action is past.

Time to act! 'Come on 113th! We're going to take Rangoon!'

'Oh, Jesus Christ!' Coleman's voice rose high pitched as Wells grabbed his arm and pushed him onward.

O'Neill gave a high pitched laugh and ran forward, chanting his Gaelic slogan.

'Come on lads,' Jack leapt in front of his men, 'join the Royal Irish!'

He ran forward, aware that the faster they covered the open ground in front of the town, the less time the defenders had to shoot at them. He heard Wells raise a cheer but only O'Neill and Graham joined in, and then they were on the flank of the 18th Foot with a red faced colonel staring at them and a company of the 40th Bengal Native Infantry marching in impassive ranks. Jack did not notice how they crossed the valley or negotiated the jungle. He was leading his men on an assault, with colonels and General Godwin watching; all eyes were on the 113th; all eyes were on him.

Jack scraped out his sword. Light flashed on the curved blade. 'Come on the 113th!' He ducked as a British roundshot howled past his head and crashed into the pagoda gate. His men were lagging, with Wells pushing them on and O'Neill five paces in front.

The British artillery fell silent as the infantry approached the gate.

'It's all up to us now,' a captain of the Royal Irish drew his sword and put his shoulder to the heavy teak. His men followed, cheering as their combined weight burst open what remained of the gate, and the Queen's and Company infantry crashed through. Rangoon lay before them.

'Onward lads!' Jack thrust his sword upwards, 'with me the 113th!'

Oh Jesus: where do we go now? This attack is a Royal Irish show: it's their decision.

The gate opened directly onto a long series of steps that climbed the centre of the pagoda's terraces, flight after flight of steep stone stairs with strange carved beasts placed in prominent positions.

'Sir?' Wells ducked as a musket ball smacked into the wall a foot from his face. 'Do you have orders, sir?'

As men of the Royal Irish pushed through the door and mingled with the 113th, Jack looked around. Burmese soldiers defended the terraces above. Some stepped on to the stairs to aim at the intruders.

One of the Royal Irish yelled and looked at the scarlet stain that spread across his chest. He dropped his musket and slowly crumpled to the ground. A moment later another grunted and clutched at his shoulder.

'Sir...' Wells aimed at the Burmese and fired.

'That's our way, lads,' the Royal Irish lieutenant pointed upward, then staggered as a musket ball thumped into his chest. He looked at Jack through wide eyes and slid down the wall.

I am the only officer here just now; I must take the lead.

'Follow me, men!' With his revolver in his right hand and sword in his left, Jack took the steps two at a time, ducking and weaving to put the Burmese musketeers off their aim. The steps were steep and seemed to go on forever, with musket balls and the larger jingal balls hammering and pinging from the stonework. There were more shouts behind him as the Burmese found their mark, but the British and sepoys continued up the stairs.

Jack saw the gilt hats and black padded jackets of the defenders as they stood on the ramparts, firing downward, yelling, inviting the British to come on, but then he was level with them on the first terrace with his leg muscles screaming for relief. He flinched as a stalwart defender fired at him, shouted as the ball skiffed his forage cap and blasted the Burman away with two shots from his revolver. A group of Burmese rushed to challenge him, hesitated, fired a couple of rounds and turned to run as the Royal Irish, and the 113th poured onto the terrace.

'Come on, lads!' Wells levelled his bayonet.

O'Neill surged past, laughing.

'Blood!' Knight roared, 'blood and death!' The men of the 113th followed in a phalanx of stabbing blades and swinging musket butts.

Leaving the 113th to deal with the lowest terrace, the Royal Irish poured up the steps, shooting and cheering as they fought their way toward the higher levels. Those of the defenders who turned to fight were killed out of hand while the rest turned and fled.

'Come back and fight!' O'Neill shouted.

A lone Burmese soldier turned to face Jack. He shouted something, levelled his musket and fired, with the flint striking a spark only a few feet away from Jack's head but no succeeding spurt of smoke.

Misfire, by God

Jack pointed his revolver in the man's direction and squeezed the trigger. He cursed as the hammer clicked on an empty chamber.

Damn it! It's empty!

With no time to reload and the Burmese coming at him with his square-ended dha, Jack dropped his revolver and swung mightily with his sword. Although he had attended a few fencing classes, nothing had prepared him for the rush and fury of a fight to the death on the terraced defences of the Golden Pagoda in the heart of Burma. His swing missed by a foot. The Burmese slashed sideways at his neck. Jack could smell the garlic on the man's breath.

Jack parried the dha with his sword, but the force of the attack sent him staggering backwards. He withdrew a step to regain his balance, saw the triumph in the Burmese soldier's face and lunged forward. The Burmese side-stepped with ease and aimed a vicious swipe that would have gutted Jack like a rabbit had he not sucked in his middle. The dha hissed past so close that it ripped one of the brass buttons from his tunic.

For a moment Jack was unaware of anything else. All that mattered was the sword fight between him and this doughty Burman. They clashed again, blade to blade, muscle to muscle, and eye to eye: Occident and Orient on either side of sharp steel and both combined by the desire to kill and a fear of death.

Jack knew he was the taller and possibly the stronger, but the Burmese warrior was fast and muscular, skilful with his dha. Within a minute Jack was on the defensive, backing away along the terrace with the Burman following, unsmiling as he concentrated only on killing this insolent British invader.

The musket shot came from behind him. The Burmese warrior stiffened and put a hand on his stomach, just as a British soldier lunged at him and thrust a bayonet hilt deep in his chest.

'And that's done for you, son,' O'Neill said, as the warrior crumpled to the ground. He put a foot on the man's stomach and hauled his bayonet free. 'Sorry to interfere, sir, but you seemed to be getting the worst of it.'

'Thank you, O'Neill,' Jack felt the sweat pouring from him. 'I rather think you saved my life there.'

O'Neill grinned. 'You can remember that next time the peelers haul me before you for being drunk and disorderly.'

Jack realised that the firing and roaring of battle had altered to cheering and shouting, with occasional loud whoops and the crash and rattle of destruction.

'What's happening?'

'The Burmese have bolted sir.'

'They've bolted?' Jack stared as O'Neill casually cleaned his bayonet on his victim's jacket.

We've won. I've led the 113th to our first victory.

'Yes sir and now we'll loot the place sideways,' O'Neill grinned. 'Come on, sir or the Royal Irish and the sepoys will get all the best stuff.'

'Stop that!' Jack yelled. 'We're not here to rob.' But he knew that from time immemorial soldiers had looted any place they had taken by storm. It was one of the few perquisites of the job.

Jack stepped to the edge of the terrace and watched as the British and Indian soldiers ran riot. Some scattered to the many smaller pagodas, laughing as their officers temporarily lost control. Most ran straight to the Golden Pagoda. Jack heard the loud cries of joy as some found loot, and raised voices as men from rival regiments disputed ownership of useless knick-knacks or priceless statuettes from the pagoda.

'Come on boys! There's gold and rubies here!'

This part of Rangoon seemed dedicated to religion, with the Golden Pagoda being only the largest of a collection of Buddhist temples. Their basic design was always the same, an irregular pagoda with a very shapely top, surmounted by an umbrella within a fringe of wind-powered bells, so every movement of the air was accompanied by a delicate melody that sat ill with the sounds and sights of battle. It was hard to reconcile the essential religious message of peace when dead bodies polluted the entrance and unheeded blood pooled at the foot of guardian statues.

There were more shrines with sculptures of Gautama, the local in-carnation of Buddha, sitting within open spaces, sometimes in solitary splendour, often with companion statuettes in alabaster or gilt-covered brick. After the thunder of battle, the call of birds sweetened the air, while the swaying of brilliant green trees cast flickering shadows over a place that had been beautiful before British shells wrought their destruction. Jack leaned on a huge stone crocodile to gather his thoughts. The woman watched him through thoughtful eyes.

'Are you back?' Jack asked.

'I've never been away.' Although the woman spoke quietly, her words were very audible. The raucous jesting of a mob of redcoats faltered as they saw her. A blood stained corporal made an obscene suggestion, then dropped his eyes as she ignored him. They shuffled past and only stared when they were a dozen safe yards away.

Safe? Why did I choose that word? A woman is a rarity in their lives. Let them look. They know only cheap prostitutes and officers' wives who would scarcely acknowledge them as being of the same species. This woman is different.

'Are you not afraid?' Jack indicated the shambles of battle's aftermath and the narrow-eyed soldiers.

The woman did not blink. 'They are only men,' she said with such devastating calm that Jack could not respond.

'Why are you here? Are you following me?'

'This is my country; why are you here? Are you seeking me?' The woman smoothed a hand over the outside of her longyi in the most sensual gesture that Jack had ever seen. He realised he was staring at her hips.

For God's sake man, you don't even like women: remember?

'You are the most infuriating woman to talk to,' Jack told her.

She straightened up again. 'Then don't talk.'

'What is your name?' Jack asked when it became apparent that the woman was not going to move away.

'What is yours?' she countered.

'I am Jack Windrush.' He waited for her to respond.

'Jack Windrush,' in her mouth the name sounded as musical as the temple bells. 'Jack Windrush.' She nodded and walked away with her hips stirring her longyi and her slender upper body as erect and straight as any guardsman. The private soldiers of the Royal Irish stepped aside to let her pass. One touched a hand to his cap.

The woman smiled softly and drifted away.

She did not tell me her name. What was the meaning of that meeting? Why do I feel so differently about her?

'Loot boys! Find some gold to take home!' That was a Midlands voice, perhaps from Birmingham, and the words seemed to remain in the sultry air.

If I found something precious, I could buy my way into another regiment. After today's action people will know my name, so they might forgive my illegitimate birth.

The thought came fully formed into Jack's mind. It overcame a lifetime of training and habit, so he nearly ran down the stairs and stopped at the entrance to the Golden Pagoda. There was a crowd of soldiers lying prone on the steps, some with their tunics open, some squeezed into whatever shade was available. Others had draped themselves an enormous statue of Buddha, on whose head one man had carefully placed a white British cap, complete with the flapping neck guard. They looked up as Jack passed, and some scrambled to their feet.

'Rest easy men,' Jack said and entered the pagoda.

The difference in temperature was immediate, with the tall conical roof keeping the interior cool and dark and pleasant. Half a dozen soldiers wandered around, staring open mouthed at the dragon statues and the huge Buddha, with their voices muted as if they were in church, which, Jack surmised, in a way they were.

He had expected to see a single statue of Buddha with perhaps rows of pews as in a church back home. Instead, he was confronted by a vast open space surrounded by an unknown number of statues in gold, porcelain and brass, with Buddha sitting cross legged with a smile of peace on his face. He did not see the source of the light that gleamed from the soft sheen of gold and reflected from a hundred precious stones.

Jack stopped in awe. He had not expected the magnificence or the beauty of this temple to Buddha, or the sheer wealth of the statuary and adornments. Nor had he expected to experience such an atmosphere of sanctity.

These are no primitive people; this is as fine a building as Hereford Cathedral; finer even and much richer.

Jack felt an urge to kneel before the shrine of this serene Eastern deity, if indeed it was a deity, he was not sure. *Is Buddha a god?* A draught of wind set the temple bells ringing, softly at first and then louder, until they seemed to fill the vast space below the conical roof. The melody penetrated his thoughts, so there were only the chiming bells inviting him to submit to their calming authority and forget the avarice and aggression of the world outside. Jack stood in front of the huge golden statue and met the almond-shaped eyes, so expression-less, yet accusing him of theft and murder and invasion.

'This is a grand place, Coley!' that was O'Neill's voice, loud and cheerful and uncaring of man, devil or eastern deity. 'There's enough gold in here to keep us in drink for the rest of our lives.'

'And women,' Coleman sounded strained. 'We could buy a brothel, Paddy, and fill it with the best doxies that London has to offer.'

The coarse, matter of fact soldier's voices broke the spell, and Jack saw the pagoda in another light. Rather than a spiritual place of awe and wonder, it became just a fancy Eastern temple with meaningless statues and a collection of gold. With gold, Jack could buy promotion, buy his way into a better regiment, maybe even the Royals, and acquire land and property in England. Without money he was a nobody, an undistinguished and impoverished ensign.

A pocketful of golden boys would pay for my step up; a hatful would make me Captain. But I am an English gentleman, a man of honour. No: I am the son of a servant! In the eyes of the respectable, I am illegiti-mate with no right to a commission in the Army. I am a fraud in a very precarious position.

The golden Buddhas sat in splendour, serene, sublime, internally un-touched by the mad wastage of man around their temple. Jack glanced around, more furtive and mean than he had ever felt in his life. He slipped over to the darkest quarter of the temple and stood beside a row of sitting Buddhas. They are only idols, false gods: they mean nothing. They were of various sizes from some small enough to slip unnoticed into his pocket to others the size of a well-grown child.

Jack took a deep breath and lifted the smallest; it was heavier than he expected, with the gold warm to the touch and smooth under his palm. For a second he pretended to examine the workmanship, checked that nobody was watching and then slid it inside the right side pocket of his tunic. It fitted comfortably.

Now I am a thief, no longer fit to be an officer of Her Majesty or a British gentleman.

With the code of honour cracked, it was easier to continue. The next Buddha fitted into his left pocket with only a slight bulge and a feeling of vague discomfort that he ignored. Jack lifted the third and was wondering where to store it when he heard an outburst of raucous singing as a group of men from the Royal Irish came toward him, their iron shod boots crashing on the floor and their voices raised in disregard for the sanctity of their surroundings.

'Oh sorry sir,' a smoke-blackened corporal said, 'we did not see you there. Attention boys!'

The men behind him stiffened to attention, with one trying to hide the loot he had picked up.

'You men keep out of trouble,' Jack acknowledged the salute with a flick of his finger he hoped looked casual.

What if they saw me looting? Dear God, what if they saw me? I've ruined my reputation and career.

We saw you, sir,' the corporal's words made Jack feel suddenly sick.

'You saw me do what, Corporal?' The statuettes were heavy in his pocket; Jack was sure that the men of the Royal Irish were hiding their accusation behind the impassive stares private soldiers adopted when facing an officer.

'In the assault, sir,' the corporal grinned. 'We saw you charge up the stairs. You were good enough to join the Royal Irish sir if you don't mind me saying so!"

Jack nearly sighed with relief. 'Thank you, Corporal, but it's hardly your place to comment on an officer.'

'Yes sir,' the corporal's smile was replaced by the same lack of expression as his men. 'Beg pardon sir.'

'And you,' Jack prodded the man who held the statuette, 'can return that where it belongs. Looting is a flogging offence.'

He walked on without another word. He hoped he had acted like a typical British officer, so there was no suspicion of his actions within the pagoda.

Gentlemen don't steal. But I am not a gentleman.

The golden statuettes seemed so weighty that Jack felt as if his pockets reached to his knees. He slowed down, grateful for the swift onfall of night to mask the guilt he knew shone from his face.

'Sir!' Well's salute was as immaculate as always. 'I've been searching for you everywhere, sir.'

'Well, now you've found me.' Jack said. *He knows about my thefts. These blasted veteran sergeants know everything; I can see the accusation in his eyes.* 'What do you want, Sergeant?'

'The general is looking for you, sir. He requests that you join him in his tent immediately.' Wells relaxed a little. 'Maybe he saw you lead the attack, sir.'

'And where will I find General Godwin, Sergeant?' Jack tried to hide the mixture of pleasure and apprehension.

'He's in his tent outside the town, sir.' Wells allowed himself a small smile. 'Good luck, sir.'

Chapter Eight

Rangoon Spring and Summer 1852

The British Army had settled in around the walls of Rangoon. The artillery had taken up defensive positions in case of a Burmese counter attack, and a score of hanging lanterns revealed busy seamen scurrying around doing twice the work of the soldiers in half the time. There was a small forest of tents ready pitched, with wooden-faced sentinels outside and harassed officer's servants hurrying from place to place searching for their master's baggage, fresh water, wine and other essentials of the campaign. Outside the perimeter, Burma waited, seemingly more menacing with the contrast between light within the British camp and the outer darkness.

General Godwin travelled in style, with smart native orderlies at attention behind his desk and two crystal decanters among the litter of papers and maps. There were other officers in the room, with coats of red or blue, and the murmur of educated voices as they discussed the next stage of the campaign. Moths fluttered around the oil-fuelled lanterns, and the high-pitched whine of mosquitoes was so common that Jack paid it no heed.

'Who are you and what do you want?' Godwin snapped when he noticed Jack standing at attention in front of the desk.

'Ensign Windrush, sir. You wanted to see me.'

When Godwin frowned, a whiskered Madras Native Infantry colonel spoke. 'This is the officer I told you about sir. He left his post without orders to join in the assault on Rangoon.'

That was not what Jack hoped to hear. The speaker was vaguely familiar but from where Jack could not say.

Godwin stared at Jack as the other men stepped back. Jack could feel their disapproval.

There was silence for a full minute, save for the buzzing of insects.

'You are a disgrace, Windrush,' Godwin's voice was quiet, but with an edge to the words. 'You were given a job to do, and you failed to do it. You broke ranks and took your men them into an operation that was the function of a different unit. You acted entirely without orders and gave an example of poor discipline in front of the entire army. God alone knows what damage you have caused.'

Jack said nothing. He had hoped for praise for his courage and initiative; instead, Godwin was treating him like a disobedient schoolboy in front of half a dozen senior officers. He felt the blood rush to his face while Godwin continued his tongue-lashing.

'You are from the 113th, Windrush.' Godwin paused for a moment. 'I had thought to give you a chance. Colonel Murphy persuaded me- assured me - that you were a reliable officer that would help redeem the reputation of that unhappy regiment.'

'Quite the opposite,' the Company colonel said. He shook his head. 'If I may say, sir, I met this officer in England and his conduct even then was quite disgraceful.'

Jack shook his head. 'I am sorry sir, but I think you must be mistaken. I do not believe we have met...'

'Silence sir!' Godwin's voice was like a steel clamp. 'How dare you contradict a senior officer? Colonel Harcourt is a man of integrity and honour, not some...' As Godwin controlled himself Jack realised that he had indeed met the Company officer before.

Harcourt: this is Lucinda Harcourt's father, the irascible man who was at the door when I brought Lucinda home that evening.

'So, Windrush,' Godwin's tone was more moderate. 'Rather than try to build a better reputation for the 113th, you have tarnished it further. You and they are a regimental disgrace. However, I will make some allowances for youth and inexperience. You acted, I hope, out of impetuosity rather than a desire to take the glory of the day from the 18th Foot. It was glory that they well deserved, together with the gallant soldiers of the Company forces.' He nodded to Colonel Harcourt.

Jack said nothing as the blood rushed to his face. He felt the Buddhas heavy in his pocket.

'I am not going to mention your actions in my official report, Windrush,' Godwin said. 'Instead, I will send a private message to Colonel Murphy, informing him of my disappointment in you. He may decide to recall you, and he may not. Either way, you can be assured that you have not advanced your career by this action of impetuosity, and have further damaged the already embarrassed reputation of your regiment. I will keep my eye on you, Windrush.'

Jack took a deep breath. 'We captured the pagoda, sir...'

'You are dismissed, sir,' Godwin said. 'Get out of my sight.'

Jack left the tent feeling as if his world had collapsed. As he stepped outside a warm drop of rain splashed on his face, a foretaste of the monsoon.

As the British Army consolidated and the Burmese withdrew north, the rains began with a succession of hammer-blows that rendered movement all but impossible. In common with the others, Jack endured the climate while suffering his private torments.

Damn Colonel Harcourt: I did nothing untoward with Lucinda. Damn all blasted women. They are nothing but trouble.

And then the image of the Burmese woman with her deep eyes and that wondrous scent of sandalwood returned, together with the slide and shift of the *longyi* around her hips and bottom.

I am uncommonly stupid. She is a native woman.

Yet she remained in his mind over the next few weeks during which the British settled into life in Rangoon and the monsoon massed its might overhead. For a few weeks there were breaks between the savage squalls, and then the skies reopened and unleashed a deluge upon them.

The nights were the worst. During the dark hours Jack's mind spun with the visions of battle and death. He saw the faces of the men he had fought and the memory of his position tormented him. Then the faces would alter, become that steady eyed Burmese woman with the *longyi* tight around her hips and Jack would reach for her, only to recoil as she dissolved into the fog that shrouded the Golden Pagoda with its stolen Buddhas. He would wake drenched in sweat and stagger up to check his men, who suffered in less-than-silence from the incessant rain, staring into the mysterious dark of this hostile land.

The days were nearly as bad for Jack. He was a guest in the mess of the 51st, but was not part of it. He shared the hospitality but not the traditions and tried to ignore the hastily cut off conversations.

'He's out of his element here, poor young fellow. It must be hard on him.'

'He was kicked out of the Royals you know. His own family disowned him, I believe.'

'I heard he doesn't like women either. I mean, what sort of chap is that to have in the army ... Here he is now.' The officers would look away in sudden silence.

Jack did not spend much time in the mess of the 51st. Instead, he explored Rangoon, visited the pagodas and continued to read whatever military manuals he could find as the rains restricted all movement and the army sulked with inaction.

'Now I know how Noah felt,' Wells sheltered under the thatch fringe of a Burmese hut as he peered toward the sodden jungle.

'How did he feel?' Knight pulled his hat tighter onto his head in a vain attempt to mitigate the worst of the rain.

'Bloody wet,' Wells told him.

Standing a few feet away, Jack hid his smile. Wells sardonic humour was always a tonic, even on the most depressing days. He peered through the curtain of rain at the naked Burmese men who guided their buffalos through the mud of the rice-fields across the river.

'They're tough people,' he said.

'They're different to the Indians,' Wells checked the tarred canvas that covered the lock and muzzle of his musket. 'They're cleaner and less excitable.' He held the musket muzzle-downward to prevent rain from entering the barrel.

'Have you served in Burma before?'

When Wells nodded, water cascaded from the brim of his hat. 'Yes, sir; I caught the end of the last Burmese war way back in '26 when I was a Johnny Raw.'

Jack noted the red, blue and red medal ribbon on Well's chest. 'That's the Meritorious Service Medal, isn't it? You did not win that in Burma, Sergeant. It only came out a few years ago.'

Wells glanced down. 'Not in Burma sir. I was in Afghanistan with the 44th.'

'Were you at Gandamack?' Jack knew about that disastrous battle where the Afghans annihilated the remnant of the 44th were annihilated.

'Yes, sir.' Wells said.

'You survived,' Jack prompted.

'Yes, sir,' Wells did not elaborate. 'I transferred to this regiment when my own was sent back to England.' He looked uncomfortable at the admission, which suggested that he had something to hide.

'What happened at Gandamack?' Jack pressed.

'A woman dragged me free from the pile of dead, sir.' Wells said.

'Why did she do that?'

The outburst of firing was so close that Jack started. 'What the devil?'

'Stand to!' Wells shouted. 'Out you come lads!'

The rain fell like an opaque grey curtain, hammering down on the muddy maidan and weeping from the terraces of the Golden Pagoda.

'Nobody fights in the bloody monsoon,' O'Neill struggled to fasten his tunic as he stumbled from the tent.

'You tell the Burmese that,' Wells said, 'they don't know the rules.'

Jack ducked as a bullet ripped passed his head. He unfastened his holster and blinked through the rain. Figures were moving out there, but whether British or Burmese he could not tell. The failing light made things worse.

'Over there!' Wells kneeled and fired into the gloom.

'What's happening, Wells? What did you see?' Jack stood ready with his pistol as Wells reloaded.

A havildar of the Madras Native Infantry rushed past in a shower of mud, followed by a score of his sepoys.

'Dacoits, sir,' Wells fitted the percussion cap on to his musket and cocked it. 'They could be anywhere.'

'Dacoit? What's that?'

'Bandits,' Wells explained. 'They could be local *badmashes* come to rob, but more likely some lot attached to the King of Ava's army. I can't see ordinary dacoits attacking a British garrison.'

Somebody yelled close by, the words in Burmese, and a score of men seemed to rise from the ground and rush across the maidan, holding muskets and waving dhas.

'Look out, sir!' O'Neill shouted, knelt and fired. One of the Burmese fell at once, with the others charging bravely forward. The leading man wore what looked like a ragged red coat, and Jack fired three shots at him in quick succession. The man in the red coat was unhurt, but another of the attackers fell, to lie kicking on the ground.

'They're not after us, sir,' Wells fired from a standing position. 'They want the general.'

Jack aimed at the red coat again and pressed the trigger, without result. He swore and stepped backwards, lost sight of his target in the teeming rain but saw another man rushing at him; he squeezed the trigger again and flinched when his attacker staggered and came on, holding his dha high in the air. Dropping the now empty pistol, Jack grabbed at the hilt of his sword, yelling loudly to heighten his courage.

'Mine, sir!' Graham lunged forward with his bayonet and ran the man cleanly under the chin.

The Madras Native Infantry havildar appeared through the rain with his men in perfect formation behind him and formed them up in front of Godwin's tent. A sharp order and there was a barricade of bayonets around the tent.

'They've all gone,' Graham said. 'They Madrasi lads scared them away.'

Jack nodded; the only Burmese he could see were either the dead or injured.

'Where have they gone?' Jack, at last, drew his sword and held it ineffectively.

'Vanished into the night, sir.' Graham placed a foot on the man he had killed and withdrew his bayonet. He began to reload his musket. 'Bloody dacoits.'

There were three Burmese and two sepoy bodies on the ground, with two Burmese wounded.

'They did not fire,' Jack said, 'why did they not fire?'

'The Burmese only have flintlocks, sir,' Wells explained. 'They don't work too well in the rain.'

'They're brave men to attack when they only have knives,' Jack said. He raised his voice. 'Ranveer!' He hardly said the name before the Sikh arrived. 'Did you see how the dacoits got in?'

'Like snakes, they crawled on their bellies,' Ranveer said at once.

Godwin appeared from his tent, sword in hand. 'What happened? What did they want?' He looked down at the wounded Burmese. 'Can anybody speak Burmese?'

'Not a word, sir,' Jack said. He looked at Ranveer, 'how about you, Ranveer?'

'No, Sahib.'

'I know a few words, sir,' Wells volunteered.

'Ask that fellow what they were thinking of, attacking a British garrison,' Godwin ordered. 'I'm sure you can be persuasive.'

'I'm sure I can, sir.' The Burman had been shot in the thigh. He lay on his back on the rain battered maidan, twisting with pain as Wells lifted his dha and thumbed the edge. 'Right my boy, time for you to tell us things.' He laid the blade alongside the bullet hole in the man's leg and spoke in halting Burmese.

When the man shook his head, Wells pushed the point of the knife into the wound and twisted slowly. The man writhed, with sweat breaking out on his face.

I thought we were English gentlemen! We don't do this sort of thing!

Godwin looked on, unmoved as Wells repeated his question. 'Where did you learn Burmese, Sergeant?'

'I was here before sir, with the 44th.'

'I see.' Godwin nodded. 'You transferred then?'

'Yes, sir.' Wells looked up. 'Shall I ask him again?'

'Please do so.' Godwin turned away. 'Let me know the moment you find out anything Windrush.'

I feel sick; this is not what Englishmen do!

'You're not looking very well sir.' Wells said tactfully. 'Maybe you'd better have a lie down out of the rain; I'll carry on here.' He raised his voice. 'Bring me some light!' Lifting his boot, he kicked the wounded man hard in the groin, ignored the resulting scream and stood on the bullet wound as the dacoit writhed underneath him.

'I'll stay,' Jack fought the nausea that threatened to unman him. *I should be able to do anything the men can do, but better and for longer, and that includes watching human suffering.*

'As you wish sir.' Wells turned the dha and ripped the Burman's loin cloth from his body and began to jab him with the blade. When the man's cries turned to agonised screams, Jack pulled at Wells' arm.

'That's enough, Wells.'

'Nearly there sir,' Wells sounded as calm as if he was merely asking the time of day.

Jack looked into the pleading eyes of the dacoit. 'I'm sorry,' he said. 'I don't like this either, but we must know.'

'Just a few more minutes, sir,' Wells placed the toe of his boot on the man's groin and pressed, twisting, as he repeated his question.

The man screamed again and gabbled something.

'That's my lad!' Wells removed his foot at once. 'That's what we wanted to hear. They were after the general sir. They knew he was in the big tent and they wanted to kill him and the staff officers.' He nodded to the dacoit who lay in a foetal ball on the ground, clutching at his injuries. 'You're a brave man, Johnny Dacoit.' He raised his voice. 'I need somebody to look after this wounded man. Take care of him.'

Stooping, Wells examined the dha.

Jack could not face the wounded man and the golden Buddhas were heavy in his pocket. He hesitated, hating himself for what he had to say next. 'I am sorry Sergeant, but there is something else I must know. Ask him why their leader was wearing a red coat. Did he steal it from a British prisoner?'

Wells nodded. 'Yes, sir.' He pulled the dacoit's head back and spoke to him again, pointing to his groin with the dha. Jack shuddered; he could only imagine what Wells was saying.

Now I am as bad as any dacoit; I have condoned torture and have encouraged Wells to inflict more pain on that unfortunate fellow.

The dacoit said something, holding onto his injuries, and Wells patted him on the shoulder.

'That was easy enough, sir. He does not know why their Bo wears a red coat, but they call him Bo Ailgaliutlo or something like that. I can't quite make out what he is saying.'

'That's not surprising considering he is a lot of pain,' Jack murmured. 'Bo Ailgaliutlo: is that the leader's name?'

Wells shook his head. 'No, sir. It's his title. Bo is a military commander. His name means the English officer or Commander English.' He helped the dacoit onto a litter with such care that it was hard to imagine he had been inflicting terrible pain on the man just a few moments before. 'I think your fellow in the red coat is an Englishman, sir.'

Chapter Nine

Rangoon: Summer 1852

'An Englishman? A renegade?' General Godwin pressed the fingers of his right hand onto the bullet scarred desk. 'I can't allow that.' He glanced at Harcourt. 'What do your fellows report, Harcourt?'

'Nothing sir. They could not find him at all. They think the dacoits came by water and escaped the same way.'

'Cunning devils,' Godwin shook his head. 'That would tie in with having an Englishman in charge. He would know that we would have the sentries watching the land frontier and we'd rely on the Navy to keep control of the river.'

'How many men can you spare, Harcourt? We have to eradicate our renegade, and your Company wallahs are best for this sort of affair.' Godwin pulled a map from the drawer of his desk. 'This entire country is one big river system; the dacoits could be anywhere.'

'I can't spare anybody, sir.' Harcourt said quickly. 'In our last war with the King of Ava, we lost thousands of men through disease. I cannot spare any of my soldiers; I will need them all.' He nodded to Jack, 'but Windrush here is not officially attached to any force, and we all remember how keen he is.'

Godwin looked toward Jack, pursed his lips and pushed his hands together as if in prayer. After a few minutes, he spoke again. 'As you seem to wish to be in the centre of things, Windrush, and obviously need a stricter hand to guide you than Colonel Murphy can provide, I am going to take Harcourt's advice and send you after this Bo Ailgaliutlo fellow and his dacoits.'

'Up river sir? How far should I go?' Jack felt rather than saw Harcourt's look of smug triumph.

'You will go as far as you need to go,' Godwin said. 'I will detach you and your blackguards from my army. I have not forgotten your ill-discipline in the assault.' He looked closer at Jack. 'I understand that young officers have fire and ambition, Windrush, but they must also obey the orders of their superiors. I will put you under the command of Commander Marshall; he knows how to control young whippersnappers like you.'

Harcourt nodded vigorously. 'Well said, sir. Windrush is a disgrace.'

'Where I am sending you, Windrush, will dampen your martial ardour and introduce you to the realities of soldiering out here.' General Godwin pulled his hands apart and laid them flat on the top of the desk. 'Follow that renegade, Windrush and get rid of him. Scatter his band of dacoits and either kill the leader or bring him back to a fair trial and the noose.'

'Yes, sir.'

I am being sent away from the main theatre of war to chase some dacoit; nobody will know anything that I do. It's the Curse of the 113th again.

'Oh come, Windrush; don't look so gloomy,' Harcourt was enjoying Jack's discomfiture. 'Look on this an opportunity to redeem yourself.'

Godwin scribbled a short note, handed it to Jack and nodded toward the entrance to his tent. 'Collect your men and report to Commander Marshall before dawn tomorrow. Give him my compliments and this slip of paper and inform him that you are his military escort. That's all.'

So Colonel Harcourt has his revenge for me meeting his daughter. I am to be sent beyond the fringes of civilisation so that Burmese dacoits can slaughter me or some disgusting disease can kill me. I am to be sent into the unknown away from the eyes of anyone who could further my career.

Jack plunged his hands deep into his pockets and slouched across the bustling encampment until his fingers touched the smooth gold of the Buddhas.

I still have these; they matter more than ever now. Once I am out of this hellish place, I will resign my commission and buy some land. God knows that with my career in ruins even before it has begun I have no future in the army. The guilt does not matter; the future does.

'Sergeant Wells!' Jack bellowed the name across the torch lit spread of the camp.

Wells appeared at his side immediately. 'Sir!' Jack smelled the drink on Well's breath. Where he had got it was anybody's guess, but British soldiers had a knack for finding something alcoholic wherever they were, and as a sergeant with long experience, Wells would know every trick in the book and many that nobody had ever written down.

'We are going on a little trip, Sergeant.'

'Yes, sir. I heard the shave, sir.'

How did he know that so soon?

'I want the men ready for instant departure, with double ammunition and rations, plus water bottles full of water and not. 'Jack made it obvious that he was sniffing Wells' breath, 'not gin.'

'The men will be ready sir. They'll have two hundred rounds each and enough rations for five days, plus twice the official water allowance.'

'Well done, Sergeant. We are not staying here; we are going away from the main British Army.'

'Yes, sir.' Wells did not look upset at the prospect. 'Where are we going, sir?'

'I am not exactly sure yet,' Jack was candid. 'We are after that renegade that attacked us.'

Wells nodded. 'Hunting dacoits is never easy, sir. It's like trying to catch smoke with a fishing net.'

'Have you done it before?' Jack asked.

'Yes sir, too often.'

'Well, we have to report to a Commander Marshall.' Once again Jack wondered if he was unbending too much in front of a ranker. He had been brought up to believe that officers should always maintain a strict distance from the men.

'Would that be Commander William Marshall sir?' Wells asked with a straight face. 'He is captain of *Serangipatam*, down in the Irrawaddy.'

'How the devil do you know that, Sergeant?' Jack did not keep the surprise from his voice. 'Never mind, just make sure we all get there, would you?' He recognised the name of that ship. The black ship of the Company, he had been told.

A soldier's life is full of variety. Three hours ago I was a bored subaltern on guard duty; now I am going beyond the reach of civilisation for days or maybe weeks.

'*Serangipatam* is one of the East India Company vessels that support the Royal Navy in this campaign. She is eighty long with two masts and a 70 horse power engine. Her hull is pierced for sweeps, and she has three twelve- pounder cannon on each broadside, one six pounder facing forward and another aft.' Commander Marshall was of medium height, wiry rather than broad and tanned so dark by the sun that he could easily have passed for a native of the country. 'We are the eyes and ears of the fleet, Ensign; we go in front and see what is happening, we take the first blows of the foe and report back when we find anything of significance, be that some new stockade, enemy forces or just shoal water.'

Jack nodded. *Serangipatam* seemed crowded by men even without his ten soldiers. Sailors in white clothes were busily coiling lines or scrubbing the deck, working in a disciplined silence that spoke volumes about either their training or the personality of her commander and the three young officers who overlooked them. 'Yes, sir, and now we are following Bo Ailgaliutlo.'

Marshall continued as if Jack had not spoken. 'Your duty is to follow my orders.' He ran a stern gaze over Jack's sweating soldiers. 'Where my vessel operates, there is no room for hesitation or dissent. When I give an order, you will obey it instantly.' His boots did not make a sound on the white-scrubbed deck as he stepped past and spoke to the 113th.

'You men; Ensign Windrush is your officer, and I expect you to do as he says. In my ship, your duty is to obey every order of your lawful officers. Anything else is mutiny, and at sea, we hang mutineers. That's all.'

Jack blinked; the Company's navy did things differently. There was no side and no pretence. He checked to see how his men had taken the threats. They looked unconcerned, with Wells watching the seamen at work, O'Neill's face as expressionless as Burmese teak and even Coleman standing at attention as if Marshall had said nothing unusual. Only Thorpe appeared worried, with his mouth working silently.

'You soldiers get below until we are under way,' Marshall turned away.

Mercifully the rains had eased that night. A flight of snipe bustled overhead as Marshall gave the order to cast off and *Serangipatam* eased into the swollen river. All around, a thin mist slithered across the mud-coloured water and concealed the Golden Pagoda of Rangoon behind a clinging damp curtain. There was silence save for insects as the seamen worked with only a minimum of orders, every man knowing his task and performing it as quickly as he could.

Now the Rains are easing, Godwin will be preparing to march on to Ava and defeat the Tatmadaw – the Burmese Army - and here I am, nosing up a river with an ill-tempered sailor in charge of my future.

Smoke from *Serangipatam*'s funnel joined the rising mist as she eased upstream with her screw frothing the water and her wake raising waves that washed against the banks on either side. Early morning fishermen or rice field workers paused to watch this strange vessel that moved with no apparent method of propulsion while birds screamed their raucous calls overhead.

'Look at that,' a red-headed lieutenant pointed to a pair of buffalo that plodded through a rice field. 'I wager they have been doing that for ten thousand years, and here we are passing by in a screw steamer. That's the difference between them and us.'

Jack remembered the patient plodding of the cattle herds of Herefordshire. 'Sometimes I think we are not all that different,' he said.

The lieutenant laughed and held out a hand. 'George Bertram. Welcome aboard.'

'Jack Windrush.'

'I know: you led the assault on the Golden Pagoda.'

Jack liked this man immediately.

Within ten minutes they were out of sight of Rangoon and chugging slowly upstream with the banks a tedious mixture of jungle and cultivated rice fields varied by an occasional little village whose fishing boats were set bobbing by the wake of Serangipatam. Twice men emerged from the patchy forest and pointed muskets at them, but nobody fired and the steamer continued, leaving a thin trail of black smoke that gradually merged with the persistent morning mist. Debris washed down the river carried by the swollen water, and once the corpse of a deer surged past.

With the ship moving and one man in the bow casting a lead to check the depth, Commander Marshall sent most the crew down below, leaving only a handful on deck.

'Your men can come up now,' he said to Jack. 'You will want to have them parade or whatever you soldiers do.' His gaze never left Jack's face, but he suddenly yelled out to the man aloft to remember to watch astern as well.

'They'll be glad of the air,' Jack guessed that the men were suffering in their cramped quarters below decks.

Marshall walked away without another word.

The 113th filed on deck, scratching at mosquito bites and buckling on sundry pieces of equipment. Wells shouted them into order, threw Jack a salute and slammed to attention. 'All present and correct sir: eight men on parade.'

'We are heading up river men,' Jack gave them as much information as he knew himself, 'hunting for Bo Ailgaliutlo, that is the renegade that attacked our camp and tried to murder General Godwin. We don't know what is waiting for us or where the trail will lead; we only know that we will hunt him until we catch him. We are well in advance of the army and on our own in a position of honour.' That was nothing like the truth but Jack thought it best to keep their morale up by boosting their self-respect. 'The Burmese will not like us being in their territory, and we all have experience of their military expertise; they are brave, they are stubborn, and they are defending their own land. We must be prepared for everything and anything.'

The expressions remained stoic, as befitted British soldiers.

'Right; let's get started then.' Jack ignored the sweat that was already trickling down his spine and dampening his forehead.

He had his men marching up and down the deck with their heavy boots thumping on the teak and the sailors openly grinning at the antics of their red-coated guests.

'Go easy on my deck!' Marshall did not raise his voice, 'if there are any scrapes it is you soldiers that will sand it level.'

Musket drill was next, with the men standing at the rail presenting and aiming at points on the banks of the river.

'Don't fire those blasted muskets, Windrush. We don't want to alert the Burmese or cause them to retaliate.'

'Aim but don't fire,' Jack amended his instructions and glanced at the quarterdeck, where Marshall was watching. 'We'll withdraw the charges later.'

By midday the heat was intense. *Serangipatam* altered her position from the centre of the river to the left side.

'Keep watch on that bank,' Jack ordered. 'Keep alert.'

In mid-afternoon, Marshall ordered manoeuvres that saw them ease onto what Jack assumed was a fork of the river. Water churned brown around them, carrying debris from upstream.

'These trees are closer now,' Wells said, 'the monkeys can spit on us when we pass.'

'Have we left the Irrawaddy?' Jack asked Bertram.

When Bertram grinned, his freckles merged, so his face appeared almost as ginger as his hair. 'Strictly speaking, Ensign, we were on the Rangoon, or the Yangon as the Burmese call it. Now we are on one of the tributaries of the Yangon, the Pegu River, but still part of the Irrawaddy delta.' He glanced astern, where Marshall stood on the minuscule quarter deck.

'What are we meant to be doing?' Jack asked. 'How do we know Bo Ailgaliutlo came this way?'

'Only the Commander knows,' Bertram said, 'and God.' He gave a brief grin, 'if the Commander told him.' He looked away and fiddled with one of the ropes that secured a small boat. 'I think we only know half the truth of anything, Windrush.'

'We are chasing Bo Ailgaliutlo,' Jack said.

'We may be,' Bertram spoke softly, with his head turned away as he inspected the equipment on board the longboat. 'We are also what you in the army would call the forlorn hope, the *verlorner hauf.*' He waited for Jack's response.

'The what?' Jack did not hide his confusion.

'We are the *verlorner hauf*, as the Germans call it; the lost party.' Bertram opened the locker in the stern of the boat and prodded the rock hard bread. 'Commander Marshall always comes back though.'

Jack grunted. 'Commander Marshall always comes back, but do his men?'

Bertram straightened up from the longboat and glanced aft to the quarterdeck. The commander stood there, aloof, dignified and still as any of the gilded Buddhas in the Golden Pagoda.

'Not always,' Bertram said. He lowered his voice to a whisper. 'Not often. Not from the places they send him.'

'You came back,' Jack pointed out.

'I came back,' Bertram agreed. 'But the other three officers on our last trip did not.' He glanced aft again. 'And we lost most of the marines; that's why you are here.'

'I'm not sure that I understand,' Jack said. 'General Godwin sent us after Bo Ailgaliutlo.'

'Oh, I know that,' Bertram said, 'and Commander Bertram will follow this Bo chap to the ends of the Earth or the furthest reaches of Darkest Asia, I assure you.' He dropped his voice. 'His methods, however, do not always bear investigation. This is a John Company ship,' he said, 'it should have Company marines or at least infantry, but their commanders refuse to send their men under Marshall.' He looked away as he spoke.

'That's ominous,' Jack said, 'how many of the marines died on your last trip?'

'Lucky thirteen,' Bertram tested the lashings of the longboat and slipped further away. 'Best keep quiet; the commander does not like idle chatter.' When Bertram moved, he was as light on his feet as a ballet dancer.

The novelty of passing jungle and rice fields soon paled. While the crew of Serangipatam occupied themselves working the ship, the men of the 113th began to fret with boredom and heat.

Keep them busy, or they will cause trouble; God only knows how long this expedition may last.

'Extra parade!' Jack yelled. *I am not some little schoolboy to creep around on tiptoes, scared to move in case I incur the wrath of an irascible school master.* 'Come on the 113th! On deck with you all! I want full kit including musket and pack!'

Only eight men grumbled on deck. 'Where is Thorpe?' Jack addressed Wells; 'get him up here, Sergeant!' Jack was very aware that Marshall was watching from the quarterdeck. 'I want him on parade in three minutes flat!'

Rather than wait for Wells, Jack followed below deck, with the humid heat increasing as he stepped down and the air so thick he fought for breath. Thorpe was lying on the tiny shelf he used as a bunk, facing upward with his eyes tightly clenched and his fists closed into balls. He wore only his shirt.

Jack grunted at his state of undress. 'You have two minutes to get into uniform and onto the deck, Thorpe!'

Thorpe said nothing.

My first real disciplinary challenge and it's on a boat in the middle of the jungle with no support. What the devil do I do now?

'Get up, Thorpe!'

Jack grabbed hold of the sleeve of Thorpe's shirt and hauled him off the shelf. Taken by surprise, Thorpe roared once and landed with a crash.

I am probably breaking every regulation in the book.

'Get on deck!' Jack realised that he was shaking, either with anger or nervousness or a combination of both. 'Move you idle bastard!' He kicked Thorpe's prone body. 'Sergeant: bring his uniform and equipment!'

Thorpe yelled and rolled on his side, so Jack landed a firm kick on his backside. 'Get moving Thorpe!' He kicked the same place until Thorpe staggered up and lurched onward, with Jack kicking every time he hesitated. 'Faster!' He shoved him up the short ladder to the deck.

The other men of the 113th were standing in small groups, watching the scenery drift past.

'Stand to attention!' Jack roared. He dragged Thorpe across the deck by his hair and slammed him hard against the rail. 'You! Hold your musket above your head and double up and down the deck until I order you to stop! Move!'

Thorpe gave him one scared glance and obeyed, with his bare feet padding off the hot wooden planks and bare legs flicking up his shirt and revealing various bits of him in a manner so ludicrous that in other circumstances Jack would have laughed.

'Keep him moving Sergeant,' Jack moderated his voice. 'And if he slows down, we will see if he likes the cat. The rest of you...' he faced the suddenly subdued men, 'I will drill myself.'

With Wells yelling at the perspiring Thorpe, Jack had the others marching and manoeuvring on the deck, presenting arms, kneeling and aiming, standing and aiming and marching again as *Serangipatam* steamed slowly up the muddy river.

All the time he was aware of Marshall standing on the quarterdeck watching but saying nothing. Jack ignored him. Let him watch; if he tries to interfere with a Queen's officer doing his duty, he will learn that I am not one of his blasted seamen.

After only ten minutes, Thorpe was flagging; after twenty he was staggering along the deck.

'Keep him at it,' Jack snarled. 'Get those legs up Thorpe!'

Only then did Jack realise there was somebody else on the quarterdeck beside the Commander. She was sitting on a canvas chair beside the rail, watching the scene on deck. The second Jack met her eyes she turned away, so he saw her profile, with the high cheekbones and determined chin he remembered from their previous meetings in Rangoon.

What the devil are you doing here, Madam and who are you to be a passenger on a John Company ship? Despite himself, Jack spared her a second sideways look.

'Thorpe! Get these legs higher! Move man!'

Let the woman take what she likes out of that. The more Thorpe moved, the higher he kicked his legs, the more his shirt flopped up, and the more of him was revealed. Jack hid his smile. If that woman chose to come onto a ship filled with men she had to cope with whatever sights were there, including a man's legs. Jack sneaked another glance at her; she still looked over the stern of the ship as if what occurred on board was of no consequence to her at all.

'Mark time!' Jack raised his voice, so it echoed from the trees on either side of the river. *If any dacoits are there, they can't miss the boat anyway, so my voice won't make any difference.* 'You men; fix bayonets!'

He shouted orders until he was hoarse, worked the men until they were drooping, worked them until they obeyed his orders without question or thought, so they became like exhausted machines. He saw Thorpe slump to the deck and lie in a gasping heap.

'Get up Thorpe!' Jack thrust the toe of his boot under the man's hip and nudged ungently. 'Get up, man!'

'He's had enough, sir,' Wells ventured. 'It's the heat, sir.'

'Blast the heat! He's a soldier...' Jack stopped, aware that his men were watching him from the corner of their eyes. *What am I doing? I'll kill the man. I am putting on a show of bravado because that sailor irritated me.* He took a deep breath of the humid air. 'Throw a bucket of water over him, Sergeant and allow him a break. In fact, stand the men down. They all look tired now.'

Wells nodded. 'Yes, sir.' He paused for a moment. 'They've never seen you like this before.'

Jack chose to ignore the unstated question. *Neither have I; what the devil am I doing?*

It's not that sailor; it's that blasted woman. She's got me all unsettled.

Wells sloshed a bucket of tepid river water over Thorpe and prodded him with a hard toe. 'Up you get Thorpey.' Bending down, he grabbed Thorpe's arm and hauled him upright. 'Now go and get dressed decent like a British soldier and not like some blackguard from the arse end of Brummagem.'

'Give him plenty of water,' Bertram advised. 'Or he will die.'

'You heard the officer,' Wells glanced at Jack who nodded his confirmation. 'Drink more water. None of that beer and rot-gut spirits you pour down your throat you ruffian!'

'Stand at ease, the rest of you,' Jack was aware that Marshall had not moved an inch. Alone in the ship, he seemed invulnerable to heat, flying insects or fatigue. 'We don't know what sort of dangers we will be facing,' he said, 'so we have to keep fit and alert. Dismiss.'

As the 113th filed below Marshall gave the order for *Serangipatam* to shut off her engines.

'Well, we're here,' Wells looked around, 'wherever here is. All I can see is more jungle and rice fields and another of these Burmese temples, sir.'

Jack saw the woman appear at his side. 'Commander Marshall asks that you join us in his cabin, Ensign Windrush,' she said.

Chapter Ten

Jack nodded. 'I am glad to see you on board.'

She wore the same short white jacket she had worn in Rangoon but with a green longyi tight around her hips and a bright orchid placed in her hair. 'Commander Marshall asks that you join us in his cabin,' she repeated.

This woman is going to give nothing away.

'Then I shall join you both with pleasure,' Jack's bow contained more respect than mockery.

'This way,' she turned without another word and walked away. Jack glanced briefly at the smooth slide of her hips within the *longyi* and looked away again.

I have no time or inclination for distractions.

'We are going ashore tomorrow,' Marshall began the conversation even before Jack had sat at the small table that was bolted to the deck, 'me, you, Myat Lay Phyu,' he nodded to the woman, 'and as many men as you think will be best for an escort.'

Myat Lay Phyu: that is an enchanting name. It suits her.

'Might I ask where we are going, sir? I take it we are hunting for Bo Ailgaliutlo and his dacoits?' Jack kept his voice level and polite. 'If I knew it would help me judge how many men to bring.'

Marshall held his eyes for a long thirty seconds before he replied. 'We are hunting for the renegade, Bo Ailgaliutlo, Windrush. Myat Lay Phyu is my translator.'

'I wondered why she was on the ship,' Jack held out his hand. 'How do you do, Myat Lay Phyu?' He stumbled over the syllables of her name.

Her touch was light and firm. 'Very well than k you Ensign Windrush. How do you do?' Her face was impassive. 'Myat will do if you cannot manage the rest of my name.'

'You speak English very well,' Jack complimented her.

'So do you,' Myat replied. She withdrew her hand and folded it beside its sister in front of her. Even in her short pale grey jacket and longyi, she did not look as out of place as he felt in that cabin.

'I am English,' Jack said.

'I know.' Myat's expression did not alter.

Myat is the only woman I have ever wanted to like me, and she most obviously does not. She treats me as if I was a buffoon.

'Now the pleasantries are complete; I will ask you both to pay attention.' Marshall shuffled some papers on his immaculate desk. 'We will be landing shortly after dawn. By then the locals will have time to recover from their surprise at seeing us here and will have called in the head man, whatever his name is,' he glanced at Myat.

'His name is Bo Loung' she said and relapsed into silence.

'Bo Loung,' Marshall repeated.

'How long will be ashore for?' Jack tried to calculate rations and water.

'I do not know,' Marshall said. 'I will talk to this Bo Loung fellow through Myat and ask about the renegade Bo Ailgaliutlo.' There was no expression on his face. 'That is my duty. I will also try to persuade Bo Loung to back the British against the King of Ava. That is my choice. Either he will join us, or we will send an expedition to flatten his little town. That is the reality.' For a second Jack thought he saw a glimmer of humour in Marshall's ice-chip eyes.

'I see we use subtlety in our diplomacy,' Jack wished he had not spoken as soon as Marshall fixed him with a stare like frozen granite.

'Force is the only thing these people understand,' he said quickly. 'They are child-like barbarians and like all children must be taught right from wrong.'

'Yes, sir,' Jack wondered if Myat appreciated Marshall calling her people child-like barbarians. *How had she learned English? Who was she?* 'They certainly build some beautiful temples, sir.'

Marshall grunted. 'You are to ensure I have peace to talk with this Bo Loung fellow. Keep away his advisers and what nots: these people always have a horde of followers and hangers-on who get in the way. If anybody tries to interfere, then stop them, whatever it takes. Any questions?'

'No, sir.' Jack wondered if he was meant to jump to attention or merely salute. Instead, he nodded.

'Good; take as many men as you think you may need.' Marshall stood up. 'That's all; dismiss.'

'Where are we, sir?' Jack was determined not to act like a young schoolboy.

'We are at Pegu; dismiss.' Marshall was curt.

Pegu: I will check that on the map.

'Easy all,' Marshall ordered. The seamen lifted their oars, so the longboat eased onto the river bank.

'They're waiting for us,' Wells said. He nodded to the group of men who stood on the river bank. There were a dozen warriors in short jackets and dark *longyis*, with spears in hand and dhas at their waists. In their midst stood a man wearing a flowing knee length *longyi* with a bright yellow cowl around his neck. His spiked hat had fine chain mail washing down the back of his neck.

The stout man in yellow is Bo Loung,' Myat said quietly. 'Please remember Commander Marshall that Pegu used to be the overlord of Burma and does not like Ava.'

'Leave the diplomacy to me, Myat. You are here to translate, not to give advice.' Marshall pointed to the man in the spiked hat. 'That will be the Bo. Windrush, you make sure that none of the others interfere.'

Jack nodded. 'Yes, sir.' He raised his voice slightly, 'you heard the Captain, men. Follow my lead but be gentle. These people are not our enemies, but we are not yet sure if they are our friends.'

He had brought all of his men with him. He had been tempted to leave some on *Serangipatam* but decided that the seamen could look after their vessel. If the Peguese proved hostile, he would need all the muskets he could get.

'Tell them we are friendly,' Marshall ordered as the warriors raised their spears. Another body of men ran to join them, some with muskets.

'Ready lads,' Jack said softly, 'but don't fire until I tell you.'

Myat balanced in the prow of the boat, facing the shore '*Min ga la ba,' she said 'kama lo k'aw-ba-deh Myat Lay Phyu'*

Even in these circumstances, Jack realised he was admiring her.

The Bo stepped forward and signalled for his men to remain still. He shouted something, and Myat replied, with the name 'Commander Marshall' incongruous among the Burmese words.

There was a pause, and then the Bo replied.

'Bo Loung says that you are welcome to come to his town,' Myat said.

'As well for him,' Marshall grunted. 'Or I would blast the place to pieces.'

Marshall was first out, Navy fashion, and then Jack led his men onto land, muskets ready for trouble.

'This is Bo Loung,' Myat introduced the ornately clad man, who gave a graceful bow. 'He is a Pegu chieftain and entitled to respect.'

Jack responded to the Bo's bow while Marshall nodded.

A smiling Burmese woman trotted up and placed a garland of bright flowers over Marshall's head. The commander gave an impatient tut until Myat advised him it was a sign of respect.

'Where will we talk? Ask him where we will talk?' Marshall was as abrupt to the Pegu chieftain as he was to his crew. 'And tell him to get these hangers-on out of the way.'

'That's our job, boys,' Jack moved forward as the Peguese warriors moved closer to the Bo. 'Come on people; let the Commander talk to your headman in peace.' He pushed gently without effect until Myat spoke to the Bo, who snapped an order and his warriors stepped back slowly, eyes fixed on Jack and his men.

'Ensure I have peace, Windrush,' Marshall ordered.

The Bo indicated a large nearby hut with a wide veranda. Ignoring the gaggle of naked children who grinned and chattered to him, Marshall pushed inside, with the Bo and Myat following.

'What do we do now, sir?' Wells asked.

'We wait.' Jack swatted at the mosquitoes that already gathered around his head.

And provide food for the flies. Is this my function now? To stand guard while a John Company Commander tries to browbeat a Burmese chief into helping us?

More children swarmed to the veranda to gaze at these strange men in outlandish clothes. Wells attempted to ignore one persistent little *chokerah* who tugged at his trouser leg, gave the boy a gentle cuff on the shoulder and then broke an army issue biscuit in half and handed him that instead. The boy withdrew with his treasure and gnawed it, watching Wells through huge eyes. One of his companions, barely more than ten years old, lit a cigar as long as his arm and puffed mightily.

The voices inside the hut rose and fell, with Marshall's dominating. Jack listened for the calm tones of Myat as the sweat trickled down his face and soaked into his shirt.

'These buggers are getting a bit close,' Wells indicated the men of the town. 'Do you want me to chase them away, sir?'

The warriors who had been with Bo Loung had been joined by many more, so there were around fifty men gathered among the huts only thirty yards from the 113th. They spoke among themselves, gesticulated toward the British and occasionally fingered the dhas they wore. About half carried spears or long flintlock muskets.

Wells squinted at the men. 'They're carrying Tower muskets sir, by the look of it; our own guns exported to be used against us.'

'They know about muskets then,' Jack said. 'Have two men aim above their heads but don't fire yet.'

'Beg pardon sir, but I might be able to chase them without threats.' Wells sounded almost apologetic. 'I know a few words of Burmese, remember.'

'Try if you wish,' Jack said, 'but be careful.' He watched as Wells shouldered his musket and walked, seemingly casually, toward the gathered Burmese. When he was about fifteen paces away, he stopped, pressed his hands together as if he was about to pray and bowed toward them before saying half a dozen words in Burmese.

'Ready lads,' Jack said softly. He placed his hand on the butt of his revolver, prepared to draw and fire if the crowd proved hostile. Instead, they seemed more surprised that Wells knew their language.

A man in the full turban that Jack believed signified a person of wealth stepped forward. In common with the others, he carried a dha at his belt, while a cheroot was thrust through the hole bored through the lobe of his left ear.

'If he pulls that sword,' Jack spoke low-voiced to O'Neill, 'drop him, but be careful not to shoot Wells.' He nodded to Coleman and Thorpe. 'You two keep watch on the other side of the hut. I don't trust your marksmanship.'

I don't trust you not to aim at your sergeant.

Wells and the Burman were engaged in a halting conversation that included a lot of gesticulation and, on Well's side, fewer words. After a few moments; it became apparent that the Burman was not hostile.

'He's a decent lad,' Wells called over his shoulder. 'He's Peguese and not Burman, and he has no love for the King of Ava.'

'You men remain here,' Jack decided. 'O'Neill, you are acting corporal God help us. Keep them under control, no shooting unless we are attacked, and be pleasant to the amiable Peguese.'

A small boy ran from the crowd of Burmese, grinned to Jack and thrust forward a mango toward O'Neill.

'Careful of the *chokerah*,' Wells called out, 'that's this fellow's son.'

O'Neill knelt on one knee and accepted the fruit, handing over a farthing in return. 'That's very kind of you, young fellah.' His Irish brogue seemed strangely at home in this exotic place.

The boy grinned widely, tucked the coin inside his loincloth and scampered away. Jack could not resist smiling back.

'I see you are making friends with the locals.' Once again Jack had not seen Myat appear. She stood outside the hut, still as any statue of Buddha.

'Sergeant Wells has it all in hand,' Jack agreed.

Myat surprised him with a small smile. 'You have a good sergeant.'

'Did the talks go as hoped?' Jack knew that Marshall would tell him nothing.

'The Bo informed us that a dacoit chief had passed this way,' Myat was more forthcoming. 'He did not know if it was Bo Ailgaliutlo or not.' Her smile was small but seemed to age her. *How old is this woman? She is not as young as I had thought at first. She is certainly older than me. In Burma, it is rude to ask a lady's age.* 'He was just glad to see the chief pass without molesting him.'

'How many soldiers – fighting men – were there?' Jack asked.

When Myat shook her head, her cylinder of hair bobbed on her head. 'He did not count them. He said there were many.' She looked toward Sergeant Wells and the thin cordon of redcoats, her eyes strangely troubled. 'Far more than you have, Ensign.'

One British soldier is worth ten foreigners and twenty Frenchmen.

'I'm sure we can handle them.'

'Please may it not happen,' Myat said and added, 'it would be better if Buddha were with you,' Myat said seriously. She held out her hand, palm uppermost. 'I will take the statuettes back to the temple for your peace of mind.'

'You tried your best there,' Jack approved, 'but my mind is quite peaceful thank you and I have need of them myself.'

'Your life and that of your soldiers are more important than wealth or worldly goods,' Myat's expression did not alter.

'I am responsible for my life, and the fortunes of war and not the smile of Buddha decide the fate of my soldiers.' Jack felt unaccustomed anger creep over him. *What right has this woman to lecture me?*

Myat's nod was graceful and unexpected. 'I will be ready when you reconsider,' she said, 'but you are far from England. In Pegu the teachings of Buddha have more power than the pursuit of wealth.'

'There's more to it than wealth, damn it!' Jack nearly shouted the words as Myat nodded her head again, her expression unaltered.

'Of course, there is, Ensign Windrush.' Although her expression did not alter, Jack knew she was reproaching him.

Jack thrust his hands deep into his pockets and fingered the smooth gold of the statuettes. *These are mine and mine they will remain. They are the spoils of a hard fought battle. It is a soldier's right.*

Is it not?

He fought away his doubts.

'The greatest goodness is a peaceful mind,' Myat said gravely. 'We are born afresh each day and what we do today is what is most important.'

'What the devil does that mean, Myat?'

'It means yesterday's wrong-doings can be cancelled out by the good we do today.' She nodded again, held his eyes for a long second and walked with short, graceful steps toward Wells and the crowd of Peguese.

'Windrush!' Marshall barked. 'I am going back to the ship. Take charge.'

Jack nodded. He was merely a spectator as three dignified elders gave gruff orders that saw a crowd of people gather. They came in ones and twos, in small groups and entire families, all talking and laughing, joking as they spoke to the men of the 113th. Jack watched as both groups conversed happily; the fact that neither knew a word of the other's language did not seem to matter. *That's British soldiers for you.*

The sound of drums made him reach for his revolver until Wells shook his head. 'It's all right, sir. The people are putting on a *pwe* for us, a sort of play.'

There was no stage or lights and seemingly no rehearsals. The crowd merely parted to reveal a party of men and women in gaudy costumes, with two principal actors making gestures every bit as dramatic as anything in a London theatre.

'Look at the crowd, sir; half of Pegu must be here.' Wells was smiling.

Jack nodded; the men of the 113th were a scarlet island in the midst of a sea of Burmese. Men and women crushed together, talking animatedly as an orchestra of instruments Jack did not recognise played happily in the background. The air reeked of garlic.

'Where's Myat? What's this all about?'

'I am here, Ensign Windrush.' Myat emerged from Wells' shadow. 'The people of Pegu have organised this *pwe* for you. It would be impolite not to watch.' She gave another faint smile. 'The soldiers might even enjoy the spectacle.'

As a young female dancer appeared beside the two performers, Jack agreed that the soldiers may well enjoy the show. Aware that this may be an elaborate trap, he kept a watch around the crowd, but every gaze was fixed on the dancer. There were no muskets on view, and the few men with dhas were watching the performance.

'The greatest meditation is a mind that lets go.'

He heard Myat's words even through the babble of the crowd and forced himself to watch the dancer. She was as slim as all Burmese women appeared to be, with minuscule breasts and flaring hips under a scarlet longyi. She was pirouetting in time to the wailing of what sounded a bit like bagpipes, leaping in the air and landing to the clashing of drums. Every eye of the men of the 113th focussed on the girl.

Eventually, the music climaxed. The girl's face was white with *thanaka* paste that protected the skin from the sun and stiff with concentration. The 113th was in unison with the Pegu crowd, cheering the dancer's rhythmic movements; they were part of this pwe, as was he. Jack allowed the atmosphere to wash over him. When the girl turned away from the audience and began to rotate her bottom to the pulsating rhythm the men of the 113th cheered loudly. *I wonder if Myat could do that.* The image of her in front of him came to his mind, and he found he was smiling, searching for her in the crowd.

Their eyes met, briefly and he looked away before she did. Then the music altered again, the girl came off to appreciative applause from the 113th, and the crowd surged forward.

A group of men surrounded Jack, nearly carrying him in their enthusiasm to make friends.

'Drink,' a man stumbled over the unfamiliar English word as he thrust a wooden cup of something into Jack's hand. He held it at arm's length until the man retrieved the cup, sipped, smiled and handed it back.

'Thank you,' Jack said. It tasted very sweet. He sipped more. He allowed the man to escort him inside a hut, where undressed teak poles held up a thatched roof, and bamboo covered the floor. Other men pressed closer, talking loudly, offering him fruit and drink, smiling, talking and so obviously wishing to prove their friendship that he relaxed. He sat cross legged on the floor beside the others, replying in English as they spoke in Burmese, but somehow language did not matter. He was among friends. He drank more of the sweet liquid and laughed out loud.

The music of the *pwe* continued to reverberate in Jack's head. He drank more and smiled as his Peguese friend filled his cup up, then saw Myat at the open door talking with an older man and waved to her. She nodded to him and moved closer, with the men moving to give her room. Myat tasted the drink in his cup.

'It's very sweet,' Jack heard the slur of his own words.

'It's made from sugar cane,' Myat told him.

Jack drank more, 'the greatest meditation is a mind that lets go,' he repeated her words.

Myat stood up; Jack watched her as she walked away. He wanted to reach out and pull her back; his mind filled with images he had suppressed for years and others he had never known before.

'Myat...'

She did not answer.

'Myat...'

She was gone. There were only men in the hut, Burmese and two soldiers of the 113th, together with a handful of women in cheap *longyis* and sandals; their black hair hung loose and open mouths displayed teeth stained red with betel juice.

Dear God: what am I doing? I am a British officer consorting here with rankers and women of the lowest morals.

Jack struggled up, spilling the contents of his cup. 'Excuse me,' he said, 'I have to go.' He stumbled out of the hut into the dark of the evening. 'I'm a visitor here,' he said to the first person he met.

Myat nodded. 'I know,' she said. Her eyes smiled at him.

Chapter Eleven

Pegu Province, October 1852

From Pegu they moved northward, deeper into Burma with the landscape growing wilder by the mile. Every day they stopped at a village, with Marshall talking to the headman as Jack and his men acting as escort in a procedure that grew so familiar it became routine.

'Bo Ailgaliutlo has a stockade only three days march from here,' Marshall emerged from the hut with what might pass for a smile on his face. 'We can be there in two by the river.' He looked skyward. 'And then we destroy them, man and boy, and burn the stockade to the ground.'

'Yes, sir,' Jack remembered the artillery and storming parties for the White House Picket and wondered how Marshall intended to capture a stockade held by tenacious Burmese dacoits with ten British infantrymen and the crew of a single John Company vessel.

'Two days to reach them,' Commander Marshall repeated, 'two days to reduce the place, another to hang the prisoners and a week to return to Rangoon. We will be back in fourteen days at the latest.'

Then what? Back to being an outcast officer with no prospects while General Godwin leads the main British Army to glory against the King of Ava.

Jack stared at the gloomy bamboo jungle. *Only the presence of Myat makes this campaign worthwhile.* A monkey gibbered to him from its perch on an upper branch.

The drums started before dawn, so quiet that Jack barely noticed them. They thrummed from the dense jungle of the Pegu Yoma hills that stretched to the north as far as he could see, echoed along the dark banks of the river and invaded everything that he did. By the time the first grey-green beams of light filtered through the trees, they were audible to even the least sensitive of men so that Coleman nudged O'Neill with a whispered enquiry.

'Can you hear that, Paddy? I think it's the Burmese.'

O'Neill swivelled his eyes and turned his head to one side. He cupped a hand to his ear. 'Of course, I can hear it Coley; the whole bloody ship can hear it.'

'Quieten down lads!' Wells said, and the drums invaded again, throbbing through that morning as *Serangipatam* pushed upstream with the 113th on deck, swatting mosquitoes as sweat dampened their clothes and ran into their eyes.

'Keep a sharp look out, boys,' Jack loosened the revolver in his holster and peered into the jungle in the hope of seeing one of the drummers.

'You won't see them,' Myat seemed to read his mind. 'They can see us, but we'll never see them.'

'Who are they? The king's forces?' Jack could almost feel the predatory eyes probing into him as the ship eased upstream.

'Maybe, or perhaps a band of dacoits. It could be anybody.'

'Keep your men alert, Windrush,' Marshall's voice was quiet as ever.

'Yes, sir.'

The river eased into a succession of bends, each one tighter than the last, with Marshall giving precise orders to the helmsman to keep in the centre of the channel.

A seaman pattered past Jack and hauled a marked length of weighted rope into the river, pulled it out and started to chant the depth.

'Quarter speed,' Marshall ordered, and *Serangipatam* slowed further.

'Careful now boys,' Wells cocked his musket, 'this is the sort of place the dacoits might choose.' A monkey screamed from the trees, joined by a score of others.

'Bloody monkeys,' Graham aimed his musket at one and closed his left eye. 'Bang, bang.'

'Load your pieces,' Jack ordered and saw the relief on his men's faces as they poured powder and ball down the barrels of their muskets and added the percussion cap. He began to pace the length of the ship, one hand on his revolver.

The sound of drums increased, echoing through the trees.

'Battle stations,' Marshall ordered, 'handsomely now!'

The sailors ran to their guns and stood alert as the smoke from *Serangipatam*'s funnel lay thick on the deck.

The leadsman continued to chant the depth as if nothing else was happening. 'Four fathoms, muddy bottom.'

The drums continued their beating, louder now as if in competition with the invasive throb of Serangipatam's engine. Jack flinched as a gaudily coloured bird exploded from the trees.

'Three and a half fathoms, muddy bottom.'

'Just around the next bend, men, there is a friendly village.' It was so unusual for Marshall to give out any information that Jack knew that the persistent drumming must be unsettling even him.

There was no village around the next bend or the one after that; only the jungle; thick, tangled and unfriendly. Creepers hung over the river with some dragged by the current. A deer watched them for a second before turning to vanish in the undergrowth. There was something else there as well. At first, Jack was unsure what it was, monkey or human but as he stared, he saw it was a man, or rather a boy, tattooed so heavily he seemed to merge with the jungle.

'I smell smoke, sir,' Thorpe volunteered. 'Not our funnel smoke. Something's burning ahead.

'Thank you, Thorpe,' Jack said. It had a different scent, more acrid, sharper, laced with some odour he recognised but could not place.

'Meat,' Myat said, 'it's like cooked meat. They have made a feast for us.'

'Human flesh,' Wells said quietly. He eased his hands over the stock of his musket. 'I've smelled that before.'

They rounded the next bend, and the village came in sight. It was a typical neat Burmese riverside settlement with a score of thatched huts and half a dozen boats pulled up on the mud, except that every house was ablaze and the boats were holed and sinking. Piled at the water's edge was a mound of corpses, smouldering and sparking within a circle of flames.

'Jesus!' Knight lifted his musket.

'Jesus must have looked the other way,' Wells glanced at Jack. 'Are we going in, sir?'

That depends on the Commander.

'Steer straight on, helmsman,' Marshall spared the village a single glance.

'There could be somebody left alive sir,' Jack suggested. 'We might be able to help them.'

'They can't help us,' Marshall unbent sufficiently to explain.

Smoke from the village merged with that from the ship as they passed.

'There may be a survivor, wounded and injured...'

Marshall did not reply. *Serangipatam* rounded the next bend and the landscape altered with banyan trees amidst swampy fields of rice on one bank and patchy forest on the other.

'These fields will be untended then,' Wells said.

'Why is that, sergeant?' Coleman asked.

'There's nobody left to look after them,' Wells jerked his head in the direction of the village. 'The dacoits have killed them all.' The drumming surrounded them, beating at their ears, rebounding from the hull of the ship.

'Where are they?' Thorpe licked his lips with a dry tongue, 'why don't they attack?'

'They will,' Wells said. 'When they are ready, and they think we are not.'

'We'll anchor in mid channel tonight,' Marshall gave the order. 'Keep sentries posted Windrush. The dacoits may try to attack in the dark.'

'They're everywhere,' Knight said, 'they're all around us.'

'There's something in the river sir,' the sailor at the masthead shouted, 'it's some sort of boat.'

'Stand by!' Marshall shouted. 'Slow ahead; cutlass men forward.'

'Ready men,' Jack echoed. He pulled his revolver from its holster as half a dozen seamen pattered past, each holding a cutlass.

Serangipatam eased on.

'There it is,' Lieutenant Bertram pointed. 'It's a raft, sir, with somebody on it.'

'Boathooks,' Marshall ordered, 'bring him in.'

'Keep alert, men,' Jack ordered. 'This could be a trick.'

The raft was about six foot square with a man lying on top. As the current brought the raft alongside, Jack saw that the man was stark naked, spread-eagled and with his hands and feet fastened to the corners of the raft. A seaman leaned over the bow and hooked the raft in so it bobbed and bounced at the side of *Serangipatam*. The man stared up through sightless eyes.

'He's dead, sir,' the seaman said.

'Let him go,' Marshall ordered.

The seaman released the boathook, and the raft resumed its lonely voyage. The drums continued, mocking the handful of British seamen and soldiers.

Despite the clammy heat, Jack shivered as night raced in. The jungle sounds always seemed louder in the dark, the cry of unseen animals and unknown birds were sinister, as though they came from a soul tortured beyond endurance.

'Double sentries, Sergeant,' he said. 'I don't want the men standing alone tonight.' He knew he did not have to explain his decision.

'They'll be tired tomorrow,' Wells took advantage of his leniency.

'They'll have more chance of being alive tomorrow!' Jack turned abruptly away.

He slumped in the stifling cubicle that was more like a coffin than a cabin. *I am too easy on these men. I should retain a proper distance to maintain my authority. They will take advantage of me. I must be a laughing stock.* The lapse of duty in Pegu still preyed on his mind. *I hope the men did not see me drunk.*

The bed was damp with the sweat of the engineer with whom he shared, and the high pitched whine of insects disturbed his attempts at sleep. Thoughts and images bustled through his mind, from the piled up corpses in the last village to the constant throbbing of the drums.

The shout penetrated the muddle of his mind, so he sat up with a jerk.

'Halt and identify yourself!'

Jack was at the door of the cabin before he realised he had neither sword nor pistol. As he turned back there was the sharp report of a musket, and then another.

'Get back you hound of hell! Back to the jungle damn you!'

By the time Jack got onto the deck, there was nothing to be seen. O'Neill was reloading as Armstrong peered into the vicious dark.

'What happened here?'

'Something in the water,' O'Neill tested the hammer of his musket. 'It might have been dacoits, it might not, but I thought best to let them see we are ready for them.'

Marshall appeared on the quarterdeck. 'Call all hands; Windrush, get your men on deck.' As always he spoke softly but his words carried throughout the ship.

'Lanterns,' Marshall ordered. 'Bertram, attach lanterns on long poles and hang them over the sides.'

The dark seemed to press upon them, dense, humid and alive with the whine of insects. One by one Bertram had lanterns lit and hung from the spars so a halo of light illuminated *Serangipatam;* she was a ghost ship trapped within a circle of predatory night.

'Now they can see us,' Wells stood at attention at the rail of the ship, 'but we can't see a bloody thing.'

'We're attracting every bloody moth and flying brute in Burma,' Coleman muttered.

For a few moments, Jack was unaware of the silence; he merely knew something had changed.

'They've stopped,' O'Neill's voice broke the silence. 'The drums have stopped.' Only the sounds of nature remained, frightening in their variety and intensity as insects and night-prowling creatures competed to make the night hideous.

'What does that mean?' Thorpe asked, 'maybe they've all gone away?'

Lantern light reflected from Myat's hair when she appeared on the quarterdeck. She spoke to Marshall. He nodded and raised his voice a fraction. 'Man the guns.'

'Out there!' Bertram shouted. 'War boats: dozens of them!'

They surged into the circle of light, long, high prowed vessels packed with warriors, each with muscular men paddling the river into white-frothed fury.

Dear God, there are scores of them.

'Aim at that first boat,' Jack ordered. 'Volley fire!' Ten muskets cracked out, 'reload, fast as Christ will let you.' He did not look to see the result but flinched as the gun crew next to him fired. The sound was shocking, the results terrible as a charge of grapeshot crashed directly into the second Burmese war-boat. The carnage was immediate with dead and wounded men flung backwards and head, arms and dismembered torsos flung up in the air. For a second Jack saw a hanging curtain of blood that pattered to the water.

'And that's done for you, you bastards,' O'Neill's voice sounded through the screams and yells of the wounded.

A spear thudded into the deck beside Jack, and a seaman yelled and plucked at the arrow that spouted miraculously from his arm.

'They're in the trees above us,' Jack shouted, 'Wells, you and O'Neill concentrate on the trees, and the rest take the war-boats.'

'Quarter speed ahead,' Marshall ordered. 'Bertram: put a man in the bows with a line.'

Serangipatam rocked as she picked up speed, nosing ahead of the slender war-boats that crowded around. One war-boat tried to close and board, but Marshall altered course and *Serangipatam* rammed her amidships and split her in two. Jack saw pieces of wreckage and shrieking men on either side of the hull, with seamen and soldiers firing at the survivors.

'Keep them at a distance!' Jack said. 'Volley fire is best; six shots to one boat are of more use than single shots to half a dozen. That boat there,' he indicated a vessel that approached rapidly from the bows. 'Give it a volley!'

Jack flinched as a Burmese ball smacked into the rail at his side, and another lifted a splinter of wood from the deck at his feet. Lantern light reflected from the hazy powder smoke that drifted in their wake.

Another two Burmese boats loomed into the circle of light and for a second Jack saw a nightmare vision of wiry, sturdy men in loin cloths and simple turbans paddling vigorously as a score of yelling warriors brandished dhas or fired long muskets at *Serangipatam*.

The man who stood in the bow of the leading boat wore a loin cloth and a much-patched coat that had once been scarlet but had faded to a dirty pink. For an instant, he gazed directly into Jack's eyes, and despite the haze of powder smoke and the flickering lantern light, Jack knew this was Bo Ailgaliutlo. This man was not afraid in the slightest; his eyes were sharp and lively as if he relished the encounter with an Honourable Company vessel and its contingent of British soldiers.

'That boat!' Jack pointed directly at Bo Ailgaliutlo, 'and that man. Give him a volley.'

But the renegade had his own plans. He shouted something and the musket men in his war-boat fired a volley of their own. The muskets, Burmese and British, crashed out together and two of the British lanterns exploded in a thousand splinters of glass.

'He's putting out the lights,' Jack yelled. 'Give him another volley!'

'I can't see him, sir; where is he?' Graham shouted.

Jack swore. The renegade had pulled his boat back into the darkness. 'Listen for the paddles,' he ordered.

All at once there was silence save for the steady surge of the river and the throb of the engines. The musketry had stilled the usual night sounds of the river.

'They've run away,' Coleman shouted. 'We've won!' He began to cheer until Wells snarled him into silence.

'Two fathoms,' the leadsman's voice sounded, as it had probably done throughout the encounter.

'Bertram: replace the broken lanterns; men, keep at the guns.' Marshall's voice sounded.

'They're out there, waiting,' Wells peered into the dark. 'I can smell them.' He raised his voice slightly. 'Make sure you are all loaded and ready, lads. The dacoits aren't finished with us yet.'

'What will their next move be?' Jack asked.

'I don't know sir,' Wells said. 'I've never known dacoits to attack a well-armed boat before. Their typical tactics are to murder sentries or parties of foragers, burn villages and rob travellers. This Bo Ailgaliutlo fellow is different to any other I have encountered before. They say...' He looked away quickly and relapsed into silence.

'They say?' Jack prompted. 'They say what, Wells, and who are they?'

'Nothing sir,' Wells was uncharacteristically hesitant.

'Spit it out, man!' Jack glanced around, 'any information could help, and hurry before they come back.'

'I heard that this Bo Ailgaliutlo was a British soldier sir.' Wells said, 'that's all.'

'We already guessed that,' Jack did not hide his irritation. 'You know something else, Wells; what is it, man?'

'It was just something I overheard in one of the villages, sir. You know that I speak a little Burmese.' Wells looked away. 'Well sir, the Burmese in one of these villages we were in say that Bo Ailgaliutlo was a British officer, not just a private or even a sergeant.'

'Good God!' Jack could not help the exclamation of surprise that burst from him.

An officer? A gentleman? English gentlemen don't do such things. I would be prepared to believe that a ranker might join the enemy but not an officer.

As Jack swung away, the Buddha in his pocket seemed twice as weighty as it had before. *English gentlemen are not supposed to loot and steal either, yet I now know they do.*

'Thank you, Sergeant,' Jack tried to keep any expression from his voice.

'One and a half fathoms,' the leadsman reported.

'Slow ahead,' Marshall ordered, an instant before *Serangipatam* ran onto something in the river.

The shock of the collision knocked most people on to the deck, with loose gear rattling forward and a line aloft parting with a sickening crack.

'We're aground!' Bertram yelled.

'Jesus God in heaven!' Knight blasphemed. 'What happened?'

'It's the Burmese,' Thorpe shouted.

Then the drums began again, a thunderous roar that came from all around, accompanied by loud chanting that raised the hairs on the back of Jack's neck.

Serangipatam's engines raced, driving her further onto whatever she had struck. 'Stop engines; check for damage below,' Marshall's voice cut through the clamour. 'Fire the bow chaser; prepare to repel boarders!' His orders came in a rapid procession. 'Full astern! Mr Bertram, check for damage aloft. Mr Windrush, the dacoits will attack now, have your men ready.'

The thunder of the drums rose to a crescendo and then stopped as a fusillade of musketry smashed against the hull and upper works of *Serangipatam*. One seaman staggered, cursed and grabbed hold of his shoulder. Bright blood seeped between his fingers. Easterhouse, the quietest of Jack's men, slumped to the deck, staring at the blood that pumped from his thigh.

'Volley fire,' Jack stepped to the rail. He knew he was presenting himself as a target for every Burmese marksman, but he also knew he had to make an example to his men.

'What's the target, sir?' Wells asked. 'We can't see a blessed thing.'

'Aim for the muzzle flashes,' Jack said.

'They're not firing,' Coleman pointed out.

'I'll make them fire.' Jack felt the increased pounding of his heart as he spread himself out against the rail. 'Come on Bo Ailgaliutlo; here I am you traitor, you black hearted scoundrel! I am Ensign Jack Windrush of the 113th: come and shoot me!'

As he had hoped and feared the Burmese responded with a fusillade of musketry, but shooting from moving boats at a shifting target on a river at night was not easy even for trained soldiers. For native warriors with poor quality muskets, it was nearly impossible. The musket balls spattered all around Jack, but not a single one came within a foot of him, while the muzzle flashes betrayed the Burmese positions. Jack cursed when a ball smashed the lantern at the starboard bow.

'Fire lads!' Wells gave the order, and the 113th fired a volley. The muzzle flashes ripped apart the black of the night.

'Slow astern,' Marshall ignored the battle that raged around as he concentrated on saving his ship. 'How is she forward?'

'We're holed sir!' Bertram replied at once. 'We ran onto a pointed stake; the Burmese have staked the river here.'

They feigned the attack with war boats to force us to move faster, so we did not see the stakes. Bo Ailgaliutlo is a subtle and dangerous man.

'Half astern; fire both broadsides.' Marshall gave the order. 'Blast them with everything we have.' He raised his voice. 'Mr Windrush, keep your men firing if you will.'

The roar of *Serangipatam*'s weaponry interrupted Jack's reply. Each flare from the cannon muzzles revealed a vignette of the battle. Jack saw images of men of the 113th loading and firing, open mouths and moving hands, red jackets and concentrating faces. He saw seamen holding cannon balls or ramrods, clouds of white powder-smoke set against the black backdrop of night, spars and masts of *Serangipatam* ripped by Burmese musketry. And then, out of nowhere, a sea of tawny faces as a boatload of dacoits swarmed up the sides of the ship.

'Cutlasses lads!' A lithe young lieutenant shouted as the vignettes merged into a tableau of violence and courage.

'With me the 113th!' There was the shriek of steel as Jack drew his sword and dashed forward. 'Just use the bayonet lads! Don't shoot the bluejackets.'

The Burmese on board surged toward the quarterdeck, slashing with their dhas in a silent frenzy as the 113th met them with bayonet, boot and musket butt. The naval officers gave sharp orders that drew the seamen together in a compact line; they drew their cutlasses and moved slowly forward, stamping, slashing, parrying and thrusting in a show of disciplined skill that Jack would have admired had he the time to watch.

O'Neill lunged toward the groin of the first dacoit and when the man dropped his guard to defend himself, lifted the point of his bayonet and spitted him under the chin. 'And that's done for you!' he roared.

Jack thrust at a fierce-eyed man in a large turban, missed and flinched as a dha hissed perilously close to his ear, recovered his aim and slashed instead, swore as the Burman parried, recovered and thrust at the man's stomach and saw him fall under the flailing butt of a British musket.

'On me the 113th!'

Then *Serangipatam* was moving faster, surging astern up the river and leaving the war-boats in her wake. Realising there was no hope of reinforcement from their fellows, the dacoits on board turned to flee, with redcoats and bluejackets cutting them down as they mounted the rail and jumped into the water.

'Eradicate them, lads!' Lieutenant Hook must have been in his bunk for he was stark naked except for a belt as he swung at the dacoits with a cutlass, shouting encouragement to his seamen. 'Send them to Nirvana!'

Within a few moments, the deck was clear of dacoits and the British stood in a panting, sweating group watching the few survivors swim out of the broken circle of light and vanish into the gloom. The silence was sudden and dense.

'Roll call,' Jack shouted. 'Anybody hurt?' He saw Easterhouse crumpled on deck with blood around his thigh and his throat sliced open. *Another of my men gone.*

Myat appeared amongst them, passing the seamen without a glance. She looked at Wells, her eyebrows raised. Only when he nodded did she approach Jack. 'Are your men unhurt, Ensign Windrush?'

Jack counted the 113th, 'one dead, all the others present and upright.'

Myat looked around; her eyes flicked up and down the length of Hook's naked body and moved away.

I wonder what that woman is thinking.

'Get this rubbish off my deck, Lieutenant Bertram. I want all these bodies removed and the decks scrubbed of all blood.' Marshall's voice cut from the quarter-deck.

'How about the wounded, sir? Shall we...'

'Throw them overboard,' Marshall did not allow Bertram to finish his sentence. 'Lieutenant Hook: we are leaking forward where that stake penetrated: fix it. Lieutenant Sinclair, check for damage aloft. I heard something fall when we hit. Get it sorted. Lieutenant Buchanan, see to our casualties.' Marshall was fully dressed including a blue jacket tightly buttoned to the neck and his uniform cap square on his head. 'Stop engines. Ensign Windrush, position your men to guard the ship; I want no more dacoits on board.'

With her engines stopped and anchors out, *Serangipatam* sat in the centre of the river, silent, licking her wounds as Bertram restored her circle of light. There was no sentiment as the seamen tossed the dacoits overboard, dealing with the wounded as casually as the dead and ignoring any pleas they may have made for mercy.

'If they caught any of us,' Wells said, 'they would torture us to death. We are kinder than they are; remember what happened to Smithy or that lad on the raft.'

Jack thought of the portraits on the wall in Wychwood Manor; generations of Windrushes looking noble in front of various battlefields. There was no romance in war on this frontier.

Dawn brought the usual mist that hung low on the river and concealed the banks, so visibility was little better than at night. Jack positioned his men all around the ship and paced the deck in a non-stop circle as the morning sounds of birds increased, and the insects hummed and buzzed around his ears.

'They'll be watching everything we do,' Wells thumbed the lock of his musket. He glanced toward the quarter-deck where Myat stood beside Marshall. 'I'll be happier once we are on the move again.'

'At least we know we are on the right path,' Jack said. 'Bo Ailgaliutlo must be out of temper with us to risk a full- scale attack.'

'It's unusual, sir' Wells agreed. 'I've never known a dacoit to attack a warship before, especially one with a military escort. I think this fellow is Burmese army rather than just a bandit.'

'Slow ahead,' Marshall ordered. 'Take us to where we hit the stakes.' He stalked to the bow. 'Mr Hook, have you plugged that leak yet? Mr Sinclair, is all sorted aloft? Mr Buchanan, get the men to breakfast if you please.' He passed Jack without a word and peered into the mist. 'This muck will be clear within twenty minutes; I want to be on the move by then. Mr Bertram, when we reach the stakes, man the launch and check ahead; remove any obstacles you find. Windrush, you take the jolly boat and escort him.'

Chapter Twelve

The jungle felt closer and even more menacing from a small boat in the open river. Jack fingered his revolver as Bertram slowly rowed forward, testing underneath the water with a long pole to search for stakes or other obstructions.

'Here we are,' Bertram reported at once. 'They've staked the deep water channel.'

'Mark the stakes with a flag,' Marshall shouted from the bow of *Serangipatam*. 'And secure a line around them.'

Rough-hewn and pointed, the stakes protruded from the water in an irregular line, securely hammered into the bed of the river and lethal. Bertram stripped off and jumped in the river to tie a line around each. 'There are more stakes underwater,' he reported.

Insects soon found the men in the boat, buzzing and biting despite any attempts to swat them.

Hurry it along.

Jack watched Bertram slide under water with a slender line. He looked around; the jungle crowded on them, overhanging trees seeming to invite agile dacoits to ambush them.

'There are no drums,' Wells scanned the riverbanks. 'Why are they not taking advantage of us when we are static?'

'Maybe we killed so many of them yesterday they have to regroup,' Jack hoped.

Bertram surfaced with a surge of water and hauled himself on the boat. 'That's one' he handed the line to one of the seamen. 'Secure this to a stronger cable, Hughson.' He winked at Jack. 'Three more and we'll have a gap wide enough for old *Seringy* to pass through.'

Taking another length of the thin line, he poised on the edge of the boat and dived in again. Green water surged and subsided. Jack watched his pale body under the surface for a moment and returned his attention to the river banks.

'That's two,' Bertram was gasping when he emerged. He rested his arms on the side of the boat before pulling himself in. 'Two more to go.'

'How's progress Lieutenant Bertram?' Marshall called.

'Half way, sir,' Bertram replied. He jumped back in the water just as the first arrow thrummed into the wooden plank at Jack's side.

'Where did that come from?' Jack eyed the imaginary shelter of the boat's low freeboard. He knew he could not duck in front of the men.

'The left bank, sir,' Wells scanned the jungle. 'I can't see anyone.'

Jack flinched as a blue-rumped parrot screeched above him. 'Keep alert,' he knew the order was superfluous.

'Yes, sir.'

The third arrow thumped into the prow of the boat an inch from a sailor.

'There's only one archer I think,' Wells was as calm as if he was sitting in an English pub.

'That's three done.' Bertram was gasping. He leaned on the gunwale for support. 'All right up here?'

'All under control,' Jack told him. 'You get your breath back before you go back below.'

'There he is!' Armstrong aimed and fired in the same instant, with the sound of the musket sending a hundred birds screaming from the trees.

'What...?' Bertram looked his astonishment.

'It's nothing for you to worry about, sir. You get a line on that last stake.' Jack ducked at the whistle of another arrow. 'Will somebody get that blasted archer?'

This time the 113th was ready, and four muskets blasted in unison.

'There he is,' Jack saw a flicker of movement in the trees, and shouted: 'don't shoot! It's only a boy!'

'He's a dead boy!' Armstrong would have fired had Jack not grabbed the barrel of his musket.

'I said hold your fire! We're not here to shoot children!' For a second the two men glared at each other, and then Armstrong dropped his eyes.

'Sorry, sir.'

Jack released the musket and pushed Armstrong away. 'Try and get that line done quickly, Bertram, could you?'

Bertram submerged with a swirl. The 113th scanned the jungle.

'Wells: shout out that we are friends. If he does not fire, neither will we.' Jack took a deep breath and stood upright. 'You men keep down.'

'I don't know how to say that, sir,' Wells said, 'but I'll do my best.' He stood beside Jack and shouted: '*twé-yá-da wùn-tha-ba-deh*,' and then lowered his voice. 'I think that means good to meet you, sir.'

'Now get down, Sergeant.' Jack remained standing until Bertram surfaced.

'Get back on board,' Marshall ordered, 'and get some clothes on Bertram. You're a naval officer.'

Bertram scrambled hastily into his uniform as sailors passed the line from the stakes to *Serangipatam*. 'Get us back to the ship, lads.'

'Half astern,' Marshall ordered as soon as they stepped aboard.

Serangipatam steamed astern with a great rush of water breaking creamy brown along the river bank. Jack joined the men in the bow as the cable tautened then began to vibrate.

'Nothing's happening, sir,' Sinclair reported.

The river at *Serangipatam*'s counter churned into a creamy froth as her engines strained and then all four stakes leapt out of the water and floated, double pointed and barbed half way down the length.

'Halt engines,' Marshall ordered quietly. 'Quarter speed ahead; Bertram, put a leadsman in the bows.'

'That's one more advantage of a screw steamer over sail,' Bertram was grinning. 'If we were only sail powered we would have had much more difficulty with these stakes.' He gestured toward the banks of the river. 'These Burmese won't understand how we can go back and forward at will without using oars or the wind or even the river current. It will be like magic to them.'

Jack looked to the dense foliage that crowded each bank of the river. 'Even so,' he said, 'it was a well- worked ambush, and they pressed forward well. Bo Ailgaliutlo knows his business.'

Bertram winked. 'Aye he does,' he said, 'but so does Commander Marshall. The dacoit chief has met his match this time. The commander will hunt him down and drag him back to Moulmein in chains, or hang him from a convenient tree.'

A few weeks ago Jack would have been surprised to hear such bloodthirsty sentiments from a fresh faced youth like Bertram, but the reality of war on the frontier had hardened him. Death and disease and the slaughter of innocents had stripped away childish illusions.

'Best thing for renegades and dacoits,' Jack agreed. He fingered the golden Buddhas in the pockets of his shell jacket. It was as well Bo Ailgaliutlo did not organise an ambush where that young archer had been.

Marshall had not shifted from the poop. 'Sinclair, put a scout boat a cable's length in front to watch for stakes and other obstacles.' He pushed his cap square on his head. 'Keep your men alert, Windrush.'

'Yes, sir.' Jack saw the figure standing static on the branch. At first, he thought it was part of the tree, and then he focussed. It was a youth, perhaps fourteen years old and so covered in tattoos that it was hard to see where the boy ended and the tree began. As soon as Jack saw him, the boy backed off a pace and sped up a creeper so fast that Jack found it hard to follow him.

'Was that a monkey, sir?' Thorpe had seen the movement.

'Something like that,' Jack said. He had seen that tattooed boy before: Bo Ailgaliutlo had sent a spy and knew exactly what they were doing.

Progress slowed to a crawl as they inched up the river, with the oarsmen replaced every two hours and the soldiers every four. There were no more attacks that day, no sound of drums, nothing except the constant swish of the river, the natural sounds of birds and the ever-present hum of insects.

'They've all gone,' Thorpe shifted on the wooden thwart of the boat. 'There's nobody left in the world.'

'Just us,' Wells waited for a few moments before he added: 'and ten thousand dacoits.'

'Are there that many?' Thorpe's eyes widened.

'There are at least that many,' Wells kept his voice low, 'and all looking for you. So be vigilant Thorpey, keep your piece loaded and watch the banks like a hungry hawk!'

'Did you hear the sergeant?' Thorpe repeated in a whisper, 'he says there are thousands of them dacoits watching us all the time.'

'There's one there,' Coleman pointed to an overhanging banyan tree, 'I see him!'

'So do I!' Thorpe pointed his musket, but before he had time to press the trigger, Jack pushed the barrel up.

'Easy Thorpe, don't let your imagination take over.' He glowered at Coleman, 'and you keep your mouth under control, Coleman.'

This expedition is insanity. Bo Ailgaliutlo has hundreds of dacoits while we are only a handful; he knows exactly where we are and what we are doing. His men are masters of the forest, and although we can always beat them in a straight fight, the dacoits are expert in ambuscade and devils for trickery. All we are doing is providing food for the insects and weakening our army.

'Anchor in mid-stream,' Marshall ordered an hour before dusk, 'and rig boarding nets.'

Jack watched as the seamen hoisted nets of rough rope to the yard arms and fastened them to the rail all around the ship. 'Keep it slack,'

Marshall gave brief instructions. 'It's harder to cut through slack rope than taut, and more difficult to climb up.'

'Do you think they are still there?' Lieutenant Sinclair asked.

'They're there,' Marshall said. 'They are watching us right now.'

Jack fought the shiver that ran down his spine. He imagined those wiry, fierce warriors hiding behind the screen of jungle with their long muskets and sharp dhas. 'Half the men on watch at all times, Sergeant Wells,' he said.

'There's one!' Thorpe pointed into the dark. 'I see one!' he pointed his musket and fired, the shot echoing around them.

'I can see one too!' Armstrong fired, 'they're coming again!'

'Cease fire!' Jack yelled. He grabbed Coleman's musket before he also wasted a musket ball. 'There's nothing there but shadows!'

'If you can't keep your men under control, Wingate, I'll have them all disarmed and confined in irons.' Marshall's chilling voice came from the quarterdeck.

'Yes, sir,' Jack acknowledged.

'Right you men!' Jack heard the anger in his voice. 'I don't want anybody to fire without permission from Sergeant Wells or me; do you understand? If anybody fires without orders I'll give them fifty at the triangle.' He took a deep breath, 'in fact; I don't want anybody doing anything without orders. I only want you to watch for the dacoits. Is that clear?'

'Yes, sir,' Coleman and Thorpe said at once.

Jack handed back Coleman's musket. 'All right; reload and keep your positions. Shout out if you see the dacoits but otherwise say nothing and don't shoot!'

Jack took a deep breath and turned away. *They can't help it. They can only work within the limitations of their capabilities.*

'Rig lanterns again, Lieutenant Bertram,' Marshall ordered, 'but darken the side that faces the ship so the light is all projected outwards and *Serangipatam* is in darkness. In other words, we can see them, but they can't see us. Have ten men ready with cutlasses and muskets, and the duty watch to be armed as well. Guns loaded with case shot and ready to fire.'

Despite their precarious position, Jack always found the sunset possessed a calming beauty. He stood beside the mainmast, watching the sun blaze orange-gold behind the tangled trees of the jungle, with the reflection flickering along the ripples of the river. There was a rare peace at moments such as this, between the heat of the day and the unknown sounds of the night.

He looked astern, where Myat sat on the stern rail, with her profile silhouetted against the dying sun as she talked to Sergeant Wells. Short nosed and with a determined chin, she was small-breasted and serene.

God, she's beautiful.

The thought came unbidden to Jack's mind, and he abruptly looked away. He was not here to indulge in any fruitless amorous adventures with the indigenous people, or with any bloody woman. He was here to enhance the reputation of the 113th, and push forward his career. The reminder caused him to put his hand in his pocket and caress the smooth gold of a Buddha.

This statuette is the first step to where I belong. This statuette is my future, not some Burmese woman.

Myat laughed, the sound as musical as temple bells on a sultry dawn. Jack looked up as Wells also laughed. He felt the surge of unreasoning anger and opened his mouth to shout, then closed it again quickly.

I'm jealous! I am jealous of a sergeant because he is talking to a native woman.

He turned away to face the darkness of the east.

'Have you thought yet, Ensign Windrush?' Myat's voice was serene as she stood beside him. The orchid was fresh and white against the dark of her hair.

'Thought about what, Myat?' He used her name deliberately although the syllables were awkward on his tongue.

'Have you thought about returning the stolen statues to their proper home?' Myat was blunt without being offensive.

'They remain with me.'

'You are a Christian,' Myat gave a graceful little nod, 'and I respect your belief, but sometimes, Ensign Windrush, it is wise to heed our religion and philosophy.'

Was that a threat?

'Thank you for your advice, Myat,' Jack bowed in return. 'However, I am sure that I will survive without the good opinion of Mr Buddha.'

Myat's expression did not alter. 'As you wish, Ensign Windrush; please remember that the greatest action is not in gaining position but in not conforming to the ways of the world. When you choose to alter your mind, please tell me.'

Jack noticed her small head shake as she passed Wells.

So that's it. Myat and Wells are in this together; he wants her to get my Buddhas.

'Sergeant Wells!' Jack spoke louder than he intended. 'Take the first watch, please. Wake me at midnight.'

The sound was slight but out of place. Jack realised he had been listening to it for some time before his conscious mind took note. He checked his watch; two in the morning, about four hours until dawn. He had been on watch for two hours.

Is it my nerves? Am I imagining things? Is my mind playing tricks on me?

The sound continued; it was like somebody was slapping the hull with his hand, a hollow, irregular beat.

'Can you hear that, Hook?' Jack only whispered.

Hook was Officer of the Watch. He listened, shook his head, removed his hat and listened again. 'I can hear something,' he said, 'I think.'

The sound continued as Jack walked the deck. 'Can you hear that Thorpe?'

'Yes, sir,' Thorpe slammed to attention.

'Do you know what it is?'

'No, sir,' Thorpe said.

'Why did you not report it, Thorpe? It's your duty to report anything unusual.' Jack fought down his exasperation.

'We was told not to fire or do anything without orders, sir.' Thorpe tried to look stoical, as befitted a British soldier.

Jack sighed. 'So you were, Thorpe. In future, if you see or hear anything that you don't think is right, report it at once to Sergeant Wells or myself.'

Can I trust Wells with that responsibility? I have no choice, damn it.

That tiny sound continued to irritate Jack. It acted as a backdrop to the natural sounds of the night as he toured the ship, trying to trace it to its source.

'Sir,' the seaman was short and wiry with eyes that shone intelligent above a nutmeg-brown face. 'I believe you're looking for a noise, sir.'

'That's right,' Jack nodded.

'It's over here, sir.' The man nearly grabbed hold of Jack's sleeve in his eagerness to help.

Jack knelt at the rail. A section of the boarding net was open, and one of the loose ends trailed over the side, tapping against the hull with every roll of the ship. 'Is this meant to be like this ... what's your name?'

'Anderson sir,' the seaman shook his head. 'No, sir. The net should be intact.' He stooped closer, 'I reckon some bugger - beg pardon, sir, - somebody has cut this, and that recently.'

Jack examined the ends. The rope was not frayed in any way but sliced neatly. He traced the squares of the net. There were five distinct cuts. 'A small man could get in here,' he said. The more he looked, the more he saw. The deck was wet in places just within the gap in the boarding net, with what might be the drying semblance of a human foot. 'Somebody has come on board here,' he said.

'One of these Burmese fellows,' Anderson agreed at once. 'There's wet footprints over here too, sir, leading to number two hatch.'

'Inform Lieutenant Hook,' Jack decided. Number two hatch led to the engine room via a short ladder and a dark passageway. Jack pulled out his revolver and cautiously negotiated the ladder. He had no desire to meet a party of dacoits in the dark. With these viciously sharp dhas, they were dangerous enough when he could see them.

Scratching a Lucifer, Jack applied the tiny flame to a lantern and eased himself into the passageway. The light pooled ahead, yellow against the dark woodwork. He held it low, seeing the damp stains on the deck and the splash of something that was not water. Placing the lantern on the deck, Jack looked closer. The liquid was dark and sticky, while the direction of the splash indicated that somebody coming away from the engine room had dropped it.

It's blood. There are three, no four, splashes of blood on the deck. Something bad has happened here.

There was another small hatch with a second ladder descending to the engine room which, together with the coal bunker, took up over half the space on the lowest deck. Jack held the lantern over the open hatch and peered down. There should be one of the two engineers on watch in the stifling heat, together with one of the four firemen, the seaborne labourers who stoked the boilers and did all the essential labouring tasks in the furnace heat below decks.

'Halloa,' Jack called softly.

There was no reply.

He shifted his lantern, so the light played on the shiny, still engine below.

'Halloa!' He raised his voice slightly.

Still no reply.

Holding the lantern in his left hand and the revolver in his right, Jack climbed down the ladder, jumped the final three steps and looked around the engine room.

Oh dear God in heaven.

Blood shimmered across the deck with every movement of the ship. The engineer lay on his back, his white shirt and dirty white trousers all terribly stained with blood. Somebody had cut his throat so deeply that his head appeared to be nearly separated from his body. A fireman lay next to him, bare chested and with his fists closed into tight balls; his throat had also been expertly cut.

'Windrush?' The light from Marshall's lantern merged with his own. 'Move aside.' He knelt beside the engineer. 'Dead,' he said, 'and the second Engineer has also been murdered in his bunk. Did your men hear nothing?'

'Not a thing,' Jack reported. 'The dacoits must have come aboard during the night, sliced through the net and moved straight to the engine room and the engineer's quarters.'

'They knew exactly where to come and who to murder,' Marshall said. 'They killed the most vital men on board, for without engineers we are entirely dependent on the wind and current.' For the first time since Jack had met him, Marshall looked worried. 'Bo Ailgaliutlo has hit hard this time.' He nodded. 'He must have had help. No Burmese dacoit would know his way around a steam screw ship.' His voice was low and cutting. 'Your soldiers should have kept a proper watch; that will be in my report, Mr Windrush; you can depend on it.'

Without another word, Marshall raced to the spar deck. 'Myat! Come here!'

It was still an hour shy of dawn, with the river black beyond the circle of lantern light and the ship stunned by news of the murders.

'They must have had help,' the words whispered from man to man. 'It was that woman; never trust a Burmese.'

Was it Myat? Would she help Bo Ailgaliutlo?

'Myat is not Burmese,' Wells said quietly. 'She is from Pegu. She would never betray us.'

'You seem to know a lot about the translator, Wells.' The jealousy returned, twisting knife-like inside Jack as he imagined Wells and Myat together, writhing naked on the bamboo mats in that hut in Pegu.

Before Wells could reply, Myat appeared on deck, walking as serene as always with her lacquered sandals making no sound on the teak planking.

'There she is, the murdering bitch!' One of the remaining firemen pointed an accusing finger. 'We should string her up!'

'None of that!' Jack shouted.

'Ensign Windrush!' Marshall did not raise his voice. 'I will take care of discipline on my ship. Your concern is the laxity of your guards that allowed dacoits to murder my crew.' He took hold of Myat's arm, 'you, madam, stand there.'

A petty officer moved closer as Marshall addressed Myat.

'Do you know anything about the murder of three of my crew?' Marshall was as direct as ever.

Myat bowed her head before the Commander. 'I knew nothing until one of your men told me,' she said quietly.

'There is no fear in her,' O'Neill said. 'She is not afraid at all.'

'That's because she's bloody innocent,' Wells' voice was hard.

Jack remembered his doubts about Myat and Wells only the previous day. Wells shifted restlessly on deck. His eyes fixed on the quarter-deck where Marshall conducted his very public interrogation.

'The dacoits boarded us last night and murdered my engineers and one of my firemen,' Marshall recounted the facts. 'They could only have known where to go if somebody had told them, and only you speak Burmese and know the layout of the ship.'

'I have had no dealings with Bo Ailgaliutlo or any of his men,' Myat said softly. 'He is the enemy of my people.'

'Told you,' Wells said softly.

'I am inclined to hang you out of hand,' Marshall mused, 'and leave your body to dangle above the river as a warning to others.' He glared at Myat, 'or I could have the ship's corporal beat the truth out of you!'

Wells stiffened. His hand strayed to the hilt of his bayonet.

Should I interfere? Should I speak up for Myat? Why? I don't entirely trust her myself, and she is the only person on board who can communicate with the dacoits: but I have seen Wells speak a few words of Burmese as well.

Despite himself, Jack put a single finger on Well's tense arm. 'Easy, Sergeant.'

'I'll do for him, sir; I'll fucking do for him.'

'Enough, Sergeant.' *He has fallen under Myat's spell as much as I have.*

'Instead, I will confine you in irons under armed guard, pending interrogation when we return to Rangoon.' Marshall spoke more loudly than usual, 'and if you attempt to escape, the guard will shoot you dead.'

Jack saw Wells relax slightly; his hand slid away from the hilt of the bayonet.

Myat did not protest as two burly seamen hustled her below; she exchanged one glance with Wells, and then the burly ship's corporal shoved her ungently below deck.

'Assemble all hands at dawn,' Marshall ordered and left the quarterdeck.

Jack fingered the Buddhas inside his pocket. 'What was that all about Sergeant?'

'I don't like to see women treated like that sir.'

Especially that particular woman, eh Sergeant?

'I understand, Sergeant, but if you had pulled that bayonet, the commander would have hanged you for mutiny.'

'Yes, sir.' Wells' face was unreadable.

Jack touched his Buddhas. *All I have to do is survive this campaign and get back to England.* He pictured the house on the western slopes of the Malvern Hills, facing the sweet fields of Herefordshire. He would have servants and lands, a carriage or two and an elegant wife. *Survive and leave.*

'Men!' Commander Marshall had donned full dress uniform including a gold hilted sword and an immaculate coat. He looked down at his assembled crew, and for only the second time since Jack had known him, he smiled. 'We have pursued this renegade Bo Ailgaliutlo from Rangoon to this God-forsaken spot; we have seen the outrages of which he is capable, we have defeated his ambush, and we know exactly where his den is.'

Marshall swept his hand toward the jungle behind him in a gesture so melodramatic it could grace a London stage or a Pegu *pwe.*

'He is there! In there from his stinking fastness he has sent his assassins and has murdered three of our shipmates on board this very vessel!' Marshall took off his cap and shook his head. 'My men and your friends, butchered without mercy.' He waited until the crew had

hooted their anger. 'Well my lads, it is time for retribution. We are going after this fox, this wolf, this evil renegade, this blood-dyed traitor.
We are going to land on that shore,' Marshall pointed to the river bank,
'and we are going to singe his beard, we are going to hunt the lion from
his den, we are going to bell this traitorous cat!'

*That is too flowery. That speech will not inspire British seamen and
soldiers.*

Jack shook his head as the bluejackets broke into mighty cheers
that echoed from the jungle on either side and silenced the sounds
of birds. He watched his men; Coleman and Armstrong cheered with
the seamen while the veteran O'Neill looked thoughtful. Only Wells
was silent. The sergeant touched a hand to his bayonet and threw the
commander a look that should have killed him stone dead.

Chapter Thirteen

Pegu Province: October 1852

Commander Marshall reverted to more mundane but practical dress as he organised the expedition to Bo Ailgaliutlo's stockade. He left only a skeleton crew of six men on board, while the remainder and all of Jack's men were to take part in the assault.

'We might need Myat as a translator, sir,' Jack did not like the idea of Myat lying in irons on board *Serangipatam* for an unknown length of time.

'There is nothing to translate, ensign,' Marshall told him. 'We are well past the speaking stage.' Marshall's tone warned Jack not to continue.

'Bo Ailgaliutlo may wish to negotiate a surrender,' Jack ventured.

'There will be no negotiation. Bo what's-his-name threw that card in the fire when he murdered my men.' Marshall fixed Jack with a poisonous glare. 'You'd do well to attend to your own business, Ensign, and leave the important decisions to your superiors.' He turned on his heel and marched away, erect and unapproachable.

Jack nodded after his retreating form. 'Yes, sir,' he said and returned to his small command.

'Take plenty water,' he reminded Wells, who nodded.

'We will, sir.'

'How much ammunition do we have left?' Jack asked.

'Ninety- two rounds per man, sir.' Trust Wells to know exactly. 'We have one man sick and all the rest fit and able to fight.' He stood at attention.

'Who's sick?' Jack asked, 'I wager it's Thorpe.'

'Not this time sir; it's Knight. He's down with fever.' Wells unbent a little. 'It's genuine sir. We've been lucky so far; the last time I campaigned in these parts we lost about seven- tenths of the men through disease and most of the rest were sick at one time or other.'

'Very well, leave him behind.' Jack decided. 'Give him twenty rounds of ammunition and distribute the rest among the men.'

Marshall had his bluejackets well trained. They used winches and pulleys to hoist both the ship's six pounders into the long boat and rowed ashore, where Jack's 113th provided a guard for a bridgehead that expanded hourly. It only took six hours to land the expedition; forty men from *Serangipatam*, seven of the 113th and the officers, with Hook left reluctantly behind with orders to guard against Burmese attack.

'I will come too, sahib.' Jack had almost forgotten about the efficient Ranveer, but now he touched the hilt of the *tulwar* he always wore. 'One sword may make all the difference.'

'You were a warrior were you not?' Jack asked.

'I was a soldier of the *Khalsa*,' Ranveer confirmed.

Can I trust him? It is only a few years since we fought two very sanguine wars against the Sikhs. What if he harbours resentment against us? What if he was the traitor and not Myat?

'Guard my back,' Jack decided to take the chance. 'This could be a bloody affair.'

Ranveer's grin reached his eyes.

At the riverbank all was hustle with some seamen fitting drag-ropes to the guns, others checking knots or piling up stores and a working party headed by the ship's corporal hacking out the beginning of a road into the jungle.

'Do we know how far this stockade is, sir?' Jack approached Marshall.

'Of course, I know.' Marshall was not pleased with the question. 'My informant at the last village was very specific about the location.'

'May I ask how far, sir?' Jack glanced back at *Serangipatam*. She floated twenty yards off the bank, festooned with boarding nets, her funnel stark and useless with no engineer to work the engines. Bo Ailgaliutlo had deprived them of their chief advantage in one night; he might well have other surprises ready.

'Less than a mile,' Marshall unbent a little. 'We should reach it this evening, take it tomorrow and be back on board the next day.'

Jack phrased his next question carefully. 'Do you wish me to scout ahead, sir?'

'Devil take your impudence!' Marshall shook his head. 'I said I knew where the stockade is, Ensign. I want you to ensure your men fight when ordered.'

'Yes, sir.' Jack stiffened to attention. 'They will fight, sir.'

'Best not ask the Commander too many questions,' Bertram advised quietly. 'He likes to keep things close to his chest.'

'So I see.' Jack said. He indicated the bustle on the riverbank 'but why is Bo Ailgaliutlo allowing us to land in peace? He could have harassing parties out shooting at our sentries and disrupting our movements. If I were him, I would make our life very difficult.'

Bertram shrugged. 'These Oriental fellows think differently from us. Maybe it's Ramadan or some other festival. Maybe they think their stockade is too strong. Maybe they just cannot be bothered.' He shook his head. 'Whatever the reason, it's better for us and so much the worse for them.'

It was early afternoon before the expedition set off from the riverbank. A dozen seamen in white shirts and trousers led the way, protected from the sun by straw hats and from the dacoits by four soldiers of the 113th. They hacked out a path for the two six-pounders with cutlasses and cursing effort. The cannon were next, hauled by sheer muscle power along the very rough track with two more soldiers as an escort. The remainder of the seamen followed with Marshall at their head and Armstrong as rearguard. Jack remembered the artillery needed to reduce the White House Picket and thought it a small enough force to try and reduce a Burmese stockade in the middle of the forest.

'Haul away lads!' Bertram ordered. He lent his wiry strength weight to the ropes. 'Keep these guns moving!'

The presence of so much sweating humanity attracted insects, so the British moved at the centre of a host of biting, stinging creatures that no amount of swatting and arm waving discouraged.

'Bloody mosquitoes,' Coleman swore in frustration.

'They like you,' O'Neill told him. 'The more that bite you, the less that come to me!'

Progress was slow, with the cutlass men having to be replaced every half hour as they toiled in the heat and Jack moving around his men in a constant circle.

'Is everything all right sergeant?' Jack slapped at a mosquito that probed at his neck. The jungle was dense here with bushes wrestling each other for the filtered light, creepers choking the trunks of trees and undergrowth hiding God-only-knew-what horrors.

Wells was in advance of the others, peering forward. 'Everything is in order, sir,' he reported. 'This jungle lasts for another hundred yards or so and then there is a bit of a maidan.'

'Any sign of the Burmese?'

'Nary a trace sir. They are as quiet as the grave.' Wells wiped the sweat from his forehead. 'Shall I scout past the maidan, sir?'

'Commander Marshall does not wish that, Sergeant.' Jack said, 'so we just press on.'

Wells nodded. 'Very good sir.' Only an experienced sergeant could say one thing while a slight inflexion of tone indicated the exact opposite.

The Burmese appeared to have vanished as the British hacked at trees and vegetation that all shed their quota of insect life onto cursing seamen and hauled guns that were reluctant to move on the yielding ground. Life was a nightmare of gasping, muscle-wrenching effort, biting insects and cursing men.

Jack only saw the stealthy movement because he was looking exactly in the right place. He started at the gleam of dark eyes; the boy looked at him briefly and vanished among the vegetation, hidden by his tattoos.

'Keep watch, men,' Jack said. 'The dacoits are watching us.' He loosened his revolver in its holster.

'I wager they have all fled,' O'Neill pushed aside a tree bough and cursed as a giant spider scurried over his boots. 'They must hear us coming, and they've run.'

'Nah,' Coleman stamped at the spider, missed and nearly overbalanced. 'They're waiting for us in their nice fort, all comfortable and safe while we wear ourselves out here.'

That tattooed boy is one of Bo Ailgaliutlo's followers. Why don't they attack while we are vulnerable?

'Sir!' Wells' salute was not as precise as normal. 'We've reached the maidan, sir.'

The sun was in the west, the colour of burnished brass as it scorched the earth below. Swathed in tall yellow grass, the maidan stretched on either side of the toiling British, as far as the jungle covered Pegu Yoma range to the south and another forest belt on the east. In front, it reached for perhaps a mile, when it ended at a small knoll backed by dark green bamboo.

The knoll stood alone, bare of trees in its lower slopes and crowned with a stockade, topped with a huge flag.

'There we are then.' Wells' voice was quiet. 'Now we can see them, and they can see us.'

That's the lair of Bo Ailgaliutlo. If we can destroy this place, then I can rejoin the main force.

'It's a relief to get out of that blessed jungle.' Bertram wiped sweat from his face. 'And in the open, we have all the advantages.' He grinned, 'the dacoits should have attacked us back there; they have missed their chance.'

Jack thought of that tattooed boy. 'They know we are here,' he said softly.

'Form a column!' Marshall gave orders. 'Windrush, throw your men out as skirmishers to guard the flanks. Push on men; I want the guns in position by nightfall.'

With sweat discolouring their white clothes, the seamen mustered a mighty cheer and continued their labours, hauling at the heavy guns. The cutlass men joined them, so despite the waist high grass, they made faster progress across the flat terrain.

'How do we set about reducing a fort?' Bertram asked.

Jack remembered the manuals he had read on his journey to India. 'We aim at the bottom of the wall and gradually work upward,' he said.

'That sounds easy enough!' Bertram patted the breech of the nearest gun.

'Listen, sir.' Wells reported. 'The dacoits have woken up.'

The drums started softly, a background throb that Jack barely noticed, and then increased to a roar that surrounded the small British force as they crawled across that sun-roasted grassy plain.

'Sir! They're behind us!' There was fear in Thorpe's eyes as he ran to report.

Jack glanced back. A score of black jacketed men stood at the fringe of the jungle they had so recently left.

'Thank you Thorpe; now get back to your place. Do nothing unless they attack.'

'Can I fire at them, sir?'

'Only if an officer or Sergeant Wells gives permission,' Jack was moving even as he spoke. The column was barely a hundred yards long, with the cannon in front and men with ammunition and stores in the centre. The handful of 113th was hard pressed to cover all angles.

'Over there, sir, on the fringes of the jungle.' Thorpe's finger shook as he pointed.

The breast high grass made observation difficult, but Jack guessed there were around twenty Burmese standing in a tight knot around a tall man in a spiked helmet.

'I see them,' Jack said. 'Keep an eye on them, Thorpe. If they look dangerous, let me know.'

'They look dangerous now, sir,' Thorpe levelled his musket. 'Permission to fire, sir?'

'No,' Jack pushed the barrel of his musket down. 'Not unless they threaten us. For all we know, they are from a friendly village just having a look to see who we are.'

The column pushed slowly on, yard after hard-won yard with the wheels of the cannon crushing the grass and seamen and soldiers looking around, hands wary on cutlass and musket. Insects clouded around them, biting viciously.

'In front, sir,' Wells reported. 'Burmese.'

There was another party of about a dozen men, watching them.

'Give them a hail, Sergeant. Ask what they want.' Jack had to raise his voice above the roar of the drums.

'Yes, sir.' Wells took a deep breath of the humid air and shouted something that Jack could not translate. There was no response.

'Keep an eye on them,' Jack advised, 'but don't fire unless they threaten us.'

There was another party on the right flank, watching but not interfering as the column moved closer to the stockade.

'They're everywhere, sir,' Thorpe's voice rose.

'They're only dacoits; we are British soldiers. Pull yourself together, man!'

'This will do,' Marshall gave a sudden crisp order. 'Set up the guns Bertram. I want both ready to fire within an hour. We'll have British colours flying above this stockade by nightfall tomorrow.'

Jack saw the puff of smoke from the stockade an instant before he heard the crack of the gun. 'That's the party opened,' he said.

'Four pounder,' Bertram gave his professional opinion, 'and very short.'

'Fire as soon as you are able,' Marshall gave a laconic order. 'Windrush; guard the flanks and rear; leave the front to us.'

The second Burmese shot slammed into the ground fifty yards to their left and the third thirty yards to their right.

'They've only got one gun, and a cock-eyed gunner,' Wells spat his contempt on the ground. 'We might take this place after all.' He looked skyward. 'The drums have stopped, sir.'

Jack nodded; the silence of the drums had not registered with him, but now he realised they had been quiet since the cannon had fired. 'Maybe the same man fires the cannon and beats the drums,' he said.

'That will be it, sir,' Wells agreed.

Bertram had both cannon pointing toward the stockade, three hundred yards distant and rising eighteen feet above the grass.

'Aim for the main gate,' Marshall ordered. 'We've no ladders, so we won't go over the wall.' He narrowed his eyes. 'Hurry it up, Bertram and we might get this over before dark today. I don't expect much resistance from a bunch of dacoits.'

'Load!' Bertram ordered, 'and allow me to aim.' He supervised his gunners like a father with a brood of children, tutting and cajoling and double –checking all that they did. 'Good man; well done. Now fire; fire!'

The double report echoed around the maidan, with the muzzle flare scorching the grass immediately in front of the guns.

'Reload!' Bertram yelled as the whole British camp stared at the stockade to see the fall of shot.

'Too far to the right,' Marshall used his telescope to observe. 'Two points to port, Bertram, and you've got him.'

'Permission to fire sir?' Thorpe's voice rose to a panic stricken squeak. 'Burmese; hundreds of them!'

Jack ran to the rear. Thorpe's hundreds numbered about twenty, advancing at speed from the jungle toward the small British force. Unlike the soldiers at Rangoon, they wore no uniform, only a variety of small turbans and loin cloths or *longyis*.

'Fire, lads,' he said, 'and keep firing until they run.' He showed the way by emptying his revolver into the mass. He did not see the result as he bent his head to reload, snapping cartridges into the small chambers of his revolver. He dropped one, stooped to retrieve it from the ground and straightened up again. The firing had stopped.

'Why are you not firing, Thorpe?'

'They've gone sir,' Thorpe said. 'All of them.'

The maidan to the rear was empty; the Burmese had vanished. The British were alone.

'They might have just gone to ground; keep your eyes open.' Jack swore when musketry began on the right flank. He ran round there, to see O'Neill reloading. 'What happened here O'Neill?'

'It might have been a probe sir, but I thought it best to let them know we were awake.' Both men flinched as Bertram's cannon roared out again, followed quickly by a reply from the stockade.

'How many Burmese were there?'

O'Neill screwed up his face in thought. 'Not sure, sir. They moved around a lot, bounding and bobbing. There might have been fifteen or maybe a score. No more than that.'

The Burmese are probing our defences; they'll try the left next.

There was only a single musket shot from the left, then a volley, followed by an irregular crackle. Jack arrived as Graham unsheathed his bayonet. 'Where are you going, Graham?'

'After they dacoity buggers, sir. Them's the ones that murdered Lacey.'

'Lacey's not dead,' Jack looked around.

'They shot him, sir,' Graham clicked the bayonet in place. 'I'm going after the bastards.'

'You'll stay put!' Jack said. He saw Lacey lying on the ground with his eyes wide open and half his chest blown away. 'What happened?'

'They appeared from nowhere sir, one rose out of the ground and shot him and then more came and they all shot at Lacey and all ran away. I fired after them.'

Another man gone; they are killing my men off one by one and testing us. Rear and both flanks; they are harassing us.

'How many were there, Graham?'

Graham took a deep breath and tried to concentrate. 'I don't know sir. Ten or so.'

'Well, they've gone now. Keep a good look out.'

There was another double bark from the cannon, another reply from the Burmese, and a wild cheer from the seamen as pieces flew from the gate of the stockade. Once again, the dacoit's shot fell short.

'Good shot, sir! That was a six if ever I saw one!' Sinclair shouted.

Jack nodded. 'Try again, Bertram!'

'Silence!' Marshall snapped the word. 'You are British seamen, not schoolchildren. Keep firing Lieutenant Bertram. I expect a hit every time, not one hit in every half-dozen attempts.'

The drumming began again, low and ominous.

'They like their music,' O'Neill said and ignored Marshall's stare.

'What's that?' Coleman pointed to movement in the distance.

'It looks like cavalry,' O'Neill said. 'I didn't know the Burmese had cavalry.'

Cavalry; the word spread around the British force; and every face turned towards this new threat.

'Keep your positions,' Jack ordered. He stepped beyond the pickets. Colourful in the distance, the Burmese cavalry loomed above the grass. With the heat and their constant movement, it was hard to estimate numbers, but Jack guessed about fifty, perhaps more. They looked lithe and efficient, with long lances and light coloured uniforms.

'Deal with them, Windrush,' Marshall ordered. 'Bertram, hurry along with that gate. I want it destroyed, not tickled.'

'Aye, aye, sir,' Bertram said.

Deal with them? I only have a handful of men!

'Right lads' Jack gave swift orders. 'Thorpe; watch the rear, Armstrong, take the left flank, all the rest come with me.'

I have five men to face an unknown number of cavalry which could be very good or very poor.

'Sergeant Wells; what are Burmese cavalry like?'

'Cassey Horse,' Wells screwed his face up. 'I hear they are well disciplined and ferocious when they think they are winning, but not so good when things go against them.'

'Well then, let's see if we can make things go against them. Form a line and follow me.' Jack made a swift decision that went against the very first maxim when facing cavalry. *I should form a square and wait for them but how can I do that with only a handful of men?*

The grass swished beneath their feet and tangled around knees and ankles, so Coleman stumbled and swore. As they moved, the cavalry advanced toward them with both forces converging in the maidan, while the cannon roared behind them and white powder smoke hung low and acrid.

'Put on your percussion caps,' Jack ordered quietly. He felt the tension mount. This would be an unrecognised skirmish in an unknown sideshow in a minor war. There was no glory here if he won and a sordid, forgotten death if he lost. Above them a pair of vultures circled, sensing death.

'Keep in line and march slowly,' Jack had heard of some regiments which could fire and march simultaneously, but he had not trained his men to do that. 'When we are at a hundred paces, we will halt and fire a volley.'

He could see the Burmese clearly now; they were watching the advance of this small handful of British soldiers with more curiosity than aggression, speaking to one another and pointing without fear.

'Halt!' Jack ordered, and added, 'dress the line, sergeant.'

By God, if I am to die out here I want to die like a soldier.

'Present!'

Five muskets clicked into place.

'Fire!'

Four muskets fired; Coleman swore. 'Mine misfired, sir!'

'Reload; Coleman, draw that charge.'

One of the horsemen had gone down in a kicking mess of horse and man. The others had halted as if they could not believe the effrontery of such a small number of men in attacking them.

Jack felt the heat like a great weight pressing on him. He wiped away the sweat that formed on his eyebrows and dripped across his eyes.

'Present: fire!'

Another horseman fell; the others wheeled about and withdrew. The downed horse kicked and screamed. Three more vultures joined the circling pair.

'Back we go men,' Jack felt a mixture of elation, relief and confusion. *Why did they not ride forward and wipe us out? The enemy is throwing away their advantage.*

The cannon roared again as they returned. 'That's the gateway heavily damaged sir,' Bertram reported. 'Four direct hits.'

Commander Marshall opened his telescope and examined the stockade. 'That's our way in then. Fire another two rounds, and then everybody double forward. We'll have that place under control before night.'

'What about the guns, sir?' Bertram asked. 'If we leave them unattended, the Burmese will take them.'

'The Burmese will be too busy running away from us to even think about a couple of stray cannon,' Marshall said.

'But the cavalry, sir,' Bertram was obviously concerned about his guns.

'Our soldiers chased them away. You saw them flee. My orders stand; get your men ready for the assault, Lieutenant Bertram.' Marshall pointed to Jack. 'Windrush; you lead the attack. Head directly for the gate and don't stop for casualties. And if there is any of that Chillianwalla nonsense I will personally shoot you like a dog and hang your men. Do you understand?'

Jack nodded, 'oh, indeed sir. The 113th will take the position of honour while you stay behind us.' The words were out before he could restrain them.

'You impudent blaggard!' For a moment Jack thought Marshall was about to hit him, but the commander restrained his temper. 'I'll report you to your commanding officer, Windrush. You have not heard the last of this, by God! Attend to your duty, Windrush.'

'Yes, sir.' Jack said.

'You've not heard the last of this by God,' O'Neill quietly repeated Marshall's words in a high-pitched tone. 'That's the first time I've heard an officer speaking up for the 113th, sir.'

I should not encourage other ranks to speak against their superiors but damn it; these men have not put a foot wrong.

'We are all 113th, O'Neill, but I am not proud of what I said.'

'That's all right, sir, I'll be proud for you.'

'And me too,' Coleman added. 'Bloody John Company tarry-arses!'

'Enough now!' Jack quietened them down, 'get yourselves ready for the assault. Now we have to show these bluejackets how to fight.' He raised his voice. 'Forward the 113th!'

'Jesus in Heaven, was Rangoon not enough?' Thorpe muttered, hesitated a little and followed the rest.

The men lurched forward, musket in hand, bayonets fixed, heads bowed as an instinctive subconscious means of protection against the musketry, jingal balls and cannonade expected from the stockade walls.

'Don't linger, boys; we're the 113th. Let's show these John Company people what real soldiers can do: charge!' It was the first time that Jack had used that word in earnest. He ran forward, increasing the length of his stride as the musketry began from the stockade. He saw long spurts of white smoke and heard the whizz and thump of balls on the ground. It did not matter; he was in command, he could not be touched: he was invulnerable.

'Charge!'

The remains of the gateway were directly ahead, gaping open as the artillery had left only fragments of wood hanging from shreds of what had once been the hinges.

'Cavalry! The cavalry are behind us!' Jack heard the panic in the shout and looked over his shoulder.

The Cassey Horse had moved across the maidan and had formed into three long lines behind the advancing British. They rode at a trot with their lances held low, like mediaeval knights. Long grass concealed the legs of their horses, so they looked deformed, horse heads and the top half of men floating above a yellow-brown cloud, yelling some Burmese war cry.

'Sir: there's infantry on the flanks as well. They've cut off our retreat!' O'Neill pointed to the side. The maidan was alive with Burmese infantry, moving through the long grass on either side of the small British force.

Coleman wavered; he half turned, until Wells pushed him onward.

'Forward Coleman! There's nowhere to go, lad. Our only chance is to take the stockade. Charge, man, charge!'

'Come on the 113th!' Feeling very melodramatic, Jack drew his sword and rushed on. He had been born to soldier; fighting was the day-dream that had occupied many of his childhood hours, leading his regiment in a death-or-glory charge toward the enemy.

The gateway was thirty yards ahead; twenty; ten; Jack could see the interior of the stockade with half a dozen Burmese watching the British charge. He heard Wells roaring a challenge, heard O'Neill whooping like an Irish banshee, heard Coleman repeating the same obscene word again and again, and then the ground opened underneath him, and he was falling, to land with a terrible thump. There was excruciating pain in his left leg, and other bodies were landing beside him; somebody was screaming in terrible agony, Wells was shouting something he could not understand, and the entire world had changed.

Chapter Fourteen

Pegu Province: November to December 1852

For a long time, the pain dominated Jack's life. He closed his eyes and fought the scream that he wanted to emit, but knew he could not. All his life he had been trained to control his emotions, as a British gentleman should. His mother – or the cold-eyed woman he had thought of as his mother - had taught him never to react to pain by inflicting more of the same, which was a lesson reinforced at the boarding school where he had suffered his childhood and youthful years.

Jack dragged back these lessons now and put the pain into perspective. There was more than one pain; there was the overall mental pain of defeat, and there was the single sharp agony in his left thigh. It was that latter pain that he found hard to control; it was that pain he had to identify and ease, or at least understand.

He looked around. He was one of three people inside the defensive pit, a hole with pointed stakes pointing upward for the attackers to fall on; a *trou de loup* as the technical experts would term it. The Burmese had camouflaged their trap with mats of dry grass, and he had led the 113th straight in. Coleman was on his left, lying on his side with blood on his head, and Graham, screaming with a pointed stake through his groin and another deep in his chest. Jack looked at his thigh; the point of the stake had gone straight through and out the other side. The pain came in waves. His sword lay between the stakes, the ineffectual glitter of its blade mocking him.

Oh dear God, we are at the mercy of Bo Ailgaliutlo. Instead of bringing honour and glory to the 113th I have led them to another defeat. The Curse of the 113th.

The desultory firing ceased, in its place came Burmese voices and high pitched laughter. When Jack looked up a circle of Burmese faces peered down at him, somebody pointed and laughed, and three wiry men in loincloths and brief turbans jumped into the pit. They ignored the British soldiers and lifted the muskets and Jack's sword, which they tossed up to their companions.

Two men stood over Graham, who continued to scream high pitched. One Burmese with a deep gouge down his face sat on him, so he slid further onto the stake, while the other laughed at the renewed screams.

'You filthy bastards!' Jack gasped, 'torturing an injured man! You dirty hounds!'

Leaving Graham, the dacoits stepped to Jack and stared at him. One kicked his injured leg while the other fingered his uniform.

'British officer,' Jack said. 'Leave my men alone!'

The two Burmese spoke again, ignoring Graham and the stake that was thrust through Jack's leg until Graham gave a long gurgling moan. Jack became aware of a man on the lip of the pit watching everything that happened. He wore a faded red jacket, but it was the eyes that were familiar.

'Halloa!' Jack heard the catch in his voice. 'Are you Bo Ailgaliutlo, the Englishman?'

The man in the red jacket looked at him but said nothing.

'Help Private Graham,' Jack said, 'he is badly wounded and needs attention. He cannot harm you in his condition. Please.' He found it difficult to be polite to a renegade and enemy to his country, but Graham was one of his men. 'Please, Bo Ailgaliutlo.'

The man in the red coat said something and one of the Burmese in the pit drew his dha and stepped toward Graham.

'No!' Jack shouted, 'help him!'

The man looked directly at Jack, and then pulled back Graham's head, so his throat was bare and slowly, deliberately cut his throat. Graham gurgled as the blood poured out of him.

'You dirty murdering bastard!' Jack tried to wriggle free of the stake but the pain intensified and he shrank back, swearing. Bo Ailgaliutlo watched expressionlessly from above, then spoke again and pointed to Jack. The Burmese with the dha stepped forward and grabbed hold of Jack's hair.

'Let go!' Jack swung a punch. He knew it was unavailing, but he was determined not to make it easy for them.

So this is how I die; murdered in a stinking pit in Burma by a dacoit. No glory and no honour, no brave last stand around the colours, no medals and no admiring witnesses. Sordid, dirty and unknown, here dies Jack Windrush: unwanted bastard.

'You leave Ensign Windrush be!' Jack was unaware that Coleman was conscious. 'I said, you leave Ensign Windrush be, you dirty Burmese devils!'

Bo Ailgaliutlo said one word and held up a hand. The Burmese knifeman paused. Bo Ailgaliutlo spoke again, and the knifeman put his dha away.

'What is your name?' Bo Ailgaliutlo spoke with difficulty as if he found the words painful to use.

'Ensign Jack Windrush of the 113th Regiment of Foot,' Jack said. 'And this is Private John Coleman of the same regiment. The wounded soldier your brute so foully murdered was Private Henry Graham...'

'He was dying in great pain,' Bo Ailgaliutlo said slowly. 'My man did him a great service by killing him. He would have lingered for hours with no hope of survival.' He changed to Burmese again, giving sharp orders.

The Burmese crowded around Jack and examined the stake through his thigh.

'What are you going to do?' Jack asked.

They ignored him, grabbed the stake and ripped it bodily out of the ground. Jack screamed, and yelled again when they hoisted him between them and dragged him to the surface.

Control yourself; British officers do not show pain.

Bo Ailgaliutlo looked closely into Jack's face, nodded and gave more orders.

Jack bit deep into his lip as the Burmese laid him on face up on the ground. Bo Ailgaliutlo stood over him as they brandished a dha and put it to his groin.

So now I am to be tortured. Well, I know nothing of any use to anybody.

One of the Burmese patted his pockets as expertly as any London pickpocket. He said something to his companion, thrust his hand in deep and came out holding one of Jack's golden Buddhas. They laughed and ransacked Jack's clothes, removing both Buddhas and Jack's pocket-book.

'So you've been looting have you?' Bo Ailgaliutlo shook his head. He held out his hand and took the Buddhas and the wallet. Flicking through the pocket-book, he tossed all the coins and bank notes to the Burmese. 'I'll look through your papers later, Ensign,' he said and spoke to his followers.

The Burman sliced open Jack's trousers from waistband to ankles and pulled them away, and then Bo Ailgaliutlo tied a tourniquet around his upper thigh.

'This will hurt,' he said, and held Jack down while the Burmese pushed the stake right through his leg and out the other side.

Jack heard himself scream and then merciful unconsciousness released him from pain.

He opened his eyes. There was mottled sunlight through darkness and the sound of rustling. Pain: always pain, in everything he did there was pain. He looked around. He was in a large wooden hut with a roof of thatch through which sun seeped in motte-filled bars. Pain. There were other people there, men, some of whom he recognised, others he did not.

'The officer's awake.' That was Thorpe's voice.

'Welcome back, sir.' There was dried blood caked from O'Neill's head to his chin, and his uniform was torn across the breast. 'You've been out for two days, near as I can judge.'

'Where are we?' Jack's head thumped with every word while both legs were ablaze with agony. He looked down; he was lying on his back, chained by the wrists to a long pole and with his bare legs raised above his head and fastened to another pole. There was a mess of leaves and ripe bananas on the wound in his thigh from where the worst pain throbbed around his body.

'In some prison hut, sir,' O'Neill said. 'A lot of the lads are here but not all. Some of the sailor boys are here as well.'

Jack closed his eyes and allowed the pain to wash over him.

I am a prisoner of the Burmese. I have led my men to defeat and disaster. I am a failure as an officer.

'Roll call,' Jack heard the strain in his voice. 'Let's see who is here.' He heard his voice as a croak. 'Sergeant Wells: call the roll if you please.'

There was silence for a moment before O'Neill spoke again. 'Beg pardon sir, but the sergeant did not make it. He's not here, sir.'

Wells dead! That wise, subtle, cunning veteran killed.

'How did he die?' Jack asked.

'I don't know sir.' O'Neill shook his head.

'Does anybody know?'

Nobody knew. Nobody had seen him fall. Thorpe and Armstrong had survived, with O'Neill and Coleman, but all the others of the 113th were gone. The seamen had also suffered casualties, with officers as well as men falling before Burmese shot and blades. There were only forty prisoners in that hut, some wounded and all despondent.

'Not the best day, then,' Bertram's voice sounded from the far corner of the hut. 'I saw the Commander taken, so he's still alive, but I don't know where. Old Sinclair is dead though. One of the cavalrymen spitted him clean.'

'So what happens now?' Lieutenant Buchanan asked weakly. In common with all the others, he was chained on his back. He rattled his chains in despair.

'We have two choices,' Jack said. 'Either we sit and wait for rescue, or we try and get out of here ourselves.'

'Let's hope that Lieutenant Hook had the sense to get back down to Rangoon,' Bertram said. 'Even without engines he should be there within a week or ten days, and there could be a relief column up within a month at the most.'

'A month!' Buchanan lifted his feet, so the chains rattled. 'I can't stand a month like this.'

'Hopefully, they'll come before that,' Jack said. He looked up as the door opened and two Burmese entered, escorting Bo Ailgaliutlo between them.

'You are Windrush,' Bo Ailgaliutlo did not waste time.

'I am Ensign Jack Windrush of the 113th Foot,' Jack agreed.

Bo Ailgaliutlo nodded. 'Are you any relation to Major William Windrush?'

'General William Windrush was my father,' Jack lifted his chin.

Bo Ailgaliutlo stepped back slightly. 'So he made General rank did he, and you are his pup.' He leaned closer, his eyes china-blue and laughing. 'You may be useful as a bargaining token, later.'

'You knew my father did you, you traitorous blackguard,' Jack's tongue betrayed him once more.

'I knew of him,' Bo Ailgaliutlo did not seem concerned by the insult. 'I am surprised you are in the 113th. That family always served in the Royal Malverns.' He nodded to the Burmese and snapped an order that saw Jack released and dragged out of the hut with his leg trailing behind him. He yelled once and bit his lip against the pain.

'Keep your chin up, Windrush!' Bertram shouted.

'Don't you hurt the Ensign you dirty bastards!' Coleman added but chained as they were, the 113th could do nothing but shout encouragement as Jack was dragged out. They were in a group of huts within the walls of the stockade, with groups of Burmese men and women walking around, some armed, others not. A few stopped to watch him.

'You treasonous blackguard,' Jack tried to ignore the shooting agony of his injured leg. 'As soon as General Godwin hears about this he'll send a relief column and destroy your fort and all your men. You'll hang, Bo Ailgaliutlo.'

'I very much doubt that Ensign Windrush,' Bo Ailgaliutlo said dryly. He said something in Burmese and the two silent guards pulled Jack to a line of upright poles set in the centre of the stockade. 'How will the good general find out when we have captured your lovely little boat?'

Jack felt the nausea rise within him as he saw that there was a man tied to each pole. 'Dear God,' he said, 'what have you done to them?'

'We killed them,' Bo Ailgaliutlo said.

'You barbarian; you murdering dog!' Jack recognised the first mutilated body as Lieutenant Hook and the second as what remained of Knight. After that he stopped looking for all the men had been sliced and hacked to death.

'Barbarian?' Bo Ailgaliutlo shrugged. 'That is entirely possible, Ensign, but only a moment ago you threatened my men and me with hanging, while your Sergeant Wells tortured a wounded prisoner; the kettle and the pot are both black in wartime, my upstanding gentlemanly friend.'

And Myat? Where were Myat and Ranveer?

'Did you kill everybody on board?' Jack asked.

'Not everybody; we are not as ruthless as the British.' Bo Ailgaliutlo did not elaborate. He spoke again in Burmese, and his men pulled Jack inside a small hut. They proved their experience in this sort of operation when they chained Jack to a log with a few skilful moves and stood back.

'Now, I have two hostages,' Bo Ailgaliutlo pointed to the far corner of the hut, 'and I only need one. Which of you will I keep alive and which will I give to my men, or my women, to dispose of?'

'Damn you, you murdering traitor,' Jack said. He peered into the far corner of the hut. Commander Marshall lay on the ground, securely tied down.

What do I do now? We are prisoners of a renegade in the heart of Burma. The Burmese have captured my ship, and all my men are dead or prisoner. Yet Bo Ailgaliutlo knows my family and to judge by his accent; he is well educated. He was no private soldier; he was a sergeant at least, or perhaps a gentleman ranker.

'Is that you Windrush?' Despite his predicament, Marshall's voice was as acidic as ever. 'Damn you for an incompetent buffoon! I sent you to chase the cavalry away, and they merely circled us. I sent you to make a path for the main assault force, and you immediately fall into a ditch.'

Jack did not try to contain his tongue. 'The whole affair was pointless, sir, attacking a stockade with a handful of men and two small cannon.'

'You give me impudence, Windrush! I will put that in my report, depend on it. Your career is at an end now for nobody will employ you after this little fiasco.'

Does this man realise he is a prisoner?

'Both our careers could be at an end, sir if Bo Ailgaliutlo decides to kill us. He has already murdered half your crew.'

'Nonsense; I am a Commander in the Honourable East India Company's navy; he knows that if anything happens to me the Company's vengeance would be swift and terrible.'

'Yes, sir, but nobody knows where we are, and Bo Ailgaliutlo has captured *Serangipatam* so there is nobody to carry the news.'

Marshall relapsed into silence.

'How long have we been here?' Marshall asked later.

'They captured us two days ago, sir, maybe three,' Jack said. 'If we are lucky General Godwin might send an expedition to rescue us in a month or so.'

That is unlikely. We are on our own. We must survive as best we can.

After a while a fat Burmese waddled in with a mess of rice and fish and fed them, thrusting his fingers deep into Jack's mouth.

Jack counted the passing of time by the visits of that man with the rice. There were periods of darkness and periods of light, and there was feeding time. Every so often a pair of burly Burmese would haul him outside into sunlight so bright it hurt his eyes and throw buckets of water over him.

'Bath night,' Jack tried to make a joke of it, although Marshall said nothing.

After the drenching, the guards took Jack back to his place in the hut and shackled him down. At first, he counted the days. After a while he stopped; it did not matter what day it was as they were all the same.

After a space of time, the guards dragged Commander Marshall away from the hut. Jack never saw him again; he did not miss him; he preferred his own company. The routine continued. Jack found that it was quite pleasant to lie and allow his mind to drift. He thought about the dreams of his early life and the tortured pleasures of public school, the abortive ambitions of military glory and the concentration on his career that allowed no time for please. Then he thought of Myat Lay Phyu.

She was not as young as he had first thought, but he found it hard to judge the age of these Burmese women. They were all wondrously slender. He thought of her serenity and that determined thrust of her chin and the way her *longyi* slid over her hips. Something disturbed his daydream. A sound.

What was that sound? It was like marching feet as if an army was on the move. Better think of Myat and...

The scratching was irritating. At first, Jack ignored it, but when it persisted, he looked over to the gloom of the far corner. 'Go away,' he whispered, 'leave me in peace.'

The scratching continued, growing louder.

'Ensign Windrush!' The voice was quiet but distinct.

'What?' Jack tried to cudgel sense into his dazed brain. 'Who's there?' He was so used to the silence that he had to work out the meaning of the words. 'What is it?'

'It's me, sir.' The voice was familiar, but Jack could not remember from where. Weeks of solitary captivity had dazed his mind.

'Who is that?' He tried to twist around in his chains.

'Sergeant Wells, sir. I've come to free you.'

'You're dead,' Jack said and giggled. 'Am I dead as well? Are you taking me to the next place?'

'You're not dead, sir.' Wells' hard tones were painful after the silence of the hut. 'Nor am I.' He was unshaven and his hair was unkempt, but he still wore his uniform. He crawled across the floor with a knife in his hand. 'How are these chains fastened, sir?' Wells examined them briefly. 'Oh I see; it's a simple catch; we'll soon have you out of here.'

'Most of the men are dead: Graham, Knight, Lacey have all gone. Myat and Ranveer too, I think.' Jack found the words tumbled out of him.

'Myat is alive, sir,' Wells worked on Jack's chains. 'This thing is rusted in the humidity, sir.' 'And Ranveer is here too.'

Myat is alive?

'Commander Marshall's dead,' Wells swore as he struggled with the chains, 'beg pardon for the language, sir but this rust is hard to shift. When were you last released if I may ask?'

Jack shook his head. 'I don't know sergeant. What day is it?'

'I don't know sir. It's the middle of November I think.'

'How about the men, Sergeant? Have you freed them too?'

'No sir; they're in a different place.' Wells gave a little grunt as he freed the bolt on Jack's ankle chain. 'That's it, sir. Can you move your legs?'

Not an inch.

'Give me a minute,' Jack knew his muscles were weak after many weeks immobile, but he desperately wanted out of the hut. He held forward his arms. 'Can you get these manacles off too?'

'Yes, sir. Hold still.' Wells freed the bolts and threw the manacles on the ground. 'I'll help you, sir.'

Jack tried to stand, but although the wound in his left leg was healing, neither leg could bear his weight. 'I'll have to crawl.'

Moving crab-wise across the ground, Jack followed Wells to a gap in the wall.

'Do you have him safe?' Myat crouched at the gap, her face as impassive as ever.

'Safe but weak,' Wells said. 'Come along, sir.'

Even the humid air of the stockade smelled sweet after the dense confines of the hut. Jack took a single deep breath and began to cough until a hard hand closed on his mouth.

'It is better to keep quiet, Sahib until we are away from this place.'

'Ranveer!' Jack could not help his grin as he pushed the Sikh's hand away. 'I thought you were dead as well.'

'If you can keep silent, Ensign Windrush, 'we might get away from here alive.' Myat shook her head in disapproval.

Only then did Jack notice the corpse on the ground. The Burmese sentry lay on his back with a single wound on the side of his neck. 'Was that you, Sergeant Wells?'

'No sir: I got that one over there.' Wells pointed to a second body at the back of the hut. 'This one was Ranveer.'

Jack looked around the stockade. 'Where are all the Burmese? The place is nearly deserted.'

'I'm not sure sir. The place has been full of warriors all this time, but the last two days Bo Ailgaliutlo gathered them all in their boats and yesterday they paddled down the river. That's how we could get you out. We've been watching the stockade since they captured you, but this was our first chance.'

And this is the man I thought was conspiring against me.

'Thank you, sergeant. I am more grateful than I can say.' Jack tried to stand again, staggered and Ranveer grabbed him before he fell. 'How are the rest of the men?'

'What's left are in that hut there,' Wells nodded to the large hut that stood in the centre of the stockade. 'There are about a dozen guards, sir, a few too many for us to handle.'

'We're not leaving them behind,' Jack said. 'What weapons do we have?'

'My musket sir, Ranveer's *tulwar* and whatever these two Burmese fellows carried.'

'Bring their muskets and dhas over,' the idea formed in his head even as he spoke. 'They don't know there are only two of you, and a woman and a weak-as-water officer. Let's make them think there are more of us than there are.'

Jack watched the sentries on the large hut for around quarter of an hour. As Wells had said, there were twelve of them, all armed with musket and dha.

'They don't appear very vigilant,' he said. 'They gossip together and smoke their cigars.'

'Why should they be vigilant?' Wells asked. 'They have had the lads as prisoners for weeks without any difficulty. Our men are chained hand and foot and fed rice and water. They are in no position to do anything.'

'We have three muskets. How much ammunition do we have?'

'I have thirty rounds, sir and these fellows,' Wells indicated the dead Burmese, 'had a few rounds, some of stone balls, some lead.'

'That will have to do. Myat: do you know how to load a musket?'

'Of course, I do, Ensign Windrush.' Jack was sure there was mockery in Myat's nod.

'Here is what we do. We will take a musket each and open fire on the sentries. With luck, we may hit some of them, but more likely we will merely alarm them. The object is to make them believe we are an entire relieving column, so shout like the devil.' He saw Wells and Myat exchange glances.

The sentries were in two groups, one at each end of the hut, with one man occasionally slouching away on some errand of his own. The acrid smell of Burmese tobacco drifted across the compound.

'We will concentrate on one group,' Jack decided. 'That way we might scare half of them away and the remainder should be easier to manage.' He pointed to the huddle of sentries who were closer. 'Sergeant, you know your own weapon best, so you keep that while Ranveer and I will use the Burmese muskets. Myat, please load for me. My hands are not working very well.'

Sheltering in the angle of Jack's former prison, they aimed at the guards. The musket felt heavy and clumsy in Jack's grasp but he fought his weakness.

I have led my men to defeat and captivity. I must do something right.

'On my command,' Jack said softly. 'Ready, present ... fire!'

Two of the muskets cracked immediately; Jack's hung fire for a second and then fired. One of the Burmese soldiers fell, yelling and the others turned in surprise to see from where the attack came.

'Reload!' Jack handed his musket to Myat, 'and shout out!'

'113th! To me the 113th!' Well's roar echoed around the stockade, joined by Jack's much weaker croak.

Ranveer had a deep throated roar: *'Bole So Nihal, Sat Sri Akal!'*

Wells fired again, with Ranveer a few seconds later and Jack third. Another of the dacoits slid down, kicking and writhing. The others were raising their muskets or had run for cover. Jack aimed at the back of one of the running men and fired. The man yelled, grabbed at his leg and fell, to wriggle on the ground.

That's for Lacey and Graham.

'Keep firing,' Jack ordered. He ducked as a Burmese ball thumped into the corner of the hut a few feet from his head. Wells shouted again and fired a third time.

'Watch your flanks!' Jack warned.

The second group of Burmese was coming around the side. They advanced at the run, some holding their muskets, others having drawn their dhas.

'Get that lot,' Jack ordered. He grabbed the reloaded musket from Myat, aimed at the centre of the group and fired. His ball took the leading man square in the chest and threw him backwards, so he collided with the man immediately behind him. Both fell. The remaining four hesitated; two turned around, and two raised their dhas high, screamed what was obviously a battle cry and rushed toward their attackers. Wells fired and missed, Ranveer fired and hit one of the retreating men, drew his *tulwar* and charged forward.

'*Bole So Nihal, Sat Sri Akal!*'

'You crazy Sikh bastard!' Wells yelled, slotted home his bayonet and ran to help. Jack took one step, staggered and collapsed. He could only watch as Ranveer sliced the advancing Burmese across the stomach and then chopped at his head. The Burmese fell at once. Wells spitted one of the retreating men and followed on to disappear around the corner of the building.

'Be careful Edwin!' Myat stood up sharply, her hand to her mouth.

Edwin? I had not thought of Sergeant Wells being an Edwin: and how did Myat find out?

'Musket!' Jack held out his hand. 'Wells can take care of himself: where is my musket?'

Myat's eyes were wide as she looked at him, and then she seemed to remember what she was doing and hastily reloaded.

For a few moments, Jack heard Ranveer's war cry alongside Wells' roars and the lighter voices of the dacoits. He took the musket from Myat as three Burmese exploded from cover with Wells and Ranveer behind them.

'I told you Wells would be fine,' Jack said. He dragged himself to a kneeling position and aimed at the leading Burman. Waiting until the man was only twenty yards away; he targeted his stomach and pulled the trigger. The weapon jerked viciously in his hands, and the Burman staggered. Ranveer finished him off with a backhanded slash across the ribs.

'Two got away,' Wells threw a smart salute. 'They ran before we could reach them.'

'You could have got killed!' It was the first time Jack had seen Myat show any real emotion. She stalked up to Wells, shouting in a mixture of Burmese and English, and slapped him hard on the arm. 'You could have died, Edwin Wells!'

Jack thought it best to look away as Wells shouted back at Myat, his English also mixed with a smattering of Burmese words. 'You are very concerned with the life of a British soldier.'

Myat looked at him with eyes that retained vestigial anger. 'Don't you realise yet, Ensign Windrush? He is my husband!'

Oh dear God in heaven! Jack stared at her. 'Wells is your husband?' He tried to control the emotions that threatened to engulf him.

'Myat.' Wells reached out a hand but paused when it was evident that he was too late. Myat had said the words. He stiffened to attention. 'Myat and I were married more than ten years ago, sir.'

'Legally?' Jack asked.

'By Burmese custom, sir.' Wells remained at attention.

A lot made sense now. That was why Wells elected to stay in India. A British soldier with a native wife would not find life easy in England. Myat would not be accepted by the convention-bound sergeant's mess, while the other sergeant's wives would have cold-shouldered her at the least.

'It was Myat who rescued you from Gandamack,' Jack said.

'Yes, sir,' Wells remained at attention.

'Was Myat the reason you transferred to the 113th when your first regiment returned home?' Jack noticed that Myat was standing shoulder to shoulder with Wells, man and wife facing trouble together.

'That's correct, sir.' Wells remained at attention, despite the fact that Myat linked her arm with his.

'Did your old commanding officer know of your marriage?' In some regiments, even non-commissioned officers had to seek the colonel's permission before they married. It would be a very broad minded colonel indeed to permit a soldier to marry a native woman.

'No, sir.' Wells said.

Marrying without permission was an offence. Wells had made himself liable to the cat and perhaps even dismissal from the army with the loss of his pension.

'Colonel Murphy may be more understanding, Sergeant,' Jack said. 'I would wait to see what his views may be before you approach him. I will ask him what he thinks of such matters and let you know.'

Wells' salute would have graced any RSM in the Brigade of Guards. 'Thank you, sir.'

Another thought chilled Jack. He remembered the thoughts that had occupied him when in captivity. He had considered a liaison with the wife of a ranker: that was one of the worst crimes imaginable for an officer. Was that his mother's passionate blood showing? He shook away the thought: he had more immediate concerns than an abortive romantic liaison.

'Now shall we get the other prisoners free?' Jack said. 'Ranveer, could I borrow your arm, please?'

Jack said nothing as Myat came to him. She touched his shoulder lightly. 'You had three battles to fight; against your country's enemies, against your conscience and against yourself. You are winning the third.'

Wells tore open the door of the prison hut. 'Officer present! Stand to attention 113th.'

It was the smell that hit Jack first. It was the smell of men locked up for weeks in a confined space with no facilities and no sanitation. With Ranveer supporting him, he stood in the doorway.

'Lie still men; Sergeant Wells and Ranveer Singh will free you. We are leaving this place just as soon as we can.'

There were not many left alive. Coleman, Thorpe, Armstrong and O'Neill crawled out of the hut, followed by five of the seamen. All the others had died of disease or neglect. Lieutenant Bertram was the only surviving naval officer, and he was yellow with fever.

'Feed these men up,' Jack ordered, 'We will stay in this stockade until we are fit to move.'

Myat pressed her hands together and gave a deeper than usual nod to Jack. 'The men stink, Ensign Windrush. They need to wash and you also need some clothes to cover yourself.' She ran her gaze down him from face to feet and back.

Jack had forgotten he wore only his shirt. He shifted uncomfortably as Myat smiled.

'Your men may be jealous.' She handed over a strip of material. 'A loin cloth,' she told him. 'Would you like me to show you how to tie it in place?'

'No, thank you,' Jack hurriedly covered himself. 'I'm sure I can manage.'

Myat wrinkled her nose. 'Maybe you should manage a wash as well,' she suggested.

'More important than washing,' Jack turned the conversation around. 'We need weapons.' He raised his voice. 'Sergeant Wells!'

'Sir!' Wells stiffened to attention and Jack ignored the winks that he and Myat exchanged or the manner in which Myat also came to attention in unsmiling mockery.

'Scour the stockade for weapons, Sergeant. Muskets if you can find them, dhas if you can't, or sharpened sticks if that's what we can get. I want every man to have at least something to defend himself with if the Burmese return.'

Myat wrinkled her nose and looked away. 'Oh, you won't need weapons, Ensign. One sniff of the stink here and any dacoit will avoid this stockade. That is if you don't all die of disease before the dacoits come.'

Wells could not resist the slight twitch at the corner of his mouth.

'And when you have searched for weapons, sergeant, organise a bathing party, could you?' Jack gave Myat a look that was meant to subdue her but instead only resulted in a slight narrowing of her eyes as she fought to control her laughter. 'Else this woman of yours will drive me to distraction.'

'Yes, sir,' Wells said. 'She's very good at that, sir if you don't mind me saying.'

I know, Sergeant, I know.

Walking without the support of Ranveer was painful. Jack forced himself to take one step, then another. He cut himself a staff and moved further, yard after yard until he felt confident in his ability to move

independently. It was another two days before he took full control of
the stockade.

'I want to get these men back to Rangoon.'

*Why am I saying so much to a ranker and a native translator? Because
they saved my life, damn it!*

'Most of the men can hardly stand yet, Ensign Windrush,' Myat
pointed out.

'I'm quite aware of that,' Jack said, 'but Bo Ailgaliutlo's men won't
be away forever and when they come back we will be trapped like rats.'

'Buddha says...' Myat began but Jack interrupted her.

'Buddha can say what he likes. Buddha was never in command of
a unit of weak men in enemy territory. We are getting out if they're
fit or not.'

Myat bowed her head in less-than-meek acquiescence.

'Sergeant, keep the sentries alert and force them back to fitness. I
am going to inspect this place.'

The interior of the stockade was simple with a scattering of huts of
various sizes around an open space. The huts were untidy, with betel-
stained mats on un-swept floors, rough-cut teak pillars rising to thatch
that rustled with rats, vermin and nothing much else.

'What are you seeking, Ensign Windrush?' Myat watched him bang
his heels on the floors and rap on the walls.

'Whatever I can find,' Jack said.

'Bo Ailgaliutlo's hut is apart from his men,' Myat spoke quietly. 'If
you seek what he took from you.'

'You seek the same things,' Jack said.

'It is your responsibility to return them, not mine to take them.'
Myat was expressionless again.

Bo Ailgaliutlo's hut was smaller and graced by more ornate décor,
a splendid brass bed and, oddly, Jack thought, a portrait of a young
Queen Victoria. Two uniform jackets hung from a beam. One had belonged to Commander Marshall, and the other was Jack's. He slipped
it on with relief.

Now I look like a soldier again.

There was nothing valuable on display, so Jack prodded at the walls, seeking hidden cavities. He was about to give up when Ranveer entered the hut.

'Is the sahib searching for something?' Ranveer looked as solemn as a servant should, with eyes that gleamed.

'Yes, the sahib is. The sahib is searching for his property that Bo Ailgaliutlo stole,' Jack did not hide his frustration.

'The two golden statues?' Trust Ranveer to know everything.

'That's them,' Jack said.

'Would the sahib like me to help?' Ranveer's face was innocent.

'Damned right the sahib would like you to help,' Jack said.

Ranveer wasted no time. He removed the rush matting from the floor and stamped with the heel of his boot, worked his way from one side of the hut to the other and said: 'here, Sahib. It is hollow here.'

There was a slot in the planking, through which Ranveer slipped his fingers, and a section of the floor lifted up. Underneath were Jack's Buddhas, a small bag of European coins and pieces of Oriental jewellery.

Is that the spoils of Bo Ailgaliutlo's dacoitry, or a nest-egg for the future?

Tossing the coins to Ranveer, Jack pocketed the Buddhas. Their weight was comforting.

Now I have hope again. Now I can buy my way to respectability.

'Right men,' Jack addressed his assembled collection of soldiers and sailors in the maidan outside the huts. 'We have to get back. Myat knows the area better than anybody here, and she tells me that we have a garrison on Pegu, a place for which we all have fond memories.'

He waited for his words to sink in. The men looked tired, sick and worn. Some of them perked up a little at the mention of Pegu.

'We are marching to join that garrison. With luck, we will be there within a fortnight, and then it will be clean beds, decent food and safety.'

It was only a short speech and not as inspiring as Commander Marshall's. There was no cheering, only a stolid acceptance of their position as the men filed slowly away.

Jack watched them go.

'We are not marching to Pegu, Ensign Windrush.' The voice was weak but determined. 'I am taking charge here.'

Chapter Fifteen

Pegu Province: November 1852

Lieutenant Bertram stood in the door of the hut. 'None of us are fit to march. We are going by water. I outrank you, remember.' His grin removed any sting from the words.

Jack ignored Coleman's harsh whisper of 'I'm not bloody swimming,' as he nodded to Bertram. '*Serangipatam* is long gone, Lieutenant. The Burmese burned her I think.'

'I'm not talking about *Serangipatam*,' Bertram lurched forward. 'This is a military stockade. The Burmese attacked us in war boats, correct?'

'Correct,' Jack agreed, 'but...'

'Bear with me, Ensign,' Bertram swayed so that one of his seamen dashed forward to support him. 'The men of this garrison came in boats and left in boats, but they did not all leave. The guards were left behind. Their boat will be here somewhere.'

'Well, let's find it then,' Jack met Bertram's smile. 'I don't like marching at the best of times.'

'You *Serangis*,' Bertram said, 'scour the edge of the river. You know how good the Burmese are at hiding traps, so their boats will not be in the open.'

'My men will help,' Jack offered, but Bertram shook his head.

'Your lobster backs wouldn't know a war boat from a walrus,' he said. 'This is a job for seamen. You and your redcoats can salute each other or march at attention or do something equally military.'

Jack felt his spirits lift. Bertram was the opposite of Commander Marshall; a man under whom he could happily work.

Weak as he was, Bertram commanded his men with skill. He divided them into parties to search. 'But watch for any of these infernal traps,' he reminded. 'We've lost enough good men, and we don't want to lose any more.'

'They won't find anything,' Wells had hardly spoken before there was a roar from the river bank.

'Here we are, sir,' a broken-nosed seaman shouted, 'hidden under these ferns or whatever they are.' He swore loudly, 'beg pardon sir but it's alive with spiders and things.' He swore again and stamped hard on the ground as Bertram limped up.

They examined the war boat as it lay close to the bank; half filled with water and with the stern covered with broken branches. There was a ragged hole in the hull near the bow, a hundred different insects scurried along the bottom, and half the paddles were missing.

'Oh dear God; we can't go in that,' Jack said.

'She's beautiful,' Bertram decided with enthusiasm.

'It's a bloody wreck,' Coleman gave his candid opinion.

'We'll have her seaworthy in a day,' Bertram ignored the insolence. 'Ensign Windrush, could you ensure that we are undisturbed? Shoot any of these Burmese rascals that come close.'

'But only the rascally Burmese,' Myat reminded, grave faced, 'not the Peguese. We are on your side, remember.'

Jack waved a hand as he checked the positions in which Wells had placed his men.

This waiting is playing on my nerves. I was all ready to march.

'What shall we call her, lads?'

Jack raised his eyebrows but said nothing. He had never heard an officer ask his men for an opinion before. He waited for their reaction.

'We could call her *Burma*, sir,' one man said.

'Or *Serangy,* after our ship.'

'Would *Mabel* be allowed, sir? That's my sister's name.' The seaman was small and very thin, with an anxious expression in huge eyes.

'What do you think lads?' Bertram shouted out, '*Mabel, Serangy* or *Burma?*'

The reply came in a babble of voices, to which Bertram listened with a small smile on his face. '*Mabel* it is then,' he decided.

'Thank you, sir,' the thin seaman whispered.

Jack wiped away the sweat from his forehead, swatted vainly at the buzzing insects and felt the reassuring smoothness of the Buddhas in his pocket. 'When will your boat be ready?'

Bertram drew a hand through his ginger hair and looked upward, where the sun was disappearing behind the trees. 'Not today,' he said.

That means another night here; another night vulnerable to dacoit attack.

'We will leave early tomorrow morning,' Bertram said. 'Give the men another few hours to recover their strength.' His grin was surprising after so many weeks in captivity.

As always there was a mist on the river and a pre-dawn chorus of insects and unseen birds as they clambered apprehensively into the narrow Burmese war-boat. Navy- style, Bertram was first on the boat and Jack last. Jack looked up at the log walls of the stockade.

'We should burn the place down.'

'Too late now,' Bertram did not hide his pleasure at being afloat again. 'Come on lads; let's get *Mabel* moving!'

The seamen studied the paddles with intense curiosity.

'Like this,' Bertram demonstrated how to paddle. 'We face the bows and push *Mabel* through the river, all the way to Pegu.'

'Watch the banks lads, and don't talk. If we're quiet, people might think we are Burmese.' Jack felt rather than saw Myat's disbelief.

Bertram balanced on the high prow, looking forward into the shifting mist. For a moment Jack thought he looked exactly like a figurehead, a young, proud man facing a God-knew-what threat as he led his men forward like Jason or Odysseus, and then reality returned.

The men of the 113th all had a musket of some sort and carried a dha in place of a bayonet. They were lean and weak after the past few months but were also tighter knit. Despite their hardships, or because of them, they looked like soldiers.

'How far is Pegu?' Coleman asked.

'Downstream with no obstructions it is three days journey,' Myat answered at once.

'Bo Ailgaliutlo put obstacles in the river to stop *Serangipatam*,' Jack reminded.

'I know,' Bertram spoke over his shoulder without looking round, 'that's why I am up here. I'll see them first.'

The thin sailor swore as he missed his stroke and his paddle caused a mighty splash.

'Keep your voices down!' Bertram ordered, 'there could be ears listening.'

The sailors were not expert paddlers; there were more loud splashes and subdued cursing as *Mabel* moved erratically down the misted river.

'I hope this fog lasts all day,' Jack said, and at that moment it began to lift.

'Slow ahead,' Bertram said, and amended his order to 'stop paddling, back water.' There was a flurry of activity as the seamen tried to master the art of the paddle rather than the oars. Eventually, *Mabel* came to an untidy halt and bobbed in the current, with two men paddling to keep her static.

'Look ahead,' Bertram pointed, 'there's *Serangy*.'

'What's left of her,' a seaman muttered, while another swore, cursing the Burmese with a string of foul oaths. Bertram did not order him into silence.

Serangipatam lay on her side on the near bank of the river. Her upper works and part of her hull were burned completely away with the remainder charcoal black and twisted by the heat. Above the wreck and hanging by his neck was the skeleton of a man, picked clean by birds and insects.

'I wonder who that poor bugger was,' Coleman asked.

'Commander Marshall,' Bertram said quietly. 'That renegade fellow told me exactly what they did to him.'

'What was that, sir?' Thorpe asked, but Bertram shook his head.

'It was not a quick death,' was all he said.

The Burmese had once again staked the river to prevent British warships from passing, but as the war-boat was narrower that *Serangipatam* Bertram managed to manoeuvre between the stakes. He steered to where *Serangipatam* lay.

'We'll give him a Christian burial,' he said. 'A British seaman deserves better than to hang forever in Burma.'

With the forest a backdrop and a chorus of birds replacing the solemn hymns of a church, they hacked out a ragged grave, and the seamen lowered in the skeleton of their commander with as much reverence as they could muster.

'Does anybody know the words?' Bertram asked. 'No? Well, I will do what I can, then.'

Jack remembered the funeral of his father. He listened as Bertram stumbled over a handful of phrases that vaguely resembled the burial service, and then he sent his men on picket duty around the boat and the gathering.

'He was a hard man,' Jack said.

'He was a good seaman,' Bertram remained loyal to his superior.

They left Commander Marshall on that muddy river bank in upper Pegu province with a roughly fashioned cross above the grave. Nobody looked back.

'Bastards,' the thin seaman said with every forceful stroke of the paddle, 'bloody Burmese bastards.'

When Jack glanced at Myat, she was sitting close to Wells, her face impassive. For once there was no need to order the 113th to stay alert. They positioned themselves around the boat, hugged their muskets and scanned the passing forest, scrub land and fields.

'What's that in the river?' Wells pointed to the side. 'It might only be an animal.'

'It's a man,' the thin seaman called out. He reached out with his paddle as Bertram steered them in that direction. 'No,' he continued, 'it's not. It's a woman.'

She floated face up with her hands spread out.

'Do we bury her, sir?' The thin seaman asked.

'No,' Bertram decided after a pause. 'We don't have time.'

'We took time with the Commander,' the thin seaman reminded.

'He was one of us,' Bertram said. 'She is only Burmese.'

Wells reached over to touch Myat on the arm. Jack looked away, aware of the jealousy that twisted inside him.

There was another body later that day, headless, and a third without arms, trailing blood within a frenzy of feeding fish.

'Bo Ailgaliutlo's been busy,' Wells said.

I led my men to defeat. Every death here is my fault for failing at the stockade.

'He's dead; everybody's bloody dead. I'll do for that murdering Burmese bugger!' Coleman pulled the dha from his belt and kissed the blade. 'I swear it!'

They smelled smoke arrived before they paddled around the bend, and the village was only a smouldering mess.

'Keep paddling,' Bertram decided. 'We can't do anything here.'

There were other villages, either burned or deserted, with the rice fields untended, the huts ruined and fishing boats holed and sunk at the river's edge.

'It is like Attila the Hun passed here,' Bertram said.

'No,' Jack shook his head, 'just Bo Ailgaliutlo and his dacoits. War here is not civilised.'

'Is war anywhere civilised, Ensign Windrush?' Myat asked softly. 'The war in the Punjab killed thousands, the war in Afghanistan saw a British Army destroyed, and all the camp followers slaughtered, and they were mere skirmishes compared to your great war with France.'

'How on earth do you know that?' Jack asked.

Myat gave a nod that did not hide the mockery in her eyes. 'I know, Ensign. I am only a native and not one of you,' her glance at Bertram was meaningful. 'I have no right to know about European history or anything else.'

Jack felt the colour rise to his face. 'I did not mean...' He did not complete the sentence. *What did I mean if not that?*

Chapter Sixteen

Pegu: November to December 1852

'There it is boys,' Coleman pointed across the maidan, 'there's the temple of Pegu.' The men gave a little cheer, sailors and seamen together.

In the evening light, the town looked more exotic than ever with its great pointed temple rising to the darkening sky, dwarfing the huts that clustered all around. The dainty sound of bells ghosted across to them.

'There's a flag flying from the temple,' Wells said, 'but I'm blessed if I can see which one.' He turned to Myat. 'Can you make out the colours?'

'It's the British flag,' Myat said at once, and when the words spread, the men cheered again.

'So all we have to do is march in like soldiers, and we'll be safe,' Jack told them. The 113th stared at the Union flag that flapped above the town as if sight alone could bring them food and clean water and security from biting insects and marauding dacoits.

'Come on lads, smarten up!' Wells lined them up. 'I've no idea which regiments are in Pegu, but I do know that they have not done what we have done. Clean your muskets, smarten what's left of your uniforms and march to attention. We're going into Pegu like soldiers, like the best regiment in the Army.'

'You *Mabels*,' Bertram shouted, 'let's show these red coats how sailors march.'

'You're going home,' Wells whispered to Myat and touched her arm.

Jack looked at the remains of his command. They looked older, harder, leaner and fitter, if much less smart. Even Thorpe looks something like a soldier.

'We've done it, lads,' Jack said. 'We've faced the worst that Burma can throw at us and survived. We will be in a British held town soon, with British soldiers manning the walls and no more worries about dacoits...'

'What's that sound?' Thorpe was first to hear it.

'It's just the wind in the trees,' O'Neill said, 'nothing else.'

'It's drums,' Coleman's voice was leaden.

'Can you hear that, Bertram?' Jack called along the length of the column.

'Halt and listen,' Bertram ordered, and the men stopped at once, eyes swivelling to the dark surroundings.

'Drums,' Jack confirmed. He did not have to say more. All the men knew what that meant.

'It could be just some local festival,' Coleman said, 'it's nearly Christmas...'

'Peguese don't celebrate Christmas,' Myat told him. 'We are Buddhists, not Christians.'

'Maybe a wedding then, or something,' Coleman continued.

Jack shook his head. 'It's the dacoits,' he said. 'Keep your eyes wide open, boys.'

'March on,' Bertram ordered, 'quick march or at the double or whatever the order is.'

The mood had entirely altered as the small column moved on. Elation had changed to tension, joy to fear and relief to doubt.

'They're getting louder,' Thorpe's voice was high pitched. He began to move faster toward Pegu, 'Jesus look! The place is alive with them!'

He's right, damn it. Damn it, damn it, damn it!

Jack looked around. The Burmese had emerged from the jungle behind them, moving with the same confident, wary vitality as they had in every previous encounter. Two distinct bodies of Burmese soldiers emerged from the forest. The stocky, muscular soldiers carried their long muskets and vicious dhas with skill and they moved together in formation.

'These are no dacoits,' Jack said shortly, 'these are regular Burmese soldiers.'

Wells nodded. 'Could be,' he said, and asked Myat her opinion.

Myat glanced over her shoulder and pushed forward a little faster.

She is scared. I have never seen Myat looking scared. For an instant, Jack fought the urge to hold her in reassurance.

'They're not dacoits,' her voice lacked its habitual calm. 'They are the king's favourite two regiments, the Invincibles and the Invulnerables.'

'Are they good?' Jack did not need to ask the question. He knew by the way the men moved that they were trained soldiers. He raised his voice, 'at the double, boys. They are right behind us.'

The Burmese were moving fast, trotting up to Pegu as the light faded behind the temple.

There is no movement in Pegu. We have to warn the garrison.

'Wells, O'Neill; fire at the Burmese!'

'They have not seen us yet, sir,' Wells warned.

'Nor have the garrison seen them,' Jack told him. 'We have to wake them up.'

The Burmese were advancing in ordered ranks, keeping their positions as if they were on parade. If the Invincibles and Invulnerables came to Pegu in such order, any unwary sentries would be overwhelmed. The Burmese would flood the defences and massacre the British in their barracks.

Wells nodded and nudged O'Neill. 'You take the Invincibles and I'll take the Invulnerables,' he said.

'All of them?' O'Neill murmured but knelt and faced the oncoming Burmese. Jack waited with them. The Burmese were almost invisible;

dim shapes in the rushing gloom. The bamboo jungle behind them seemed like a solid black wall.

'Don't aim, just fire,' Jack said, 'we are warning the garrison more than trying to halt the Burmese.'

'Aye, sir,' O'Neill made the words sound like an insult.

Hurry along for God's sake. Jack looked over his shoulder as Bertram led the column toward Pegu. *We are isolated here.* He touched his leg; the wound was aching damnably.

'Ready Corporal?' Wells sounded casual.

'Ready Sergeant.' O'Neill gave a small grin, his teeth white in the dark. 'You give the word.'

'Fire,' Wells was laconic.

Both muskets barked; there was the orange flare of the muzzles, and the smoke jetted acrid and clinging white. The Burmese line faltered slightly. Jack heard voices through the dark and the sharp tones of commands. A dog barked in Pegu, joined by a dozen more.

'Give them another,' he ordered, although all his instincts told him to flee for the sheltering muskets of the garrison of Pegu. *They must have heard that, surely?*

'Yes, sir,' Wells was already reloading, ignoring the now rapidly advancing Burmese as he balanced the percussion cap on its perch.

'Fire when ready,' Jack said, 'and then retire as fast as you like.'

O'Neill fired first and was on his feet and running even as Wells' continued to aim. Jack waited until Wells musket flared and then began to move. He heard the noise from the Burmese increase and a ragged volley followed, but he knew that in the dark it would be a lucky musket-man indeed who could hit a single moving man. *Jesus*; Jack staggered as he came down hard on his injured leg. *Ignore the pain: pain is temporary, honour lasts forever.*

'They're coming fast,' Myat sounded scared.

'Not long to go now,' Wells came beside her. 'Keep close to me. The garrison will be alert.'

They were. British voices sounded in the night. 'What's to do? Who goes there?' Light pooled from a swaying lantern.

'Friend!' Bertram shouted out, 'followed by thousands of un-friendly Burmese. Let us in please.'

'Advance friend,' the voice sounded quite relaxed, 'until I can see you.' The light moved slightly, stretching out in an elliptical illusion of security surrounded by hostile darkness.

'Come on man; the Burmese are behind us...' one of the seamen started, but Bertram hissed him to silence.

'Keep quiet and do as the man says.'

'But the bloody Burmese...'

'Who's there?' A new voice of authority cut through the dark.

'Lieutenant Bertram of *Serangipatam*,' Bertram replied at once, with 'Ensign Windrush of the 113th Foot and the survivors of both.'

'Good God!' There was a second's silence broken only by the sound of the Burmese swishing through the grass behind them, and then that same voice barked again. 'Let these men in right away.'

'There are thousands of Burmese right behind us,' Jack warned.

'Stand to!' the officer's voice rose to a shout. 'Get these men inside for God's sake!'

'Right lads, follow me,' Bertram said.

The first shot sounded from behind them, followed by another. Thorpe flinched.

'They're shooting at the lights,' Jack said.

'Come on!' A British soldier stepped into the pool of light and waved them on. 'Hurry it along!'

'Sahib!' Ranveer shouted the warning, spun round and fired so close to Jack's ear that he flinched.

A Burmese soldier fell with his dha flying from his hand.

'Thank you,' Jack said.

'There's more,' Wells said briefly. He snapped his bayonet in place. 'They're all around us.'

'Time to go, boys,' Bertram shouted, 'run for it!'

Exhausted, battered, feverish and weak, the survivors limped to-ward the light. It felt like the race for Bo Ailgaliutlo's stockade, without the elation and hopefully without the ditch. Jack felt the pain in his wounded leg increase and the breath burn in his lungs.

'In you come, boys,' the Dublin accent of the burly soldier was welcome. 'And close the door behind you; keep the draught out.'

'You say sir when you talk to an officer,' Wells spoke automatically.

'Beg pardon sir, I didn't know you was an officer,' the private sounded genuinely shocked.

As more lanterns appeared, the light flickered on a line of red coats and grim faces, with levelled muskets and heavy black boots.

'Which regiment?' It was too dark for Jack to recognise the facings.

'Madras Fusiliers,' Wells said at once, 'Company infantry.' He glanced further along the perimeter of Pegu where another unit was forming up, 'and that's the Madras Native Infantry' he said. 'I'm not sure which regiment.'

'Present!' An officer of the Madras Fusiliers yelled the words. 'Fire!'

The volley ripped through the night, followed by a few roars and a more ragged return volley from the Burmese. As the Burmese fired, Jack saw a succession of images of flat Burmese faces and yelling Burmese mouths, of muzzle-flares glinting from the wicked blades of dhas and of an advancing press of determined men. The Invincibles and Invulnerables were obviously not deterred by a single British volley. Temporarily blinded by the musket-flares, Jack waited until his night vision returned and stared into the dark.

'Fire!' the Fusilier officer yelled again, and his men loosed another volley.

'Fire!' that came from further along as the Madras Native Infantry added their fire to the defence.

Musketry came in return, an irregular spatter, and then there was silence. The acrid stench of powder smoke drifted across Pegu to slowly dissipate in the sultry air.

'They'll be back,' somebody said and stepped into the circle of lamplight. 'Major Hill of the First Madras Fusiliers,' he said, 'I'm in charge of the garrison of Pegu.' He studied Jack for a second. 'Well Ensign Windrush, we heard that all on board *Serangipatam* were dead. I am glad you survived.' He looked up as firing broke out from the direction of the river. 'They are attacking the river picket.'

Jack looked at his men; ragged, exhausted, thin, they had not waited for orders before reloading their muskets while the men of the Fusiliers watched these refugees from the jungle. 'Do you wish us to march across sir? If you could supply us with a few muskets rather than these Burmese things I know we could give a good account of ourselves.'

Major Hill shook his head. 'No, Windrush. Lieutenant Brown will have to manage for himself tonight.' He nodded to the scarecrows of the 113th. 'Get your men inside the pagoda, Ensign, feed them and find some rest. It looks like it will be busy here. That goes for you too, Lieutenant Bertram.'

It was a relief to be in the midst of British soldiers again and to hear British voices giving commands and the regulated crunch of British and sepoy boots on the ground while the multi-crossed Union flag hung serene and proud from the pagoda above.

'Well Windrush,' the major's face was lined with fatigue, 'it seems that you have stepped from the frying pan into the fire. It would have been better if you had kept on downstream to Rangoon but too late now.' He paused for a moment, 'the Burmese have closed the ring around us. Pegu is under siege.'

Chapter Seventeen

Pegu: November – December 1852

Pegu was not as Jack remembered it. British and sepoy infantry patrolled between the huts where laughing Peguese had entertained him and his men with their impromptu *pwe*. Garrison troops and commissariat stores filled the upper storey of the three- storey pagoda and cannon poked black snouts from behind hastily built walls.

Jack stood back and studied the defences. Years of neglect had reduced parts of the pagoda to disrepair with silvery reedy grass growing through the crumbling brickwork nearly everywhere he looked. It was not an impressive barrier behind which the garrison rested.

'We are in a bad position here,' Major Hill spoke to his officers as they stood on the walls. 'We are cut off from the main British army and outnumbered by a considerable Burmese force. We must make our stance at the pagoda.'

'This place is even larger than I remembered,' Jack said.

'The upper platform has four sides each of about 220 yards.' Hill was a man who liked figures. 'We use the brick wall for defence where we can, but the west wall, as you see, is virtually non-existent, God knows what will happen if the Burmese make a determined rush there. The north east is nearly as bad.'

They toured the town, taking notes. The garrison had partially repaired the low buildings around the pagoda and occupied them as barracks. European and Native infantry exchanged banter and repartee as if they were not in a besieged town deep in enemy territory.

'Are these the officer's quarters?' Jack pointed to larger houses that stood slightly detached from the troop's huts.

'Yes indeed. These buildings were the ponghee- priests'- houses but the priests have all gone elsewhere. They're not perfect but better than being outside with the mosquitoes. 'Hill killed his smile and pointed to a hut that stood slightly apart from the others. 'That one is the magazine. God knows it's not full enough to withstand a long siege, but it's all we have.'

'What's on top?' Jack indicated the highest level of the pagoda to which over thirty flights of steps ascended.

'Nothing.' Hay said quietly. 'Except the temple.'

'There are other temples,' Jack indicated a group of small pagodas near the east face. 'These will give the enemy cover. Can we not raze them to the ground?'

Hay gave a distinct shiver. 'Good God, no! That would be interfering with the religious susceptibilities of the people, and one just cannot do such a thing.'

'Yes, sir. Even when it means our men are in more danger?' Jack thought of the hardships his men had already endured. It seemed unfair to put them through more.

Hay's eyes widened. 'Our men joined the army by choice, Windrush. Nobody forced them to take the Queen's Shilling. They knew it meant danger.'

Jack nodded; arguing his point with a senior, and more experienced officer would do him no good at all. 'Yes, sir.'

'That is much worse,' Hay pointed to the jungly hills that overlooked Pegu to the north and east. 'The Burmese will be up there now, watching every move that we make. We cannot prepare for a counter attack or a sally without them seeing us. They have the advantage of surprise and numbers; we have nothing.' He stopped, possibly because he realised he was mouthing defeatist talk. 'Except a brave garrison of course.'

Jack looked around the pagoda and the surrounding town. There seemed very few scarlet jackets to patrol a settlement the size of Pegu 'How many men do we have, sir?'

'Including both native and European troops, we have 435 bayonets to defend a perimeter that requires at least three times that number.'

'We brought you a few more,' Jack reminded cautiously.

'You brought us a handful of starving skeletons that will be lucky to stand straight yet alone withstand a siege by a Burmese army.' Hill caught himself again and raised his voice to include the small group of officers that had gathered around him.

'We will base our defence on the pagoda,' he announced. 'We cannot defend the entire town with the men we have.' Suddenly Hill straightened up and became very decisive. 'I want the upper platform of the pagoda barricaded and three of the entrances blocked. That will leave only one for us to defend.' He swept his hand over the approaches to the town. 'All that tall grass affords cover to the enemy so they can creep up and murder our sentries and the innocent Peguese. I want it cut down. Our Peguese all carry dhas and are expert at that sort of work.'

'Yes, sir,' a young lieutenant began to move away.

'Stay!' Hill ordered. 'I have not finished yet. We captured three cannon when we stormed the town: I want one mounted at each blocked gateway, so they control the entrance, and I want our company gunners there permanently.' He looked around. 'I want a captain to command each face of the pagoda. If your neighbour needs assistance, I expect you to support him.'

The officers nodded. Jack listened, taking in each new idea as Hill continued with his defensive strategy.

'I want patrols out to see what the Burmese are doing. I am aware that they are watching us; I want them to see that we are active and hope to bring the fight to them. We will not tamely sit here and allow the enemy to take the initiative. We need to find out all about these people, so we know how to defeat them.'

'Sir,' Jack said, 'may I say something here?'

'Please do, Ensign. We are a small body of officers and every opinion is valued.'

Jack blinked. After the stifling command of Marshall, Hill's openness was refreshing. 'Thank you sir; the Burmese soldiers who attacked last night were regulars from the *Tatmadaw*.'

'The what?' One of the captains asked, 'speak English, damn it, man!'

'The *Tatmadaw*,' Hill said, 'is the Burmese regular army. Are you sure, Ensign?'

'Yes, sir. They were not local levies.' He hesitated, 'they fought as a disciplined force.' For a moment Jack wondered exactly how much he should say; he had no desire to appear as a know-it-all in front of these professional fighting men. 'Local levies fight under their chiefs, in a mob. They are brave enough but hardly eager, while these men had order and training. I believe they were the Invincibles and the Invulnerables regiments.'

Hill hid any surprise he may have felt. 'I thought they might have been. They attacked like professionals and not merely dacoits.' His eyes narrowed slightly. 'How do you know that, Ensign? You seem rather young to have such knowledge of our enemy.'

'The native woman who was with us is from Pegu,' Jack said. 'She was our translator on *Serangipatam*.'

'Can we trust her?'

Jack fought his resentment at what was a natural question. 'Implicitly sir. Her people have no love at all for the Burmese.'

'Good: she may be useful as a go-between with the Peguese.' Hill frowned. 'All right; you all know what to do. We must hold out here until relief arrives.'

The 113th looked a little better after a night's sleep and some British rations. Still ragged, still skeleton-thin, they were gaunt, hollow-eyed and wore uniforms little better than rags, but stood at attention when ordered and their weapons were clean, oiled and well maintained. They were soldiers.

'I thought we were going to be safe here,' Coleman gave the inevitable grouse.

'You're a soldier Coleman; you took the Queen's shilling. Now bloody earn it.' Wells gave the equally inevitable reply.

'We are stationed on the north wall of the pagoda.' Jack told them, 'we'll join the Fusiliers there.' He touched the Buddha in his pocket. 'We've improved our position a great deal; we are no longer prisoners, and we are no longer alone. There are hundreds of Company troops fighting alongside us now.'

'And thousands of bloody Burmese just waiting to spit us on their knives,' Thorpe said sullenly. 'Look at them out there!'

Thorpe was correct. The open maidan to the north of Pegu was busy with men. There were parties of soldiers moving purposefully from one side to the other, and an occasional squadron of cavalry.

'Cassey horsemen,' Captain Stephenson handed his binoculars to Jack, 'I've heard they are efficient in their own terrain.'

Jack studied the cavalrymen. 'We met them briefly,' he said, 'but had no real opportunity to see what they were like.' The cavalry moved in small groups, well-disciplined on their stocky ponies. 'They look a handy crew.' Wearing red tops, blue trousers and a neat turban, they handled their long spears with the casual familiarity of long experience.

'Sir!' Thorpe pointed to the edge of the forest. 'Big bloody elephants, sir! With men riding them.'

Before Jack could focus in that direction Stephenson had snatched back the binoculars. 'You're right private; those look like their chiefs on the elephants so no doubt they are planning something nasty for us.' He put one foot on top of the parapet wall and peered down. 'I wish I knew who these fellows were.'

'Our translator might know, sir,' Jack volunteered. 'I could send for her if you wish.'

Stephenson kept his attention on the Burmese officers. 'Do that,' he said briefly.

When Myat arrived, Stephenson handed her the binoculars. 'Ensign Windrush tells me you know the Burmese commanders; see if you can identify any of the men on the elephants.'

'I know two of them,' Myat confirmed after a few moments. 'The one on the right with the faded red coat is Bo Ailgaliutlo. He is the dacoit chief who attacked General Godwin in Rangoon.'

Jack felt a shiver run through him.

That makes sense. Bo Ailgaliutlo must have left his stockade to join in this attack on Pegu. That is why we escaped so easily.

Stephenson frowned. 'I know that name. I've heard that he is a renegade, an ex-British soldier who joined the Burmese. Is that correct?'

Jack nodded. 'I believe it is, sir. He is also the one who murdered Commander Marshall and many of our men.'

Stephenson focussed the binoculars on Bo Ailgaliutlo. 'Too far for our cannon to reach: I would like to get rid of that one. And the others?'

Myat pointed to a shorter, more elaborately dressed man who rode a larger elephant. 'The one in the centre is Muong-Kyouk-Loung, one of their most senior commanders. He's no dacoit chief but a regular soldier.'

'Muong-Kyouk-Loung: his name is known,' Stephenson murmured. 'According to our intelligence, he is an officer of general rank with some 11,000 men under his command. If he is here, then they are taking the siege of Pegu very seriously indeed.' He lowered his binoculars and looked at Myat. 'Your people are redoubtable warriors,' he said.

'The Burmese are not my people,' although Myat spoke softly, there was steel in her voice. 'I am Peguese. These are invaders from Ava in the north.'

Stephenson nodded in apology. 'Do you know who that third officer is?'

'That is Muong Gyee,' Myat said at once. 'He is Muong-Luong's brother in law.'

'Ah,' Stephenson nodded again. 'I know of him as well.' He did not flinch when there was a puff of smoke and the sharp report of a jingal from the edge of the forest. 'They've noticed us here. Best tell the major.'

Major Hill looked worried when he arrived at the wall. 'Bo Loung himself? That is bad news. He would not come merely for a raid.' He pursed his lips. 'The King of Ava has lost two of his prize possessions, the Shoe-Dagoon pagoda in Rangoon and this one;' he jerked his thumb at the pagoda, 'what they call the Shoemadoo Praw. It must hurt his pride to be bearded at his own backdoor.'

He grunted. 'All right: I want Brown's picket withdrawn from the riverbank and taken inside the defences; it is too vulnerable there with the Burmese in such force. And bring Lieutenant Mason to me. I will send him to Rangoon with notice of our situation.' He glanced at Windrush, 'how are your men, Ensign?'

'Well enough, sir.'

'Good. I have forty sick already and rising. If things go on as they are we'll have more men in hospital than on the defences.' He scanned the perimeter with his binoculars. 'We are surrounded by hostile Burmese I see.'

The next day the local people began to filter into Pegu for protection. At first, they came in singly and then in family groups. Soon the whole population of villages arrived with men driving the huge Burmese bullock carts with the family sitting on top. Hill watched them for a day and ordered a stockade built just outside the pagoda. 'There's too many for us to accommodate and defend; let them do what they are best at.'

'Even old granny's coming, all looking for British bayonets to protect them from the Lord of the Golden Foot,' O'Neill said.

'That's why we are here,' Jack told him. 'That is what the British Army does; we protect the weak from the bully-boys.' He watched the Peguese arrive in squealing carts and with hope in their eyes.

'Sir!' A young Fusilier lieutenant panted up the stairs and saluted Stephenson. 'There are a couple of British soldiers out there being chased by the Burmese.' There was the sound of scattered shots, the brassy clamour of gongs and distant voices shouting.

Jack stared across the maidan. Is there no peace? The men wore the scarlet tunics of British soldiers. 'Madras Native Infantry,' Stephenson said at once. 'They're in a bad way. Bring them in Windrush, would you?'

The sepoys staggered as they ran, with the leading man waving his hands as soon as he saw Jack's 113th. There were a score of Burmese bounding in pursuit, dhas raised, and as Jack watched, a unit of the Cassey Horse trotted from the jungle fringe. The rearmost sepoy looked over his shoulder, shouted something and ran faster.

'Give the cavalry a volley,' Jack ordered. He suddenly felt very exposed out here on the maidan. The cavalry increased their speed to a canter.

'Form a line, boys,' Jack kept his voice calm, 'aim at the horsemen.' Five muskets levelled. O'Neill thumbed back the hammer of his musket with a calloused thumb. He was chewing tobacco with a steady rhythm. 'Fire,' Jack ordered, and the men fired as one.

My 113th are veterans now

The jets of white smoke gushed out. One of the horsemen fell.

'Reload,' Jack ordered.

The remaining Cassey Horse came on undaunted; lances held low. The sepoys were running in something like panic, blundering through the grass, looking over their shoulders.

'March forward,' Jack said.

It was madness for a handful of infantry to oppose a larger number of cavalry in open country, but after the last few weeks, he trusted these men and the sepoys needed help. He would be failing in his duty if he left them to be cut down by the Cassey Horse.

The sepoys staggered to them, dishevelled, bare footed, one with blood seeping from a cut on his scalp.

'These lads look done in, sir,' O'Neill ejected a mouthful of tobacco juice.

'They do,' Jack agreed. 'Take another dozen steps and give the cavalry a second volley. That should allow the sepoys time to escape.'

With both forces closing on each other Jack could now make out details of the Cassey Horse; with the high supports behind their saddles and the long spike on the butt of their spears they looked too formidable to allow near.

'Right lads, kneel and give them another volley.'

The Cassey horsemen were uncomfortably close. *Have I waited too long? Have I miscalculated?*

'Fire!' Jack tried to sound calm.

The muskets became more effective as the range shortened. Two horsemen fell, one to rise immediately and kick his horse as if blaming it for being shot. The body of the other man disappeared among the long grass. The remaining horsemen pulled up short and hesitated.

'Give them another, sir?' Wells was already reloading. He seemed eager to continue the fight.

Drive it home or get these men out safe? The time taken in firing might tip the balance between safety and disaster.

Jack calculated the distance between the cavalry and his men and decided not to risk it. 'No: reload and withdraw. If we fire now and they charge, they could reach us before we reload.'

'Yes, sir,' Wells accepted his order without hesitation.

Jack glanced over his shoulder. The sepoys were already fifty yards to the rear.

'Withdraw slowly,' he ordered, 'keep facing the enemy and if they approach too closely, present but don't fire unless I give the word.'

The Cassey Horse followed at a distance, never closing the gap but never falling back until Jack's men were within easy range of the garrison of Pegu. 'Right boys, in we go.'

'Nicely done,' Stephenson said briefly. 'Now let's hear how these two scallywags came to be wandering through the Burmese forest.' He gave a bleak grin. 'First, it was you and half the Company navy and now a brace of sepoys. I don't know what we'll have next: the brigade of Guards perhaps, or Dalhousie himself and his retinue.'

That was perfect; my boys acted like veterans, they are as good as any infantry in the army.

Once the sepoys had been fed and greeted by the officers of their own regiment, they gave their story. It seems they were from a party of twenty- two native infantry led by a *Jemadar*. They had been coming by river from Rangoon to Pegu, but the Burmese had ambushed the boat and captured it after a fierce battle. The sepoys had lost one man killed and two wounded, but these two had escaped and run to Pegu for help.

'My lads would give a good account of themselves,' a captain of the Native Infantry said.

'They have a good name,' Stephenson agreed at once.

'What about the rest of the men on board?' Major Hill asked, and one of the regimental officers translated the question.

The sepoys looked away as they replied.

'Either dead or prisoners,' the officer said.

Major Hill nodded. 'Well, we can't have more of our men held by the Burmese. We all know the treatment Windrush, and his men had, and the death of Commander Marshall shall forever be a stain on the Burmese Army.'

'That was Bo Ailgaliutlo,' Jack reminded, 'a dacoit chief and probably a British renegade. I don't think the Burmese Army has committed any atrocities against us during this campaign.'

'Obviously, you have more information than we have, Ensign,' Major Hill's voice was acidic.

I should have kept my mouth shut.

'I want a patrol sent out to try and locate our people,' Hill glanced at Jack. 'That means you Windrush. I know you have had a bad time and are pretty knocked up, but you know the country better than anybody else. I want you to take out a picket, try to locate where these poor fellows are being held and report back so I can organise a rescue expedition.'

'Yes, sir,' Jack said. 'Shall I try and rescue them?'

'Use your best judgement, Windrush. You have a reputation for impetuosity, which I hope your recent experiences have tempered. Do not attempt anything unless you are sure of success.' He raised a sympathetic eye. 'Are you game?'

'Of course, sir.' Jack saluted. *Thank God; that will erase any memory of my previous comment.*

Hill nodded to the topmost level of the pagoda. 'Go up there, liaise with the captains and get the lay of the land. If you can't locate these sepoy fellows, then find out how many of the Burmese are regulars and how many just dacoits that will scamper when things get serious. You may take as many men as you think fit; your own, the Fusiliers or the Native Infantry.'

'Yes, sir.' *There is no decision to make. I will take my own men.*

Jack checked his equipment: he had a Burmese dha, a borrowed pocket compass, water bottle and revolver, and a roughly drawn map of the area showing where the sepoys had been ambushed and in which to insert anything he discovered. He peered out into the dark: he had two hours before the rising moon painted a silver sheen over the surrounding countryside. Two hours of true dark to get past the Burmese sentries around the small pagodas, across the maidan and scout the belt of bamboo jungle. After that, the trees should hide him.

'Ready, Windrush?' Hill asked.

'Yes, sir.' Jack had chosen a small party of only two other ranks, plus Myat and Ranveer. If he ran into trouble, even fifty men would not be enough against Muong- Kyouk-Loung's thousands, while they would undoubtedly make more noise. He had swithered about Myat, but in the end, he had asked if she would come.

'I don't like putting women in danger,' he told her, 'but your translation skills are invaluable to us, and you know the country far better than anybody else.' He hesitated for a moment. 'I won't force you to come if you don't want to.'

She looked at him, unflinching, unemotional and patted Wells' arm. 'I will go with Edmund.'

Wells frowned. 'Don't call me that,' he whispered.

Myat had smiled and squeezed his arm. 'It is your name,' she said.

Wells opened his mouth, but whether to protest at this blatant proclamation of a name he apparently disliked or to try and persuade Jack to leave Myat behind, Jack never knew for he closed it again without saying a word.

Ranveer had proved himself as a loyal man. Jack trusted him.

'Last check, men,' Jack kept his voice quiet as he fought his nerves. He hated these last few moments before things happened.

It's not fear or not all fear. It is a mixture of apprehension and nerves. I am more afraid of doing things wrong than I am of being killed. It would be worse to be severely injured and left a blind cripple, or hideously malformed. A slight wound would be all right; a scar to let others see that I have been in action might help my promotion prospects.

'Are you all right, sir?'

Wells words brought Jack back to the present. 'I was working out our route.'

The Fusilier sentries stepped aside to let them through, then closed ranks again, wordless but with expressions that suggested they were glad to be staying behind. Only the dark remained, and the long grass, the bamboo jungle and the enemy. There were no gongs sounding, no commands ringing from the unseen Burmese ranks. Instead, there was the soft, sinister rustle of the grass, the sudden roar of a distant tiger, the call of a deer and the constant underlying whine of insects.

'No heroics, boys,' Jack reminded. 'We are here to scout the Burmese positions and look for these sepoys, nothing else. We will be back before dawn.' He glanced over them. Despite the frowns of senior officers, he had ordered that they take off their scarlet jackets and wear clothes of darker colours to merge with the jungle.

'British soldiers wear scarlet,' Captain Stephenson had disapproved.

'I want to keep my men alive,' Jack replied, 'and they have more chance of surviving if the Burmese don't see them.'

Stephenson nodded reluctant understanding. 'I see; well good luck, Windrush.' He had held out his hand.

Now they were once more outside Pegu but this time in the dark and without the knowledge of friendly eyes watching over them and a hundred British muskets waiting to keep back any possible Burmese enemy. Now they were alone with the dark, the *Tatmadaw* and the dacoits of Bo Ailgaliutlo.

Jack had a last glance at his men; he was in command of an operation where there was no superior officer to ask for advice: there was no Commander Marshall, not even a Lieutenant Bertram: just himself and his own resources.

The leather neck stocks were long gone and not regretted. The men carried percussion Brown Bess muskets with bayonets and forty rounds of ammunition, a water bottle and a pound of bread for emergencies. Ranveer also carried his *tulwar,* while Myat had refused any offers of carrying a weapon.

'I am a Buddhist,' she told them. 'I don't kill.'

'The enemy is Buddhist too,' Jack reminded her. 'At least carry a dha just in case.'

'No,' Myat shook her head firmly. 'I am a Buddhist.'

Jack sighed, patted his golden Buddhas and stepped into the dark.

The Burmese sentries among the small pagodas were lying on their backs, smoking and talking as Jack led his party past them. He ignored Ranveer's hopeful touch on his *tulwar* and moved on, tense until they merged with the dark of the maidan. A soft wind swayed the grass around them, hiding their movements as they padded toward the jungle edge. Sometimes the Burmese had cavalry patrolling the maidan but not that night. Jack's picket threaded through the tall grass without incident, and the jungle greeted them like an old foe, clammy, dense and echoing with unknown noise.

'This is the elephants' track,' Myat took over without any fuss.

'Follow it,' Jack said, 'but be careful, there may be sentries.'

Myat's expression did not alter. 'Yes, Ensign,' she said.

Jack moved slowly, testing each step for hidden traps, stopping at every possibility of Burmese activity. Twice they stopped at a stealthy sound, to see a large animal pass in the dark.

'Deer,' Myat mouthed the first time, and 'tiger' the second. Neither animal looked at them.

They moved on, with their nerves taut and throats dry as they probed deeper into the bamboo forest. Once they heard the drift of conversation and Jack led them in a wide detour around a Burmese outpost, and once the tang of tobacco alerted them to a passing Burmese patrol.

They heard the noise as they reached the encampment, the low murmuring of a thousand men, the muttering of conversation and the sound of somebody singing. Next was the flickering of torches reflecting through the trees and a sudden burst of cheering.

Jack motioned them to halt.

'Noisy buggers,' Wells spoke with the disdain of a professional soldier. 'We could march past with drums and flutes, and they wouldn't notice.'

'We won't try that today,' Jack said. Let's have a look at them as we're here.'He glanced at the others. 'You stay here; Wells and I will go alone. If anything happens to us, O'Neill, you are in charge; take the rest back safely and report this camp to Major Hill.'

Without waiting for a reply, Jack moved forward. As before the sentries were relaxed, smoking or talking with their muskets leaning against the boles of trees and their attention anywhere but on guarding the camp.

'Sir?' O'Neill touched the hilt of his bayonet.

Jack shook his head.

The Burmese looked quite settled in their clearing, with a collection of makeshift huts and a score of torches flaring in the night. There was a boxing match taking place with the contestants punching and kicking to the delight of the spectators, while another group of men were sitting in a large circle smoking and laughing.

'They certainly don't look like a defeated army,' Wells said. There was no need to whisper with the constant roar of noise.

'No, more like an inexperienced rabble,' Jack said. 'How many are here do you think?' He tried to count them, but in the flickering torch light and with the movement of so many bodies, he had to resort to guesswork. 'About five hundred?'

'Maybe more; maybe a thousand sir,' Wells said.

'You could be correct,' Jack agreed. He withdrew again, leaving the Burmese to their pleasures and the sentries to their sloth.

Myat favoured Wells with a brief nod, and then they were moving again, soft footed as any dacoit as they eased along the elephant track.

'We best be careful here Ensign Windrush,' Myat stopped them again. 'There is a valley ahead, a gulley.'

'Perfect place for an ambush,' Wells murmured, 'shall I have a look, sir?'

Jack nodded, 'go carefully, Sergeant; I don't want to answer to your wife if we lose you.'

The path dipped into a deep gorge with thick undergrowth on both sides and the trees above merging. The dark was dense, nearly tangible, frustrating even Myat's night vision. Jack loosened the revolver from its holster and crouched at the side of the path. He ignored the insects that feasted on the sweat that trickled down his face.

'All clear,' Wells reported.

The moon rose as they reached the river, ghostly white above the wispy fronds of the tall palms and reflecting from the slow slither of the water. A bird glided past, hunting some of the myriad insects whose hum enlivened the night.

Jack consulted his map. 'The sepoys were attacked about a hundred yards down river from here.'

Wells put a hand on Myat's shoulder, 'may I take the lead here, sir?'

Jack nodded. He would have preferred the position of most danger but knew that Wells possessed vastly more experience.

The sergeant eased past with hardly a sound. They moved on, slow and quiet, keeping even their breathing subdued as they followed the bank of the river.

'Ahead!' Wells said softly and motioned them to stop. 'Over there.'

There was nothing much left of the man. His arms and legs had been chopped off, and his head was missing. Only his torso remained, with the darker colour of skin an indication that he had once been Indian rather than Burmese or Peguese.

'One of our sepoys, I wager,' Wells said quietly. 'What a place to end your life.'

Ranveer stepped over the body and touched the hilt of his sword, saying nothing.

'Rest easy, soldier,' O'Neill touched the body as he passed.

They crept with their hands restless on the triggers of their muskets and the sweat cold as it trickled down their spines. Jack fought his nausea.

'Sahib,' Ranveer placed a hard hand on his arm and gestured ahead. There was the sound of Burmese words, a brief high-pitched laugh and a low muttering moan that Jack could not place.

Wells raised his eyebrows in an unspoken query. Jack nodded, and Wells vanished into the night, his feet making no noise on the soft river bank. Myat looked after him and then composed her face, folded her arms in front of her body and relapsed into total silence.

'It's our lads right enough,' Wells had returned so quietly that Jack had not heard him. 'The Burmese have them in the river or tied to trees.' He crouched at Jack's side with his mouth close to his ear. 'I counted a dozen guards, but there might be more.'

'Show me,' Jack said.

The sepoys were held fifty yards further down the river, with some tied back to back and up to their necks in the river with the Burmese watching them with muskets, occasionally taunting them with insults or throwing sticks or tree branches at them. Other Sepoys were fastened to trees. Jack saw their wide eyes in the dark as their captors passed them with the occasional punch or slap. Somebody laughed.

I have a choice: leave these lads here to the mercy of the Burmese and inform Major Hill or attempt to rescue them here and now. If I tell the major, he will undoubtedly send a column to rescue the sepoys, but some may be dead by then. If I try and free them and fail, the Burmese may kill them out of hand and my people as well. I have discretion: the decision is mine alone.

'What do we do sir?'

As Wells asked the question, one of the Burmese drew his dha and sliced at the nearest sepoy. The man writhed and tried to pull back, but tied to the tree there was nowhere he could go as the Burmese thrust the knife into his arm and slowly pulled downward. The sepoy's scream echoed through the jungle.

'We rescue these lads before they are all chopped to pieces,' Jack decided. 'Go and get the others.' He took hold of Wells' sleeve, 'not Myat though. Best she keeps clear of this.'

We are four men against twelve Burmese, with hundreds more of the enemy within calling distance. It was foolhardy, but Jack knew he could not leave these sepoys for the Burmese to torture to death.

There are twelve Burmese sentries, but only four are looking at the prisoners. Jack checked the odds. *Three are lying smoking, two are dozing, two talking together and one has vanished.*

'Sir,' Wells' whisper sounded through the silver-gloom of the jungle. 'Orders, sir?'

Jack touched his Buddhas for luck. The feel of their golden solidity was reassuring. 'I want these sentries disposed of quietly,' he said. *Disposed of, what an ugly euphemism; I am talking about stealthy murder here.*

'Sir?' Wells prompted. 'Which ones shall I take?' The sound of his unsheathing his bayonet was as sinister as anything Jack had ever heard.

'You and O'Neill take the three that are sleeping and the two smoking. Try to make as little noise as possible.'

Wells grin lacked mirth. He nudged O'Neill and vanished without a sound.

The tortured sepoy screamed again.

'That leaves the rest for us, Ranveer,' Jack said quietly. 'Are you game?' It was the same question as Hill had asked him.

'Yes, sahib,' Ranveer said. He drew his *tulwar* and kissed the blade in a gesture Jack found melodramatic but strangely reassuring.

The two Burmese talking together were too surprised to put up any resistance. Ranveer simply sliced the head off his man while Jack killed his victim with a bayonet thrust into the side of his neck.

Isn't it frightening how easy it is to kill a man? One minute he was alive and the next he was dead.

That left five, of whom three were watching the fourth slicing at the screaming sepoy prisoner.

Ranveer did not hide in the shadows. He calmly walked forward and thrust his *tulwar* into the throat of the first of the watchers, and then gave a backhanded hack at the second. The man looked in astonishment at his intestines as they spilt onto the ground. He screamed once before Ranveer sliced his *tulwar* onto the back of his neck.

Jack was not as efficient. His man turned as Jack was in the act of thrusting the bayonet, so the point missed and raked across the man's face instead. When the Burmese squealed and put both hands on his face, Jack followed up by an evil kick to the man's groin that doubled him up and crashed his ammunition boots onto the man's head until he lay quiet.

The last Burmese swivelled as he was in the act of cutting the sepoy's throat. He shouted for help a second before O'Neill rammed a bayonet deep into his chest.

'And that's done for you, you murdering bastard!'

'Free these men,' Jack cursed his clumsiness, 'and get away as fast as we can.' He sliced through the bonds of the nearest sepoys. The tortured man collapsed on to the ground. 'He's dead. There's nothing we can do for him.'

Jack realised he was shaking with reaction. *I have just ordered the death of eleven men.* He touched the Buddhas again, drawing strength from their presence.

The remaining seventeen sepoys all talked volubly as Jack's men sliced the ropes that held them, all thanking their rescuers.

'Keep quiet,' Jack hissed, 'else the Burmese will hear us!' He cursed that he had no gift for languages as Wells and O'Neill barked at them in a mixture of English, Gaelic and, Jack guessed, half a dozen Indian languages.

'You try, Ranveer,' Jack invited.

Within a minute the sepoys lapsed into silence.

'Ensign Windrush,' Myat appeared from a stand of bamboo. 'Burmese soldiers are coming toward us.'

'Thank you Myat,' Jack said. 'You- sepoys – grab a musket and some ammunition. Hurry now!' Jack mimed the actions and pushed the men as Ranveer barked at them.

'Sir,' Wells peered into the jungle. 'I can hear them now.'

The gongs were beating in the distance, and Jack imagined the long columns of lithe Burmese soldiers threading along half-seen paths.

'Back the way we came,' Jack ordered. 'Wells, you and Myat lead; I'll take the rearguard; Ranveer and O'Neill help the sepoys along. Some are pretty weak after their ordeal.' He glanced at the line of sepoys, some were pushing the others in their haste to get clear of the Burmese, and others were staggering with comrades helping them. One naik – the sepoy equivalent of a corporal - stood apart; he held his captured musket and slammed to attention in front of Jack.

'Reporting for duty, sahib!'

'Very good, naik,' Jack returned the salute. 'Just you help your comrades along.' He forced a smile, 'I see you speak English?'

'Some, sahib!' The naik's smile gleamed through the dark.

'Well done, naik. Now watch for the Burmese and let's get away from here.'

They withdrew faster than they had come; less concerned about making a noise and more with putting distance between themselves and the Burmese. After only a few moments they heard shouts and cries from behind them.

'They've found that the sepoys are released,' Wells guessed.

'And their men are all dead,' Jack added.

'Oh they'll be after us now,' O'Neill turned to face behind him. There was an uncanny ring to his laughter. 'On you come, boys!'

'Keep moving,' Jack pushed him onward. He took two steps and gasped as the wound in his thigh opened.

'Sahib?' The naik hesitated until Jack pushed him on.

'Look after your men, damn it; they need you.'

He could feel the blood seeping down inside his trousers, weakening him with every step. The harsh English public school training had taught him to ignore pain and hardship. He strode on, biting off his curses. The gulley was straight ahead.

He heard nothing; it was an instinct that made him turn, and something drew his gaze to a pattern among the undergrowth. There was something not right, something not natural; he realised he was looking directly at the tattooed Burmese boy he had seen before. And then he was gone.

Bo Ailgaliutlo's dacoits are close.

Although he was alert, the burst of musketry still took him by surprise. He heard the zip of a ball passing close by and saw the muzzle flares through the foliage ahead.

'Ambush,' Wells fired as he shouted.

For a second Jack hesitated. *Sit still or break out?*

If we sit still the numbers against us will only increase. 'Fix bayonets and charge through!' he yelled. 'Go right for the throat.' He pushed the nearest sepoy forward, 'go on, man, move!'

The naik gave a loud yell and charged forward as O'Neill gave his high-pitched, unnerving laugh and led the attack. Wells hesitated, reached behind him and grabbed Myat. 'Come on!' Jack kept in the rear, encouraging the weaker of the sepoys with hard pushes as he fired his revolver into the undergrowth on either side of the gulley. He slipped, jarred his injured leg and swore.

Moonlight vanished as the deeper dark of the gulley closed in, broken only by the muzzle flares of muskets on both sides. 'Keep moving,' Jack knew the sepoys would be disorientated and no doubt in shock by their recent experience but if he allowed them to falter they would be killed at best and captured for further ill-treatment at worst. He felt cruel pushing them on, but the alternative was far worse.

'Keep going! Don't stop!' He saw a nightmare of trees and undergrowth, of flaring muskets and teeth glaring in Burmese faces, of waving dhas and jabbing bayonets, of a sepoy sliding down as a Burmese man thrust at him with his dha, of the naik clubbing at a Burmese soldier with the butt of his musket. He fired his revolver, saw a man's face dissolve in a porridge of brains, blood and bone, fired again as another Burmese soldier aimed a long musket, saw the man fall and moved on.

'Keep running, push through them!' He lifted a sepoy from the ground by his collar and landed a kick on the seat of his trousers, 'get going!'

'Sir!' Wells was ahead, grappling with a Burmese soldier. 'Sir!' The Burman jumped in the air and kicked out, sending Wells sprawling on his back. Jack pushed forward to help, but Wells pointed frantically behind him 'Myat, sir!'

Myat was on the ground, struggling to get up as a Burman stabbed at her with his dha. Jack levelled his revolver, hesitated and lowered it again. Even at that range, he was not sure he could hit the Burman in the dark without putting Myat in danger.

'Myat!' Jack knew he was no more responsible for Myat than for any of his men, but all his instincts and training told him to look after a woman. A pair of sepoys rushed past; the naik yelled as he threw himself on a Burman and Wells turned despairing eyes on him as his opponent kicked the musket from his hands.

'Sir: please!'

Myat tried to roll away. The Burmese soldier took hold of her hair and dragged her bodily into the undergrowth. He was grinning, holding his dha in his left hand, enjoying his moment of triumph.

Jack lunged forward, swearing as fluently as any private soldier as a second Burman rushed at him. He fired without thought and the second Burman vanished. Myat was screaming, kicking her legs as the man hauled her away. Her hair had come unfastened from its customary tight cylinder, and her *longyi* was torn, so her thighs showed through the rents.

'Sir!' Wells sounded frantic.

Jack staggered as a root caught his ankle, recovered and thrust forward his pistol. The Burman was too intent on capturing his prey to look up. Jack saw the panic in Myat's eyes and heard her incoherent scream.

The Burman laughed and pulled at Myat's hair. Only when Jack pressed the muzzle of the pistol against his chest did his expression alter, and then Jack squeezed the trigger. He did not hear the report as the bullet crashed into the Burman's body. The force of the shot pushed the man backwards. As Myat screamed beside him, Jack fired, again and again, sending two more bullets into the writhing man on the ground before the hammer of his revolver clicked on an empty chamber.

'Sahib!' Ranveer put a hand on his sleeve, 'Sahib; we must leave!'

Jack found he was gasping. He took a deep breath as sanity returned. He nodded. 'Myat…' She lay there, dazed, mouth open. Her *longyi* was in rags, high up her thighs and her hair a tangled mess around her face. She had never looked more attractive.

'Myat!' Wells was bleeding from above his eye and his mouth. He lifted his wife in his left arm. 'Come on!' He glanced at Jack, 'thank you, sir.' For a second their eyes met, and Jack saw genuine gratitude.

'Sahib,' Ranveer wiped the blood from the blade of his *tulwar*.

Jack looked around. One of the sepoys lay bleeding on the ground along with half a dozen Burmese. 'Keep going,' he ordered.

Wells supported Myat for the first dozen steps, and then she pushed him away and said something sharply in Burmese.

O'Neill had halted the sepoys fifty yards past the gully. 'Thank God you are here, sir. I was getting worried, and these lads are a bit upset.'

'No wonder after what they've been through,' Jack tried to count the men; they were shadowy figures in the dark, milling around and some were talking. He raised his voice slightly. 'Naik!'

The naik appeared, teeth white in a wide smile. 'Reporting for duty, Sahib.'

'Keep these men quiet, can't you?'

Ranveer repeated the order in Urdu, and the naik passed it on. The noise ended at once.

'I will lead from here,' Jack decided, 'Wells, look after Myat; she needs you. O'Neill, keep the men together and Naik, I want you to be rearguard.' He heard Ranveer speak to the naik as he pushed his men to where he wanted them to be. 'Right, move.' He led the way, careless of the noise they made. He needed to put as much distance between his men and the Burmese. Bo Ailgaliutlo was not a man to give up after a single reverse.

Rather than pass the Burmese encampment, Jack dived straight into the forest, hacking with his dha and hoped the noise he made scared away any poisonous snakes and insects.

'Keep together,' he reminded. After every fifty steps, he stopped to check his compass and ensure his men were together.

'Sir,' Wells pushed to the front, 'begging your pardon sir, but may I ask something?'

Jack nodded. 'Go ahead sergeant.'

'Are we heading back to Pegu, sir? Or have you another destination in mind?'

'Pegu,' Jack said.

'Well sir, 'Wells hesitated. 'It's in that direction.' He pointed at right angles to their line of march.

Jack glanced at his compass. The needle gyrated. He shook it. 'This is broken; are you sure?'

'Sure that Myat says so, sir.'

Jack grunted. 'Is Myat fit?'

'Yes, I am, Ensign Windrush.' For the first time, Jack noticed strands of silver in Myat's hair. With her face bruised and her *longyi* ripped, she looked more determined than ever.

'Lead on then, Myat.'

In the night time jungle, one direction looked like another to Jack, so he followed Myat with blind faith. Within minutes she had found an animal track that allowed for better movement, and half an hour later he sighed with relief as they emerged into the open maidan. The lights of the Pegu watch lanterns flickered in reassuring welcome.

'Get your men in order,' Jack said to the naik. He looked at the quarter mile of maidan. 'Keep together; there might be cavalry patrols out here. If we are scattered, head for the lights and shout loudly when you near Pegu.' He glanced over his shoulder. 'Lead on, Sergeant and don't stop for anybody.'

Except for Myat of course; you will stop for her. As would I, damn it!

The maidan presented different problems from the jungle. There was not the stifling confinement and the fear of ambush, but neither was there the knowledge that they could slide into the undergrowth and hide. Instead, there was the feeling of exposure to cavalry and the vulnerability of space if the enemy saw them.

Once all the others were away, Jack followed, taking the position of most danger. No officer should put a private soldier in a position more dangerous than his own. It also meant he could hide his limp. Only quarter of a mile of maidan to cross and they would be safe; it was a success for the 113th.

The hands had closed around his throat and mouth before he was aware there was somebody behind him, and Jack was dragged back into the forest.

Chapter Eighteen

Pegu December 1852

Oh God, what's happening?

Jack kicked with his right foot and tried to flail his arms in a vain attempt to break the stranglehold. The man who held him was too powerful. Jack saw the open space of the maidan vanish as he was pulled further into the dark blur of the forest. He thought of his revolver, but even as he reached for it, his attacker threw him to the ground and kicked him savagely in the ribs.

There were three of them, bare- chested Burmese, standing around him. One thumbed the edge of his dha and smiled.

Is this death?

The vision came to Jack. *He was standing at an old gate on the western foothills of the Malvern Hills. It was dusk with that soft pale pink hue settling over the glorious patchwork of fields and orchards that stretched all the way across Herefordshire to the blue hills of Wales. The terraced slopes of the British Camp were to his left while a pair of owls exchanged soft calls in the gentle air. That was his country: his England. That was where he belonged.*

I am not dead yet, by God!

Jack relaxed for a moment, allowing the Burmese to think he was too petrified to move, and then grabbed for his revolver. Flicking open the small stud that fastened the holster took only a second, but that fraction of time enabled the first Burmese to leap up and stamp on his wrist. Jack winced at the flaring pain.

No: don't give up; pain is temporary, death is eternal. Buddha says that suffering is the essence of life.

He roared, switched hands and drew the pistol with his left.

Dear God, did I load it after the ambush in the gully?

Jack pulled the trigger. The hammer rose and fell with a sickening click. Empty chamber! He tried again and the revolver bucked against his wrist, and the shot cracked out. The nearest Burmese jerked as the bullet thumped into his stomach. He looked down in astonished curiosity as the blood began to seep out and then covered the wound with his hand as he crumpled to the ground.

As Jack fired again the second Burmese ducked; the bullet flicked past his turban to lose itself somewhere in the dark undergrowth behind. Jack swore and aimed for the same man even as the third threw himself on him.

He felt savage satisfaction as his bullet hit the Burmese in the arm, spinning him round, but then the third man was on him. Jack tried to aim, but the Burman kicked the revolver from his grasp. He swung a punch, missed and felt something hard crack against his jaw. The force was sickening. The second blow caught him in the stomach, and he doubled up, gagging.

The revolver was two yards away, lying under a fallen branch and just within his orb of vision. *Can I make that?*

The pain in his stomach was intense. He steeled himself for it to increase as he lunged, and then two more figures came into view.

One was the tattooed Burmese boy. The other casually lifted the revolver and pushed Jack with his foot.

'Oh so it's you, Ensign Windrush,' Bo Ailgaliutlo said. 'I wondered who would be foolhardy enough to rescue our sepoys. I might have known it would be the wild Windrush boy.'

Jack tried to shake himself free of Burmese hands, thinking quickly. *This man has been a British officer: he will understand the notion of honour and truth.* 'You should surrender,' he said. 'If you surrender and voluntarily give information that helps us, Major Hill will ensure you have a fair trial. He is a good man, and I will speak up for you as well.'

Bo Ailgaliutlo surveyed Jack. 'That is an interesting offer, Ensign Windrush. Jack isn't it? You don't mind if I call you Jack; it is an unusual name for a Windrush; they are usually William, Adam or George.' He stepped back. 'I know your family, you see. You are suggesting that I give up my position here to willingly become a prisoner of the British, at best to endure years in jail, at worst to dangle from a rope.' He shook his head, 'Of course, your words would save me for General Godwin would listen with great attention to one of the Windrushes; even a lowly ensign.'

Bo Ailgaliutlo's laugh echoed through the trees. 'Last time I was going to hold you as a hostage in case the British were victorious, but now I have seen the blundering slowness with which General Godwin moves I have no fear of being caught.'

Jack shrugged. 'So kill me then.'

Don't give this renegade the satisfaction of seeing I am afraid.

'We will, but don't rush to death, Ensign; it will wait for you.' He spoke sharply, and the Burmese began to drag Jack back toward the river. 'You may welcome it after my men have finished with you.'

The tattooed boy watched as two sturdy dacoits dragged Jack to his feet and pushed him all the way to the riverside where Bo Ailgaliutlo had his encampment, a rudimentary clearing where the river gurgled at the sterns of war-boats drawn up on the bank.

'Home sweet home, eh, Jack?' Bo Ailgaliutlo looked closer at him. 'How's the leg? Still sore?' His eyes were diamond bright.

Jack realised that the night was waning when he could see across the river to the far bank. Wisps of morning mist were settling on the rippling water, swirling around floating branches that flowed down to Rangoon and freedom.

Bo Ailgaliutlo cracked out another order, and the Burmese began to wrestle Jack's jacket off. When one stuffed a hand deep inside the pocket, let out a yell of triumph and dragged out one of the Buddhas, his companions crowded round. For a second Jack was unattended. He rolled away and jumped up, pushed over a surprised Burmese, grabbed his dha and staggered toward the river.

He had no plan and no idea; he only hoped to put some distance between himself and the dacoits. He heard Bo Ailgaliutlo shout something, glanced back and saw half a dozen dacoits running after him, shouting and brandishing naked dhas.

Jack felt the weight of the Buddha in his pocket. That was his treasure; it would pay for the next step in his career, make him a lieutenant. He had lost half already; he needed the remaining Buddha. He tripped and staggered as his leg failed him. The mud was warm and comfortable beneath his face.

No; move Jack!

Jack pushed himself up and staggered on, swearing, with tears and sweat stinging his eyes.

The dacoits were closing, shouting, calling after him. Bo Ailgaliutlo was at their head, running with an expression close to hatred as he powered along, holding Jack's revolver in his hand.

That tattooed boy stood in his path, grinning, holding a curved dha. Jack swerved away from the river bank and plunged into the jungle. He swore as his jacket caught in the thorns and branches of the undergrowth. He tugged, looked behind him, checked his remaining Buddha was secure, tore his jacket free and swore again. The Buddha thumped against his thigh with every step. What was his plan? To where would he run?

If I stay in the jungle, they will catch me. The Burmese are fresher and more used to this kind of terrain. That boy is between me and the river. I have to find somewhere to hide.

There was nowhere. There was only the jungle or the river itself, dark and muddy and probably teeming with carnivorous fish.

Jack swore again, loudly. He had to slow down the dacoits, so he could hide in what remained of the dark. Once the dawn swooped up properly, he would be too visible. He needed a few moments.

There is only one solution.

Swearing, unhappy but aware he had no choice, Jack pulled his remaining Buddha from his pocket and turned around. There was a single beam of sun filtering through the trees, and he held it up, so the light caught the gold and reflected it in the faces of the rapidly advancing Burmese.

Bo Ailgaliutlo shouted what was possibly a warning, but when Jack tossed the Buddha over their heads and into the bush about half the dacoits dived after it. Three hesitated and then followed their companions, which left only Bo Ailgaliutlo and the boy to chase after Jack.

I can fight one man no matter how experienced he is. I can fight him. I have a chance.

Jack dropped his jacket, turned and fled, gasping at the stabbing agony of his leg. He heard Bo Ailgaliutlo's footsteps pounding behind him, turned and tried to still the beating of his heart. Bo Ailgaliutlo came to an abrupt stop and raised his revolver, but before he pressed the trigger, Jack had ducked and charged.

An instant before he made contact he lowered his shoulder and met Bo Ailgaliutlo with a solid thump. He knew the renegade must be much older than him, but he was solid muscle and bone, so the shock of contact made both stagger.

Bo Ailgaliutlo grunted and smashed the butt of the revolver onto Jack's neck. Jack winced but held firm, as the gun thumped down again and again. He locked his hands around Bo Ailgaliutlo's back and tried to lift him, swearing. Both men were snarling now, grunting with effort.

Jack suddenly jerked his head up, catching Bo Ailgaliutlo under the chin, so he staggered back. Jack followed up by hooking his right leg around Bo Ailgaliutlo's left and throwing him backwards. The renegade clung onto Jack, so they fell together and rolled in the mud beside the banks of the river.

Jack grabbed Bo Ailgaliutlo's hand and tried to prise his fingers from the butt of the revolver. 'You bastard!' Bo Ailgaliutlo snarled, 'I'll finish you!' The renegade put forward his head and bit into Jack's arm, worrying until Jack swore, but did not let go.

'That's foul language from an English gentleman,' Jack grunted, 'and you were a gentleman once weren't you?' He felt the renegade's teeth grinding in his arm, felt his flesh tearing open and the hot blood flowing. 'You can be English again. If you confess your past and give up to the general.'

He brought up his head again, trying the same trick as before but this time Bo Ailgaliutlo moved his chin aside. Instead, Jack thrust forward his knee, hoping to find the renegade's groin.

'Is that how gentlemen fight now?' Bo Ailgaliutlo opened his mouth to taunt. 'In my day we faced each other with fists.'

'So stand and fight like a gentleman,' Jack invited, 'and not like a Burmese dacoit.' He wrenched his arm away from Bo Ailgaliutlo, balled his fist and smashed it into the renegade's face, again and again. He felt a bone breaking, but Bo Ailgaliutlo was stubborn.

Jack released his hold so suddenly that Bo Ailgaliutlo fell forward; his grip on the revolver loosened and Jack lifted his boot and raked it down his shin. It was an old trick but effective as the renegade swore loudly and lifted his leg; Jack punched him in the throat, grabbed the revolver and stepped back.

What do I do now? Kill a man in cold blood? Waste time in tying him up? No by God; imagine the glory if I bring him back with me. It would make my name and bring instant promotion; I lost my Buddhas, but this is even better.

'Now, you traitor, you're coming with me!'

Bo Ailgaliutlo's mouth opened. He glanced into the forest. 'My men will be here soon.'

'Your rabble is fighting over trinkets,' Jack's single contemptuous word dismissed the Buddhas that were to bring him advancement.

Bo Ailgaliutlo looked directly at Jack. 'Shoot me then, Jack Windrush, but you can't take me prisoner to the British.' His smile was sudden, 'but you won't kill me either, can you? You're an English gentleman; you can't commit cold-blooded murder.'

Jack gestured with the revolver, 'move, Bo!'

'You should be in the Royals, Jack Windrush, not the lowly 113th,' Bo Ailgaliutlo's eyes gleamed with an expression so familiar that Jack paused. 'Why are you in the 113th, Ensign Jack Windrush of Wychwood Manor? The Windrushes always gained commissions into the Royals. What did you do to fall out of grace?'

'Keep quiet!' Jack snapped. He could hear the dacoits moving close by. *Is it Bo Ailgaliutlo's plan to keep me occupied until his men arrive?* He jabbed the muzzle of the revolver toward the renegade. 'Get moving toward Pegu, or by God I won't kill you clean. I'll shoot you in the stomach and let you die by inches!'

'If I shouted now,' Bo Ailgaliutlo lowered his voice, 'or if you fired a single shot, my men would be here in minutes. They would track you down, and your death would take days.' There was that look again, that devil-damn-your-hide glint in his eyes that Jack knew so well.

'But consider, Jack,' Bo Ailgaliutlo said, 'ask yourself why I did not kill you when I had you as a prisoner. I told you that I kept you alive as my bargain in case the British were victorious but you surely knew that was a lie. I could not kill you just as surely as you cannot hand me in for the pleasure of Major Hill.'

'Why the devil not?'

'Don't you know yet? Blood calls to blood; I am a Windrush, just like you,' Bo Ailgaliutlo held out a hand. 'How do you do? If you are Will's boy, then I am your Uncle George.'

Oh Dear God in heaven. Jack's mind rushed back to Wychwood Manor and the portraits in the hall. He remembered tentatively flicking back the curtain that concealed Uncle George, the man with the devil-damn-your-hide eyes; the man who had defied convention to join the East India Company army and who had supposedly died out East.

'Your portrait is covered up,' was all he thought to say. He did not take the proffered hand.

'I am surprised it is even there at all.' George said, 'what do they say about me?'

'That you married a native woman and drowned at sea.' Jack told him. He kept the revolver pointed at his uncle's stomach. There was a new sound in the background, a throbbing beat that did not belong in this forest.

'Both wrong,' George said, 'I lived with a few women but never married them; there must be a round dozen little Windrush bastards running about the East somewhere, one of my boys is around here, flaunting his tattoos like a picture book. Nor was I lost at sea. I suppose that was a convenient lie to hide the truth. Your father knew I joined the King of Ava of course...'

'I don't wish to know your sordid past,' Jack lied. The mention of Windrush bastards hurt. 'Come on: we are going to Pegu.' He motioned with the pistol once more.

'Yes, Ensign Windrush,' that devil-damn-you glint was stronger than ever. 'Let's tell Major Hill everything, how the traitor Bo Ailgaliutlo is a Windrush and your uncle.' He raised his eyebrows. 'Now you had not thought that, had you? Imagine what that will do to your career, and the reputation of your family.'

Jack paused.

He's right. If the Army learn that Bo Ailgaliutlo the renegade is a Windrush, I will never advance further and my name will suffer.

'Difficult choice isn't it?' George was smiling again. 'You'd better decide quickly. My men will be along any second. Come on now, Jack, what will you do now? Murder your uncle, or hand him to the hangman and destroy your career and the family name? Or escape now and tell nobody. If you leave now I will hold my men back – that's a promise, and you know that we Windrushes are honourable English gentlemen...'

As he spoke, George threw himself forward and grabbed at the pistol. Instinctively Jack squeezed the trigger, but where the ball went, he did not know. George was on top, his hand on Jack's throat.

'But of course I discarded all that gentlemen nonsense years ago,' he lifted the pistol high and released his grip. 'Go free, Jack. Run, boy.'

Jack saw the blur of movement to his left but could do nothing as Wells thrust his bayonet straight into George's side and twisted the blade to enlarge the wound. George's eyes opened wide, still with the devil-damn-you look, and then he stiffened, and blood gushed out of his mouth. Wells lifted his boot and shoved the still writhing renegade off his blade.

'And that's him dead and gone,' he said. 'One traitor less,' he spat his contempt on the twitching body. 'I would have liked to see him hang though.'

For a moment Jack could only stare at the corpse. He had found and lost an uncle within the space of five minutes. He was numb, unsure what he should think.

'Sir...' Wells said, 'we'd best be going. The Burmese are close.'

'How did you get here?' Jack found his tongue. 'I ordered you to get the men back safely to Pegu!'

'All back safely sir,' O'Neill emerged from the shade of a banyan tree. He gave a smart salute that did nothing to quell the impertinence of his grin. 'And the sergeant asked Major Hill's permission to come and look for you.'

'You're a pair of utter fools,' Jack told them.

'Yes, sir, and us too sir,' Coleman, Armstrong and Thorpe added themselves to the list, 'and Ranveer is here as well, sir.'

Before Jack could think of a suitable retort, there was the report of half a dozen muskets.

'Back to Pegu, boys,' Jack ordered, 'the dacoits are back.'

Wells led the way into the forest, only to duck down. 'There is more this way, sir. Best try along the river bank.'

Burmese gongs were sounding now, adding to that deep chunking throb that Jack had heard a few moments ago. He had a vision of half a dozen dacoits emerging from the shelter of a clump of bamboo, the smoke and flame of musketry and the zip of a bullet passing him close.

'They are there as well.'

What to do now? There are two choices: jump in the river or fight it out.

'Form a square, boys,' Jack ordered.

If they had not come for me they would be safe in Pegu; now they will all die by the river. The Curse of the 113th.

They lay down behind whatever cover they could find. Jack burrowed into the mud behind a rotting tree trunk and tried to ignore the ants that scurried around him. A few months ago he would have recoiled from their bites, but now they did not matter. He looked around; his men were in a semi-circle with the river at their back and the Burmese in the jungle all around, firing at every movement.

'Lucky these Burmese lads are poor shots,' O'Neill winced as a ball lifted the hat from his head.

'It's the heat,' Coleman reloaded as he spoke. 'It rots the brain.'

'You should be all right then, Coley: you don't have a brain, to begin with,' Wells aimed and fired. 'Got the bastard!'

Ranveer laughed out loud. 'Do you British always joke when you are about to die?'

'Who's about to die, Ranveer? We're winning!' O'Neill said. 'In a few moments they will come out with the white flag and surrender, you see if they don't.'

O'Neill's optimism appeared unjustified as the sound of gongs intensified, and the numbers of Burmese increased. The volume of fire was so intense that it became difficult for the men of the 113th to raise their heads. Jack watched with some curiosity as a small column of ants began to explore his arm, intent on protecting their territory.

'Here they come!' Wells had to shout above the increased noise of the drums and that strange throbbing sound.

The Burmese emerged with a rush, a solid wall of men carrying dhas and muskets.

'Here we go, lads,' Jack said. 'Fire!'

The six shots seemed a pathetic response to the massed attack. Two of the attackers fell: the rest continued onward.

'Reload,' Jack said.

I am not afraid now. I am going to die, and I am not afraid. I am dying with men I now consider as friends and equals. These men of the 113th are as good as any soldiers in any regiment including the blasted Royals.

The Burmese were thirty yards away, twenty, fifteen; their faces contorted with hate, their dhas raised.

'113th!' Jack roared, '113th! Fire!'

The muskets barked, bringing down two of the attackers.

'Fix bayonets!'

The sound of bayonets clicking into place was lost in the hellish batter of gongs and the yelling hordes of dacoits. Jack stood up and stepped to the forefront of his men. He had no ammunition left so held his revolver by the barrel.

The volley of musketry came from behind them and knocked a dozen of the dacoits flat on their back. It was followed by a loud 'reload' and then 'fire!'

'What the devil...' Jack looked over his shoulder. A paddle steamer was thrusting up the river, with a score of Company soldiers standing on the paddle boxes, firing at the Burmese. Even as Jack watched, the men on the starboard paddle box fired again, dense white smoke hiding them for a moment and clearing in time for the men on the port paddle box to present and unleash another volley.

'Where did they come from?' Wells asked.

'It's the relief column,' Jack guessed. 'Remember Major Hill sent the boats away?'

He looked up as a file of Madras Fusiliers trotted on to the river bank. 'We heard the firing,' a young lieutenant said, 'and guessed that you might need some help.'

'You guessed right,' Jack said. He was not sure whether to salute or not.

The lieutenant seemed equally unsure, so they shook hands instead. 'Now could you fellows direct us to Pegu? I know it's around here someplace.'

'Just allow me a moment,' Jack said, 'there's something I must retrieve first.'

Chapter Nineteen

Pegu January 1853

'Did you hear the news?' Sergeant Wells asked, 'Dalhousie has annexed the whole of Pegu province from Burma. The war is over except for chasing away what's left of the *Tatmadaw*.' He glanced up at the great pagoda. 'This is British territory now.'

'Do you think the regiment will be needed?' Only Myat could make the act of smoking a cheroot appear so elegant that Jack's heart raced as he watched her.

God, she is beautiful.

'No, Myat,' he tried to keep his voice neutral. 'The regiment is being sent back to Moulmein. We won't be involved in the clearing up process.'

Myat patted Wells' arm. 'Good. Then Edmund and I will stay in Pegu.' She removed the cheroot from her mouth, examined the glowing tip and returned it.

'What do you mean? You will travel with us to Moulmein and later, maybe, to England.'

Wells shook his head. 'Sorry sir, my time is up now. You know I transferred to the 113th rather than take Myat to England? Well, we've decided to stay in Pegu now that it's under British control.'

Jack stared at Myat rather than at Wells. The words came automatically. 'I don't want to lose you,' he said. He closed his eyes for a second and thrust his hand deep into the pocket of his tunic. 'Here, Myat; these are better with you than with me.' Pulling out the two golden Buddhas he had retrieved from the dead bodies of the dacoits at the river bank, he handed them over. He let his fingers linger on Myat's for one tiny fraction of a second.

'You don't want them anymore?' Myat asked.

'No, I don't want them anymore.'

What changed? My men came for me. The men I fought beside, the men of my regiment, the 113th, not the regiment of the family that discarded me.

Myat placed the Buddhas beside her. 'You had three battles to win, Ensign Windrush. You had to defeat your country's enemies, the enemies within your family and the enemy within yourself.' When Myat's eyes met his Jack realised she understood how he felt about her. 'You could not defeat the first two until you defeated the third.' She lifted one of the Buddhas, 'now you understand more what is important in your life, Ensign Windrush.'

You are important in my life, Myat, yet you are unobtainable.

Myat looked at Wells, 'there is something I must do, Edmund.'

'What is that, Myat?'

'This,' Myat stood up and gave Jack a long kiss on the mouth. She tasted of aromatic tobacco. 'That is for saving my life,' she said, and not until then did Jack see Lieutenant Lindsay watching with a look of surprise on his face.

About the Author

Born and raised in Edinburgh, the sternly-romantic capital of Scotland, I grew up with a father and other male relatives imbued with the military, a Jacobite grandmother who collected books and ran her own business and a grandfather from the mystical, legend-crammed island of Arran. With such varied geographical and emotional influences, it was natural that I should write.

Edinburgh's Old Town is crammed with stories and legends, ghosts and murders. I spent a great deal of my childhood when I should have been at school walking the dark roads and exploring the hidden alleyways. In Arran I wandered the shrouded hills where druids, heroes, smugglers and the spirits of ancient warriors abound, mixed with great herds of deer and the rising call of eagles through the mist.

Work followed with many jobs that took me to an intimate knowledge of the Border hill farms as a postman to time in the financial sector, retail, travel and other occupations that are best forgotten. In between I met my wife; I saw her and was captivated immediately, asked her out and was smitten; engaged within five weeks we married the following year and that was the best decision of my life, bar none. Children followed and are now grown.

At 40 I re-entered education, dragging the family to Dundee, where we knew nobody and lacked even a place to stay, but we thrived in that gloriously accepting city. I had a few published books and a number of articles under my belt. Now I learned how to do things the proper way as the University of Dundee took me under their friendly wing for four of the best years I have ever experienced. I emerged with an honours degree in history, returned to the Post in the streets of Dundee, found a job as a historical researcher and then as a college lecturer, and I wrote. Always I wrote.

The words flowed from experience and from reading, from life and from the people I met; the intellectuals and the students, the quiet-eyed farmers with the outlaw names from the Border hills and the hard-handed fishermen from the iron-bound coast of Angus and Fife, the wary scheme-dwelling youths of the peripheries of Edinburgh and the tolerant, very human women of Dundee.

Cathy, my wife, followed me to university and carved herself a Master's degree; she obtained a position in Moray and we moved north, but only with one third of our offspring: the other two had grown up and moved on with their own lives. For a year or so I worked as the researcher in the Dundee Whaling History project while simultaneously studying for my history Masters and commuting home at weekends, which was fun. I wrote 'Sink of Atrocity' and 'The Darkest Walk' at the same time, which was interesting.

When that research job ended I began lecturing in Inverness College, with a host of youngsters and not-so-youngsters from all across the north of Scotland and much further afield. And I wrote; true historical crime, historical crime fiction and a dip into fantasy, with whaling history to keep the research skills alive. Our last child graduated with honours at St Andrews University and left home: I decided to try self-employment as a writer and joined the team at Creativia ... the future lies ahead.

Also by Malcolm Archibald

- Jack Windrush -Series
    - Windrush
    - Windrush: Crimea
    - Windrush: Blood Price
    - Windrush: Cry Havelock
- A Wild Rough Lot
- Dance If Ye Can: A Dictionary of Scottish Battles
- Like The Thistle Seed: The Scots Abroad
- Our Land of Palestine
- Shadow of the Wolf
- The Swordswoman
- The Shining One (The Swordswoman Book 2)
- Falcon Warrior (The Swordswoman Book 3)